WENDY BLANTON

RED SKY IN MOURNING

Book Cover by MiblArt

First edition 2025

ISBN

Hard Cover 979-8-9876972-8-3

Paperback 979-8-9876972-7-6

Ebook 979-8-9876972-9-0

Contents

Pronunciation Guide

People

Aengus—Angus

Ailin—AY-lyn

Aithne—EYE-th-na

Briant—Brian-t

Ceann—Shawn

Cruthadair—CREW-ha-dare

Dermod—DER-mod

Dougal—DOO-gal

Gitta—GET-ah

Hamish—HAY-mish

Lassair—LASS-air

Laoch—Lay-ock

Maccha—MA-ka

Magda—MAG-da

Moira—MOY-ra

Murine—Mern

Raya—RAY-a

Ruan—RU-an

Sine—Sheen

Siril—Seeril, sort of like cereal but without the a

Dragons

Aegon—AY-gon

Saphir—Sa-FEER

Gautier—GO-tee-ay

Oriel—OH-ree-el

Peio—PAY-o

Dyatrisse—Dee-ah-trees

Places

Balphrahn—BAL-fran

Mevan—MEE-van

Gynhalion—Ghin-HAY-lee-un

Jobs

Raca—RAH-ka

Wreiddon—RYE-don

Wybren—WHY-bren

Lavban Dia—LA-v-bahn DEE-ah

Bealban Dia—BELL-bhan DEE-ah

Curses

Galla—GAH-la

Uffern—UHF-ern

CHAPTER ONE ~ MEVAN

Bron lounged on the throne and surveyed the audience chamber. Of course, it was large and ostentatious; the nobility of Mevan had grown pretentious over the centuries. Floor-to-ceiling windows revealed the eclipse was ending. The returning sun cast a warm light over bodies which littered the marble floor. The terror from the crowd huddled in the furthest corner rolled over her in waves. It soothed her, and she took a deep breath of blood-scented air.

"Landry?"

The chamberlain stepped forward. His gray hair was clubbed, and he wore a spotless red and black livery, not the pretender's blue and yellow. Unlike those who had been rousted from their bed, he had been ready and waiting for her like an obedient servant. "Yes, Raca?"

"Show me to my chamber."

"Of course, Raca."

Bron stood. "Prince Tiernay, you'd better tell the queen what's happening." She followed Landry through an antechamber, up a flight of stairs, and down a corridor. She felt his controlled fear, and she smiled softly. Her watchers were better trained than she realized.

He led her through a door at the far end into a sitting room with padded furniture and paneled walls. Candles burned in gold candlesticks on tables flanking the walls and on the mantle over the fireplace. It looked newly furnished, but she knew there hadn't been time for that. Through an open door, she saw maids and footmen bustling to remove the pretender's belongings under the supervision of her own staff.

She sat on the sofa in front of the fireplace. Landry added wood to the fire before going into the bedroom to hasten progress. Landry's voice grew harsh after a loud thud, but she ignored what he said. She basked in the way her presence unnerved the palace staff.

One of her maids approached, keeping her eyes down. "Raca, Evanna has requested an audience."

"Evanna? The necromancer with the tanad animals? Interesting. Send her in."

The maid nodded toward the door, and Evanna approached, holding a large moonstone. Her hand trembled as she gave it to Bron.

It fit in her palm, its energy throbbing like a heart. "What is this?"

Evanna kept her eyes on the floor. "Raca, I heard there were dragons at the landing site near here, so I went to see if it was so. I found an injured hatchling and an adolescent."

"What does that have to do with this gem?" asked Bron, allowing a touch of impatience into her voice.

The girl's feet shifted as if she wanted to run. "I reversed the process used to make tanad animals to extract the life force from the dragons, and channeled it into the gem."

Bron's eyebrows raised. She rarely found herself surprised. Momentarily speechless, she sat back and said, "Go on."

"You can access the power in whatever way you deem appropriate. When the power is depleted, the gem will break."

"The process to make such a gem will work with full-grown dragons, yes?"

"Raca, I could do it, but I'd require assistance."

"Assemble those you think appropriate, and include Slannish mages if they have the ability. Tell Landry what materials you need."

"Yes, Raca." Evanna inclined her head and backed away, turning and striding out only when there were people behind her.

Bron examined the moonstone. Accessing the power would be a simple matter. Too simple. She would need to layer safeguards into the gem to keep others from accessing the power.

She heard wailing coming from a nearby room. Tiernay had told his mother. Good. The question was, had he only told her the king was dead, or did he reveal how he'd died? If he had told her he'd killed his father, she could send him dragon hunting with Evanna. It would do the boy good to get into the field for a while, experience hardship, and prove his loyalty.

The side of her mouth curved up as she turned to hold the gem up in the light. If he fell to a dragon, it wouldn't be a great loss.

Bron leaned back in the padded chair at the late King Tiernay's desk and looked out the large window in the adjacent wall. That he had a glazed window this big in his study spoke to the complacency, or arrogance, of the Slannish leadership. She considered having it walled in, leaving transom windows, but strengthened it with magic instead. It overlooked the south side of Mevan and the wooded hills beyond, and she watched the activity in the city for a few minutes until she sensed

Landry's approach. She waved her hand, and the door swung open.

Landry entered cautiously. "You sent for me, Raca?"

She felt his apprehension. The reality of her arrival had set in. She smiled a little, and his anxiety moved toward fear. Excellent.

"Did Evanna find you?"

"She did, Raca. I took her to the treasury myself to choose what she needed."

Bron nodded and picked up the large moonstone. "What sort of gems did she take?"

"The largest ones we had—two opals, two lapis lazulis, a jasper, a garnet, and two turquoise."

She rocked the gem in her palm. "Do we not have anything more precious?"

He shook his head. "I offered her sapphires and rubies, but she said they were too hard. In order to access the magic she is infusing them with, one must be able to fracture the gem."

"I see. And she took what she needed?"

"I told her to take as many as she wished."

"Good. Is there anything else I need to know?"

"We had two pockets of resistance, but they have been dealt with. Those who were injured are in the infirmary."

Bron nodded and put the gem on the desk. "Has Laisrin found a suitable space for my workroom?"

"He said he has, but I'm not so sure. It's in the dungeon."

Bron shrugged. "As long as the walls are thick enough, it will be fine. The construction of the room is more important than the location, and if something goes wrong and I kill a prisoner, it is no matter." She turned toward the window. "Send Prince Tiernay to me, and arrange an introduction with the queen this afternoon."

"As you wish, Raca." He backed out of the room, and she heard his footsteps recede.

She turned her attention to the first of the dispatches from Berengar and Rory. They'd successfully taken the Keeps with minimal casualties. The *tanad* armies were effective. Even better, the necromancers converted the dead from the opposition, swelling the *tanad* ranks. She began drafting messages to return to her commanders when she heard footsteps.

A moment later, Tiernay stepped into her open doorway. "Good morning, Raca."

"Tiernay. Come in."

His face went blank when she didn't return the pleasantry. He hesitated on the threshold for a heartbeat before pulling his spine straight and marching to stand in front of the desk, his fingers laced behind his back.

"I have a job for you. My apprentice, Evanna, will be leaving to hunt dragons. She is a talented necromancer and will be infusing gems with their essence. I want you to go with her."

"Me, Raca?"

"Is there a reason you should not? I thought you would be eager to prove your loyalty to me."

His face paled, but to his credit, he didn't waver. "No, Raca. Is there anything in particular you want me to do?"

"Guide them to the Western Keep. The dragons are trapped in their lair. I'm certain you'll find other ways to help."

He raised his chin. "I will do my best, Raca."

"Good. Landry will tell you when to be ready, but it's best to begin preparations now. Send Landry back to me."

"Yes, Raca." He waited a beat before backing out of the room in a cloud of anxiety and confusion.

A moment later, Landry returned.

Bron picked up the dragon stone. It pulsed with power, warming her hand. "Escort me to the infirmary." She sensed Landry's confusion as he led her through to halls. He didn't understand why she wanted to visit the wounded. She didn't elaborate. It wasn't his place to know in advance; he'd see soon enough.

She smelled the infirmary before they turned the last corner—astringent cleaning herbs, blood, gangrene. They approached the door to find two healers waiting for them, a man and a woman, concern on their faces. They were Slannish, and their distrust was palpable.

"You have separated your patients?" asked Bron.

"We have," said the male healer.

Bron arched an eyebrow when they didn't move. "Take me to them."

The woman looked at the man and nodded, and they stepped aside. The woman gestured to the group on the right. "These are the ones who are willing to pledge fealty."

Landry narrowed his eyes and stepped in front of her. His voice was a low rumble. "They will pledge fealty, *Raca.*"

The male healer nodded. "Yes, they will, Raca."

Bron took a step toward the group. "You have taken the oath and met with my healers?"

They nodded as one.

Bron reached out with her magic, skimming their minds. She sensed the standard obedience spell in all of them. Her apprentices had been busy. "You will find obedience is rewarded in kind."

She reached for the well of healing magic she'd gained from her current body and gripped the dragon stone, holding it up in front of her chest. She spoke the words of the spell for healing a group, tapping the magic from the stone rather than herself. It glowed red, and she felt the power of the dragons race through her, exiting from her body like a cloud and settling on the group to her right. Ignoring the cries of fear and the shouts of relief, she pushed the magic over them in swirling waves until it settled and sank to the ground.

She pulled the magic back and regarded the shocked group. Their wounds were closed, leaving scars that looked years old rather than seconds. One moved his broken leg and gasped, reaching down to tear off the splint. One by one, the others examined their own healed wounds.

Bron turned to the healers. "These are fit to return to duty. Examine them if you must."

She turned to the group on her left. "You have seen how I treat those who obey me. Would any of you like to change your mind?"

Half of them nodded.

"Not all of you, then." She scanned the group with her magic and found an old soldier who had served the former ruler for decades. He was older, with gray hair, the beginning of a paunch, and a splinted leg. "What about you?"

"I pledged my fealty to King Tiernay and his heirs as a boy. I gave my word and cannot take it back."

"Very admirable. Too bad you chose the wrong option." She held up the dragon stone and reversed the healing spell, using it to pull the remaining health from the man's body. His eyes widened, and he moaned. She pulled harder, and the moan became a hoarse yell as the man aged before their eyes. His limbs bent as if affected by old age, and when she sensed his pain was nearing the threshold of unconsciousness, she stopped.

He groaned, eyes wide. His mouth opened and closed, but he couldn't find the words. She looked at the rest of the group, picking out a few more potential trouble-makers. They were close to changing their minds, so she directed the same magic at them.

The others in the group jumped as random men aged rapidly. Their screams rent the air. Behind her, she sensed Landry holding the healers back.

When she was done, she regarded those remaining. "Would any of you like to change your mind?" She smiled at the chorus of yesses. "Good. Landry, send for my apprentices to see to them." She turned to the healers. "You will continue to care for the ones who came to their senses. As for those who did not, treatment will waste resources. There is nothing to do for them. Move them to a place where they will not disturb those who are left. It will take them some time to die."

She tucked the dragon gem into her belt pouch as the healers gaped at her. She stepped toward the door and stopped. "On second thought, move our living examples of treachery to a place where others will see them to help others to decide."

"I'll see to it, Raca," he said.

She walked out the door and sauntered back to her study, pleased with her work and with the newfound power source.

Chapter Two ~ Annwn

Aithne crouched in the bushes, listening as the fae searching for her moved away. Without the moon or the sun, she couldn't tell which direction they were going, but she knew which way they didn't go. She hoped she'd have something to navigate by soon.

A bird flew over, and she looked up but saw nothing more than a black form moving in the darkness. She heard a caw, and a raven landed in the bushes. In the gloaming, she saw it transform from a bird to a human form.

"Girl?" hissed the protector's voice.

She stood, and he gasped and jumped back.

"Sorry, I didn't mean to startle you. I thought you knew where I was."

His eyes went wide. "I did know, but when I flew over, I couldn't see you."

She shrugged. "Well, it is dark."

"Your form should have been at least visible to me."

"I asked Cruthadair to hide me until it was safe."

His jaw went slack, and he touched his heart with his right hand. "Holy Goddess, you *are* the Lavban Dia."

She nodded slowly. "I don't know what that means, but I appreciate your help. I don't want to get you into trouble, so I'll be on my way."

"Where to?"

"To find my dragon. She will keep me safe until it's time to go home."

He frowned. "How will you know that? And how will you remain safe until you find it? No, it is my task to look after you. Let's go."

She shifted her feet to run, even though she knew he would turn back into a raven and follow her. "You don't have to go with me. I can find my way."

"There may be more trouble."

She shifted her pack. "You're not getting me back in that cave."

He shook his head. "It is not safe there." He gestured in the direction she'd planned to go. "Come. It's not smart to stand here arguing."

She bit her lip, then nodded. She didn't trust him, but he was right. Getting as far away as possible before the sun returned—if it returned—was the priority, and she'd elude him, too, as soon as she was able.

The sky lightened into a clear day. Aithne hoped she'd be able to find Saphir sooner rather than later. She didn't want to sleep in the snow any longer than necessary, and she'd be warm with Saphir.

The terrain was open and rocky by mid-afternoon. When they came to a sheltered ledge, the protector stopped short, almost causing her to collide with him.

He looked down his nose at her. "This is a good place to camp."

Aithne shivered; even in the shelter, it was still cold. She couldn't call it a cave. It was more of a large crevice scooped out of the rock. "If you say so. I don't see much firewood."

"There is no need." He dropped his pack and rummaged through it.

"There's no need because you have something, or because you don't plan to have a fire?"

He snorted. "Of course, we'll have a fire. It is too cold to be without one."

She shrugged out of the straps on her pack. "I'm glad we agree on one thing, at least."

He pulled a bundle out of his pack and took out what looked like a woven willow wreath. Replacing the bundle in his pack, he brushed snow from a spot inside the shelter near the front. He placed the wreath on the stone and waved a hand over it. As he turned back to his pack, the wreath smoldered. A tiny ember appeared under a cloud of smoke and spread around the wreath.

Aithne took her blankets out, folding one to sit on, and wrapping the other over herself. "That's impressive."

"Why?" The protector's voice was thick with disdain. "Do you not have fire laurels in Slan?"

"No, I've never seen one."

He grunted and took another from his pack, passing it to Aithne. "I make them through the summer and let them dry."

She turned it over in her hands; it was woven with branches, as she'd suspected, but it wasn't entirely dry. "Is it infused with magic somehow, or is it fresh? It's dry, but more intact than it should be, at least by Slannish standards."

"Slannish, or non-magical?"

She shrugged and passed it back. "I don't know. Either? Both?"

He pulled a bag and two water skins from his pack. He handed her a skin and a large piece of something that looked like jerky.

Her brow furrowed. "Is this—"

"Dried fruit and crushed grain. It is common travel food among my people. That should last you for a couple of days."

She nibbled the edge. It was hard but sweet. She wrapped the edge of her blanket around the water skin and pulled it against her body to keep it from freezing. She nodded to his pack. "You must be an efficient packer to have so much in there."

He shrugged. "I don't have to be. It is spelled to carry more."

Aithne shook her head. "I was impressed with myself for being able to use spells, but you have magic infused into everything."

"Not everything, but many things, I suppose. I don't think about it."

"Why would you? Will I be able to do that someday? Infuse things with magic?"

The protector shrugged. "I don't know. I don't have Lledrith."

"How do you know Lledrith?"

He tilted his chin down and looked at her, eyes wide, as if she were a stupid child. "Your magic. It's called Lledrith."

"No, she's a person. Sort of. She's either made of light or reflects it. Cruthadair sent her to me."

His eyebrows shot up. "Do you really not know? Lledrith is your magic."

Her face heated. "Why would I ask a stupid question if I knew the answer? We don't name magic in Slan. It's magic." She pulled the blanket tighter and turned away. "I don't even know why the Seers sent me here. From what I can see, it's a waste of time.

He grunted. "That seems like a logical conclusion for you to reach."

Aithne snorted and sat up straight. "Why are you even here? And do not give me that tired 'I have to protect you' garbage. If you're only going to do is tell me how stupid I am, go away. If I die, it's not going to affect you."

He was quiet for several minutes. "It will affect me. It will affect all of us."

When he didn't continue, she shook her head and turned away. *Saphir, do you know how much further I have to go? Will I be able to reach you tomorrow?*

Saphir's voice was quiet, as if she communicated from a great distance. *I do not know, beloved. My senses are still muddled. Perhaps tomorrow I will be able to tell you more.*

Aithne took a deep breath to still her irritation. *If I can't shake this jerk, I'm going to need you to incinerate him for me.*

We will deal with that when the time comes. We may yet need him.

Great. Just great.

Chapter Three ~ Commain

Briant focused on the right sequence of hand motions to keep the shield up. He'd lost count of how many times he'd repeated the pattern that formed the spell, but his shoulders ached from the constant movement. The *tanad* army surrounding them shifted like the tide. One of them shambled to the shield and peered inside, as if looking out a window. Briant gasped. It had his mother's face.

His hands stopped moving as grief swamped him, and he stifled a sob. He knew several members of his family had fallen to the necromancers. He saw them during the battle of Nokton, when he killed the mage who had caused so much trouble. But they were far below on the battlements of the ruined castle he and his dragon, Vask, had circled during the fight. Coming face-to-face with one wasn't something he'd imagined.

Tears streaked down his face as the top of the shield opened. Oswin smacked his leg, and Briant snapped his attention back. He squeezed his eyes shut, pushing grief and horror down to focus on maintaining the shield. He felt the opening close again, and he used the hand motions to strengthen it further.

Outside the large barn they occupied, the dawn faded back to night. The stars shone brightly. It would have been peaceful if it were not for the reversal of time and the raging battle outside.

Oswin and Raya flanked him, pale, their hands resting on their swords, silent as the sleeping dragons behind them. Little remained of the barn, but those remnants felt confined. The sea of undead surrounding the shield had torn out the doors, frames, and all.

Oswin gaped at the ocean of bodies. They faced all directions, some of them wandering aimlessly, others standing still or swaying. Dozens of them seemed to be the same person. Clones. A couple of them brushed the shield, but didn't appear to notice. "What are—"

"*Tanad*," whispered Raya. "Undead fighters. I didn't know they were so far east. I thought they were only near the Western Keep."

"Me, too," murmured Briant. The thump of ballistae fire reverberated through the ground. Someone shouted for a battering ram.

Oswin leaned toward him and whispered, "Why do they look like each other?"

Briant clenched his jaw. "The necromancers can make several undead from one body. Now, shut up and let me work!"

"Sorry. I don't have Lledrith, but can I help hold the shield?"

Briant nodded and turned to face Oswin, opening his eyes to ensure he did the right movements. Only Laoch—no, Cruthadair—knew how long the shield would need to stay up.

Oswin moved closer, watching Briant's hands, and copied the wide motions.

Briant felt a subtle shift. The shield had no physical weight, and the power to make and hold it came through Briant, not from him, so the sensation of having someone help was odd. It felt as if Oswin removed rocks from a bucket of water, allowing more water to come in and fill the container.

Outside, someone shouted insults, telling others they needed to get inside to find the Bealban Dia.

Oswin's face paled, and his hands stilled.

The weight taken from Briant returned. In his mind, he saw the rocks drop back into the water bucket with a splash, and the right side of the shield collapsed. The *tanad* standing near it turned.

Oswin cursed and tried to repair the damage, making it collapse further.

"Stop," said Briant. He clenched his jaw and increased the magnitude of the hand motions. The shield filled in, thin at first. He layered strength into it.

"What happened?" asked Raya.

Oswin's face went red. "I dropped the shield. They've come for the Bealban Dia."

Why would they be interested in her?

"I don't know." His voice wavered, and he took a shaky breath. "The dragons I understand, but why Adrienne?"

Raya's brow furrowed. "Who is Adrienne?"

"The Bealban Dia. She's my sister, and I can't get to her."

"Are you sure?" asked Raya. "Briant, could you lower the shield so Oswin can leave?"

"No," said Oswin. "Not so much the dropping part, but rebuilding takes a lot of power, and he just got it back up." He ran his hand back through his hair. "No, we need to stay here. She has bodyguards; they'll get her to safety."

"How? At least from here, it looks like the abbey is surrounded."

Outside, they heard a series of horn blasts, and the *tanad* blocking their view moved in a single wave out of the barn, taking part of the main wall with them.

With the view now unobstructed, Briant saw bodies on the ground and people—maybe *tanad*—loading them in carts to take somewhere on the other side of the abbey.

People in every window of the abbey defended it with spells. Concussive strikes shook the ground. The air stank of death. He heard shouted commands, the clash of steel, and screams from the wounded.

Raya turned away from the fighting. "I never thought I'd want *tanad* near me, but at least they're blocking what's happening out there."

Oswin nodded, squinting in the dark. "Holy Goddess, what is that? Do they have more reinforcements?"

"Where?" asked Raya.

"Coming from the other side of the abbey."

"Probably *tanad,*" said Briant. He closed his eyes to increase his focus. "They must have necromancers with them. Raya, check the dragons." He heard rustling.

"They're still out, but it seems like it's getting a bit lighter outside. The eclipse might be finishing.

"Your lips to Cruthadair's ears," said Briant.

"Is that when the dragons will wake up?" asked Oswin. "We need their help, and I don't know what's become of my sister."

A loud thump rang out. "They're going to breach the door," said Oswin, his voice rising in panic. "We have to do something!"

"What?" asked Raya. "What can we do? We're too far away to intervene!"

"I—I don't know! Maybe we could--"

A feminine voice rang out, cutting through the noise. Briant opened his eyes without meaning to as columns of fire fell from the sky. He flinched, but kept the spell going.

"Uffern!" shouted Raya, but her voice was drowned out by the sounds of screaming and fire.

The fire from the columns spread, stopping abruptly several yards from the barn and the woods in a circle around the abbey.

There was a moment of stunned silence as the fire died down. The sky brightened as light slowly crept across it.

Briant took a deep breath. "Was that—"

"Adrienne," whispered Oswin as shouts from the woods shattered the silence. Briant felt the now-familiar thump of ballistae as bolts flew out of the woods, sailing toward the abbey. A few arced over the roof, and he heard screams.

Briant squinted in the gloaming. He saw the Bealban Dia in her gold robes on top of the abbey, surrounded by female warriors. The first rays of the sun fell on her, and she raised her arms as another volley of bolts flew toward the abbey.

She shouted, and the bolts reversed course with enough force to impale fighters on the ground with the blunted ends. Invaders who had come out of the trees, some with bows, and some with a battering ram, dropped their weapons and ran. For a few seconds, the noise level dropped to deafening silence. A group of enemy soldiers resumed fighting, but their ranks were thinner, and the defenders held them back.

The Bealban Dia dropped her arms and turned to the women guarding her. They took a step back as she spoke. The Bealban Dia turned and stalked to the stairs that led to the roof, leaving her guards where they stood.

Oswin sank to the ground and covered his face. Briant turned away from him, and Raya caught his eye.

In his mind, his dragon, Vask, stirred, but he seemed to be in a deep sleep. Briant's shoulders relaxed; at least he was alive.

Raya stroked her dragon's head. "Isidro is dreaming."

"Vask, too, I think."

She looked past Oswin and frowned. She went to Gautier, holding her hands over the green dragon's nostrils. Her jaw went slack. "I don't think she's breathing."

Briant pushed back a ping of alarm and murmured, "Vask said the eclipse would incapacitate them. Maybe she was in a deeper, whatever that was, than the others?"

"I don't know. I hope so."

"We were preoccupied for most of it, so neither of us thought to monitor them."

"True." She looked closely at him. "Are you all right? Do you still need to maintain the shield?"

"No," called a woman's voice from outside. "You no longer need the shield."

Oswin's head shot up, and he rolled to his feet. "Adrienne?"

Briant released the shield in front of Oswin, holding the remaining sections in case they needed it again.

Oswin ran out of the barn. Briant heard their voices, but not their words. Raya crouched beside Isidro. Briant concentrated on holding what remained of the shield in case they needed it again, ignoring Oswin and his sister's escalating argument.

"And that's the problem!" shouted Bealban Dia. "You think you have to protect me, that your loyalty should be to me! That's why things are going bad so quickly! Your allegiance should be to Cruthadair, not to me!"

"You can't blame all of this on me," said Oswin.

"Of course I don't; you're not the only one with misplaced loyalty. Go quickly and prepare for your journey. You need to go as soon as the dragons are ready to fly, and I need to secure things here."

"You're not going back to Gynhalion, are you?"

"I will go when the Goddess tells me to go. You, however, will go when I say. Go *do your job*, Oswin, and realign your priorities. It's not *my* good graces you need to win back."

"Yes, Bealban Dia."

A moment later, the Bealban Dia walked into the barn and looked around. Light streamed in through all the broken doorways on the east and south sides. She shook her head and walked toward Briant.

"You are unharmed?"

Raya stood. "We're fine, but we may have lost a dragon."

The Bealban Dia walked over and put her hand on Gautier's head. "You are correct; she will no longer fly in our skies." She caressed Gautier's face before turning to Briant and Raya. "I have ordered Oswin to take you away someplace safe. Or safer, I suppose, than you would be here or in Gynhalion. As soon as the dragons can travel, you will need to go."

"With all due respect," said Raya, "we don't know why Gautier died. We need to find her Wybren."

"Why? Doesn't the Wybren die when the dragon dies?"

Raya stiffened. "Most of the time, but there are exceptions. It is likely in this case. Even if she is dead, none of us wants to see her body turned over to necromancers.

She wouldn't want that; she'd want a Wybren funeral. Our custom is to cremate the dragon and Wybren together with dragon fire."

Bealban Dia's eyebrows raised. "I will not stand in the way of your custom, but you will not burn my barn. I have need of it." She looked around. "What's left of it. I will have her body moved to the field."

Raya scoffed. "Where the necromancers can come back for her? Yes, a *tanad dragon* is exactly what we need."

"They could easily take her from the barn, and I cannot spare people to guard her."

Raya ran a hand back through her black hair. "Fine, we'll leave when the dragons are ready, but what about Ruan and Dermod?"

"I will consult the healers about them. Oswin will bring the rest of your belongings and travel rations for you. Briant, put aside your enmity with my brother, or your failure will be the death of us all."

Briant swallowed hard. "Yes, Bealban Dia."

She touched her heart with her right hand. "May the Goddess be ever before you, Lavban Dia."

Before he could reply, she strode out. In his mind, Vask stirred again. *Lavban Dia.*

Briant sat on the dirt floor of the barn, leaning against Vask, but his mind was in his mental meadow, soaking up the sunshine. The butterflies were nearby, but they didn't seem inclined to interact.

It was quiet outside. Whatever the Bealban Dia had done to chase away the invaders had worked better than Briant imagined. Even the last of the *tanad* had fled before he settled down to meditate.

He heard Raya distantly. She was readying their belongings while keeping watch for trouble. Air displaced near his body with a thump, and guessed she'd brought Vask's saddle over. He breathed through his mouth to avoid gagging on the smell of blood and feces.

Vask stirred in his mind, and he heard a scaled tail sweep over the dirt.

Are you all right, Vask?

There was a pause as Vask considered the question. *I am alive, and the pain has nearly gone.*

We'll need to leave as soon as you and Isidro are able.

Sorrow tinged Vask's voice. *We should see to Gautier first.*

Raya wants to find Finley before we do that. He pushed his own sorrow away; he didn't have time for Finley's death to be more than theoretical at this point.

The sound of another person approaching brought him out of his meditation. Oswin strode in carrying several packs. Raya jogged over to take some of the load, and they carried them to the dragons.

"Will they be ready soon?" asked Oswin.

Briant got a wave of agreement from Vask as Raya said, "It shouldn't be long now. Briant, let's see if we can get them saddled."

Briant rolled to his feet and reached for the saddle as the dragons lumbered up clumsily.

Oswin paled. "You're sure they'll be able to fly?"

Isidro turned to him. "Worry about yourself, human."

Raya placed the saddle on his back, patting his neck as she ducked to buckle the straps. "It's been a long time since you were this grumpy."

As she straightened, he sank back down with a grunt.

Briant smiled a little as he finished Vask's straps and ducked away so Vask could rest. He heard the dragons talking to each other as he transferred their belongings to saddle bags.

"Oswin, we'll have to wear as much weight in the packs as possible since Vask will have to carry us both."

"Why? The weight will be the same whether we wear it or not."

"It will be balanced differently. Besides, you've never flown before. He'll have to compensate for you, too. I hope we won't have to go far."

Oswin shook his head. "Our destination is about a league from here."

"Raya, what can we do about Gautier?" asked Briant. "If she's dead, Finley must be too."

Raya swallowed hard. "Her death may have killed Gautier. I'll see if I can find her. You focus on your magic." Her head jerked toward the front of the barn. "Isidro hears something coming. We better go."

I hear it also, said Vask. *It sounds like the movement of siege engines. Do you have everything stowed?*

"Yes, everything is ready," answered Briant, out loud so Oswin could hear. "Should we mount in here or outside?"

Best to do it in here.

Vask lumbered to his feet, and Briant pushed Oswin toward him. "Get in the saddle. I'll strap you in."

"What about you?" asked Oswin.

"Never mind me. Someone is coming. We have to go." He slid his foot into the nearest stirrup and vaulted onto Vask's back behind the saddle. "Come on."

He grabbed the straps as Oswin clambered into the saddle, making Vask grunt.

Raya finished buckling her straps. "Hurry, Briant. Vask, you launch first. We'll draw fire if we need to."

Briant strapped the two of them in. "Go, Vask."

Vask lumbered toward the entrance furthest from the source of the noise, working up to a jog. He passed through the opening as a wave of *tanad* ran screaming from the woods toward the abbey.

"Lean forward!" shouted Briant as Vask launched.

Oswin leaned over Vask's neck, and Briant leaned over Oswin's back, wrapping his arms around him to hold on to the saddle.

Briant closed his eyes and clenched his legs into Vask's sides as they climbed. He heard a twang and the whistle of a ballista bolt, and he threw a shield around them. *Please, Goddess, don't let Raya or Isidro get hit.*

Briant, which way?

Briant leaned forward a little more. "Which way, Oswin?"

"South!"

Vask turned, heading toward the densest part of the woods. Another bolt flew toward them and bounced off the shield.

Isidro streaked past. Raya leaned low over his neck, raising one hand toward Briant as they flew by.

I told Isidro to let us draw fire, said Vask.

Good idea.

A few minutes later, they flew over dense woods, out of range of the weapons, and Vask slowed.

Briant sat up, moving his hands to the back of the saddle. Evergreen trees streaked past below.

Oswin shivered and shouted, "There should be a game trail in the trees, but I've never seen it like this before." He looked around. "There! A little to the right, there's a clearing. Go that way."

Vask altered his course and beat his wings to gain altitude. Several minutes later, Oswin pointed to his left. "Land in that clearing with the evergreens ringing the birch trees."

Briant felt a wave of relief from Vask as he circled the clearing, landing harder than usual. They slid off his back, and Briant unloaded the saddle bags.

Oswin nodded toward the trees. "I have those trees warded for hunting. It's big enough for you to rest in, Vask."

Briant unbuckled the saddle and pulled it off. "Thanks. Where can we find you later?"

Oswin frowned. "We?"

"Well, me, I guess, since Vask will have to hunt eventually."

Vask turned to look at Briant. *You must go with Oswin.*

Briant frowned. "What? No, I'm not leaving you."

"I will be safe here inside the wards, yes, Oswin?"

"I've had a few different kinds of animals come to the trees and look right at me without seeing me."

Briant scoffed. "What about people?"

"People don't come out this far. There isn't even a homestead within a league's radius."

"But the enemy could have seen Vask land."

Vask huffed and lumbered into the trees. *Come find me, Briant. Tell me which way I face.*

Briant rolled his eyes and walked to the clearing. It looked empty. Putting his hands on his hips, he looked more closely. He walked into the tree ring, and the magic protection wards snapped at his skin. Two steps later, he walked into Vask, and he became visible. He sighed. "Fine. I'll go with Oswin if you're sure you'll be safe."

Vask laid his head on his paws. "I will be fine. Go away so I can sleep. You have a job to do, and it will not be accomplished if you sit here watching me rest."

Briant left the hunting blind, and the wards snapped him again. He clenched his jaw and hoisted Vask's saddle onto his shoulder. "Which way do we go?"

Chapter Four ~ Western Keep

Tanwen hardly dared to breathe as she crouched in the berry thicket. Cold seeped through her clothing, and the dozen teenage trainees around her were still as statues, frozen in fear. A branch poked her side, and she focused on it, trying to calm herself.

Quillon? Her dragon's silence didn't surprise her, but it remained alarming. In all the years since they'd paired, she'd never lost contact with him. She'd looked for him as they ran out of the escape tunnel in the lair. Going to find him was out of the question, especially with so many trainees looking to her for leadership. Their lives were in her hands.

She heard armor clinking and leaned to see who was coming. Her husband, Liam, and their friend, Colum, rounded the corner of the Keep. She stiffened as the trainees relaxed. She held up a hand before anyone stood. Several soldiers followed the men. Liam pointed at the tunnel where Tanwen and the others had just exited. She jumped when Gitta leaned close.

"What are they doing?" she hissed in Tanwen's ear.

Tanwen angled toward the others without taking her eyes off Liam. Pitching her voice low, she said, "I don't know what's happening, but we have to assume they aren't there for the welfare of Slan. When I give the order, you boys need to throw your most destructive magic at them and run. Hit them hard, but don't overdo it. The girls and I will finish them, and we'll rendezvous at the creek. Lucas, you're in charge of the boys."

She glanced at the pale faces and wide eyes.

"But Liam—" whispered Lucas.

"That's not Liam. We saw *tanad* who look like him at Nokton." She looked back at the enemy, and her breath caught as three men in mage robes stepped in front of the tunnel. "What are they doing?"

Lucas' jaw dropped. "I don't know that spell, but it's directed at the dragons."

Anger jolted through Tanwen. *Quillon!*

Still no answer. "Rendezvous at the creek. Boys first, with Lucas. Girls, you're with me. Give it everything you've got, and then run."

The boys shifted, and Lucas nodded at Tanwen.

"Now!" she hissed.

The boys sprang up, shooting magic toward the enemy, hammering them with fireballs and lightning strikes.

The enemy shielded after the first mage fell. Tanwen saw magic strikes bounce off, but some penetrated. Colum and Liam stood still, surrounded by the enemy and protected with shields.

One by one, the boys darted out of the berry patch and ran away from the Keep. They stayed under cover for as long as possible, but Tanwen saw the enemy take notice. She watched Lucas, and when he stepped back, she leaped to her feet. "Wybrens!"

The girls followed, shouting as they engaged those who met them. The mages at the tunnel began their spell again, and Tanwen moved to strike the nearest one in the back. She couldn't see his shield, but hitting it would disrupt the spell.

She turned her blade and swung at the shield, swatting it hard with the flat of her blade. The man inside jumped.

"Tanwen!"

Glancing over her shoulder, she saw Liam advance. He swung his sword at her head, and she ducked, thrusting hers toward his torso. He danced back.

She stepped forward, channeling her fear for Quillon into fury. "Not this time!" She swung for his neck, and he blocked it, taking another step backward.

She moved around him, trusting the girls to guard her back, making him turn as they traded blows. When she faced the tunnel, she stepped forward and kicked him in the belly, shoving him against the mages. She swung her sword at his head, forcing him to duck. The mages fell over, and he tripped on them, but she kept up her momentum so he was too busy to cast magic.

Around her, the sounds of fighting diminished, and she smelled blood. She heard Lassair shout her name. Tanwen ignored her, hissing as Liam's blade cut the side of her coat. Someone asked Gitta if she was all right, distracting Tanwen for a single heartbeat, long enough for Liam to roll to his feet.

She felt a vibration in the ground under her feet, and rocks slid down the rocky face of the Keep foundation. She screamed and charged into Liam as the tunnel collapsed, pushing him into the path of the falling rocks. Someone grabbed her arm and pulled her back as small rocks bounced off her. She stumbled back, landing on her upper back outside the rock slide.

Lassair pulled her up. "Tanwen! We have to go!"

Tanwen tried to move, but she stood rooted to the spot until Lassair pulled her toward the woods. She followed, but her legs were wooden, refusing to obey her mind, as the enormity of what happened became clear.

She had killed her beloved husband.

Tanwen stumbled on a tree root and fell to her knees.

Lassair grabbed her arm and dragged her up, hissing, "Don't you give up on us! Don't you dare!"

Tanwen found her feet and ran, pushing the shock and horror as far away as possible. It would be worse if the younglings didn't make it.

She heard running water—the stream was close. Something moved, and she bit back a scream. Lucas ran from the shadows to meet her.

"We've got everyone. What do we do now?"

Tanwen herded the girls to the spot where the boys were hiding, noting that Gitta and Lassair were wounded. She had to get them to safety. "Lucas, how far is the first stop to the hunting camp?"

"A couple of hours north, but we'd have to go past the Keep to get there, and Liam and Colum know where it is. Is the other way better?"

She closed her eyes, shoving away the thought of Liam buried in rock. She took a steadying breath and looked at them. "Lassair, Gitta, can you communicate with your dragons?"

They shook their heads as they turned their pale faces toward her.

"Does that mean they're dead?" asked Gitta.

"I don't know, but it's not good. We'll head for the Southern Keep. Lucas, you're second in command. If the dragons are dead, I won't have much longer. Lassair and Gitta will probably survive, but girls, I won't lie. It's going to hurt. If anyone dies, leave them and keep moving. Getting as many of you to safety is the priority."

Lucas nodded, but she saw fear in his—in everyone's—eyes.

She scanned the rest of the group. "Nothing like this has happened in our history. We're all afraid, but bravery means doing what scares you. At this point, it's all we can do. Let's go."

She led them southeast along the creek, focusing on her surroundings. As the sky lightened and obstacles became visible, they moved faster.

Dead leaves crunched under their feet despite their attempt to move silently, and the smell of disturbed earth made her sneeze. When she heard chain mail jingling nearby, she herded the younglings under the branches of a fir tree, and they clung to the trunk until the sound disappeared.

Tanwen crept to the edge of the nearest branch, pushing it aside, looking and listening. Motioning to the others, they crept out and kept going. The sun peeked over the horizon, sending a golden glow between the tree trunks.

She was relieved to see daylight, but it didn't help her ignore the forest. A shiver ran through her as the trees seemed to bend toward her.

They kept going as the sun rose. When they reached a wide spot in the stream, she motioned for them to stop. She crouched to drink and wash her face. Her hands trembled as she scooped up a mouthful of water to drown the panic blooming in her gut.

The Keep was under attack; it may have already fallen. Quillon was likely dead, or close to it, and she had two dozen trainees to protect. They had no food or shelter. Most of them didn't have adequate clothing. The darkness had passed, giving way to milky sunlight and shadows that looked wrong. The sky was gray and cloudy, and the air smelled like snow.

"Tanwen?"

She jumped to her feet, her hand going to the hilt of her sword. Lassair stood several feet away, well out of sword range.

Tanwen released her sword and pushed her hair out of her face. "Don't ask me what we should do. I don't have nearly enough information."

"I know. I came to see if you needed any help."

"With what? Do you know something I don't?"

Before Lassair answered, Tanwen heard a noise and held up her hand, snapping her fingers to get the younglings' attention. She made a circle in the air with her hand, and they snapped into formation alongside and behind her. Tanwen's heart hammered until she heard the hoot of an owl. She answered with one of her own, and a moment later, a shadow detached from the woods and Moira led another group toward them.

Tanwen swallowed a sob and stumbled into Moira's arms.

"I knew you'd make it," Moira whispered.

"I don't know how much longer. I can't find Quillon."

Moira stepped back, her jaw slack. "You too?"

Tanwen shook her head. "None of us have heard from our dragons."

"Laoch, preserve us," muttered Moira.

Tanwen looked past her as Dinsmore joined them. Blood spattered his clothes, and his salt-and-pepper hair and beard were tousled.

"I'm glad to see you," he said. "Good job getting the trainees out. There's a lot of carnage at the Keep."

"It's fallen then?"

He nodded. "It looked that way to me. I called a retreat, and everyone around me scattered. Where are the dragons?"

Tanwen?

She gasped, her hand covering her mouth. Moira's eyes widened in shock. *Quillon?*

Yes. His voice in her head was distant and muffled, as if he spoke from far away.

Are you all right? What happened?

Raine said the sun's disappearance caused it. She called it a wandering darkness.

"What's wrong?" asked Lucas.

She swallowed tears of relief. "Quillon." She looked at Lassair and Gitta, whose faces were drained of all color.

Quillon, are Peio and Haur alive?

We are all alive, and we all have empathy for the times when you are unwell.

Moira's voice was thick with emotion. "Raine says they're alive. You will hear from them soon."

Gitta covered her mouth, stifling a sob, and she and Lassair embraced. Dinsmore's shoulders sagged with relief.

Tanwen swallowed the lump in her throat. *I'd be glad, but you have to get somewhere safe. The Keep has fallen. Eventually, the enemy will figure out you're there.*

Alarm pinged through their bond. *You are safe?*

She glanced at the surrounding woods. *Yes. Sort of. We are heading to the Southern Keep. When you get out of the lair, we'll activate our beacons.*

I do not think we will be able to leave right away. We are weak. I will inform Raine that we must protect the tunnels until our departure.

"Are the dragons on their way?" asked Dinsmore.

Tanwen shook her head, dashing tears off her face with both hands. "Whatever that darkness was, it incapacitated the dragons, and they're too weak to move now."

His jaw went slack, and he put his hand on the nearest tree to steady himself. He looked around at those surrounding them, and his jaw clenched. Before she could ask Dinsmore's advice, she felt a jolt of surprise from Quillon.

Tanwen, we seem to be trapped.

Tanwen's heart jolted against her ribs as Moira's face paled.

Moira sank, sitting beside the nearest tree, tucking her head between her bent knees.

Dinsmore crouched beside her. "Moira?"

Tanwen gasped, trying to breathe, as her vision went dark at the edges. She sank to the ground beside Moira, ignoring everyone's concern. *What do you mean?*

The tunnels out of the lair have collapsed.

All of them?

All the ones we can see. It is possible we might find a way out when we have recovered.

Tanwen closed her eyes, forcing air into her lungs, and relayed what Quillon had told her to the others.

Dinsmore went pale, and he turned to one of the other Wreiddons. "Shaw, take the others and gather firewood, water, whatever you need to do to keep everyone busy for a while."

Shaw nodded. "Everyone with me." He led them away and began assigning tasks.

Dinsmore crouched, forming a tight triangle with Tanwen and Moira. "If we go to the Southern Keep, it will be safer than keeping the younglings out here in the open."

Moira closed her eyes and took a deep breath. "If you want to go to the Southern Keep, take whoever wants to go with you. I'm not leaving until Raine is out of the lair."

"Me neither," said Tanwen. "The enemy, whoever it is, collapsed the tunnels on purpose. I saw them collapse the one we came out."

"Why?" asked Dinsmore. He shook his head. "Never mind, that was dumb."

Moira leaned in closer. "If they trap the dragons, they don't have to worry about fire."

Tanwen bit her lip. "I think it's worse than that. I think they want to starve them to make dragon *tanad*."

Dinsmore went white. "I wonder if they know what happens to you when the dragons die?"

"I don't know, and I'm not sure I want to find out," said Moira. "What I do know is we need to free the dragons."

Tanwen glanced over Moira's shoulder at the others. "I wish that was the only thing." She shifted her gaze to Dinsmore. "We have a few dozen people, maybe a dozen seasoned fighters. It's winter. We don't have adequate shelter, clothing, or food. Our survival depends on retaking the Keep."

Dinsmore looked around, tapping the fingers of his right hand against his knee. "There are a few with us who can create food and water."

"Will it be enough for everyone?" asked Moira.

"Unlikely," said Dinsmore, "but it will help. We'll set up camp here. The hanging branches will block some of the wind. I'll put together a hunting party. You two focus on learning as much as possible about the dragons' situation." He touched them both on the forearm as he rose and strode away.

Tanwen leaned against Moira. "I didn't know things could get this bad."

Moira put her arm around Tanwen's shoulders. "It is dire, but we'll figure it out. Or we won't." She leaned her head against Tanwen's. "Laoch, preserve us."

Tanwen busied herself gathering firewood with a group of young children. She did her best to appear calm to avoid frightening them more than they already were, but the circumstances couldn't get much worse.

"Tanwen?"

She jumped and dropped her bundle. A couple of children scrambled to pick it up as Tanwen looked over her shoulder. Lassair and Gitta caught up with her. She took a deep breath and shook out her hands.

Lassair stepped closer, leaning closer, so the children didn't overhear. "Sorry to scare you, Tanwen, but we've been talking. We don't know anything about the people who attacked us—not who they are, or their numbers, or anything. How about a small group of us sneak in to get food, clothing, and our saddles? It will give us a chance to scope out what we will face later."

Tanwen wanted to shut them down, but the time for protecting them was over. In her heart, they were still first-year trainees, but she had to face the fact that they were fully trained Wybrens. It was too much to bear. "Have you fleshed out a plan beyond that?"

Gitta's eyebrows flew up as she looked at Lassair.

"Not yet," said Lassair. "We wanted to find out what you thought first."

Tanwen shook her head a little and blinked moisture from her eyes. "I think it's a terrible idea that might get you killed. But it could be sound tactically and strategically, even logistically if it works. Put together a few options, but keep it between us for now. There's no point in getting rumors started; we have enough to worry about. Plan as if you need approval from Sine. If you think like her, we may stand a chance."

"Yes, Wybren Tanwen," answered the girls together, grinning in amazement at each other as they dropped back.

That was a sound response, said Quillon. *Their dragons will help them, and they will come to me if they have questions.*

Good. You think like Sine more than I do.

You are improving.

A trickle of relief passed through her, and she took a deep breath. *Has anyone recovered enough to explore?*

The younglings are doing that now. Wait, they are returning.

Tanwen concentrated on the buzz of dragon communication to block out her unease of the forest. The wind rattled the dead branches as if telling her it wouldn't be that easy.

Tanwen, we are trapped. They thought there was one open tunnel, but magic shields block it.

The trickle of relief froze solid. *Shields?*

They took the first one down with fire. The next one is impervious to flame.

"Uffern!"

Those near her twisted to look at her. She saw her frustration mirrored on the faces of the other Wybrens.

"Lassair, come help these younglings with firewood." She stomped back to Dinsmore. "The dragons found

what they thought was an open tunnel. It's blocked by
a fire-proof shield."

Dinsmore's shoulders relaxed. "Only one shield? We
can fix that."

She resisted the urge to throw her hands in the air.
"How?"

"Leave that to me. Between us, we have more kinds of
magic than dragon fire."

Chapter Five ~ Commain

Adrienne sat in the window seat in her study, watching the barn and unbraiding her blonde hair. She saw Vask and Isidro launch with riders. They headed south, and she breathed a little easier when she saw Oswin in Vask's saddle with Briant behind him.

She shook out the last braid on the left side of her head and started on the right. "Thank you, Goddess, for getting them safely away."

She rose and pulled the bell cord, returning to the window. She felt sure the fight wasn't over. As if she'd conjured them, *tanad* swarmed out of the woods. She heard shouting from the parapet and saw the defenders' frost cones fall past her window, freezing the *tanad* solid. Immediate concussive strikes thundered from above, and the *tanad* and remaining ballistae shattered.

The door opened. "Yes, Bealban—?" Kevia's voice trailed off.

Adrienne turned, ignoring Kevia's shocked expression. "Gather the apprentices, acolytes, and guards. I want everyone not defending the abbey in here. Now."

"Y-yes, Bealban Dia."

She removed the last of her braids, shaking out her waist length hair and massaging her scalp.

A tray of food sat on her worktable, and she wandered over. The last thing she wanted to do was eat, even though she knew she needed to. She ate a handful of berries and pushed back against the dread that something was about to happen.

Help me, Goddess. Help me focus on what I need to do now.

She heard voices in the outer room. Someone demanded to know why Kevia had summoned them, and Adrienne felt irritation rising in her gut. "Stop dithering and come in!"

The door opened, and they filed in. She ignored their stunned expressions—no one had seen her without braids in years.

She motioned them closer. "The Goddess has begun Her purge of the unbelieving. We must be in tune with Her will in all things. Remove your braids and put away your robes. We will dress as common people, so we blend in. The enemies of the Goddess will seek to destroy all who belong to Her, and none of us is safe.

"Toireasa and Steren, go to the tabernacle for morning prayer. Roisin and Orlaith, you will relieve them in two candles. We will rotate day and night so that someone is praying at all times.

"Kevia, you will be my companach. Move your things to the consort chamber beside mine and pack my robes away. The trappings of my office need to be secured."

Steren protested, and Adrienne silenced her with a look. "It is not for any of you to question your assignments."

Kevia's shoulders tensed. "But I'm the lowest acolyte, Bealban Dia."

"I'm aware of your status. I have made my choice based on the leading of the Goddess. One more thing: When I say the trappings of my office need to be secured, I mean every one of them. You cannot use my title until I tell you otherwise. Starting now, I am Adrienne."

Several of the older women gasped.

She paused for a moment, meeting their eyes. "It is going to be dangerous for us. The enemy is powerful, and I am a bigger target than the rest of you. If the enemy comes, I must not stand out. I will need all of you to shield me, and to do that, we cannot use titles."

Kevia squared her shoulders. "We will do as the Goddess wishes and as you command, B—" She took a breath. "Adrienne."

Adrienne stood. "Let's change clothes and get to work."

Raya gripped the front of her saddle, watching for trouble. *Isidro, are you all right?*

No, I am not. But we cannot stay where we were, and we must find Finley if possible.

Raya swallowed hard. She knew the difficulty of working through illness, but dragons didn't get sick. She pushed aside her concern for Isidro and focused on watching for the enemy. They followed the road, and Isidro flew low. Although dragons were difficult to target, the situation was far from typical. Whatever had blocked the sun had gone, but the warmth from the light did little to warm her.

A few minutes later, Isidro said, *I see something on the road ahead.*

Raya looked over his head. She saw a carriage and a wagon in the middle of the road. The horses were gone. *Is there room for you to land on the road?*

Yes. He circled past the spot in a tight spiral and landed several yards beyond, facing it.

Raya slid out of the saddle and jogged toward the wagon. She didn't see anyone, but when she reached the wagon, some gifts they'd brought for the king were in it. Her stomach dropped, and she hurried to the carriage. Apart from some scattered belongings and blood on one seat, it was empty.

This is not good, Isidro. Can you hear people?

No.

She closed her eyes for a moment, leaning against the side of the carriage. *Since Gautier is dead, we have to assume Finley is, too.*

I agree.

Sorrow welled inside her, and she pushed it down, dashing tears from her eyes with the back of her hand. She went back to the wagon to check for anything useful. Gifts and belongings were scattered haphazardly. She snatched up the warm clothing and bundled it into a spare cloak.

I think we need to get back to the abbey and cremate Gautier. This could have been done by bandits, but I doubt it. If Dorchadans did this, it's a safe bet they already have Finley.

Are you sure you do not want to track them?

I do want to track them. I want to find Finley and take her back to Gautier, but funerals are for the living. I won't risk our lives to find her body. She walked back to Isidro and stuffed the clothing into the saddlebags. *Let's get back to the abbey.*

I will make it back there, but I must rest when we arrive.

It hasn't been too long since we left. Chances are they haven't moved Gautier yet, so I'll see to that while you rest. She climbed into the saddle. *Let's go.*

Chapter Six ~ Commain

Briant trudged after Oswin, shifting the saddle to his other shoulder. They passed through two more large clearings. He started to ask Oswin why his hunting blind was so far away, but Vask scoffed in his mind.

You heard what the Bealban Dia said. Put aside your animosity.

You heard that?

I heard more than you think.

Oswin turned to the edge of a clearing and walked to a large oak tree. He recited what Briant assumed was a spell, pressed his hand into the trunk, waited, and then nudged. A door swung opened, and he shifted the packs. "Come on."

Briant shifted the saddle and followed him into the tree.

Oswin used another spell to light oil lanterns, one on each wall and one on the table in the middle of the room. With a wave of his hand, he shut the door behind Briant and dropped the packs on the corner of the hearth.

Briant looked around the small cottage with its tiny loft. Oswin walked to the space under the attic and opened curtains which were veined like leaves, the delicate strands allowing dim sunlight to filter through. The walls were rough-hewn logs, placed vertically instead of horizontally. The hearth was a hollowed rock set into the wall.

Oswin nodded to the ladder on the left side of the loft. "Put the saddle in the corner and take your pack up there."

Briant didn't trust himself to speak. He put down the saddle, retrieved his pack and climbed the ladder. The loft had covered windows at each end. A few bins and barrels lined the front edge, providing access while affording some privacy to the beds against the back wall. A faded rag rug covered the floor. He put his pack on the bed and went down the ladder.

Oswin was measuring tea into an earthen teapot. A copper pot glowed in the hearth, and Briant walked over to look at it.

"Don't touch it," said Oswin. "I'm heating water."

"How?" asked Briant. He sank to his haunches, trying to see a heat source.

"Magic, obviously."

Briant scoffed. "I can see that. Open flame in a tree sounds like a bad idea."

"We're not actually inside a tree. The cottage is spelled to look like a tree to hide it."

Briant's jaw dropped. "It's not an actual tree?"

"Oh, there's a tree. I built the cottage under it and used it as the basis for the camouflage. It's similar to the birch tree hunting blind."

Briant, if you are at your destination, it would be helpful to verify your location relative to mine.

Should I step outside and raise my beacon?

There was a pause. *Yes.*

"If I step outside, will the tree let me back in?"

Oswin's brow furrowed. "How far do you plan to go?"

"Hopefully, only a few steps. Vask needs to verify our relative locations."

Oswin gestured toward the door and followed Briant out. "How?"

He drew the beacon from his shirt and held it up. "Part of becoming a Wybren is to make a beacon. When we get separated, it helps him find me again."

"You communicate over that distance?"

Briant shrugged. "That's not really that far for us."

I was correct, said Vask. *His voice had a note of sleepiness. Are you going to tell him our range is unusual?*

I haven't decided. Get some rest.

I shall.

He dropped the beacon back into his shirt and realized Oswin looked even more confused than before. He nodded toward the door. "Let's go back in and I'll explain."

Oswin shook his head and went in, closing the door behind Briant, and sat at the table.

Briant sat across from him and took the beacon off, sliding it toward Oswin. "One of the last steps in Wybren training is to go into the woods alone to find a stone to use as a beacon. When you find it, the dragon blows fire on it to make the beacon. Any of the other Wybrens will tell you there is a ceremony to do that, but it's not necessary. Vask and I were on a mission when we made mine, and it increased our range of communication."

Oswin's hand hovered over the beacon before he pulled it back and folded his arms across his chest. "So you are able talk to him when he's nearly half a league away?"

"Our range is closer to a full league, but it's longer than most. Our bond is unusually strong."

"Why?"

Briant resisted the urge to say something boastful. "We haven't figured that out yet. Maybe it's because Vask is old."

It is not; Aithne and Saphir also have an unusually strong bond.

Do you have any thoughts on why, then?

I do not. My bond with Niall was not as strong.

Briant shook his head. "Vask says it's not his age, and he doesn't know why it's stronger than usual, but my friend Aithne and her dragon also have a strong bond."

Oswin poured tea into two cups. "Perhaps it will become clear later." He focused on his cup for a moment and then leaned his arms on the table. "Since it appears we need to work together for a time, I guess we should figure out how to get along."

Briant nodded. "That might be harder than we think, given that our cultural differences. It doesn't seem like we have much in common."

Oswin grunted in assent. "We have almost nothing in common."

"Nothing—not magic, religion, even the food is different. Is that why the Goddess sent me here? Because we need to learn to think like each other?"

"I cannot say. What would your people do in this situation?"

"Figure out the magic, since that's why I'm here. That part hasn't changed, and I'm glad. It's a relief to have magic work the way it's supposed to when it never has for me before."

Oswin cocked his head. "How did it not work?"

"At first, I couldn't do anything except use an accuracy spell. After I bonded with Vask, I was able to use a shield spell, and my light wisps were brighter, but I shot lightning with a fireball spell. It's only been since I learned about Lledrith that I've made any real progress."

"That had to be frustrating."

Briant shrugged. "You learn to live with it. It was better after Mam made my brothers stop teasing me about it. Anyway, it's working now, and I'm glad to have something to focus on, but it feels urgent, like I've made progress but there's more to do that I have time for."

"I have that impression also," said Oswin. "It's hard to know where to start. Perhaps the Goddess will have some instruction."

Briant shifted. "It's going to take some time before consulting the Goddess becomes the default for me."

"That's to be expected, considering." He pressed his lips together, and his jaw twitched. "I will try to keep it in mind. You seemed to have encountered those people before, yes? The ones surrounding us in the barn?"

"The *tanad*? Yes, unfortunately."

"What are they? Why did so many of them look alike?"

"They're reanimated corpses. We think the enemy's necromancers can make multiple tanad from one body."

"Did you know any of them?"

Grief lanced through Briant. He took a breath and nodded. "Some of them were my family."

Oswin sat back, staring at Briant. He touched his heart with his right hand. "May the Goddess comfort you."

Briant blinked back tears. "If you don't mind, I think I'll go upstairs and meditate for a while."

"Of course."

Briant left the tea and bolted up the ladder before his tears fell. Comfort from the Goddess? Not so far. He took off his boots and settled, cross-legged, on the bed.

He tried to imagine the meadow in his mind where Lledrith used butterflies to teach him spells, but his mother's face swam before his eyes. A single butterfly edged into his periphery, and he physically turned his head to look at it, even though he knew it was unnecessary.

It shimmered, and he heard a woman's voice. *Let go of your fear.*

Guilt stabbed him, but he couldn't say why. Surely, concern for his family wasn't a bad thing.

The image of his mother spoke to him, but it wasn't her voice. *You can do nothing for them. Fear will halt your progress.*

He swallowed against the lump in his throat. *But if I knew they were all right...*

She cocked her head. *What will it change if they are not? You must trust them to survive on their own.*

And if they don't?

She leaned toward him as her eyes turned black. *None of you will survive if you fail.*

He gasped and opened his eyes. The words were like cold water on his skin, and he shivered. He took a few calming breaths, looking for something to focus on, but found nothing but existential dread. Briant covered his face with his hands. They were doomed.

He felt Vask stir through their link. *That is counterproductive.*

Briant lay down and curled into a ball. *Thank you, Vask. So is telling me it's not helpful.*

You are young and easily overwhelmed. You must pick a direction and move.

Tears ran down his face into the pillow. *How? What direction do I choose?*

That is between you and the Goddess. Go back to your meditation.

He closed his eyes and, again, saw his mother's face. This time, he turned around. In his mind, he was still in the barn, surrounded by *tanad*. But the butterflies swarmed around him, settling on his head and shoulders. When he mentally sank to the ground, sitting up straight, the butterflies didn't move. He closed his eyes, and when he opened them, they were in the meadow. He saw a column of gold, human-shaped, moving toward him, but he wasn't afraid.

Good. You're back.

Briant frowned; it was the same woman's voice, but this time it came from the glowing silhouette. *Do I know you?*

I am Lledrith.

He frowned as the butterflies fluttered away. *My magic?*

Just so. You will learn many things in the coming days. You must both keep an open mind and pay attention.

He smelled crushed grass and heard a single footstep behind him. *Both?*

She means me, too, said Oswin, sinking to the ground beside him.

Briant started to ask where he'd come from, but Lledrith continued.

Time flies; much remains. You must follow my lead, even when it makes little sense.

We will, said Oswin.

Lledrith turned toward him. *You are the guardian. Harm to the Lavban Dia affects everything. There is no time for animosity.*

Before Briant could ask what that meant, Lledrith disappeared in a flash of blinding gold light, and Briant jolted upright on the bed. "What—"

Oswin climbed the ladder and sat on the rug. "Ask your questions."

Briant snorted. "I don't even know what to ask."

"Then let us start with Lledrith. The woman we saw is the embodiment of your magic. It comes directly from the Goddess and is only given to certain people. She will teach you the magic, and I will, apparently, see to it that you are safe. You will likely have questions as you progress about the Goddess. I will answer those, but questions related to magic must go to Lledrith."

"I keep hearing Lavban Dia. What does that even mean?"

"It means Arm of the Goddess. For reasons known only to Her, the Goddess chose you to do her work." He got up and opened the curtains, lingering at the window. "I suspect it's because someone a long time ago misunderstood her teachings and sent us in the wrong direction. You know nothing about Her, so there is nothing to unlearn." He turned back to Briant. "Perhaps this will be as much of a learning experience for me as it is for you. Already my beliefs have been shaken. We believed the Lavban Dia would be a priestess, someone who has served the Goddess her entire life."

"So a male Wybren was the last thing you expected."

"Yes." He started down the ladder. "Come. We need to eat and begin adjusting our paradigms."

Adrienne allowed herself the indulgence of checking her reflection before Kevia returned to put away her robes. She hardly recognized herself with her hair loose, dressed in trews, a tunic, and sturdy riding boots. She didn't look as she had when she was younger. She looked like her earliest memories of her mother. And Sagart.

She shivered. If there was one person she didn't want to look like, it was her arrogant, entitled aunt. Adrienne had no idea how her mother and her aunt were so different. Her mother wanted to serve the Goddess and their people. Sagart served herself.

The reflection of something gold outside the window caught her attention. She spun. Isidro? What were they doing back? He landed clumsily in the field beside the barn, and Raya—if it really was Isidro—slid out of the saddle. Isidro lumbered into the barn, and Raya ran out the opposite door.

Adrienne strode to the adjoining room, startling Kevia when she jerked the door open. "Did you see the dragon?"

Kevia frowned. "What dragon? Just now?"

"Yes, I think it's Isidro!"

Kevia dropped the tunic she'd been folding on the bed and ran for the door. "I'll go see what's happening."

Adrienne nodded and looked out the window. It was Isidro—he spiraled to the ground, close enough for Adrienne to recognize Raya. She ran for the door, oddly surprised at how much faster she could move without the robes encumbering her. She strode through the hall, brushing past people, and down the stairs.

Raya and Kevia were near the door, and Raya looked alarmed. She looked up at Adrienne, looked away, and looked back. Frowning, she turned back to Kevia.

When Adrienne got to the bottom of the stairs, the other two came to join her.

Raya's eyes were wide. "Why does everyone look so different in regular clothes?"

Adrienne shrugged. "Desperate times. Why are you back so soon?"

"I found the carriage and wagon that the rest of the diplomat party took to Gynhalion." She glanced around.

Kevia cleared her throat. "Bel—Adrienne, perhaps you should talk in your study? I'll fetch some food for Raya and arrange to have something taken to Isidro."

Raya's eyebrows raised. "Adrienne?"

Adrienne nodded. "Come. We will share our stories."

Raya put a hand on Kevia's arm. "Thank you for thinking of Isidro. I suspect it's going to take a day or two for him to recover fully."

They didn't talk until they got to Adrienne's study. As soon as the door shut behind them, Raya turned to Adrienne.

"Please tell me you had Gautier's body moved, and Kevia didn't know about it."

Adrienne's breath caught, and she sank into a chair. "I hadn't gotten that far."

Raya bit her lip and sat gingerly opposite her. "She was dead, right? Maybe she wasn't, and it seemed like she was?"

"No, she was dead. How can she not be there? Briant's shield isn't active."

"Are you sure? I don't know a thing about magic."

Adrienne shook her head. "Briant would have to be here to shield her. Is her saddle still there?"

A line formed between Raya's eyes. "Isidro says no." She pinched the bridge of her nose. "Uffern."

"What did you find?" asked Adrienne. "You said something about the carriage and wagon?"

Raya picked at the hem of her tunic. "It looked like it had been ransacked. The people and horses were gone. I found a little blood, but not enough to account for serious casualties."

"So the whole diplomatic party was captured?"

"I think we should assume they have. If they come back here, you'll need a way to verify they are not tanad."

The door opened, and Raya jumped up, reaching for her sword, as Kevia came in.

Kevia stopped. "I am sorry, I didn't mean to scare you."

Raya sank back into her chair. "I'm a little over-whelmed."

Adrienne stood. "I'd say more than a little. Kevia, put that on the table and join us. Perhaps we can help ease the Wybren's anxiety."

Raya's eyes went wide. "How?"

"Prayer, of course, if you'll allow it."

"I don't know what good it will do, but sure, if it makes you happy."

Adrienne didn't take the time to explain. She knelt beside Raya's chair, and Kevia knelt on her other side. They joined hands and placed their other hands on her shoulders. She felt Kevia slip seamlessly into meditation, and Adrienne closed her eyes. Humming softly, she reached for the Goddess. The words of a psalm came to her, and she sang the words, letting them flow naturally as the power of the Goddess filled her. She pushed it through Raya to Kevia, who channeled the power back to her, creating a loop of power that eroded fear with a stream of peace.

In her mind, Raya looked like a silhouette filled with red lightning. Adrienne wasn't surprised, but she was a little relieved. This, at least, was something positive she could do. She channeled more power from the Goddess into Raya, and her voice dropped to a whisper as she prayed. She watched as the magic flowed over Raya. Kevia gathered it and channeled it back to the Goddess. As Raya's lightning diminished, Adrienne's fears also calmed. When Raya's inner being smoothed and turned deep pink, Adrienne stopped the flow. Raya's concerns were still present, but the fear and panic subsided.

Adrienne ended the prayer, keeping contact with Kevia through Raya as the power of the Goddess smoothed to a steady glow. When she opened her eyes, Raya's face was wet.

"What was that?" she gasped.

"Was it painful?" asked Kevia.

Raya shook her head, wiping her sleeve over her face. "Not at all. I don't understand it, but thank you."

"It's been a stressful day," said Adrienne, moving back to her chair. "I needed that, too."

"As did I," said Kevia. She rolled to her feet and nodded to the tray on the low table. "You both need to eat. I'll see that you're not disturbed, but you're not leaving until that food is gone." She swept out the door and closed it.

Adrienne chuckled. "I promoted her this morning, and suddenly she's bossing me around."

"We all need a friend who will do that," said Raya, pouring tea into both cups. With a pang, she thought of Finley and wondered if Ceann was all right.

"I haven't had a friend here since I took the gold. Except Oswin, but he's not here all the time."

"It didn't sound too friendly between you this morning."

Adrienne chose a sweet roll and put it on a plate. "When I became Bealban Dia, well, being the Mouth of the Goddess isn't as great as people think. It's hard to be responsible for the spiritual well-being of all the people in Commain, but I'm the youngest one in centuries, and having a twin brother doesn't help much. It's been an adjustment for us both. Anyway, back to the task at hand. Do you have thoughts about what happened to Gautier?"

Raya stared into her cup. "Yes, and I hope I'm wrong."

Fear spiked through Adrienne, and she clasped her hands tightly in her lap. "You think the enemy got her?"

Raya nodded. "I don't know how. I saw people on the roof; have they been there since the attack?"

"As far as I know."

"I'd say it doesn't matter now, but it does. Someone must have seen something, or whoever took her is scary powerful."

"Is there any precedent for a dragon disappearing?"

"No." She put down the cup and scrubbed her hands over her face. "Isidro says he tried to see if she was dragged out, but there are so many footprints in the sawdust it's impossible to tell. It's probably best to assume the enemy has her and everyone from the party traveling to the capitol. You should prepare people. The necromancers for the enemy know how to make several tanad from one body. Or they make one and replicate it. I don't know, but the Western Keep Wybrens reported seeing people they knew all over the place."

"Sounds awful."

"I suspect it'll be worse than awful. What about Ruan and Dermod? Did they demand to be let out to fight during that incursion?"

Adrienne frowned. "I haven't heard. To be honest, I'd forgotten about them."

"There's been a lot going on. Leave them to me. After all, I was left here to liaise on their behalf."

A trickle of relief flowed through Adrienne. "You should probably start with Mercia."

"I need to take care of Isidro first. I left his saddle on, hoping you could tell us where Gautier was so we could take care of her, and I don't want him left alone in his present state."

"I understand. Take some food to the barn and rest for a bit. I'll have Kevia organize a group to watch over him while you are away. Apparently, we need more people on watch on the parapet, too."

"Thank you. I suspect I'll have to find somewhere more secure for him."

Adrienne thought of the temple and its inner courtyards. They were big enough for dragons, but the landscaping would be ruined, not that she cared about that. "Leave that to me. We'll talk later."

Raya leaned against Isidro. He slept deeply, and she caught bits of his dreams. She closed her eyes, resting her head against his side, holding tight to the peace she'd gained from Adrienne and Kevia. She'd never known peace like it before, and she wondered if there was a way she could find it for herself.

She heard voices outside the ruined barn. One sounded like Kevia. She rolled to her feet, trying not to be afraid, and strode to the nearest opening.

Kevia raised a hand in greeting, not pausing her instructions to those who walked with her. Raya saw two men and three women, and she had to remind herself that Commainish men didn't fear dragons like Slannish men did.

She glanced at the abbey and saw more people patrolling the parapet. It seemed Adrienne had made good on increasing security. It appeared that they had been divided into four groups, each focusing on one side of the building.

Kevia and the others drew near. "Wybren, I have organized shifts to protect Isidro until he is well. Are you ready to come with me?"

Raya pushed back against the anxiety of leaving Isidro and nodded. "He's asleep. I hope you are all bored to tears when I come back."

Kevia chuckled. "May the Goddess grant all of us boredom for a while."

"Amen," said one of the women, and the others echoed her. They walked past her into the barn, surrounding the sleeping dragon and facing away from him.

Kevia touched Raya's shoulder. "He will be safe, and we have procedures in place for others to come to their aid if needed."

Raya bit her lip and looked over her shoulder. "He's safer with five of them than with one of me." She shook her head. "Now I know how new mothers feel."

Kevia smiled and wrapped her arm around both of Raya's shoulders. "Come. Let us see to other things. You will be back with him soon, and I will leave others with you."

Raya nodded, reaching out with her mind, and fumbling to grab hold of the peace she'd felt earlier, and followed Kevia into the abbey to the infirmary.

Kevia stepped in ahead of her. "Healer Mercia? This Wybren would like a word." She turned to Raya. "I will tell Adrienne you will speak with her shortly."

Raya remembered the healer from a couple of days before—had it really only been a couple of days?—and she joined her at the waist-high table. Mercia was pounding herbs in a large mortar.

"Have you come to talk about Ruan and Dermod?" asked Mercia.

"I have. Adrienne was going to check in with you, but I thought it would save time if I did it. How are they? Have you had any luck narrowing down the spell?"

Mercia's eyebrows rose when Raya said Adrienne's name, but turned her attention back to her work. "I may have. Or, rather, I think my colleague has. It appears to be a dormant spy spell, but the men seem not to be aware of it. Based on the location in the brain, this is entirely possible. If it is the type of spell we think it is, it would allow the caster to see and hear through the spelled person."

"How do you know that?"

"Our ancestors used a spell like it during the ancient wars. It hasn't been used for centuries, as far as we know. It took a team of us to figure it out, including a neuromancer and a historian."

"What does that mean for them? Is there a way to negate the spell?"

Mercia put down her pestle and leaned her forearms on the table. "I cannot say, at least not yet. As I said, the spell appears to be dormant, but the nature of it would allow the caster to turn it on and off at will, and we have no way of knowing yet when it's active. Honestly, I don't know if we can know without monitoring them around the clock, and we have other priorities now, as I'm sure you can imagine."

"I can. How much have you told them about your findings?"

"Not much. We don't want to give anything away to the enemy if they are being monitored."

"Could I talk to them? I'd like to check on their welfare."

Mercia seemed to consider for a minute and then nodded. "Apprentice Caol? Have the Slannish men brought to my study, please."

"Right away, Healer."

Mercia laid a cloth over the mortar and led Raya to a small room with a desk and shelves crammed with scrolls. One of the other apprentices brought in extra chairs, scooting out the door as the men arrived.

Raya noted they looked well cared for and even reasonably rested, which didn't surprise her.

"Raya! How's Briant?" asked Dermod.

"He was fine the last time I saw him."

Ruan grinned. "You say that like you weren't with him a little while ago."

Raya's brow furrowed, and she glanced at Mercia.

"He has recovered from his spell," said Mercia. "How do you feel?"

"Like I've been sleeping for days. I'm going to need something to do soon," said Dermod.

"Me, too," agreed Ruan.

Raya forced a sympathetic smile. "I'll see if I can find you something. There's nothing worse than unrelieved boredom. Almost makes you wish there was a battle to watch or something."

Ruan chuckled. "I don't know if I'd go that far. It might be worse to be locked away and not able to do anything but watch."

"We are old fighters, after all," said Dermod. "Having something useful to do would help, though. Even mundane tasks help me gauge the time I've spent. I've been losing track of time, and I don't like that."

Raya nodded. "I understand. I'll find something for you. You've been treated well otherwise?"

"Apart from being cooped up, yes," said Ruan. "It was nice to get outside for a while earlier."

Dermod nodded. "And they've allowed us to share a room, so I don't feel so isolated."

Mercia leaned forward. "I'm glad that's helped. I was wondering, have you had any strange dreams in the last few nights?"

Ruan frowned. "I don't remember any dreams." He turned to Dermod. "I don't remember anything much at all, do you? It's like I have blank spots in my memory."

"That's a good way to put it," said Dermod. His brow crinkled. "I have blank spots, too, but there's something that wants to be there, like when you know someone is hiding in a room. You know they're there, but you can't see them."

Mercia tapped her lips with one finger. "That sounds like something you should discuss with Geralt." She glanced at Raya. "He's our neuromancer."

Raya scrambled for something to say when someone knocked at the door.

"Pardon the interruption, but Kevin has sent for Wybren Raya. Shall I have someone come to return the Wreiddons to their room?"

"No," said Mercia. She had a crease between her eyebrows. "I'll keep them here for a bit, but I would like Geralt and Heddwyn to join us."

"I'll see to it. Wybren?"

Raya stood. "Stay the course, gents. I'll see about finding you something to do." She followed the young woman from the room and through a series of halls that all looked the same. Eventually, she led Raya into an outer study and knocked on the inner door.

Raya heard a voice from inside, and the girl opened the door for her. There was a table set up in front of the fireplace, and Adrienne stood near the window.

When she turned to face Raya, she looked older than her years, as if she hadn't slept in days. "Thank you for coming," said Adrienne. "Kevia wants you get a hot meal before returning to Isidro."

Raya inclined her head. "That's kind." She joined Adrienne at the table. The smell of bread and meat made her stomach grumble. "I don't remember the last time I ate a proper meal. It seems like I should be hungrier."

"I feel the same way," said Adrienne. "Stress has a way of stealing one's appetite. How is Isidro?"

"Still sleeping," replied Raya, taking the cover off her plate and smiling with relief when she saw roasted meat and several kinds of root vegetables. "The eclipse took a lot out of him, and having to fly so soon after was difficult for him." She pushed a carrot around her plate with her fork. "I don't like having him in a vulnerable place. I think we're going to have to find someplace more secure, but I don't know where that would be."

"I have an idea. The temple in Gynhalion has a large inner courtyard surrounded by deep porticoes. It's nearly twice the size of the barn he's in now, and while it's not entirely enclosed, it is partially sheltered."

Raya allowed a tiny trickle of hope as she tore open a hot roll. "So we'd have to move to Gynhalion. How far is that?"

"By the shortcut, two days on horseback. We'd have to work out the logistics of getting everyone there."

"Everyone? You're abandoning the abbey?"

"No, I have a small group planned."

"What about Ruan and Dermod?"

"I don't have a clear leading about them. Did you talk to Mercia?"

"I did." She spread butter on the bread and told Adrienne about their conversation.

"Interesting." Adrienne turned toward the door. "Kevia?" When Kevia appeared in the doorway, Adrienne said, "Send for Mercia, but tell her there's no hurry. We need to talk about our male guests."

"I'll let her know."

The door clicked behind her, and Adrienne turned back to Raya. "I think it's going to be a long night."

Raya stabbed a piece of meat with her fork. "I think this is going to get worse before it gets better. We should take advantage of quiet and hot food while we can, and I want to hear your thoughts on getting people to Gynhalion." She dragged the meat through a puddle of gravy before eating it.

Adrienne nodded. "If nothing else, eating will keep Kevia from fussing at me." She chewed a mouthful of potato and sighed. "I've missed having someone fuss at me."

Raya snickered. "I know exactly what you mean."

Chapter Seven ~ Annwn

Aithne woke when something damp hit her face. She opened her eyes in the darkness. It was snowing.

The fire was still burning, and the protector was asleep, leaning against a tree, his feet crossed at the ankles. For a moment, she wished she had some snares. If she could slip one around his feet, it might buy enough time to get away from him. That, and asking the Goddess to hide her again.

She reached for her pack and lifted it into her lap. Watching him, she eased to her feet and crept into the woods, hoping if he heard her, he'd think she was going to relieve herself. She had a waterskin and a day's worth of food if he was telling her the truth. Surely she'd be able to get to Saphir more quickly on her own.

Snow fell thickly, but the wind was calm. She stopped after several minutes and folded her blankets, stuffing them in her pack, which she threw on her back before jogging north. She watched for slippery spots, trusting the snow to cover her tracks.

Dawn was gray, and the snow fell in curtains. *Saphir? I'm on the move.*

She heard the sleep in Saphir's voice. *It is early, beloved.*

I know. If I activate the beacon, can you track me?

I believe so. Is your guide behaving?

I ditched him. He was asleep when the snow woke me.

There was a long moment of silence before Saphir said, *I am not sure that was wise.*

Aithne clenched her jaw. *You're not the one traveling with him.*

Perhaps not physically, but I am aware of him.

Are you aware of how insufferable and rude he is?

Yes. That does not mean you do not need him.

She dug her beacon out of her shirt. *Whether or not I need him, I still need you to track me. I don't have a warmer/colder pendant to find you, and I think we agree getting to you needs to be the priority.*

Do we? Have you mastered your magic yet?

Aithne stopped. *What are you saying? That I should stay here where people are hunting me? I've learned how to access the knowledge I need. When I'm back with you, I can continue to work on it. Just because I come to find you doesn't mean we have to go home right away.*

Have you mastered it enough to keep from harming people? From accidentally hurting me?

She gasped at the question. *Saphir! How can you think that?*

You did not intend to hurt Rylin.

Tears sprang to her eyes. *Does that mean you won't help me?*

No, beloved, but I cannot assist with your magic, and your work is not yet complete.

Snow fell off a branch onto her shoulder. She looked up and saw a raven. "Great." She snorted and started walking. "Don't tell me. I sound like a dragon walking in the woods, and even the snow couldn't hide where I'd gone."

The protector fell into step with her. "I admit I had to look a bit before I picked up your trail. The snow did hide your tracks, and you are surprisingly quiet. I found you because I had an aerial view and no leaves for obstruction."

"Good for you. I'd have that, too, if I could get back to my dragon."

"Do you know where she is?"

Adjust your course to your left, beloved.

Aithne pointed in the general direction. "That way, or so she says."

Saphir continued to guide them through the day, and by midafternoon, the protector finally spoke again. "We can find shelter in a cabin to the east."

"How far east?"

"We can be there before dusk."

She shrugged and gestured for him to take the lead. "I don't want to impose on whoever lives there."

"No one lives there. It is one of mine."

"One of yours? How many do you have?"

"A few. My patrols take me all over Annwn. I find it useful to have shelters scattered about."

"Hopefully, we don't find a bear hibernating there."

"It is protected by magic."

She snorted. "Of course it is."

He turned toward a dense wood, and she had to turn her attention to watching where she was going. When he stopped, she nearly walked into him. He gestured as if removing condensation from a window, and Aithne saw a small cabin through the trees. He led her to it, stopping outside the door and reversing his previous gesture.

"What was that for?" asked Aithne.

He opened the door, stepped in, and looked around.

"I reset the wards so they recognize you. No bears. Come."

She stepped over the threshold into a small room with a fireplace and a bed. She sent a light wisp toward the ceiling and saw a chest next to the bed.

Saphir?

I hear you. The wards do not prevent communication.

That's something, at least.

He put his pack down beside the fireplace and removed a laurel wreath. He put it in the fireplace, and it smoldered. "There is firewood and food through there." He gestured to a door beside the hearth she hadn't noticed until he pointed it out.

Putting her pack down, she opened the door and found a large closet. Passing out several pieces of firewood, she said, "I thought your wreath didn't use fuel."

"It will last longer and heat the cabin faster with wood. You will find some dried potatoes and onions in there. I will make soup, and we will talk about what you need to know."

She found several clay crocks with dried vegetables, and when she took them out, he walked in the door from outside with a copper pot filled with snow. He put the pot on the hearth and added vegetables before pushing it closer to the fire. "The snow is heavier than before. If we are careful, we should be safe here for a few days."

"Days? But—"

"I must assess your control before we go further."
He turned to her, cutting off further protest. "There is
much you do not know. We must seek the will of the
Goddess before proceeding. There are several paths we
could take, and we need to find Hers."

She wanted to protest, but knew he was right. She
shook out a blanket, folded it, and dropped it on the
floor to sit on. "Fine. Where do we start?"

He stirred the soup. "It will take some time for this to
be ready. You meditate, and I will see to our needs."

She bit back a sigh and closed her eyes. Breathing
deeply, she tried to quiet her mind, but her thoughts
raced. Part of her wanted to escape, but he would find
her again. He hadn't spoken as they walked, but she
thought she felt less hostility from him. It made no difference to her feelings, but she knew it was better if she
didn't actively offend him.

She smelled roses instead of soup, and her brow furrowed. She opened her eyes and found herself in the
clearing where she'd met with Lledrith. The sunlight
bathed it in gold light, and warmth seeped into her
bones. A sound made her turn, and she saw the Western
Keep surrounded by *tanad*. The gate, or what was left of
it, hung from its hinges, and the door into the Keep was
missing. She turned in a circle and saw blood, bodies,
and more *tanad* than she'd thought possible.

She felt a presence. Lledrith stood beside her.

"Is this real?" asked Aithne.

"It is."

Shock shot through her. "It's real right now? The Keep was attacked?"

"It has begun. It is up to you to help defeat her."

"Her?"

"All will be made clear. Stop resisting and pay attention."

Darkness swirled around her, and an icy wind chilled Aithne. She opened her eyes and saw the cabin. Quinn appeared to be meditating.

Saphir?

I saw. Quillon has confirmed it is. Not only that, the dragons are trapped. He has ordered us to remain here and focus on the task at hand.

She shivered. *Did he say anything about casualties?*

Your mother is alive, and the other Wybrens. I do not know more.

She swallowed hard, and the protector opened his eyes. "Did she show you a path?"

"I'm not sure."

"What did she show you?"

"My home was attacked. Saphir confirmed it and told me the dragons at the Western Keep are trapped. Is that what you saw?"

He shook his head. "I saw only darkness and blood, but it is disturbing that it is not only here."

Vask says Commain was also attacked.

Aithne shivered and told the protector. He ladled soup into a bowl and passed it to her. She picked up her spoon, and he lifted his brows. He bowed his head over the bowl, so she did, too. "Gracious Goddess, we thank you for the provision of food and shelter. Allow them to strengthen us to follow the path You will lay before us."

He nodded and began to eat. "You said Lledrith showed you your home?"

"Yes."

"What does she look like?"

"Human and female, but made of gold light."

"Has she said anything about your role in all of this?"

"Only that I need to pay attention so I can help defeat the enemy, but I don't know who the enemy is, or how I'm supposed to help defeat her."

"Her?"

"That's what Lledrith said—the enemy is female." She thought of the mages who had kidnapped her. "I think—I think this has been going on longer than any-one realizes."

"What do you mean?"

She told him about being kidnapped, first by the necromancer, and then by the female mages who were taking her to Raca. She'd eaten two bowls of soup by the time she finished the story.

He was quiet for a long time. "The Goddess has begun dismantling the dogma we have adhered to for so long. Even now, many of my people are sure you are supposed to be a male warrior."

"Why would they think that?"

"Our tradition says the Lavban Dia will be a male warrior who will lead the attack against the darkness." He snorted and shook his head. "*I* am more convinced than ever that you are who we've waited for."

The side of Aithne's mouth quirked up. "It sounds like it hurt you to say that."

"It did."

She smiled despite her circumstances. "Fair enough. I don't want to be here either. You keep saying a phrase I don't know."

"Lavban Dia is a title. It means Arm of the Goddess. She is using you to bring peace to our world."

"Why do you think it's me if you've been expecting a male warrior?"

"Lledrith communicates with you directly, the Goddess hears and answers your prayers, and the glomachs defended you."

She put her bowl on the hearth. "Glomachs? Are those the little furry rodents?"

He sighed and pinched the bridge of his nose. "Yes. Do you not have them in Slan?"

"Not that I've seen, but maybe in unpopulated areas."

He grunted. "They do tend to be reclusive."

"How did they defend me?"

"They healed your wounds from the grimalkin attack enough to keep you from dying, and they shielded you from predators who would have sensed your magic or smelled the fire dragon."

"They can do that?" She shook her head. "Never mind. Sorry, I'm not questioning you. It's something we do when we're surprised."

"Slannish? Or human?"

She paused. "Both? I don't have a lot of experience with anyone outside those groups."

"Likely as much experience as I have with them."

She jumped as the wind slammed into the wall. "We might be stuck here a while. It will be marginally more pleasant with a truce."

"What do you propose?"

"That we agree not to get offended when one of us doesn't understand something, we address each other with our names, and that we won't kill each other in our sleep."

His eyes narrowed. "You have low standards."

"We have to start somewhere."

"I can't argue with that. I want to, but I can't."

Her chest loosened. It was a tiny victory, but a victory all the same. "Lledrith told me your name is Quinn. I'm Aithne."

He inclined his head. "I know."

Aithne woke the next morning to the sound of water dripping. She sat up and squinted in the dim light of the banked coals. Quinn wiped the floor beside a small bucket sitting under a leak in the roof.

He glanced over his shoulder. "Good morning. Add some wood to the fire, please."

She yawned and reached for a log. "Just what we need today, right? A leak in the roof?"

"It is not how I would choose to start the day. We'll have to patch this before we go."

She scratched an itch on her right forearm. "That might not be all bad. You said you have to evaluate my magic."

He grunted. "I suppose that's as good a way as any to do that. We'll start after breakfast."

"I'll get some snow." She got up and grabbed the copper pot, pushing hard on the door to open it. She scooped snow from the nearest drift and came back in. Her arm itched again as she put the pot over the fire, and she pulled up her sleeve. Something looked wrong, and she held her arm out to the fire to get a better look. There was a black mark on her skin, and faint lines swirled out from it in all directions. "What is that?"

Quinn looked up. "What is what?"

"There's a strange mark on my arm."

He came to look at it. "I've never seen anything like that, but there are stories in our lore of the Goddess marking fae She chose for specific purposes. Perhaps that's a Goddess mark."

Aithne sat on the hearth, staring at it as he pulled out food. When he reached for the pot, she got up and pulled her sleeve down. Staring at it wouldn't make it go away.

She made tea while he prepared the food. When they'd finished eating, they dressed in their warmest gear, and Quinn shouldered the door open.

The sky was gray, and snow fell, shrouding everything and muffling sounds from the woods. The trees rattled as a whisper of breeze made her shiver.

"We will need to clear the snow off the roof to get to the leak. A wind spell will do the trick."

"I don't know how to do that."

"I suspected as much. I'll show you."

She watched as he recited the spell, holding his hands in front of him, palms facing out. A gentle breeze blew snow away from the cabin.

He dropped his hands, and the breeze stopped.

Aithne's brow furrowed in concentration. "Say it again, please."

He repeated the sequence twice, and she said it with him the second time.

He stepped back and crossed his arms. "Yes, that's correct. Now you do it."

She blinked. "Without meditating first? I've never done that."

"You won't always have the option to meditate first, and this is a simple cantrip."

She pushed the unease away and nodded. "Does it matter how I hold my hands?" She raised them, and he adjusted the angle of her left hand. She recited the spell exactly as he'd taught her. Her sleeves dampened, and instead of a breeze, a stream of water arced from her hands. It melted the snow where it fell before freezing. She closed her fists, and the water stopped.

"I—what happened? What did I do wrong?"

Quinn stared at the ice, his jaw slack. "Nothing. If I hadn't watched what you did, I'd say you used the wrong spell, but you did it exactly as I did." He shook his head slowly. "I don't understand it."

"Should I try again?"

"No! No, I'll do this a different way. Go inside and meditate. See if Lledrith will tell you what went wrong."

Aithne wanted to protest, but went back inside. She took off her coat and toed her boots off. Settling on her blanket beside the hearth, she closed her eyes. For a moment, her mind went to what Lledrith had shown her about the Western Keep the day before, but Saphir soothed it away, and Aithne sank into the warmth of her meditation.

She breathed deeply, and soon Lledrith appeared.

Her voice had a tinge of amusement as she said, "Quinn is correct when he says you cannot meditate before you cast a spell. Meditation is for learning, and you must learn the basics, starting with this: the spells he teaches you will never work correctly. My spells are not the usual spells; they are more potent, but easier for you to control. I will teach you a wind spell. While you are inside, you must whisper the words. When you have mastered it, you will go outside and practice. The louder your voice, the stronger the wind."

Aithne smiled. "That should be easy to remember."

Lledrith flowed toward her, and gold light surrounded Aithne's head. She sighed in the warmth as words formed in her mind. Lledrith moved back and shifted to a more human shape. "You have the words. Now I will show you the movement, but do not say the words yet."

Aithne watched Lledrith's hands for a round before joining her. They repeated the movement several times, and the cadence of the words became clear. When they started the next round, she whispered the words and felt the air move. Lledrith drew her hands back, so Aithne copied her, and the air stopped. They did it twice together, and then Aithne did it herself, adding a bit of volume, and a breeze made the fire dance.

"Just so," said Lledrith. "Now go outside and practice. Vary your volume, and do not blow Quinn off the roof."

The glow faded. Aithne rolled to her feet and slipped on her boots. Shrugging her coat back on, she stepped outside and started the spell, quietly the first time, and the top layer of snow blew away. She drew her hands back and turned to the bank that had blocked the door. She repeated the spell a little louder, and it cleared. Grinning, she drew her hands back slowly, and the breeze became an air current. She stopped the movement, and it remained constant. Curious, she extended her hands, and the wind picked up, blowing the snow away layer by layer.

She turned in the general direction they'd traveled from the day before and pushed her hands forward. She moved a few layers of snow within a few steps. Tilting her head to the side, she pulled her hands back and started the spell in a louder voice. When she pushed her hands forward, she cleared a path. A slow smile spread over her face as she walked forward, following the path that spread before her.

"What did you do?"

She gasped and yanked her hands to her chest, spinning toward the cabin. Quinn stood on the roof, his eyes wide, and his face red from the cold.

She propped one hand on her hip. "Please don't startle me during my practice."

He crossed his arms. "Show me what you did."

She repeated the spell for him to hear and directed the snow against the wall of the cabin, making a snow bank. She laughed, her heart lighter than it had been since before her stone quest, and she felt a surge of happiness from Saphir.

Quinn shifted his weight and shook his head. "Clearly, I am not the one to teach you about magic."

She pulled her hands back and looked up at him. "Lledrith told me any spell you teach me will backfire."

"Good to know. I'm nearly done."

She nodded. "I'll go make tea."

"That would not come amiss."

She chuckled, noting that he hadn't thanked her, and went inside. She added another log to the fire, then took the pot outside to scoop snow from the bank she'd made. When she went back inside, she left her boots and coat by the door and hung the pot over the fire. The log hadn't lit, and she knelt to blow on it, but stopped herself and whispered the spell, directing a small air current into the coals. The flames leaped, and the log caught. She yanked her hands back. "Yikes. Best not to do that inside."

Saphir chuckled in her head. *Quinn will not be amused if you burn down the cabin after he has fixed the roof.*

Aithne laughed and stood to get the teapot. The sound of dragons talking to each other buzzed in her mind, but she didn't pay attention until she felt a wave of something she couldn't identify from Saphir.

Beloved, I have news. While unsure of Tanwen's consent, Quillon feels you must be made aware.

She set the pot aside and sank onto her blanket. *What is it? Is Mama hurt?*

Tanwen is whole and uninjured. However, Liam did not survive the attack.

Aithne's breath caught, and for a moment, she couldn't think. *What—what happened? Does Quillon know?*

He was not conscious during the event, but Tanwen told him he attacked her, and she pushed him into the rockslide that closed a tunnel when they trapped the dragons.

Aithne's heart pounded. *Mama killed him?*

It was self-defense, beloved.

She nodded and opened her mind to Saphir to show that she didn't blame her mother despite the shock and disbelief. Saphir sent a wave of empathy, wrapping it around Aithne's consciousness like a hug.

Aithne choked on a sob, pulling her knees to her chest and resting her forehead on them. Through her weeping, she heard the water boil and poured it into the teapot without burning herself.

Saphir, is he really gone?

I'm afraid so, beloved.

How is Mama?

As well as possible, under the circumstances.

Aithne started to ask what that meant, and then decided she didn't need to know. *You'll tell me if anything changes?*

Certainly.

She sniffled and checked the tea.

The door opened, and she jumped, wiping the tears off her face with both hands as Quinn entered. She poured a cup of tea and passed it to him.

He sipped it and frowned. "What is this?"

"Tea."

"But not my tea."

"No, I didn't want to rummage through your pack, so I used mine."

He sipped it again, scowling. His brow softened, and he nodded. "Not bad. I'm going to—what's wrong?"

Aithne swallowed against the lump in her throat. "Saphir told me my stepfather was killed in the attack on the Western Keep."

Quinn's face went blank. Setting his cup on the hearth, he leaned forward to cover her hands with his. "May the Goddess comfort you in your sorrow."

She blinked back tears, clenching her jaw as she started to thank him. "That is kind, but he will not be the last we lose." She took a shaky breath. "You said you are going to do something?"

He picked up his tea and cradled the cup in his hands. "I will warm up and then go scout a bit. I want to check the weather and make sure no one is following us, and that will be easier as a raven."

"In the absence of a dragon, a raven will do nicely."

"I'm so glad you approve," he said dryly.

Quinn had been gone for quite a while, but without the sun shining, Aithne didn't know how long. She'd had time to wash and mend the tunic slashed by the grimalkin's claws on her first day in Annwn, and she'd refilled their water skins. She was about to start a pot of soup when she heard the call of a raven outside. A moment later, Quinn ran in and slammed the door.

"We have to go!"

Aithne stood. "Now?"

He nodded. "I saw a group of scouts heading this way. We have an hour at best." He grabbed his pack and stuffed his things inside.

Aithne packed her blanket and the tunic she'd washed. "Why are they still tracking us?"

"Most likely my sister sent them." He jerked open the closet door and dumped onions and potatoes into his pack. "Can you ride a horse bareback?"

"I don't know; I've never needed to."

He muttered under his breath. "We'll have to do our best. You'll have to carry both packs since we don't have saddlebags."

"But we don't have a horse."

He shot an incredulous look at her and rolled his eyes. He tipped the contents of the pot over the fire. "Do you have everything?"

She looked around. "Looks like it."

"Good. Come on." He thrust his pack at her and rushed out the door.

She shrugged into the straps of his pack and settled it on her back, and then threaded her arms through the straps of her own pack and pulled it onto her chest. When she walked out the door, she saw a white horse standing beside the snow bank she'd made earlier. Pulling the door shut, she strode over and scrambled up the bank to climb onto Quinn's back. "I'm sorry if I pull your mane."

He whickered and walked away from the cabin.

Aithne turned and whispered the wind spell, raising her hand to erase their tracks.

Quinn walked into the woods, and she turned back to grab a double handful of mane as he found a game trail and trotted.

She squeezed her legs, and when she shifted, it was harder to move. "Are you using magic to make me stick?"

He whinnied in a way that sounded affirmative.

She snorted. "You use magic for everything. I can't imagine."

The trail widened, and he broke into a canter, forcing her to pay attention to their surroundings and duck to avoid low branches.

Well past dark, he stopped near a grove of pine trees. Aithne slid off his back, surprised at how stiff she was, and blew on her hands to warm them.

Quinn shifted back to his normal form. "We'll have to camp tonight, but we should get to the next shelter before dark tomorrow." He strode into the grove and chose a spot.

Aithne followed, stretching her stride, and dropped the packs on the ground. She rubbed her sore shoulders and stretched her neck. "I guess we need firewood."

"Fire is a bad idea. Has Lledrith given you a spell to warm yourself?"

"Not yet, but I'll ask for one."

"We need to keep watch. You meditate first, and then I'll take a turn."

"Are you sure you don't want to go first? You ran with a burden for hours."

He shrugged. "I'm going to eat before I meditate. I'd rather have travel rations than graze."

She chuckled and pulled out her blanket. Dropping it on the ground beside the tree, she settled onto it, pulling her coat closer to her body and stuffing her hands into the sleeves.

Shivering, she sank into meditation and opened her eyes in the meadow. The sun shone on her, but it lacked warmth.

Lledrith prompted her to put her hand on the ground while imagining her body expanding as if taking a deep breath. She wasn't sure she understood, but she tried it. Magic flowed from the earth into her body. She said the words Lledrith whispered to her, and she became warmer.

She lifted her hands in the air and inhaled more magic. It flowed from around her like dust motes in the sunshine. After a few minutes, she felt full and stopped drawing magic, but she understood how Quinn used magic in ways she thought frivolous. He'd said it was what the fae did, and she wondered if they would run out of magic in the future.

Lledrith chuckled in her head. *It will never run out for you.*

Chapter Eight ~ Western Keep

Tanwen stood in front of the collapsed tunnel, sword in hand, as the rocks shifted. She wanted to run, but she was rooted to the ground. She couldn't contact Quillon.

Rocks rolled toward her, pebbles bouncing off her boots, and a hand rose from the rubble.

Panic rose from deep in her gut, boiling up as the hand pushed the debris away, and Liam rose, hatred in his eyes.

Someone touched her, and she screamed.

"Tanwen, it's me!"

She blinked as Moira's face coalesced in the darkness. Her breath came in short gasps, and Moira gripped her shoulders.

"You're safe. Take a breath."

Tanwen shook her head, vainly attempting to control her panic to breathe. She gripped Moira's upper arms and closed her eyes.

"It was a dream," murmured Moira.

Tanwen focused on Quillon. *It was a dream, Tanwen, and I will wait to ask what it meant.*

A gasping sob rose in her chest. *It means I killed Liam when the tunnel collapsed. At least, I think I did. I don't think it was a tanad. He bled when I stabbed him.*

Quillon sent calmness through their connection. *We will puzzle out what happened later.*

"Tanwen, Dinsmore needs us," said Moira.

Tanwen nodded, swallowing hard, clinging to the wave of peace from Quillon, and staggered to her feet. She trembled as she followed Moira, and when they joined Dinsmore and three Wreiddons, she clasped her arms over her chest, nodding a greeting so she wouldn't have to speak.

"We need to see what the current status of the tunnels is," said Dinsmore. "Seamus will be in charge while we go and assess the situation."

Graham shifted. "I still think Shaw should go with us. If the tunnels have collapsed, he'd be the best one to figure out what to do."

"You know he's not going to leave Tarian here while his wife is missing," said Sullivan.

"If he's the best man to figure out how to free the dragons, he needs to come," said Moira. "Tarian can come with him."

Dougal snorted. "You really think having a child with us is a smart idea?"

"No, I don't, but I'd rather have a child there than compromise the dragons' survival," said Moira.

Dinsmore nodded. "We'll have bigger problems if the enemy is successful in making all the dragons *tanad*. Graham, go get them and let's get this done."

The sun had begun to rise when they arrived at the Keep. They stood in the tree line in front of the tunnel where Liam was buried. She shuddered and turned away, focusing on the line of light on the horizon.

Focus, Tanwen, said Quillon.

She nodded and forced her lungs to expand. Shaw stopped beside her, and Tarian murmured something sleepily, his foot brushing her arm.

The men murmured beside her. She wanted, more than anything, to walk out of the woods and go inside the Keep to go to her study and start a mundane day; she felt a pang of grief for that part of her life.

Someone whispered her name, and she jolted back to reality. "Sorry, Dinsmore."

"I want to go inside and get to work." He shook his head. "Come on, we're going to see if there is anything they missed that we can exploit."

They walked around the Keep in the tree line as much as they could. All the tunnels except one were blocked with rock. The one that wasn't blocked clearly had a magic shield that even Tanwen saw.

They stopped when they ran out of cover.

"Do we dare scout the other tunnels?"

"I can do it," said Lucas. "I learned a new shield spell that will camouflage me."

Sullivan snorted. "Yeah? Let's see it."

Lucas glared at him and invoked the spell. The shield rippled, then Lucas disappeared.

Dinsmore glanced sideways at Sullivan, whose jaw hung slack. "Satisfied? Go on, Lucas. Be quick. Meet us back here."

"Be right back, sir," said Lucas.

Tanwen saw a ripple as he started away from the trees. But she knew no one would see it if they weren't looking for it. At least she hoped so. "What's the plan? Do you think we can do this? It's going to take magic, right?"

Dinsmore nodded. "Without a doubt, it's going to take magic. We need to figure out how much. We don't know how heavily those tunnels are blocked."

Sullivan crossed his arms, his eyes going unfocused for a moment. "I wonder how to drop that shield?"

Dinsmore nudged her. "Is it possible for Quillon to go down there?"

I'm already heading that way, said Quillon. *I see the daylight.*

When he stepped into the tunnel, she saw his face, blurry through the shield. For the first time since the eclipse, she felt a trickle of peace.

It almost evaporated when Quillon said, *This is as far as I can go.*

She relayed that to the others.

Graham cursed. "Of course, they shielded with multiple shield spells. That's what I'd do, but I hoped they weren't that smart."

Tarian wandered away. Tanwen glanced at him, but thought nothing about it as the sound of dragon communication buzzed in her head.

"So, how do we drop the shields?" she asked. "One at a time, I assume."

Graham nodded. "We need to get closer to see if it's a spell we know."

Sullivan snorted. "It's probably not."

Lucas appeared beside them, startling Sullivan. He grinned. "All the tunnels have collapsed except the one that opens to the field. That one is shielded three times over that I counted. I tried to drop the spell, and it didn't work, which wasn't surprising."

Dinsmore squeezed Lucas' shoulder. "Well done."

"I'm sorry, I don't have better news."

"We don't expect good news right now."

Beloved, said Quillon, *since there are two shielded tunnels, perhaps we should open one with fire.*

Tanwen nodded. "Quillon wants to know if fire will drop a shield."

Shaw's eyebrows raised as he glanced over her shoulder. "If it doesn't drop the shield, might compromise the rock anchoring it." He shifted his weight to his right. "Tarian! Come back this way."

I will try the one near you, said Quillon. *I do not want to make it easier for them to get us out if the worst happens, and the other tunnel is the logical choice for that.*

Tanwen shivered. "Quillon is going to try to fire the shielded one near him."

She heard Quillon warn the other dragons before light burst inside the tunnel. The men flinched, and Graham and Sullivan dropped to their knees.

Dinsmore fidgeted as the light faded.

I am through the first shield!

Tanwen pumped her fist in the air. "It worked!"

I must wait a moment before proceeding to the next one to ensure the fire has not compromised the walls.

She nodded. "He's waiting for the walls to cool to make sure the rock wasn't weakened."

Before anyone answered, the ground shook, and the tunnel to Tanwen's right slid down one side in a thundering pile of rubble and dust. Tarian ran back to them and grabbed his father's legs.

"What was that?" asked Sullivan.

"I don't know, but we'd better take cover," said Dinsmore, heading for the woods.

Tanwen followed. Behind her, she heard Tarian whimpering. When Shaw caught up, clutching Tarian against his chest, she said, "It scared me, too, Tarian."

What was that? asked Quillon, his voice alarmed.

Rock slide at the next tunnel. You need to get someone to check it out.

They took cover under an outcropping of rock, and Lucas shielded them to watch the Keep.

Tarian whimpered an answer to a question his father asked, and Shaw's jaw dropped. "*You* did that?"

Tanwen crouched beside Tarian. Behind her, Sullivan sputtered, and she saw Dinsmore elbow him.

Tarian dashed the tears off his face with the backs of his hands. "I saw a rock that looked loose, so I used my magic to pull it out, and the wall came down."

"Someone is coming," hissed Lucas.

Tanwen felt a ping of alarm from Quillon. *Is there a way to keep them away from the shielded tunnel? The walls are still glowing.*

Tanwen glanced around the edge of the wall. *I don't know, but it looks like they're focused on the one Tarian compromised.*

The enemy soldiers fanned out into the woods. Shaw nudged Tarian closer to Tanwen before he and Dinsmore shielded the surrounding area. Tanwen wrapped her arms around the boy, holding his face against her shoulder. His heart hammered against her chest, and she tightened her hold, comforting him silently as the enemy walked past them. She held her breath to slow her heart.

His breath tickled her neck, and for a moment she remembered holding Aithne when she was a child and afraid of a storm.

The moments dragged on. When Tanwen had to suppress the urge to scream, they heard the person in charge call everyone back. The people who had walked past jogged back to the Keep, and tension trickled out of Tanwen's shoulders.

Dinsmore and Shaw nodded to each other. Before they dismantled the shield, they heard voices. Two more people, a man and a woman, strode out of the woods in front of them.

"How will we know dragon riders from every other woman?" asked the man.

The woman shrugged. "I know only what the riding jacket looks like, but what if they do not wear it?"

They passed within feet of the shield, and Tanwen didn't hear the man's reply. She didn't have to; she knew they were looking for Wybrens.

They went back to their makeshift camp in silence. Tarian held her hand the whole way, and she took a little comfort from it.

They were looking for Wybrens. The thought chilled her. Did they know that killing a Wybren could kill a dragon? They couldn't take anything for granted. They had to assume the enemy knew everything about them.

As they neared the camp, Tarian looked up at her. "Wybren Tanwen, did I mess everything up?"

"Not everything, but it could have been a dangerous mistake." She glanced at his father. "You need to stick close to the adults and do what they say."

"I will. I didn't know the whole thing would fall apart, honest!"

Tanwen nodded. "That's the effect of unintended consequences. Sometimes, things don't go the way we think they will, so it's important to think things through and try to imagine what could happen rather than what we think."

"That sounds hard."

"It can be, but it's a good skill to learn young." They paused while Sullivan signaled the watch. When they got the reply, they walked into the camp. The younglings had constructed crude shelters that blended with the surroundings.

Shaw said, "Tarian, go with Lucas. He'll find something for you to do."

"Yes, Papa." He smiled at Tanwen and released her hand to trot after Lucas.

"Thanks for handling that, Tanwen. I was too scared to be logical."

Tanwen smiled. "It's easier to do when it's not your child."

"I don't believe in much right now, but I believe that."

They started toward the area Dinsmore had chosen for strategy discussion.

Tanwen, said Quillon, *the rock has cooled sufficiently to proceed.*

Tanwen stopped walking. *Are you coming out?*

We cannot. There is another shield. Based on the positions of the shields we know about, we have hypothesized there are at least two in between.

Tanwen's heart sank, and she hastened her pace to the gathering of strategists. "Uffern. Quillon says the tunnel has multiple shields."

"That's not surprising," said Shaw. "It's what I'd do, and we knew there were two. There was no reason to think there wouldn't be more."

"I know, but I hoped there weren't."

"We all did," said Dinsmore. "Now it's confirmed. So, how do we proceed?"

"I'd say we start by building a fire," said Moira. "It looks like we'll be here a while."

CHAPTER NINE ~ WESTERN KEEP

Tanwen sat on a fallen tree, eating a steaming piece of venison. She didn't care that they had nothing to eat with; everyone cut meat off the carcass with knives.

As she chewed the last bite, she heard an alarm call from the watch. She stood and pulled her sword, waiting for more information. A moment later, she heard the all clear. Sheathing her sword, she went to the fire for more meat.

A commotion made her look up to see a half dozen ragged-looking people stumble into camp.

Tarian jumped up. "Mama!" He ran toward the group, and one woman knelt, holding her arms open. Shaw followed Tarian, falling to his knees to embrace them both.

Tanwen cut another strip of meat off the haunch. Feeding more people might leave nothing later. She was relieved to see more survivors, but couldn't help feeling a pang of grief that her loved ones weren't among them. Liam was dead, and Aithne might not come back.

Do not think like that, said Quillon. *Aithne is alive and will soon reunite with Saphir.*

Tanwen's legs trembled a little as she sank back onto her log. *You're sure she's whole?*

She assures Saphir she is.

Tanwen's hand trembled a little as she bit into the meat. *I guess that's something, then. She's got a handle on her magic then?*

Her level of control is unknown, but she is leaving Annwn. The fae suspect she orchestrated the wandering darkness and the attack there.

Tanwen almost choked. *An attack in Annwn?*

Yes, and in Commain. Part of the diplomatic party, including Gautier and Finley, are unaccounted for.

And when did you plan to tell me?

I only just heard from Vask.

She drank from her water skin, ignoring his sharp voice. *Is there anything else I need to know?*

There are tanad in Commain.

"Uffern!" The people nearby turned to look at her, and she stood, looking for Dinsmore. He was talking to the newcomers, and she noticed Siril for the first time.

Relief that he'd survived washed away a little of her fear. *Does Vask have anything good to say?*

Briant is fine. He says there is more, and he will tell me when he finds a secure location. I will relay what he says.

She stuffed the rest of her meat in her mouth, stalking toward the group. She caught Dinsmore's eye and nodded to a spot away from the group. *We need to get you out of the lair.*

Agreed.

Tanwen and the others rose well before dawn the next morning, dividing everyone able to fight into two teams, leaving the wounded, small children, and caretakers to tend their camp.

Tanwen tightened her sword belt, ignoring the hunger rumbling in her gut. Moria walked toward her, and Tanwen met her halfway.

"You ready?" asked Moira.

"As ready as I can be. You?"

Moira shrugged. "No, but that's normal. If I'm ready for a fight, it rarely turns out well. Be careful."

Tanwen hugged her. "I will if you will."

They parted, and Tanwen turned to her group. It was small, but she knew a large group would attract unwanted attention. They headed for the site of Tarian's rock slide.

Tanwen chose her footing carefully, not wanting to trip on a tree root and give away their position.

Quillon, is everyone inside ready?

We are. Activate your beacon when you get close. I will move everyone away from the tunnel.

Do you think they're making the right choice?

I do not know. I agree it will be quieter, but perhaps simplistic.

That's what I'm afraid of. Each decision looks right at first glance; however, it's probably not that straightforward.

Let us hope that it is.

The moon was setting when they arrived. Tanwen pulled out her beacon, holding it aloft until Quillon acknowledged it. He sent a wave of love and reassurance through the link, and Tanwen felt better despite the circumstances.

Moira and Tanwen gathered the younger Wybrens, and Graham cast a shield spell around each of them.

Tanwen shifted as the magic clung to her skin like moisture on a humid day. "This feels odd."

Graham nodded. "It does, but you'll get used to it. When the fighting starts, you'll forget it's there."

He finished the spells and disappeared into the trees to maintain the magic.

Siril appeared at her side. "Are ye ready?"

"I'm ready for this to be done and the dragons to be free."

"We all are. They're about to get started. The dragons are clear?"

"Yes. Quillon has them ready to go when the shields drop, but they're out of sight until that happens."

"Good. We don't need our own men running away in a panic." He tapped her shoulder and grinned. "See you on the other side."

Tanwen nodded and caught Moira's eye. They fanned the girls out between them in an arc. She took a few steps away, watching for the enemy, her sword ready. The magic shield tingled on her skin, and she wondered why they hadn't started doing this sooner. Unbidden, she heard Briant's voice in her memory say, "Because they've always done it the other way."

In her mind, Quillon said, *He is not wrong.*

I suspect a lot of things will have to change now, she answered, turning her attention to her surroundings.

Frost crunched under her feet as she set her stance, and she felt the wind gust, but the shield blocked the cold. A rodent rustled in the brush at the tree line, and she ignored it.

She heard a muted sound from the men and glanced over her shoulder to see them enter the tunnel. *Quillon, it looks like the first shield is down.*

A moment later, she heard shouted commands above them and glanced up to see human-shaped silhouettes peering over the parapet.

"Get ready," she said, her voice pitched low.

"How did they know?" gasped one of the girls. No one answered as a half dozen arrows rained down. Tanwen braced herself, but they bounced off the shield.

She didn't have time for relief. Several men ran around the Keep toward her, and she braced herself. "Incoming," she called, not bothering with stealth anymore.

The nearest man swung at her neck, and she blocked it, gasping as someone slammed against her side as he ran past. As she deflected a strike aimed at her torso, she heard more fighting behind her than she expected. She parried a third blow, knocking the man's sword hand wide and stepping in to stab. The tip of her blade penetrated his armor, and he growled, swinging at her head. She ducked, letting the blade pass over her head, and landed a blow on his unprotected side. She pulled her sword back as she stood, slicing through his armor.

He stepped forward, his face blank, and a chill ran down her spine. *Tanad?*

She pulled her dagger from the sheath. Taking a step back, she feinted with her sword, but he didn't fall for the trick. Instead, he stepped toward her again, stabbing at her gut.

She sidestepped his blade and reversed the feint. Her blade sliced through his arm, and the sword fell. He didn't yell or bleed, but he did flinch, giving her a tiny window of time to plunge her dagger into the side of his neck.

The expected gush of blood did not erupt. Tanwen's stomach twisted, but she didn't have time to give in to her revulsion. Another *tanad* heaved a war hammer at her head, and she jumped to her right.

A volley of arrows shot from the parapet, and she heard a wet gurgling sound in the brush. Her skin stopped tingling as she ducked away from the hammer again, driving her sword into the wielder's side nearly to the hilt. She tugged it out as he fell.

Beside her, Lassair yelped. She'd tripped on a root and fell backward. Tanwen saw a man with his sword tip down over Lassair, and she ran, shoulder blocking him in the side. He fell, and she sliced him from shoulder to hip, diagonally across his torso as a loud crash sounded from the tunnel.

"Retreat!" Dinsmore ran from the cave, followed by the other men. "Retreat!"

Tanwen hauled Lassair to her feet and stepped forward, but not before a knife cut the outside of her thigh. She gasped and turned; it was the hammer wielder. Thrusting her blade into him, she yanked it free and ran, limping, into the woods.

The enemy pursued. She dared not look back, focusing instead on putting as much distance between herself and Quillon as possible. Footsteps pounded behind her. Her heart hammered, and her injury prevented her from running faster.

"Tanwen!"

She glanced back. Her pursuer was Lucas. She slowed and let him catch up. He grabbed her arm and pulled her under a pair of trees, muttering a spell. She leaned against a tree trunk, gasping for breath, and Lucas shushed her as three *tanad* ran past. Her breath caught in her chest. One looked like Colum.

Lucas dropped to his knees, ignoring the enemy, and clapped his hand on Tanwen's leg.

She stifled a yelp as her skin warmed. When he removed his hand, blood covered it, but her wound had closed.

He wiped his hand on the tree and stood, looking around. He leaned in and whispered, "That's the best I can do to heal you. When it's safe, I'll find you a walking stick."

Tanwen nodded mutely. Safe? Would they ever be safe again? She pushed her back against the tree. *Quillon, what happened?*

They got through two shields. A lightning spell warded the third. One of the Wreiddons is dead.

She braced herself for the wave of grief, but it didn't come. *I think Graham is, too. The shield spell he put on us failed.*

Are you well?

I have a cut on my leg, but Lucas fixed me up for now. We're hiding.

She felt a wave of frustration through the bond. *They were so close.*

We aren't giving up, Quillon. We'll get you out.

I hope it's not too late.

Me too.

Lucas took a step away, looking around. He picked up a fallen branch, watching to make sure the immediate danger had passed.

Tanwen followed him and took the branch. "We'd better get moving," she whispered.

He nodded, and they turned for camp. When they arrived, she saw the remaining leaders in a tight circle, and Moira faced in her direction.

"Are we still shielded?" she asked Lucas.

"I dropped it. I wanted to get us back here in one piece."

"Thank you, Lucas. Well done."

He ducked his head, his face turning pink. "I wish we could have gotten them out."

"Lucas!"

Tarian ran toward them, making Tanwen smile. Moira strode toward her.

Moira grabbed her. "I was worried when you didn't come sooner."

"I'm sorry."

"No need for that. Come on, we're talking strategy, and we'll have a healer tend your leg."

Tarian pulled the hem of her tunic. "Wybren Tanwen? Are you hurt?"

She tousled his hair. "It's nothing a healer can't fix. Run along. I'm sure we need some wood collected or water fetched."

He sketched a salute and ran after Lucas.

Tanwen watched him go as she followed Moira. Something niggled in her mind, and she frowned.

As she neared the group, Tynan said, "If they did that once, they'll do it again, and they might change up spells. We don't know their abilities."

Dinsmore turned to her. "Tanwen, I'm relieved to see you. How is Quillon?"

"Frustrated but alive."

"So are we. Why don't you see a healer? We're figuring out how to negate their shields."

"Why?"

Sullivan snorted. "To get the dragons out, obviously."

Tanwen tamped down her irritation. "Negating the spells seems risky, given that, as Tynan said, we don't know what the enemy can do. Opening a rockslide will be more work and more noise, but there's less chance of unknown magic."

Moira touched Tanwen's shoulder with hers. "That's what I've been saying, too."

Tanwen looked Dinsmore in the eye. "I'm sure it's what Sine would suggest." She scanned the others. Most seemed unconvinced. "Tarian showed it is possible. He can't be the only one able to pull rocks from a distance."

"He's not," said Shaw. "I can do it, too, but it's not my best skill."

Tanwen drew herself to her full height. "Do what you've already failed at again if you think it's the right course of action. I'm going to see a healer, and then I'm going to pull rocks by hand, if that's what I need to do. I won't leave the dragons in the lair to starve and be turned. I will also point out that if Quillon and Raine die, so do Moira and I. The younger Wybrens will be incapacitated for an unknown amount of time." She looked at Sullivan as anger flared in her gut, clouding her judgment. "*You* might think that's an acceptable loss, but I'm sure not everyone will agree."

Sullivan sneered. "Don't talk to me about acceptable loss. *You* didn't lose anyone in dragon fire at Nokton. If it were up to me, we'd leave the dragons where they are, but since it's not, I say we work on the shields."

She turned on her heel and limped away, ignoring Dinsmore when he called her name.

Scanning the area, she spotted a healer and strode toward him.

He reached for his medical kit. "I thought we got everyone fixed up already."

"Sorry, Eoghan, I was delayed. Lucas patched me up enough to stop the bleeding."

Eoghan gave a curt nod. "Good. Come, let's get you fixed up."

She followed Eoghan to the small fire he'd been sitting by. As she eased onto the log he directed her to. Lassair knelt behind her, out of Eoghan's way.

"What happened? Peio says someone was hurt taking down a shield."

"I don't know what happened in the tunnel, but Quillon said one of the Wreiddons is dead."

"Any idea what their next move will be?"

She bit back a sigh. "I just got back, Lassair. Moira is advocating for us, but I'll tell you this. If I have to dig them out by hand, I will."

"Me, too. We all will."

Eoghan cleaned the dried blood off Tanwen's leg. "Not yet, you won't. You won't do Quillon any favors if you die from infection or blood loss."

"Do what you need to do, Eoghan," said Tanwen. "Lassair, tell the other girls I'm working on a plan."

"Yes, Wybren Tanwen."

Eoghan worked silently until Lassair was well away. "Do you think it will come to that? Digging the dragons out by hand?"

"I don't know. They were talking about negating the shields again. I don't know anything about magic, but I do know if something doesn't work, it's better to try something different." She shook her head. "Briant chafes at how we've done the same thing forever. I wish he were here to suggest something hair-brained."

"You can't communicate with him?"

"I think the dragons have been preoccupied. We all have been, or we might have tried that already."

"No time like the present. Sit still. I need to stitch this wound."

"Lovely." She braced herself on the log. *Quillon?*

I heard. Eoghan is right. That should have occurred to us. I have reached out to Vask and asked Raine to as well.

I hope one of you can reach him. I don't think this will end well if we don't try something unorthodox.

Agreed.

Chapter Ten ~ Commain

A few days after their arrival at the cabin, Vask woke Briant near dawn.

Briant, I am going to hunt and find better cover.

Briant sat up and yawned. *Is the hunting blind too small?*

The space is sufficient, but there is no roof. I do not wish to be covered in snow.

Snow? He squinted at the window near the head of his bed. Fat snowflakes fell and melted on the window ledge.

Across the room, Oswin stirred in the other bed. "What's wrong?"

Briant lay back down. "Nothing. It's snowing. Vask is going to hunt and find a cave or something."

They dozed until milky light woke them. A blanket of snow had accumulated. Oswin went downstairs to start breakfast, and Briant sat up, wrapping his blanket around himself, to meditate.

Instead of finding himself in the clearing, he stood outside the cabin facing north. The trees were bare, the trunks and branches partially transparent, and he could see mountains in the distance. Snow fell on his skin, but he couldn't see it.

Something that looked like a small bird circled the nearest peak and disappeared behind it.

Vask chuckled in his head. *I was bigger than that when I hatched.*

Briant smiled and rolled his eyes. *I'm sure the size was to show me you're far away. You found shelter, then?*

I did. The cave faces southwest, so you cannot see me, but the view is toward Slan.

A small wave of grief and homesickness washed over him, and he let it pass instead of pushing it away.

He heard the door open and close. Sighing, he dressed and went down the ladder for breakfast.

Oswin came inside with a cloth bag. "I had a few potatoes and onions planted, so I went to harvest them before the snow got too heavy." He dumped the contents on the table. "The snow is already banking on the west side of the cabin. Can you fill the bucket with snow so we have extra water?"

"Of course." Not bothering with his coat, he took the bucket and scooped snow into it. Oswin's garden patch was behind the cabin. He saw cabbage and what looked like carrot tops being covered by the falling flakes.

They both bundled up and went outside after breakfast. Oswin went around the back to harvest the rest of his garden, and Briant stayed in the front to work on his magic.

Dropping into the semi-meditative state he used for practice, he watched as the butterflies showed him how to move earth. His hands made the motions, pushing the snow into a pile and exposing the soil and leaves underneath. At the sight of the mess, he wrinkled his nose, and the butterflies reversed their motion. By mimicking their pattern, he moved the earth back, but it was still mixed up.

Oswin ran around the cottage and motioned for Briant to follow him. Irritated by the interruption, Briant opened his mouth to protest. Oswin put a finger against his mouth, holding the door open with the other hand, so Briant followed.

"What's going on?"

Oswin jerked the lower level curtains closed and whirled to shush him. He pointed to the ladder and whispered, "Strangers."

Briant climbed the ladder and looked out the window on Oswin's side of the room. Several people in red and black uniforms crept through the woods, a few arm spans apart in a line from the east.

He heard Oswin come up the ladder. He murmured, "They're going to see the garden patch any minute."

Briant frowned and begin the hand motions the butterflies had shown him. "Maybe not." He muttered the spell, and the snow smoothed over the remains of the garden. He shifted to cover Oswin's footprints, and then went to the other window and covered his own before the strangers entered the clearing.

One of them noticed the snow swirling and called to the others. Oswin moved to Briant's window to cast a spell that broke a sapling in the woods behind them, and the strangers turned. He muttered another spell, and a wolf howled. It sounded close, and the strangers ran around the cabin and back into the woods.

Oswin scrubbed his face with his hands. "That was too close."

Briant nodded. "I wonder if there are any others nearby."

"We'll wait a little while. When we're sure it's clear, we need to get back out there. You need to cover whatever looks like it's not part of nature, and I need to set wards in the woods. It's too dangerous to be caught unaware."

"I'm so glad Vask left," said Briant. "It would be awful if they found him."

Oswin's eyes went wide. "I'd better make sure the wards on the hunting blind are active. There's no hiding that a dragon was there."

There is no need, said Vask. *It snowed heavily while I flew. I am certain it covered the area sufficiently.*

Briant told Oswin, and Oswin's shoulders relaxed a little. "I hope he's right."

Briant's breath steamed in the cold air, and he shivered. Snow covered the tops of his feet and he was glad for warm stockings and sturdy boots.

The snow made him reconsider working outside. He didn't want tracks outside the cottage. But Lledrith had been clear that he needed to be outside, so he chose a spot in the sun and stood for a moment, eyes closed, sending his mind to the meadow.

When he opened his eyes, the butterflies were there, hovering in front of him. When they flew in a pattern, he copied it with his hands. They moved back, and he followed, frowning a little. So far, they hadn't taught him anything that required moving his whole body. They led him through a series of motions that felt like a dance. When they stopped, he was in the position he'd started in. He saw his footprints in the snow and fought back dismay as the butterflies returned.

He followed their lead again, and they looped through it twice with barely a pause. He recognized the pattern as the movement seeped into muscle memory. The fourth time, Lledrith whispered words in his head. Repeating them, the trampled snow shifted and filled in the footprints. He grinned as the butterflies stopped, hovering an arm's length to his right.

Getting the sense that he was supposed to try it on his own, he began the dance again. This time, he said the words louder, and the snow banked around him. Frowning, he increased his volume more, increasing the size of the hand motions, and the snow bank grew higher. He finished the series and looked around. A snowbank that reached his knees surrounded him, and the ground, two arm spans around him, was clear of snow.

An idea formed in his head, and he started again, reversing the motion when the banks grew. Two rounds later, the snow lay around him pristine, as if it hadn't moved.

Another idea, which he now recognized as a leading from Lledrith, formed in his mind. He started another round with his back to the cabin door. He used the same motions as he had to replace the snow, stepping back with large steps, and forward with small ones. At the end of the round, he stood under the tree where the snow was patchy, and his footprints were gone.

The door opened, and Oswin said, "Impressive."

Briant's stomach growled, and he squinted at the sky. The sun was halfway to its zenith, and he frowned. "How long have I been out here?"

"Long enough that you need to come in and eat again. Come on, the tea is hot."

Briant turned, glancing over his shoulder at the pristine snow, before stepping back in and shutting the door. He toed his boots off and hung up his coat. "That could be a useful spell."

"I have a feeling you're going to get a lot of practice."

Briant took the cup Oswin held out to him. "Has the Goddess told you something?"

Oswin shook his head. "Not specifically. It's a feeling in my gut, like things are going to go bad quickly."

Briant shivered and sipped his tea. The movement had warmed him, and he hadn't been cold when he came in, but a chill seeped into his core. "I think you're right. I don't want you to be."

Oswin slid a plate of mushrooms and sausage to him. "Neither do I. It seems like we both have a lot of work to do."

Briant started eating. The food was savory and reminded him of his mother's cooking. He let the pang of grief flow through him. "I used to take this kind of food for granted. I might even have asked my mother why we had to eat mushrooms again. She cooked with them a lot."

Oswin looked at him. "My mother didn't cook. We lived in community with others. My aunt was a cook, though, and she let me help after my lessons were done." He looked back at his plate. "Sometimes she was more of a mother to me than my mother. But then, she was training to succeed Grandmother."

"Did Adrienne succeed your mother?"

Oswin shook his head. "My mother died before taking the gold. My aunt, too, from the same illness. My other aunt thought she would take the gold, but the Goddess chose my sister instead. Aunt Sagart has been a thorn in our sides ever since."

Briant's eyebrows shot up, and he choked on a bite of mushrooms. "Sagart is your *aunt*?"

Oswin nodded. "Sadly, yes. She was one of the very few people who thought she was fit to rule. You know Hashna? Adrienne's guard?"

Briant nodded.

"She's Sagart's daughter."

Briant put down his fork and sat back. "I'm sorry."

Oswin chuckled. "Me too. I have been my whole life, but never more so than after Adrienne took the gold. They went from treating me like an inferior being to acting like I was a threat to my sister." He shook his head. "Frankly, I'm glad to be away from there. But that doesn't change the fact that we have a lot of work to do, so we'd best get back to it."

Briant polished off his food, swiping a piece of bread over the plate to get every bit. A few minutes later, he went back outside. This time, the butterflies led him in a different dance. He got the hang of it faster than he had that morning and found himself in a dense cloud of mist. It clung to him, and the dampness seeped into his clothes. The butterflies showed him how to dissipate it, and he watched the mist break apart, the wisps floating into the air. He repeated the cycle several times before the butterflies flew away, and he went back in, hair and clothes wet.

Oswin raised an eyebrow as Briant removed his boots and coat, padding to the hearth in stockinged feet that left damp footprints.

"Lledrith showed you how to banish the mist, right?"

"Yes," answered Briant, holding his hands toward the heat.

"So if you do that part of the spell again, maybe it will dry your clothes."

Briant frowned. "Is it really that simple?"

Oswin shrugged. "What's it going to hurt to try?"

Briant considered it for a moment before moving into an open space. He went through the spell that sent the mist back into the air. Two cycles dried his hair and clothing, and he turned to Oswin. "How did you think to suggest that?"

"You dissipated mist into air outside. It wasn't much of a stretch to think it will work in other capacities."

Briant sank into a chair. "Back in Slan, I drive everyone crazy asking why they do everything the same way all the time. I thought I was innovative, but I'm starting to realize I need to think about things differently, too." He shook his head. "When this is over, no one will tolerate me."

Oswin laughed. "Who says you have to go back there? For that matter, what makes you think we'll live through this?"

Briant's eyebrows shot up. "Wow. That's morbid. Makes sense, but morbid. Thanks for the encouragement."

Oswin nodded once. "Glad to help."

Raya glanced over her shoulder as she buckled Isidro's saddle under his belly. Adrienne came in, her hair in a single braid, carrying a large pack.

"It's starting to snow," said Adrienne, boosting the pack to a more comfortable position.

"Here, let me have that," said Raya, walking toward her.

Adrienne scowled. "I'm more than capable of carrying it myself."

Raya grinned. "I don't doubt it. But it will balance the weight of my pack if I put it in a saddle bag."

Adrienne blinked. "Oh." She shrugged her arm out and slid it off. "Sorry. It's been nice being able to do things for myself lately."

Raya put the pack in a large saddle bag and buckled it shut. "You're the boss, you know. People to back off if you tell them to."

"I did at first. But everyone is so steeped in tradition, and my predecessors liked being taken care of. So do I, to a point, but as soon as I took the gold, everyone started treating me like a fragile vase."

"That wouldn't work for me," said Raya. "Do you have a scarf?"

Adrienne cocked her head as if she didn't understand. "A scarf? Yes, but what does that have to do with how I'm treated?"

Raya chuckled and double-checked the cinch straps. "Nothing, but you're going to want to cover your face in the air. It's safer if you ride in front of me. Tuck your braid into your coat too, so it doesn't whack me in the face."

Adrienne pulled a knitted yellow scarf out of the neck of her coat and threaded her hair in. "I had my scarf tucked in so it wouldn't attract attention."

"I doubt that will be an issue. Isidro will fly high enough that even if people do realize who you are from the color of your scarf, they won't be able to get to you, at least until we get to Gynhalion." She climbed onto Isidro's back, taking her place behind the saddle, and reached her hand toward Adrienne. "Hop up and I'll strap you in."

Adrienne took a deep breath and nodded once before pulling herself into the saddle. "Is this like riding a horse?"

Isidro grumbled in Raya's head, and she chuckled. "Not really, but don't worry. I'll hold onto you, so if you move like I do, we'll be fine." She fastened the straps around Adrienne and herself. "Ready?"

"No," said Adrienne, "but don't let that stop you."

Let's go, she said to Isidro as she reached around Adrienne to grip the pommel. Isidro walked out of the barn into the snow, and Raya clenched her legs as his muscles tensed.

Adrienne gasped as he launched, gripping the front of the saddle. Raya leaned forward, pushing her, and said, "It might help if you close your eyes."

She kept her arms clasped around Adrienne as Isidro spiraled up. When he caught an air current, she sat up and smiled. *It never gets old, being in the air with you.*

I hope it never will, answered Isidro.

She grinned and pulled her scarf up over her nose, and then pulled Adrienne's up. "You good?"

Adrienne was still stiff, and she shook her head a little. "I don't know!"

Isidro angled southwest, and she saw the abbey glimmering in fresh snow. "Look down to your left."

Adrienne gasped. "It's so different from up here! It's almost beautiful!"

Raya laughed. "Amazing what a layer of snow will do."

Two hours later, Isidro started his descent over Gynhalion. The city, built on a hill in a curve of land next to a river, had a tall stone wall surrounding it. She saw wrecked siege engines and evidence of pyres outside the city. Inside, streets lined with buildings curled toward the top, twisting at random times. Raya saw several dead ends, and she nodded with approval. From the ground, getting to the top would be a challenge for anyone who didn't know the way.

Is that the temple at the top? asked Isidro.

Raya leaned forward and asked Adrienne.

"We need to land in the large courtyard in the center," shouted Adrienne.

Isidro adjusted his course, spiraling in concentric twists.

Raya leaned close to Adrienne, guiding her movement as she clasped the saddle, and a moment later, he dropped to the ground inside the courtyard.

What do you think? Raya asked.

Isidro looked around. *The porticoes are higher than I imagined.* He crouched to allow them to dismount. *I believe it will suffice, at least for the short term.*

Raya undid her straps. *Good. I'll get your saddle off. Are you going to hunt?*

I am, unless Adrienne planned for food.

She unbuckled Adrienne's straps. "Did you arrange for food for Isidro?"

Adrienne gasped. "I never thought about it!" She covered her mouth with her hand.

"It's fine. He'll go hunt."

Adrienne slid out of the saddle and stepped in front of Isidro. "I'm so sorry! And after you carried me here!"

"It is of no matter," said Isidro. "Hunting will allow me the opportunity to gain perspective of the city."

Raya dropped their packs on the ground and pulled the saddle off. "He's going to reconnoiter."

Isidro looked over his shoulder. "That is what I said."

Raya chuckled. "Adrienne, will you grab the packs?"

"Of course." She scooped them up and followed as Raya shouldered the saddle and headed for the portico.

When they neared the wall, Isidro launched. The wind from his wings blew the snow on the ground into the air.

A door at the end opened, and Kevia strode out. "I hoped you'd get here before the snow started. You must be frozen through."

"It was cold up there," said Adrienne, "but so beautiful. I would love a hot bath."

Kevia took the packs from Adrienne and glanced away. "I have that underway for both of you, but first, Hashna needs to talk to you."

Adrienne blinked. "That sounds ominous."

Kevia turned back to the door.

When they got inside, Raya said, "If you point me in the right direction, I'll leave you to whatever you have to deal with."

"You should be there, Wybren," said Kevia. "You can leave the saddle here, in the corner."

Raya frowned and put the saddle down, following the others through a couple of corridors to a sitting room. She went to stand by the fire to warm up as a young girl bustled in behind them. She handed Adrienne and Raya steaming mugs of tea and bobbed a quick curtsy to

Adrienne before scurrying away, nearly colliding with Hashna as she came in.

"Lav—Adrienne, I'm glad you're here safely."

Adrienne inclined her head. "As am I. You have news?"

Hashna squared her shoulders as if expecting a reprimand. "There was an incident on our way here. The Wreiddons escaped."

Raya's jaw dropped, and she put her cup on the mantle before she dropped it.

Adrienne sipped her tea. "What do you mean?"

"The second night, we had to stop early because of the snow. We had the men tied together to a tree. During the second watch, Sorcha was on watch and heard something in the woods. She turned away from the men to see what it was, and when she turned back, they were gone. The rope binding them to the tree was cut."

"Cut?" asked Raya. "Why did they have a knife?"

"They didn't, Wybren. We were careful to make sure they weren't armed."

Adrienne glanced toward the window. "Did you look closely enough at the rope to see if it still fit around the trunk?"

Hashna's brow furrowed. "I don't understand."

"There are several spells they could have used to free themselves. One would fray the rope and disintegrate a piece of it." She shook her head. "How they escaped isn't important. I trust you tried to find them?"

"We did, but we lost their tracks in the snow."

Raya sank onto the hearth. Ruan and Dermod had escaped. On one hand, she feared for them, but part of her was relieved. *Isidro?*

I shall watch for them, he answered.

"Isidro will look for them while he's hunting, but they're probably heading back to Slan."

"I agree. Hashna, did you take corrective action with Sorcha?"

"Beyond dressing her down? I told her you will decide her punishment."

Adrienne sighed and sank into a padded chair. "I will consider it and send for you both when I decide."

Hashna nodded and backed out the door.

Kevia stepped forward. Raya hadn't realized she'd tucked herself into a corner behind the door when Hashna entered. "Wybren, I'll take you to your quarters."

Raya stood on shaky legs. "I'm not sure there's time for that. How far is the place where you lost them?"

Kevia crossed her arms. "Wybren, if Hashna couldn't find them right after they went missing, I doubt you'll be able to find them now. Besides, Isidro is hunting, and having him seek two men who know how to hide will only put him at risk."

Raya pinched the bridge of her nose. "I know, but they're my responsibility."

"Not when they went missing," said Kevia. "They were Hashna's responsibility."

"She's right," said Adrienne. "Go get your bath while the water is hot. We both need time to think. We'll meet in my study for the mid-day meal."

Raya nodded, swallowing against the sorrow welling up in her chest. She knew they were right. She also knew Ruan and Dermod were likely not the last of the friends she would lose. Kevia touched her arm, and Raya turned and followed her.

I will keep looking, beloved, said Isidro.

Thank you, but they're right. Don't risk your hide looking for those two knuckleheads.

CHAPTER ELEVEN ~ ANNWN

Someone shook Aithne's arm and hissed her name. She opened her eyes to see Quinn's outline in the dark.

"Aithne, we have to go."

She rolled to her feet, and Quinn passed her pack to her. He led her through the woods, threading back and forth, avoiding patches of snow.

A thin line of light showed through the trees. The clouds hung low and gray in the sky.

They skirted a clearing, and Quinn slowed, looking around as if to get his bearings.

"Where are we going?" asked Aithne, her voice pitched low.

Quinn swallowed hard. "I need a moment. I usually fly to my cabins, and I need to get my bearings."

"Why don't you fly? I will shield and follow you."

"I'm not sure I'll lead us the right way."

Aithne clenched her jaw. "How close are the people tracking us?"

Quinn shook his head. "I don't know."

"Then we need more information. I'll hide and shield. You get in the air and figure out what we need to do."

He scoffed. "I can't leave you."

Aithne crossed her arms. "So, unless you can transform into something large enough to carry me in flight, remaining with me seems more harmful than helpful." He looked doubtful, and she shook her head. Gathering magic, she put up a shield with a thought, and his eyes went wide.

"Did Lledrith teach you that last night?"

"I don't know, and it doesn't matter. Go find the cabin!"

He opened his mouth and then closed it. He turned and ran toward the clearing, changing to his raven form mid-stride and flying away.

Aithne looked around. The trees were bare. She wouldn't find cover in their branches, but they would get her off the ground. She went to the one that looked the strongest and hoisted herself onto the lowest branch. Once she got her feet under her, she studied the higher branches and decided she'd climb higher only if she had to. Instead, she leaned against the truck and drew magic from the tree to strengthen her shield.

The sun was nearing the bottom of her branch when she saw a raven. She kept her shield up and held her breath as the bird landed and morphed back into Quinn. Releasing her breath, she thinned her shield so he could see her jump from the tree.

She startled him, and she was surprised that it wasn't as satisfying as she expected.

He shook his head and started walking.

She caught up to him, and they walked until the sun disappeared behind the clouds, and the light became milky. The air had a metallic tang. Lovely. More snow.

Quinn stopped and grabbed her arm. She heard a bark.

He pulled her arm. "Hurry, we're almost there."

Aithne ran behind him, gathering magic as she went. She didn't know if she'd be able to use magic to defend them, but she meant to have enough to try.

Quinn grabbed her arm, running faster. He raised his free hand, palm out, and muttered something unintelligible.

Aithne's boot caught on a root, and she stumbled, righting herself before she and Quinn both fell. When she looked up, they were a few feet from a large oak tree. Quinn ran headlong toward it, with no sign of diverting. She yelped, closing her eyes.

He stopped abruptly, standing close to her.

She opened her eyes. It was dark. "Did you kill us?"

"Shh."

She heard voices, and he squeezed her hand. Dogs barked, and she flinched, closing her eyes again. Her heart hammered, blood pulsing in her ears. She wanted to run, but felt rooted to the spot in the darkness. The Goddess' name came to her, and she focused on it, thinking 'Cruthadair' over and over.

The voices trailed off. They stood still a moment longer, and then Quinn let go of her hand and whispered something.

Aithne opened her eyes and turned when she heard a panel slide open.

"Come on," whispered Quinn. He moved away, and she heard three footsteps.

A light wisp almost blinded her, and she blinked. "Aithne."

Quinn was on a descending staircase. He beckoned, and she followed him. The panel slid closed behind her. The stairs spiralled down, and she reached for her connection with Saphir.

Her dragon's voice was strong in her head. *You are safe?*

Yes. I think we're inside a tree. She conjured a light wisp. The walls looked like dirt. She touched one and dragged her finger through the damp grit.

The bottom of the stairs opened into a small empty room. It smelled like freshly turned earth, and she saw a layer of rock next to the floor. It ran around the room like a baseboard.

Quinn crouched in front of the stairs and pushed the third riser from the bottom. Aithne heard a click, and he lifted the tread, taking out a wooden box. He closed the stair and sat on it. "We will stay here for a while in case they double back. You will need to make room in your pack for this." He held out the box with both hands. It was a handspan wide and deep, and twice that in length.

She crouched and slid her pack off. "Why does it need to go in mine?"

"Because you need them." He turned a hook on each of the long sides and lifted the lid to reveal a row of slender scrolls. "Hynef doesn't know I have a copy of the scrolls. She'd have taken them from me if she did. The Goddess has revealed that I was keeping them here safe to give to you." He put the lid on and closed the hooks, passing the box to her.

"What's written on them?"

"Our scriptures. Everything you need to know about the Goddess is in that box."

She ran her hand over the lid. Dark wood, unexpectedly light, gleamed smoothly. "It seems too small for all that knowledge."

He shrugged. "That's probably true. If we really knew everything we needed to know, the world would be a better place."

She slid the box into her pack on the side with the straps and sat on the floor with her back against the wall. "Why do you think they're still chasing me?"

"Oh, I'm certain it's more me than you. No doubt, they think I'm a traitor. At the very least, they think I've been deceived by a false prophet."

She snorted. "That's not something I thought I'd be called."

"I doubt your people give any thought at all to prophets, so why would you?"

A small wave of sadness rolled over her. "They have no idea what is true."

"But now you know it. Making a change in yourself is the first step to changing a society."

"Oh, yeah, I'll be able to change my entire culture. No problem."

"Maybe not by yourself, or in your lifetime. Do the work the Goddess sets before you, and she will raise up others to help."

"She has so far. I'd say it stands to reason she will continue, but I don't understand anything that's happened since I entered Annwn."

"Then it's a good thing you don't have to understand to do the work."

CHAPTER TWELVE ~ COMMAIN

Raya strode toward the ballroom that led to Isidro's garden when an acolyte caught up with her. "Wybren, a woman has arrived who claims to be from the Slannish diplomatic team. She said her name is Sine."

Raya's heart skipped a beat. "Take me to her." She followed the acolyte to the waiting area outside the audience chamber. Raya almost didn't recognize her. She looked small, dirty. Almost defeated. A small backpack lay at her feet. "Sine?"

The woman looked up. Her eyes glistened with tears, and a slow smile spread across her face. "Raya. I'm so glad you're alive."

Raya strode across the remaining distance and knelt in front of Sine. Over her shoulder, she said, "She's going to need food and a bath. Who can I ask to have them brought to my room?"

"I'll see to it," said the acolyte.

Raya took Sine's hands. "What happened?"

Sine swallowed hard. "We were attacked an hour after we left the inn on the second day. We were trying to figure out why it was getting darker instead of lighter." Her voice trailed off for a moment before she shook herself and continued. "I only escaped because I'd drunk too much tea with breakfast. I was in the bushes when I saw a group of *tanad* come out of the woods on the other side of the road. They killed, or at least wounded, everyone in our party. They took the bodies and horses, but left the carriage and wagon in the middle of the road." Her voice trailed off, and her eyes focused on something behind Raya.

Raya touched Sine's arm. "You're safe now. Come with me. We'll catch up while you have a hot soak." She stood and scooped up Sine's pack, threading one arm through both straps.

Sine rose to her feet like an old woman. "Is Isidro here?"

Raya felt a frisson of surprise from Isidro. "Yes, they've set aside the central courtyard for him."

"Is that on the way to your room?"

"No, but I'll take you there." She led Sine through the corridors.

"Why are you here? Is everyone else with you?" asked Sine.

"Only me, for now. Briant left with Oswin. Dermod and Ruan were with the servants who came ahead of Adrienne—the Bealban Dia—and me, but they disappeared."

Sine gasped. "Disappeared?"

Raya nodded and pushed open the door to the courtyard. "The healers isolated the spell in their brains, but they haven't fully analyzed it. They knew was it was a spy spell of some kind. When the abbey was attacked, we thought it best to come here. I don't know anything more than that."

Sine stopped in her tracks. "The abbey was attacked, too?"

"Yes, during that strange eclipse." She stepped into the courtyard. "Isidro, look who I found."

Isidro lowered his head. "I am pleased to see you, Sine. I took the liberty of telling Quillon you are here."

"Thank you. I'm glad he's still alive."

"Alive. Yes."

A line formed between Sine's brows. "That sounded cryptic."

"The dragons are trapped in the lair," said Raya. "The Western Keep was attacked when the abbey was, and Isidro hasn't been able to reach any of the Eastern Keep dragons yet."

Sine went pale, and Raya braced herself to catch her if necessary. "Brigid and Laoch, preserve us."

Isidro growled. "I wished to go and help, but Quillon has ordered us to remain here."

Raya nodded. "It's been frustrating to sit around with nothing to do. Come on, Sine, they'll have food waiting for you. Isidro will listen while we talk."

Sine pushed a hand through her tangled hair. "I know." She put her hand on Isidro's paw. "Thanks, Isidro, I needed an anchor."

"I have never been an anchor, but I am pleased to help. I will relay what is relevant in your conversation."

Sine's lips pressed together in what could have been interpreted as a smile as a cold gust of wind blew into the courtyard. With a brief nod, she allowed Raya to lead her back inside and up the stairs.

Raya was relieved to see maids leaving her room when they turned into the corridor. One of them carried buckets, and another maid with buckets stepped out behind them.

The girl who had informed Raya of Sine's arrival walked to them as the maids scurried away to the back stairs.

"Wybren, the bath is still very hot, but thankfully so is the food. I took the liberty of pinching a bottle of wine that hadn't been consecrated yet. I'm afraid we haven't anything stronger here, but I can send someone to the market."

"No," said Sine, holding up one hand. "Thank you, wine will be more than enough. It was kind of you to think of it."

The girl opened her mouth and closed it again. She dipped a curtsy, turned on her heel, and strode down the hall.

Raya led Sine into her room and closed the door. The maids had built the fire up, and the water in the tub steamed.

"That looks heavenly," said Sine. She toed off her boots, kicking them into the nearest corner, and dipped her hand in. "Hmm. Still a little too hot."

Raya went to the table in front of the window that hadn't been there that morning. "Come eat while it cools."

Sine padded across the floor and sank into a chair with a groan. "I haven't been this stiff and cold since my first training flight."

Raya poured a mug of tea and handed it to her. "Isidro told me Tanwen is relieved you're here."

"Is she safe?"

"As safe as she can be at the moment, but the situation there isn't good."

"It's not good anywhere. Have you heard anything about who has done this? It sounds like it's bigger than I thought."

"I haven't heard anything yet."

She jumped at a jolt of surprised from Isidro. *Beloved, I have contact with Dyratrisse! She and Ceann are alive!*

Raya's jaw dropped, and she stammered the news to Sine. *Where are they?*

In the mountains southeast of the Southern Keep. Ceann was visiting her sister when everything happened. He paused for a moment. *The Southern Keep has fallen, as has the Eastern Keep. She knows of no survivors from either location. Her family is sheltering with her.*

Raya's breath caught, and she told Sine.

Sine wiped tears from her face. "Where is she going to go? Can she come here?"

They have not decided, said Isidro. *It is likely Vask and Briant will come at some point, and space here is limited.*

Keep us posted, please. And tell Dyratrisse that hearing from them has been the best news all day.

I shall.

Raya poured two glasses of wine and passed one to Sine. "We haven't had much to celebrate lately, but you and Ceann being alive is reason enough for me right now."

Sine picked up her glass. "I'll drink to that."

Briant sat at the table in the cabin. He felt like he was being watched. At the door, he looked outside but saw nothing. Nothing seemed amiss as he walked around the cabin. But he was sure that he was supposed to leave, so he went back inside, packed up his belongings. As he left, he headed north, although he didn't know why. It was snowing, but he used his earth-moving spell to cover his tracks. As he traveled, the sense of being watched decreased, but didn't go away.

When it got dark, he fashioned an igloo. When the sun came up, he spotted a city on a hill. There was a tall building with spires at the top of it, and a dragon flew around the spires. He couldn't tell who it was, but the sight made him smile, and he carried on toward the city.

A sound made him turn around, and when he turned back, he found himself in the cabin. He packed his things and left the cabin, traveling north. When he reached the tree line, he woke up.

He sat up, looking around. Everything seemed normal, but the sense of foreboding was still there. He heard Oswin downstairs, so he pulled on his clothes and went down to find Oswin packing food while breakfast cooked.

"I guess I don't have to tell you about the dream I had."

Oswin looked at him. "Did it tell you it's time to go to Gynhalion?"

"If Gynhalion is on a hill with a building on top, yes."

Oswin stirred the pot steaming in the hearth. "I got the same message from the Goddess."

Briant poured a cup of tea and topped up Oswin's. Outside, he could see snow falling in fat flakes. "It doesn't look like it's going to be a fun trip."

"It can't be helped," said Oswin. "I got the impression that staying here past sunset will mean a fight that will kill us both, and Lledrith said if you die, we're all dead."

Briant shivered. "No pressure. I'll get my things." He took his cup to the loft and pulled his backpack out from under his bed. *Vask, are you awake?*

I am. I saw the dream and intended to tell you to leave if you did not make plans on your own.

Did you see the dragon flying around the spires?

I did. It was not me. I will ask Quillon if we have anyone in Gynhalion.

Briant tucked his clothing and weapons into his pack. When he took it back down the ladder, he saw Vask's saddle and groaned.

"What's wrong?" asked Oswin.

"The saddle. I'm going to have to take it."

Oswin squinted at the corner where the saddle was. "That will be cumbersome, but we don't have a choice, do we?"

"Afraid not. I still have some room in my pack. What do you need me to take?"

Oswin straightened and looked around. "I have most of it, but extra blankets won't come amiss if we're traveling in snow the whole way."

"Good thinking," said Briant. He climbed the ladder again and tossed down the blankets from both beds. He went back down and was folding the first when Vask spoke.

Briant, Isidro and Raya are in Gynhalion. Isidro says there is room for me with him. I suggest we rendezvous and fly there.

Briant grinned. "Vask suggested we meet him and fly to Gynhalion."

Oswin poured oatmeal into bowls and pushed one toward Briant. "That would make the trip faster. And, hopefully, easier."

Briant sat at the table and dug into his food. "If nothing else, we won't have to carry the saddle all the way to Gynhalion."

Briant and Oswin rendezvoused with Vask in the first clearing near the cabin. They were swiftly airborne, and Vask climbed out of ballista range.

Briant was nearly frozen through when he looked over Oswin's shoulder and saw the temple in Gynhalion come into view. It was nothing like the abbey.

From above, Briant saw it perched on a plateau, providing plenty of space for the temple complex. The temple had arched doorways that Oswin had said were twice his height. From the air, Briant wondered if he had underestimated. The roof pitched to a peak, and large transom windows lined each of walls. Flanked by wings that formed the outer wall of the temple complex, it sparkled even in the muted light of winter. The bottom floor was a walkway partially enclosed in arches with two floors above. The guards patrolling the large parapet didn't react to Vask.

They flew over the temple complex, and Briant saw two large courtyards in the middle. The smaller one had garden beds, a greenhouse at the outside end, and espaliered fruit trees and berry bushes covering the remaining walls. The bigger garden appeared to have once been ornamental. Isidro walked into the middle of it, and Vask spiraled down toward him.

The snow fell in large flakes as Vask landed. They fumbled with the straps, fingers stiff from the cold, and Oswin slid out of the saddle as one of the doors in the deep portico opened. Kevia came out, rubbing her arms in the cold, as Briant dismounted.

"Welcome," she said. "The Goddess told us to prepare for your coming, but we were surprised when Raya said you were on your way."

Briant pulled Vask's saddle off as Oswin shouldered the packs. "Communication is a lot easier with dragons," Briant said, hoisting the saddle onto his shoulder.

Kevia stepped back. "Come inside. Leave the saddle there." She pointed to a corner, and Briant saw Isidro's saddle. He took it over and put it on the marble floor, and when he turned back, Oswin and Kevia were talking in low tones.

"Briant!"

He turned and saw Raya stride through a door, followed by Sine. Grinning, he took four long steps and hugged them both. "You have no idea how glad I am to see you, Sine."

She smiled a little. "I'm glad to see you, too. That's not something we can take for granted anymore."

Briant frowned. "That's cryptic."

Raya linked her arm through his. "Time enough for stories after you warm up. Kevia, do you have him in our wing?"

"I do, across from Sine."

"Here's your pack," said Oswin, holding it out.

Raya took it and slung it over her free shoulder. "Come on. Let's get you settled."

Chapter Thirteen ~ Western Keep

Tanwen sat by Eoghan's fire, drinking a second cup of willow bark and lemon balm tea, when Quillon nudged her.

Raine has gotten through to Vask.

That's good news. Have they come up with anything yet?

Briant asked for some time to ponder it. He approves of digging out the tunnel, but we are concerned about the time it will take.

So am I. Truthfully, but I suggested it more to shame the men into helping, or at least giving up the shield idea to think of something different.

I will let you know what he says.

Moira came to sit beside her. "Raine is talking to Vask to get Briant's input."

"So is Quillon." The wind gusted, and Tanwen hunched over the hot tea. "What's the consensus with the others?"

"They're still divided."

"Can we get Shaw on our side?"

"We have him, and Dinsmore is leaning our way. Unsurprisingly, Sullivan and a few others want to work on the shields; however, the others are struggling to decide which side to support.

Tanwen fought back the urge to throw the cup against a tree and scream in frustration. Instead, she put the cup beside her foot and closed her eyes, pinching the bridge of her nose. "I'm at a loss, Moira. We've had women in leadership all along. When did our society become a boys' club?"

"I don't know if it is. Tanwen, what happened to Liam?"

Tanwen's heart lurched into her throat, and she kicked the cup. She scrambled to pick it up. "Stupid. It takes time to brew this."

Moira took the cup from her hand. "Tanwen."

Tanwen looked at the ground as the tears started. "I killed him," she whispered. "He attacked me, and I pushed him into the rock slide."

Moira put her arm around Tanwen's shoulders.

Tanwen sobbed into her hands. When the wave passed, she asked, "Why are you asking about him?"

"Sullivan overheard Lassair and Gitta talking about it. He made an off-hand comment about listening to someone who didn't know her own husband was a traitor."

Grief and anger stabbed her heart. She sputtered, unable to form a coherent thought. Taking a deep breath, she whispered, "What else?"

"You don't need to know it all."

"I do, Moira. What am I up against?"

"I don't know yet, but there are a few who don't trust that you have our best interests at heart. There was the implication that you killed him so we wouldn't suspect you're a traitor too."

Fury overrode the grief, and she looked at the group of men. She shifted her weight to stand, and Moira held her back. "Calm down. Dinsmore, Shaw, and I shut that down, fast and simultaneously. We don't have room for anger, Tanwen. We need to free the dragons."

Quillon stirred in her mind. *Tell me which one he is. When I get out, I will finish him.*

The side of Moira's mouth curved up. "Raine said she'll eat him for you. She got word from Vask. Briant says if it were up to him, he'd blast a hole in a wall. The dragons are looking inside for weak spots in the rock slides. Tanwen, you're still the liaison. You lead the Wybrens, at least. What if I take Lassair and Gitta and have a look at the outside? You clearly need to stay here and rest, and Dinsmore will want to talk with you."

Tanwen nodded. "Yes. Take Lucas to shield you."

Moira nodded and stood. "I'll let you know what we find." She strode away, and Tanwen picked up her cup again.

Quillon, you heard that, right?

I did. Raine and I have split the younglings between us and are each taking half of the lairs. Tanwen, you know none of that was your fault.

Tanwen swallowed another batch of tears. *I try to convince myself of that, but I'm doubtful. We don't have time for that now. How are you doing? Is everyone hanging in there?*

We cannot do anything else.

She leaned forward to add a log to the fire. The snow started again, and she pulled her collar closer to her neck.

Dinsmore joined her at the fire. "How are you feeling?"

"Terrible, but I expect all of us are."

"Don't minimize yourself. I need your head in the game."

Tanwen snorted. "Do you?"

"Of course I do. We work well together. I value your opinion."

"My opinion didn't seem to count for much earlier. My influence will diminish as long as people blame me for Liam."

Dinsmore blinked. "Tanwen—"

She waved a hand. "Nothing we can do about that now. Have you come up with a game plan?"

"That's the thing. They have strong opinions, and most of them want another shot at the shield. I need to know what you think."

Tanwen took a deep breath, tamping down the simmering anger. "Moira took a team to see if there are any weak spots to exploit. I'll know more when she gets back. Briant said he'd blast a hole in a wall."

Dinsmore frowned. "That's—different. It will be loud."

"If there is a weak point, it won't take as much to make an opening. I didn't say it would work, but we have to explore more options. Digging them out by hand will make noise, too, and it will take even longer if—no, when—we have to stop to fight."

"That was our concern, too. That's why they're focused on the shields."

Tanwen hit the side of the log with her fist. "Uffern! Why? Why does everyone think we have two options? This is not the time to think small!"

Dinsmore's jaw hung slack. He stared at her for a few seconds and then put his hand on her shoulder. "You're right. We do need to think bigger. Let me go back to them and see if we can come up with more options."

Tanwen picked up her walking stick. "Good. Let's go."

"No, let me do this. I'll talk to them." He stood. "We know your focus is getting the dragons out, and you're right. That's the priority. You rest."

He walked away, and Tanwen stared after him in disbelief. Her anger boiled, and it bubbled over the top when Sullivan turned to Dinsmore and smirked.

Do not do it, Tanwen, said Quillon. *I agree he needs to be put in his place, but this is not the time.*

It appears it's not the time for anything!

I agree with you, but shift your focus back to the task at hand. Two spots will serve our purpose, but they are elevated. Figure out how to get someone high enough to compromise them, or think of more options. We need backup plans and contingencies. He paused. *I have asked Isidro for Sine's input.*

Tanwen sighed. *Thank Laoch, she's alive. Tell her to hurry.*

The sun was going down when Moira found Tanwen huddled under a fir tree, away from the others.

"Why are you hiding?"

Tanwen snorted. "I'm not hiding. You found me."

Moira sat beside her. "Raine told me about your conversation with Dinsmore."

Tanwen shook her head. "He treated me like a woman who shouldn't worry her pretty head."

"Tanwen, none of us is at our best now. It's more likely he didn't want to deal with you and Sullivan together."

"That works for me, but it would have been better if he'd said so."

Moira laughed. "Are you sure you'd have been fine with it in the moment, or would that have offended you, too?"

Tanwen's face warmed, and she looked away. "What did you find?"

"Two weak spots at the top of the rock slides. They're going to be difficult to break through, and even harder for the dragons to get out of. If we hit them with concussive strikes, the rock will cave in, and that won't help matters. Shaw thinks the best of the bad choices is for him and Tarian to pull out the rocks below the best weak spot to make another avalanche that will make a hole big enough."

"Hmm." Tanwen sighed and leaned her head against the trunk of the tree. "We've barely started this conflict, and already I'm tired. I want to curl up in a warm bed and go to sleep and let someone else deal with this."

"You're not the only one."

Beloved, Sine suggests you ask if any of the Wreiddons will enter the tunnel to push rocks out. She also suggests creating a diversion to draw the enemy as far from the tunnel as possible.

Tanwen picked up her walking stick and clambered to her feet. "Quillon told me what Sine recommends. Come on, let's go find Siril."

They found him chatting with some of the other teachers in what looked like an impromptu planning session to get the younglings back in training. He nodded to Tanwen.

"Did Eoghan get you fixed up?"

Tanwen shrugged. "Yes, but he says I can't fight unless it's a matter of life and death."

"Healers always say that," said one teacher. "It looks like you have something to talk to Siril about, so we'll leave you to it."

Siril rubbed his beard. "If you need my help to free the dragons, things must be getting desperate."

"They've been desperate," said Tanwen. She told him what Sine said and turned to Moira. "Tell him what you found."

"I took a team to the Keep to survey the outside. Two of the tunnels have spots that look weak at the top of the rock slides. If we can't get volunteers to go in, do you know of a way to open them enough for the dragons to escape?"

Siril tapped his mouth with his finger. "Sine is right. Theoretically, precise strikes from the inside will push the rocks out instead of falling in. I know the dragons can launch from a standing position, but the space will be confined."

It would be difficult, said Quillon. *Perhaps with a running start, and even that presents problems.*

Moira shifted her weight. "Raine has doubts about getting everyone out through a small hole."

"Quillon agrees," said Tanwen. "He said they might be able to fly out if they get a running start, but again, how would they do that in a tunnel?"

Siril squinted, looking around the clearing. "Let's ask Shaw what he thinks."

Tanwen followed him as dragon communication buzzed in her head. The sound calmed her in a way it wouldn't have before she'd lost contact with Quillon for those few awful hours.

Beloved, we have consulted Vask. Briant suggests we explore ways to open the tunnel from the inside, and he thinks we need a diversion to buy time once it starts.

It's good to know he and Sine agree. That will give the idea more credibility. She waited while Siril brought Shaw up to speed, adding, "Briant agrees with Sine's suggestion."

The side of Siril's mouth quirked up. "The lad is handy to have around even when he's not around."

Shaw nodded. "A diversion will be necessary. Making a hole big enough for dragons to get out without blocking them in more is going to take time. Is it even possible to work from the inside? Do we have something you can use?"

Moira scoffed. "I talked to the smiths about making magic weapons for us, but I don't think they ever started."

"They didn't take you seriously," said Tanwen. "We have dragons; why do we need magic, too?"

Moira shook her head. "They better stay away from me."

"We can't do anything about that now," said Siril. "It's complicated enough as it is. First, if we do have someone to send in, how do we get them in? And how do they open the tunnel without dropping rock on themselves? There are a couple of ways, but they need equipment we'd have to take in through the Keep."

Shaw leaned against a tree, rubbing his beard. "A couple of mages could do it." He held up his hand when Moira and Tanwen protested. "Hear me out. This started when Tarian pulled out a rock. Pulling rock means we can also *push* rock. So we figure out how to get two mages inside the tunnel, one to push out rocks and another to shield."

"Yes, but who? Oh! Could they use the debris to make a ramp?" asked Moira.

Siril's eyebrows went up. "That's an interesting thought."

Moira grinned. "It's not mine; it's Raine's."

"Even so," said Siril, "it bears exploring."

"It does if there is someone willing to go in," said Tanwen. "Moira and I will be useless for that."

"I'll go in if I don't have to deal with the dragons," said Shaw. "I'll need help, and I won't take Tarian, but I think it has a better chance of success than messing with the shields."

"We could get the dragons to stay out of sight while you work," said Moira.

Siril glanced around. "Let's take this to Dinsmore. There are more things to consider than who goes in the tunnel."

Chapter Fourteen ~ Western Keep

Small fires lit the way from one side of their camp to the other, aided by the full moon's light. The wind was frigid, but Tanwen felt a little better about the situation.

Dinsmore looked at those assembled to plan. "So we're agreed? Tanwen's team will work on freeing the dragons, Siril's team will create a diversion, Sullivan's team will work on the shields, and my team will raid the salle for supplies?" When everyone nodded, he added. "We'll leave at the end of the third watch."

They split up, and Tanwen, Siril, and Dinsmore went their separate ways to gather their team.

Quillon, has Briant had specific thoughts about how to open the tunnel?

He has, answered, Quillon, *but I will tell you when everyone gathers.*

She started to protest until Lucas jogged toward her. Meeting him part of the way, she chose a spot away from the others. "Lucas, I have a question, and I need you to answer honestly. You can even take some time to think about it if you need to."

His face went slack. "That sounds ominous."

"Not bad, but definitely challenging. At Briant's suggestion, we want to drop a couple of mages inside the tunnel to blast out the rock from the inside. It's going to take men with excellent shielding spells, and you're the best here that I know of. You will be inside the tunnel, but the dragons will stay out of sight until the hole is big enough."

His eyes widened a little with every detail. "You-you want me to be in the tunnel with the dragons?"

"Essentially, yes, but only if you're willing. Shaw has already agreed to it, although he won't take Tarian with him."

Lucas' shoulders relaxed a little. "At least one person has a little sense. Inside the tunnel is no place for a little boy."

"Absolutely not. It's likely I'll take charge of Tarian since fighting isn't my best option right now."

Lucas bit his lip and looked at the ground. "Do you have others in mind if I say no?"

"We'd have to figure that out. Come sit in on the strategy session if you want to."

He nodded. "Do I have the option to say no?"

"Of course. We need to know soon to figure out another option. The job will be too big for Shaw to do alone."

"I'll join the strategy session, then."

Tanwen barely slept that night and finally got up when the first hint of light appeared on the horizon. She yawned and reached out to Quillon.

I hope you got more sleep than I did.

I have slept little since the wandering darkness, answered Quillon. *Peio and Haur worked into the night on the spot we agreed on. They made a few small cracks, but nothing more.*

She stood and stretched, rubbing the sore spots from sleeping on the ground. *We'll take what we can get. You've warned everyone to stay out of sight, right?*

I have. We will remain at the entrance to the council chamber, ready to move quickly.

Good. She peered across the camp. *Laoch willing, we'll be in better shape tonight than we are now.*

An hour later, the stars were fading as the camp split into three groups. Tanwen and Moira led the other Wybrens, Shaw, Tarian, Lucas, and Aiden to the weak spot.

Sunlight touched the horizon, so they took cover to wait for the signal that the diversion had started. Tanwen stood beside Shaw and Lucas. "Are you ready?"

Lucas looked like he wanted to vomit. "Ready to go into the tunnel with the dragons? Sure. Yes."

"Are you trying to convince yourself?"

"Yes, and before you ask, it hasn't worked yet."

Shaw squeezed Lucas' shoulder. "I'm not looking forward to it, either, but I'll focus on shoving as much rock out of the tunnel as possible, and you focus on the shields."

Tanwen put her hand on Lucas' other shoulder. "The dragons are staying in the council chamber until you finish. Keep your back to that end of the tunnel and make the hole as big and fast as possible."

Shaw nodded. "When it's done, we'll duck and cover until the dragons are out, and then we'll get ourselves out."

"Yep. I know. It'll be fine."

Tanwen glanced at the horizon. "It won't be long now. Shaw, do you have a plan to get out?"

"I have a couple options. You swear you'll get Tarian back safely?"

"I'll pretend he's Aithne."

Shaw looked like he wanted to laugh, but he couldn't bring himself to. "Tarian, you know what to do, right?"

"Yes, Da, I'll stay with Wybren Tanwen after you go in the tunnel."

Shaw tousled his hair. "Good lad." He pressed his lips together and gave a sharp nod. "I thought you'd be older when you started fighting."

"I'm not fighting, Da. I'm pulling out rocks."

"That's what you told Mam, isn't it?"

"Yep!"

They froze when something exploded on the other side of the Keep.

"That's our signal," said Tanwen. "Let's go!"

Shaw, Tanwen, and Tarian went to the edge of the woods while the others took up positions around them, ready to defend them if necessary.

Tanwen lifted Tarian onto her shoulders so he could see the area to focus on, and he and Shaw began the spell. Through the link, she sensed Quillon readying the other dragons.

She heard the enemy responding to the explosion—shouting at first, and then horses galloping. *Please, Laoch, keep Siril and the younglings safe.*

She jumped when a louder explosion boomed. Moira nudged her. "Sounds like the boys are having fun."

"They can have it," said Tanwen. Her shoulders ached.

Pebbles cascaded down the side of the wall, followed by a few larger stones.

Lucas and Aiden joined them, adding concussive strikes to the area, and a small hole opened.

Tarian and Shaw swept rocks down the side, creating a steep ramp, using the debris they caught from the concussive strikes before it fell inside the tunnel.

In a few minutes, they'd opened a hole large enough for a small man.

Shaw and Lucas started climbing the makeshift ramp while Tarian and Aiden continued working. A shower of stones flew into the air, bouncing off Shaw and Lucas' shields, and Shaw glared at the others.

"Stop for a minute, boys," said Tanwen, watching as Shaw and Lucas dropped through the hole.

Moira leaned toward her. "I'd feel a lot better about this if we were able to develop some magic weapons."

"Me too," said Tanwen. "I'd rather be in there than out here."

Rock exploded from the edge of the hole, and Tanwen flinched.

Tarian and Aiden caught the debris and pushed it away from the hole. The smaller rocks flew toward the woods. They bounced off tree trunks with a loud crack and ricocheted into the Keep walls.

"Oops! Too much!" said Tarian.

For a moment, rock tumbled down the side.

"Incoming!" hissed Lassair from Tanwen's right. Half of the other Wybrens moved toward her. The other half watched the other side, ready to defend the left flank.

Tanwen tensed. "Tarian, we have to move."

"I think I can see from the ground now."

She put him down, and they ran for cover, ducking into a sumac grove as the first of the enemy defenders ran around the corner.

Tarian continued pulling rock out of the wall, whispering to himself as Tanwen watched Moira and the girls engage the enemy. Aiden stood back a few feet, hurling rocks at the enemy.

Another group came from the other side of the Keep, and Tanwen pointed them out to Tarian. Gitta and Alina engaged them; Tarian started throwing rocks at them.

Gitta screamed as her opponent landed a blow. She struck back but missed as a shower of rock exploded from the wall, startling them all. Magic shields rippled, and the Wybrens ran out of range.

Two of the enemy soldiers didn't get their shields up fast enough; they fell as stones pelted them. One, who was shielded, fell under a large rock.

Beloved! Cover the opening!

A thrill ran through Tanwen. "Tarian, make sure no one stops the dragons!"

"They're coming out?"

"I think so. Don't be afraid."

She put her arms around him, as much to reassure him as to keep him from running.

Venka burst through the opening, sending a cascade of rock tumbling down the wall. She felt Tarian tense.

The remaining enemy fell back, but one had the sense to alert the guard on the roof. He got a single yell out before Tarian hurled a rock at him. It hit him in the head, and he fell.

Hurry, Quillon! You won't have much time before their weapons are ready!

Haur burst out of the opening, followed by Ludo, each increasing the opening. Venka roared and flew north. Haur and Ludo followed her, climbing out of weapons' range. With each dragon, Tanwen's fear increased. Would Quillon make it out with them?

Peio flew out of the hole, wings flapping so hard that Tanwen felt their wind. He shot into the air at an impossibly steep angle and circled to blow fire over the parapet. The screams of the enemy and the smell of burning flesh, inexplicably, sent a trickle of relief through Tanwen.

Tarian relaxed a little, and his mouth hung slack as Raine jumped out of the hole, pausing on the edge to launch.

"Don't be afraid," she murmured in his ear. "They're almost done."

"I'm not afraid," whispered Tarian. "Have they always been so wonderful?"

Tanwen's brow furrowed, but she had no time to waste wondering. When Quillon climbed out, and she scanned the area for threats, her heart was thudding. Both she and Tarian jumped when Quillon roared. Two of the enemy fled back around the Keep, and Aiden ran for the woods.

Nearby, Lassair screamed, "Wybrens!" She ran after those retreating, and the other girls followed her, but before they reached the corner, Tanwen heard the other dragons buzzing through the link. The girls stopped and turned for the camp. Quillon launched, flapping his wings hard. She saw Moira on the other side gather the girls with her. She waved at Tanwen as they bolted for the woods.

Tanwen heard the thrum of a ballista, and Raine banked, blowing flame on the roof of the Keep as Peio and Ludo flew away. Quillon soared over the Keep, breathing fire on the far side, and Tanwen felt his relief as he flapped hard and turned north to follow the others, blowing flame at the enemy as he went.

Tarian jumped up, his fist in the air. "Yes! Get them!"

Tanwen heard shouting. The Keep was on fire, but she couldn't feel sad that it might be destroyed. She stood, grabbing Tarian's hand. "Come on, let's get out of here!"

He laughed and ran beside her. "We did it, Wybren Tanwen! We did it!"

She couldn't answer. She choked back a sob of relief and ran for camp as joy flooded her connection with Quillon.

Thank you, beloved.

She laughed despite the danger still surrounding them. *For what? Saving my skin? Get away from here.*

We are going to the mountains to hunt. You should talk to Dinsmore about splitting up the Wybrens. It's clear that someone is specifically targeting the dragons. Losing several of you at one time could be the end of us.

Tanwen shivered. *I think that's been in the back of all our minds, but we hadn't gotten far enough to find a solution.*

We had other priorities. The mages need to figure out how to protect you.

We've told them we need magical weapons, but of course we didn't know how high the priority was. I'll talk to Dinsmore when we get back. Are you away from immediate danger?

We are.

Tanwen's chest loosened, and she took a deep breath for the first time in days, blinking back tears of relief. "Come on, Tarian, let's hurry back." She held his hand as they ran back to camp. When they saw it through the trees, Tarian shouted, "Mama!"

He let go of Tanwen's hand and bolted to his mother. She caught him, dropping to her knees and holding him at arm's length to inspect him thoroughly.

Tanwen smiled and followed him. "I know that feeling. How are things here, Dara? Has anyone else come back?"

Dara stood and scooped Tarian into her arms. "Part of Siril's group is here, and Aiden is back. We had a few minor casualties, but it was manageable. Thank you for keeping him safe."

Tanwen scoffed. "He kept me safe. When the dragons busted out, rocks flew everywhere."

"Mama, it was the best thing ever! The littlest one shot through the opening we made like an arrow, and then all of them came out! You should have seen it!"

Dara's eyebrows shot up. "You weren't afraid of them?"

"Naw, they were amazing! Aiden ran away, but I didn't. Why does everyone say they're scary?"

Dara's eyes widened as she looked at Tanwen, the question written on her face.

Tanwen shrugged. "I can't explain it, but something has been happening since we have a male Wybren for the first time in centuries."

"I want to be next!" proclaimed Tarian.

Dara's face went white, and she put him down. "You—you want to be a Wybren?"

He nodded emphatically.

Tanwen crouched in front of him. "We can't start training again right away. You know that, right?"

"Yes, Wybren Tanwen."

"Which dragon did you like best?"

"Quillon, of course." He looked at Dara. "When he came out of the hole, he made sure we were safe. He roared at the enemy, but he didn't burn them 'cause there were Wybrens there, too. That's how I want my dragon to be—brave and fierce and protective."

Tanwen smiled and tousled his hair. "If they're not, they're not allowed to Choose." She looked across the camp when she heard raised voices. Standing, she put her hand on her sword and moved between the sound and Dara. A moment later, she saw Dinsmore and re-laxed. "Thank Laoch. Dara, you might have some work to do, but everyone is moving under their own steam."

Dara's face was still white. She glanced at Tarian and back to Tanwen. "So, do you think—"

Tanwen touched Dara's arm. "Time enough to worry about that later. He's young, and it's a long process. Come on, let's see if anyone needs help." She strode to the newcomers.

Dinsmore grinned and clasped Tanwen's upper arms. "We saw them! Well done!"

"I did the least of everyone, but they're reasonably safe for the moment."

"For now, that's the best possible scenario. Who is back?"

"Tarian and I just got here, but Dara said Aiden and part of Siril's group is here. The other Wybrens left when I did, but they might not come directly back in case they're followed. I need to talk to you."

He nodded, and they walked away from the others.

"Quillon says the mages need to figure out how to protect the Wybrens, and we should split up. If we stay together, the enemy might kill several of us at once, and that would be disastrous."

"Indeed. Do you have thoughts on how to split the group?"

She shook her head. "I haven't had time to think about it."

Dinsmore squinted. "The others will be back soon. I hope they will, at least. Let's give it some thought, and we can talk about it with the others. We're going to have to move camp, anyway, in case someone is followed here."

"Good point. How did your mission go?"

"We got some travel rations and water skins from the salle. We got pinned down in the stable for a little while, but while we hid, we grabbed some blankets. It's not enough, but it's more than we had."

"Everything will help."

Chapter Fifteen ~ Annwn

They moved on the next morning with Saphir guiding them northeast. Quinn seemed nervous. He watched their surroundings, his hand never far from his sword.

His nervousness made Aithne nervous. She leaned closer and whispered, "Do you think they're still following?"

"They will not stop looking."

"What will you do when you get me out of Annwn?"

His brow furrowed. "I had not thought that far ahead. I will deal with that after you are safe. Letting them catch me is the most sensible approach to confirming your death."

She stumbled and caught herself. "Will I be dead?"

"Not if I have breath left in my body."

Aithne forced air into her lungs. The corner of the scripture box dug into her back, and her tattoo itched. She shifted the pack straps and looked for a slender stick to scratch her arm with. "Was there a particular reason you had an unauthorized copy of your scriptures?"

"There are none considered authorized, so mine were not contraband in the sense I think you mean. Long ago, the acolytes of the Goddess made copies of the scrolls for their personal use. It was only after they had copied each letter correctly that they were considered for promotion to apprentice. I decided to revive the practice, even though I wasn't an acolyte."

"Why not?"

"I am a ranger. Hynef blocked my chance serve the Goddess directly."

"That doesn't seem right."

"Your culture may have some questionable aspects, given what you know now."

Aithne thought for a moment. "I suppose there are. How long did it take you to make your copies?"

"Several years. I had to limit my work to the times Hynef was away. Fortunately, she was fostered in the early phases of her training, or I might still be working on them. You will see my growth in the writing as you read them."

Aithne smiled. "Are you sure you want me to take them? They must mean so much to you."

"You are the rightful owner." He grabbed her arm and stopped. Aithne froze, looking and listening. The woods had gone silent. There hadn't been a lot of noise, so the further lack of it felt ominous.

Quinn looked over his shoulder. His body went rigid. He dropped her arm and turned.

Aithne turned with him. A bird flew off a tree branch, transforming when it landed. Hynef walked out of the woods.

"Good. You're still together. That makes it easier."

Aithne scanned her surroundings. There were several ravens on low branches. *Saphir, looks like we have company. Don't come here; but find the pass.*

I am looking for anything suitable near your location.

Quinn walked toward Hynef. "What do you want?"

She snorted and rolled her eyes. "You know what I want. Are you going to come quietly?"

"I will if you let Aithne go."

"Let her *go*?" She barked a laugh. "She's fully corrupted you."

"As far as you're concerned, I didn't have far to go. You think I was corrupt at birth."

"The thought had occurred to me."

Aithne took a deep breath, mimicking a meditative state and gathering magic.

Five of the birds landed, transforming before they hit the ground, and stalked toward them.

"Come along, then. The council is waiting for us to return." She looked at Aithne. "I'm eager to learn why you came ahead of your invading force. Are you a leader or a scout?"

"Neither," said Aithne. "They've invaded my home, too."

Hynef smiled, but her eyes were cold. "I'm looking forward to your interrogation."

The men jogged past her, and others landed. More ravens flew into the area.

Quinn raised a hand and shot a wide beam of magic toward the approaching men, and Aithne raised her hand, shouting the wind spell, and directed it at the sky. Ravens cawed as the wind blew them away. She drew a shield around herself like a cloak as a bolt of magic raced toward her. It deflected off her shield, but pushed her back a step. She widened her stance, planting her feet, as she shot a bolt of magic in the direction it came from.

Something pushed her from the side, and she looked at the men who were closing in on each side. She turned, positioning herself back to back with Quinn and extending her shield around him. Panic crept in along the edge of her consciousness, and she reached for Lledrith. Calm filled her, and she added a deflection spell to her shield. Magic ricocheted off in bright streaks. She noticed different colors in the magic but couldn't take the time to wonder about what, if anything, that meant.

A spell hit the shield in front of her, but it didn't bounce. Instead, it spread in a black blob, and she felt the power draining. She snarled, pulling magic from the earth through her feet, and shouted a spell to burn the blob off with fire. For a moment, flames engulfed the shield. When she pulled the fire back, it glowed like the sun.

The fae closed in around them, and she felt Quinn step out of her shield.

Fear crept into Aithne's mind, and she shoved it away. She grabbed a knife from a leg sheath and threw it at the nearest adversary. He yelped as it sank into his shoulder, and she sent another spinning toward the next one. Behind her, Quinn hissed.

She invoked the wind again, pushing her hand out as far as she could and turned in a semicircle. When she saw Quinn, he was bleeding from a wound in his shoulder, and an arrow protruded from his leg. He shouted something, pushing both hands forward. Two men dropped, blood blossoming from their throats, and Hynef jerked back, her hands covering her chest. Rage crossed her face.

"Run," said Quinn.

"Right behind you," Aithne answered.

"No! You! Go!" He pushed Hynef back three more steps. "RUN!"

"I'm not going without you!" She slammed her shield around him again as he swore. "Let's go!"

He limped a few steps, still swearing.

She put her arm around his waist, forcing him to encircle her shoulders, and ran. His weight slowed her, and she pulled the shield tighter. He mumbled another spell, pushing out with his free hand as their pursuers closed their flanks to trap them. The men on the right side stumbled back, and he whispered something else, which allowed him to run faster.

Aithne whispered a spell that came to her head; she heard shouting behind her.

"Good choice," he murmured in her ear, and she didn't waste breath asking what he meant. He added something to her spell and pointed to a game trail on the right. The angry shouting behind them became cawing ravens.

The trail led to a smooth shelf of rock that sloped gently up. Quinn grunted in pain as they followed it to a tiny cave. He pointed to it, and they ducked in. He slid down the wall with a groan.

Aithne grabbed her bow from its spot on her pack and strung it. Ravens circled above the trees as she plucked an arrow from her quiver. "We can't stay here long. There's not enough cover."

"We don't need cover with your invisibility spell."

Shock made her hand tremble, but she kept her eyes on the birds. "Is that what I said?"

"You didn't know?"

She shook her head. "I repeated what Lledrith said to me."

He gasped, and blood trickled toward her foot. She stepped away from the ledge and turned to look at him. He'd pulled the arrow out of his leg; it lay beside him on the rock. His wounds poured blood, soaking his clothes. He was white as a sheet, trembling with a sheen of sweat on his face.

She knelt beside him. "We need to bind your wounds. They'll be able to track us when they see your blood."

She shrugged her pack off, and he put a hand on her arm.

"You have the scroll box, right?"

"Yes, but—"

"You need to go. Take my pack. You'll be able to carry more."

She looked around. The ravens still circled, searching for them.

Saphir? Where are you?

I am nearing what appears to be a pass, but it is narrow.

She pulled out her beacon, watching the birds. *Am I near it?*

Yes, but it is too narrow.

Aithne pressed her lips together in frustration. *Is there anything else nearby?*

That depends on if you can go up.

Cautiously, she stepped out of the shelter and looked around. *I'm going to wait until they give up looking for me.*

She felt a surge of frustration from Saphir. *I wish I could provide a distraction.*

Me too, but that would draw attention to you. Maybe I can distract them.

"Quinn, we need to—" She stopped as she turned to look at him. He stared at the opposite wall, and she dropped to her knees beside him. "Quinn?"

He didn't respond, and she touched his neck, seeking his heartbeat. Sorrow flooded over her when she couldn't find it. "Oh, Quinn. I'm sorry."

What happened?

She leaned back against the wall as tears rushed down her face. *He was wounded in the fight, and now he's dead.*

There was a moment of stunned silence. *Aithne, you need to go. If they catch you, you will get blamed.*

She swallowed hard and leaned forward to brush Quinn's eyes closed. *I'm going to leave my beacon out so you can track me.* She threaded her arm through the bow, tucking it on her shoulder with the riser on her back, and stepped around Quinn to the ledge, snagging his pack with her free hand. It felt like there was nothing in it, so she spared a few seconds to look inside. With no time to examine the contents, she stuffed her pack inside his, shocked when it fit. She buckled the flap and slung it over her shoulder.

A noise made her look down. Her pursuers were picking their way up the hill toward her. She scrambled away from the shelter, climbing on top of it and picking her way up diagonally, careful not to give away her position.

A rock slid under her hand. She swallowed a startled gasp, gripping the rock before it fell. The men had almost reached the ledge, and once they reached it, they would see Quinn. She glanced at them, relieved to see they were looking down. She threw the rock, and it bounced off a tree trunk.

Her pursuers turned toward it as words came to her. She whispered them, letting her hand drift like a feather from her shoulder to hip height. The bushes on the ground swayed. She shook her hand as if she was shaking the dirt off plant roots, and the bushes shuddered. She heard them rustle, and then a shadow detached from the bushes and ran away from the direction she was going. The scouts followed it, running silently. She looked around. There were no signs of birds.

What did you do?

Aithne jumped, and her free hand flew to her chest. *Saphir! You scared me!* She took a low, deep breath. *I don't exactly know what I did. I think I cast an illusion of myself running away.*

Then you better get far away from there before they realize they are chasing a shadow.

Aithne nodded, even though Saphir couldn't see it, and increased the speed of her climbing. Reaching a ledge, she ran. It wound up the side of the mountain and doubled back. At the top, she glanced down. She saw bodies on the blood-stained earth where they'd fought, but Hynef wasn't among them.

A pair of ravens circled in the sky, and she shoved the grief away, making her way around the peak to the other side. As she started back down, she held up the beacon. *Saphir, do you know where I am?*

I sense your location. I am unsure which side of the border you are on. Keep moving and I will find you.

Aithne climbed down, holding her arms out for balance. Her feet slid on loose rocks, and she slowed to place her feet more carefully. Somewhere nearby, a raven cawed, and she looked up as it slammed into her shoulder.

She yelped but kept her balance, ducking to avoid another bird.

A shadow passed in front of the sun. Relief flooded through her, and she looked up to see where Saphir was.

It wasn't Saphir; relief froze solid in her chest as a flock of ravens descended. She dropped to her knees, bracing herself in a ball with her arms protecting her head and neck. She gasped at the impact. They felt like rocks as they hit her. Some of them landed on her back, scratching and pecking. She smelled the metallic tang of blood combined with something herbal but with a musty edge.

More birds dove, and she heard the hiss of an arrow as it flew past her. She batted the birds away and rolled to her feet, running and zig-zagging so she'd be harder to hit, ignoring the loose rocks under her feet. An arrow grazed her leg, and she stumbled forward as another slammed into her pack.

She slipped on an icy patch and fell, and a raven dragged its claws over her face. She screamed and tried to get to her feet, but the birds kept flying into her, keeping her on the ground. From the sparse tree line to her right, she saw three cudions running toward her.

Strong jaws bit her left upper arm, yanking hard, and she screamed. She punched at its head, hitting it in the eye. It let her go as it yelped, and she screamed a spell that sent it tumbling down the hill.

The sound of a sword leaving a scabbard made her jerk her head up. The fae changed to their human forms, and one stalked toward her, his sword arm raised.

A bow string twanged, and an arrow buried itself in the man's side. He crumpled with a yelp, and a grimalkin bounded out of the woods. It pounced on his chest and bit a chunk out of his neck before springing at another fae nearby.

Aithne froze, fear gripping her muscles. She heard more arrows and looked to her left. Two men targeted her attackers, hitting them one by one and letting the grimalkin finish those who didn't die immediately.

Her chest loosened enough to take a deeper breath, and she clambered to her feet, keeping her eyes on the grimalkin.

The last fae fell, and the grimalkin turned to look at her. It prowled toward her and she backed away. The rocks slipped under her feet and she and tumbled, landing on her hip. One stranger whistled, and the grimalkin loped back to them.

Aithne scrambled to her feet as the men turned to look at her. They dressed like the mages who had attacked her when she arrived in Annwn.

Ahead, she saw another group of ravens flying toward her.

The men took a few steps toward her, and one asked, "You are Slannish dragon rider?"

She stifled a gasp and turned, running down the hill. One raven grazed her shoulder. She swerved and skidded, but kept her balance. *Saphir!*

I am coming!

Something moved in her peripheral vision, and she saw Saphir bank, breathing fire. She heard shouting as

Saphir landed on a small ledge, inhaling for another round of fire.

Aithne! Come!

Aithne stumbled and ran, hauling herself onto Saphir's back. The ravens dove again, and Saphir blew fire at them. The stench of burning flesh and feathers filled her nose, and she gagged.

Saphir launched, and Aithne crouched low, holding Saphir's dorsal spines and gripping with her legs. She extended her shield to Saphir. They circled to gain altitude, outpacing the birds, and turned east.

Aithne's heart hammered, and she closed her eyes, trying to calm herself. *Where are we going?*

I have consulted Quillon and Vask. They want us to go to the temple in Commain.

Surprise spiked through Aithne. *Do you know where that is?*

I do not. Vask said to fly east to find a rendezvous point.

How do they know there is a temple in Commain?

Vask and Isidro are there with Briant and Raya.

A trickle of relief flowed through Aithne, and her eyes misted. She would be with people she knew, people who would not try to kill her. *Did Vask say how far it is?*

He did not. We will pass the Southern Keep on our route. Perhaps it is wise to stop there to seek the help of a healer.

Aithne wanted to tell her not to, but her wounds throbbed, and her clothes were wet with blood. *That's going to cause problems of its own.*

Let me worry about that. For now, drop your shield to conserve your energy.

When she released the shield from Saphir, the wind slammed into her legs. Gasping, she shoved it back into place. *That's not the best idea. It's blocking the wind.*

Can you move it away from my wings without compromising your safety?

I'll try. She pulled the shield away from Saphir, bending her legs more to keep them in the shield as much as possible. It was awkward, but warmer. *Wherever we're going, we need to get there fast.*

Chapter Sixteen ~ Commain

Aithne clung to Saphir's back in a meditative state to gather as much magic as she could from the air. To staunch the bleeding and dull the pain, she diverted the excess energy from her shield to her wounds.

Saphir's voice filtered into her consciousness. *Beloved, we are nearing the Southern Keep. I am going to approach. Quillon says you should signal your distress to the guards on watch.*

Aithne pulled out of her meditation, holding on as Saphir banked gently. She opened her eyes; the Keep was close enough to distinguish men on the battlement. She raised both arms over her head, waving them in the standard distress signal. They motioned for them to circle the Keep, and Saphir tilted into a gentle spiral that took them closer. The men on the battlement ran in an organized manner, as if moving to battle stations rather than fleeing the dragon.

Saphir, does their movement seem odd to you?

Odd how?

She turned the corner, and Aithne saw the ballista. It loomed in her vision, blocking everything else out, and fear made her shield waver.

"Saphir!"

The bolt exploded from the weapon as Saphir banked, and Aithne shifted her legs to keep her seat. The bolt sailed past, but the sound of the ballista had drowned out the twang of bowstrings. Two arrows embedded in her leg, and several more bounced off Saphir's scales.

She screamed, grabbing Saphir's dorsal spikes and clinging to them. "Go, Saphir!"

Saphir banked away, and another arrow tore through her wing membrane, thudding into Aithne's thigh. Several more arrows bounced off Saphir's scales, and another ballista bolt skimmed her tail.

With a powerful eastward flap, Saphir gained speed and altitude, while Aithne clung to her spikes.

How badly are you hit? asked Aithne.

I can still fly. You?

Three arrows in my leg.

She felt a ping of alarm and heard the buzz of dragon communication.

A moment later, Saphir said, *Extend your shield to cover your whole body and hold on. Vask and Isidro are on their way to a new rendezvous point.*

Hurry!

Briant! Aithne is in trouble. Raya is here, saddling Isidro, and she will start mine, but you need to come now!

Briant dropped the scroll he'd been reading on his bed. He shrugged on his thickest wool sweater, strapped on his sword belt, and grabbed his flight jacket, shoving his arms into the sleeves as he jogged to the courtyard.

"Briant? Is something wrong?"

He glanced over his shoulder and saw Kevia. "I think so, but I don't know for sure what it is. Come with me so you can tell Adrienne."

She lengthened her stride, following him.

He knew the polite thing would have been to wait for her, but he didn't have time for politeness. Not with the tone of Vask's voice. Winding through the labyrinth of corridors, he stopped, not sure which way to go. Great. Just great.

"Right," called Kevia. She was jogging now, and he paused. "Go, I'm right behind you!"

He turned right and ran. A moment later, he entered the cavernous audience hall and sprinted across to the courtyard, his open jacket flapping against his sides.

Raya had put Vask's saddle on him, and he ducked for the straps. "What's happening?"

Kevia burst out of the door. Raya jumped, one hand gripping her sword hilt as the other flew to her heart.

"Sorry," said Kevia. "What's happening? Hurry and tell me so you can go."

"We don't know much," said Raya. "Saphir called for help. Vask told her which way will get her here. We're going to look for her."

"Just Saphir?" asked Briant.

"Aithne is with her, but she's wounded. Saphir is, too."

"Hurt, but not injured," said Vask. "I told her about the clearing where you were detained. Hopefully it is clear of the enemy."

Isidro grunted in agreement. "If it is not, it will be."

Raya climbed into the saddle. "Let's go, Briant!"

"I'm right behind you."

Isidro walked to the center of the courtyard. Briant and Kevia shielded their heads with their arms as he launched. The door behind Kevia opened, and someone handed her a bundle.

As Briant mounted, Kevia strode forward and tucked a blanket in his saddlebag. "Vask, is there anything else I need to tell Adrienne?"

"Tell her the Southern Keep is compromised, and to prepare a room and alert the healers."

"And tell Sine!" added Briant.

Kevia nodded, backing toward the door as Briant strapped in.

A moment later, they were circling the temple. He scanned the ground as Vask climbed. He flew until he caught a thermal, smoothing his flight and making it easier to see the ground rushing by. The wind was cold and stung his face, but he ignored it. *Vask, how is the Southern Keep compromised?*

It seems the enemy has captured it. They have installed ballistae on the parapet and have archers ready. Arrows that went through Saphir's wing membrane shot Aithne in the leg.

Briant shivered, but he didn't ask anymore questions. He wasn't sure he wanted to know. That much information had his gut roiling.

He was so focused on the ground that it surprised him when Vask descended. He squinted at the sky and saw Saphir banking toward the ground. Aithne was riding bareback, and relief flooded through him.

He stayed quiet as Vask circled. Isidro landed, and Raya vaulted from the saddle when his feet hit the ground. He saw Aithne slide off Saphir's back, landing in a heap on the ground. She didn't move, and Briant's mouth went dry. His hands shook as he gripped the front of the saddle.

Vask descended sharply, and for a moment Briant's attention was on staying in the saddle. The straps dug into his skin, and he pushed his feet forward in the stirrups, bracing so Vask could land quickly.

Raya bent over Aithne as Vask landed, shielding her from the debris his wings stirred up. Briant unbuckled his straps, holding on tight as Vask landed. He slid from the saddle and hit the ground running. "Aithne!"

Raya looked over her shoulder. "Briant, she's too cold! Tell me you have a spell."

"I do. Aithne, I'm going to have to touch your skin."

She nodded. Her lips were blue, and she shook with cold. He invoked his heat spell, reaching under her clothing to press one hand to her belly and one to her back. She gasped, and her eyes flew open.

"We need to get her back," said Raya, "and she can't fly on her own."

"I'll take her," said Briant. "I can warm her while we fly. Kevia put a blanket in the saddle bag."

Raya ran to get the blanket, and Briant moved his hands to lift Aithne into his arms. "Saphir, I'm going to get her to the temple. Are you all right to follow?"

"We'll guide her back," said Raya. She covered Aithne with the blanket as she walked beside Briant. "Hang on." When Briant paused, she pulled Aithne's beacon out of her clothing.

"Good idea," said Briant.

"It was Isidro's," said Raya. "Let me have her. You mount and we'll get her into the saddle."

Briant handed Aithne to Raya and climbed onto Vask's back behind the saddle. He strapped himself in, stretching to brace his foot in the stirrup as Raya passed Aithne back.

Aithne moaned as they jostled her, getting her into the saddle and strapped in. Raya moved the stirrups back so Briant could get his feet in them as he snugged himself against Aithne's back.

"Go," said Raya. "We'll get Saphir back."

Briant nodded and Raya ran a few steps away, turning her back as Vask launched. Aithne moaned again. "You're okay, Aithne. You're going to be okay."

"Will I?" She went limp in his arms, and Briant's breath caught. For a moment, he feared the worst, but she was still breathing.

He felt relief from Vask. *Where there is breath, there is hope.*

Yes, and I hope we get back in time.

Chapter Seventeen ~ Slan

Greer stood in the tree line of a clearing, looking up at the sky. It was sunny for the first time in days, but she smelled the change of weather coming—loam, wood smoke, and snow. She heard footsteps behind her, but didn't turn.

Evanna came to stand beside her. "The Western Keep mages seem nervous."

Greer shrugged. After living in Slan for so many years, the Dorchadan accent seemed foreign to her. "The curse may be fading, but it's not gone. I'm not sure why you want to train them to make dragon *tanad*. Surely any other animal would do the trick."

"I have already shown them to make *tanad*. Now we make dragon gems."

Greer looked at her. The girl had fair skin and a long black braid, so much like Lassair, she had to look twice. She kept her voice even, almost bored, when she said, "Dragon gems?"

"It is why Raca sent me here. There are no more dragons in Mevan. She said you could get them here."

Greer wanted to scoff. Raca had her sister's body, but made it clear she was no longer her sister. She hadn't wanted anything to do with Greer until she needed a favor. *Razo? How long?*

I am sending Argento down now.

Greer squinted as a large shadow passed over the clearing. Behind her, the three Western Keep mages gasped, and the young man traveling with Evanna told them to hold steady. She'd introduced him as Tiernay with no other elaboration, but the man's bearing and looks told her he was the heir. She wondered what he was doing on such an errand. Was Raca holding his family hostage? It would be like her.

Evanna began a spell as Argento, one of the youngest dragons, spiraled down, settling in the clearing and looking around. His silver scales glittered in the sun as he turned, looking for the enemy. He stopped moving, frozen, and snorted. Greer saw his muscles tense, but he didn't move. Evanna beckoned to the others and stepped into the clearing. Greer stepped back. She had known Argento since he'd hatched. Watching him die was not high on her priority list, but she didn't dare show it lest Raca find out.

A twig snapped, and she turned as Berengar tossed the broken branch in his hands to the ground. "Did she start yet?"

"Just now."

Berengar nodded. "The girl is impressive. I see why Raca singled her out."

Affecting boredom, Greer covered a yawn and looked away from the clearing. "I suppose so."

"You don't think so?"

"I think I'm ready for her to finish so she can go back to Raca. We have enough going on without escorting one of her pets."

Berengar chuckled. "You're jealous."

"Of what?" Greer demanded. "Do I think I should have a higher post because Raca is—was—my sister? Absolutely. Will I get it based on that? Not bloody like-ly."

"Raca does what she will, whether it makes sense to us or not."

Greer heard a stifled roar and a loud thud. Nausea roiled in her gut. "Are you going to stay and watch?"

"Of course. Aren't you?"

"I have no desire to watch her kill a defenseless drag-on. Keep an eye out, will you?"

Berengar regarded her for a long moment. "It is per-haps your attachment to dragons, to Slan, that is keep-ing you back from a prominent position with Raca."

"Even if that's so, I'm not staying to watch." She stalked away. The sound of crunching leaves and snap-ping twigs did little to drown out the chanting behind her, and she lengthened her stride. If she was lucky, she'd never have to witness such a thing again.

Razo, are we on the right side?

I believe we are. Casualties are inevitable, beloved.

I know. But I didn't think it would hurt that much to watch.

I had no difficulty sending him down. His wings promised mountains, but his wisdom whispered of molehills.

Greer snorted. *He was a little on the arrogant side. Still—*

Beloved, he will be of more use to Raca as tanad, and if his life helps elevate you to a higher status, so be it.

I suppose, but I hope we die in battle, not restrained and helpless.

That is my preference as well.

A large shadow passed over her, and she turned, looking up. A bird flashed past, and she saw only blue feathers before it disappeared into the trees. The wind gusted, blowing small, sharp snowflakes in her face. Shivering, she hurried to the Keep.

Stopping in the kitchen for a cider ration, she went to her quarters. She expected to see Muirne when she arrived, but wasn't disappointed to find the rooms empty. Building a fire, she settled with her mug and let the alcohol soothe her battered emotions.

Before she could set aside her mug, someone knocked at the door.

Greer sighed. "Come!" She scoffed when Gallia stepped in far enough to see her. "Oh, it's you."

"Yes," Gallia sneered. "Berengar wants you."

"I already saw him outside."

"He's inside now and has sent for you."

Greer rolled her eyes. "I'll be there after I've banked the fire, unless you'd like to do that."

Gallia laughed and shut the door.

Greer drained her mug and set it on the hearth. Banking the fire took only a moment, and she sauntered through the halls to the study he'd claimed.

The door was open. Berengar and another man stood beside the map table, talking in low tones. They looked up when she entered.

"Ah, Greer," said Berengar, "I've had a message from Raca. She wants you to go to Mevan."

Greer frowned. "What's the catch?"

The stranger's eyebrows raised. "Why would there be a catch? You've been summoned by Raca."

Berengar nodded and stepped away from the table to pour a cup of water. "That's really all we know. I understand you're used to getting reasons for doing things here, but when Raca commands, we obey."

Greer scoffed. "Of course. Did she give any indication of how long I will be there?"

Berengar frowned and looked at the man, who shook his head. "Not specifically. I'd pack for a couple of days, and if she wants you there permanently, you can send for the rest of your things."

"Permanently?"

Berengar walked back to the table. "It might be. She was your sister. She might have something important for you to do."

Greer nodded slowly. She wasn't sure if they were serious or pulling an elaborate prank, but she knew if Raca summoned her, she had to go. She turned on her heel and strode out, heading for her chambers.

Razo, you heard that, right?

I did. What time suits you for departure?

Greer paused at a window. The morning was late, the weather fair. *It depends on how long it takes to find Muirne. If this is to be permanent, she'll be joining me.*

I will await your decision.

Greer continued down the hall. Hope blossomed in her gut. Would all her years of hard work finally pay off? She lengthened her stride. Time was of the essence.

Razo landed at the Mevan landing site, and Greer unbuckled the straps. Muirne slid out of the saddle and stepped back to retrieve their packs from the saddlebags.

Greer walked around to Razo's head and cupped his face in both hands, touching her forehead to her nose. *It's finally happening! You won't have to deal with the Keep dragons anymore!*

You have done well, beloved. I will look forward to our new positions in the kingdom.

She grinned. "Enjoy your pampering!" She took a pack from Muirne. "Let's get down to the stable. They won't know we've been summoned."

They descended through the tower, not paying attention to the activity around them. None of the usual people were there. Greer assumed Raca had killed or captured them. Exiting the tower, they crossed the courtyard to the stables. No one was there.

Greer scoffed. "Of course, there are no stable hands. Why would anything be done our way? Come on, Muirne, we'll have to do it ourselves." Walking toward the tack room, her vision blurred. She reached for the wall to steady herself.

Alarm flooded her link with Razo. *Beloved! Evanna...*

Greer sank to her knees, her heart pounding.

"Mama?" She heard fear in Muirne's voice.

Razo, what's happening?

His voice was faint and strangled. *Evanna. Gem. Love...*

Her heart hammered so fast she thought it would explode. The buzz of dragon communication filled her head. "Muirne. Run. Find Moira."

She collapsed in the sawdust, and Muirne fell to her knees beside her. "Mama!"

Taking a deep breath, Greer rolled onto her back and reached for Muirne. Her hand landed on Muirne's arm, and she grasped it. "Razo. Dying. Go. Moira." She gasped, panic filling her, and squeezed her eyes shut so Muirne wouldn't see it. Muirne's cries and a long moan from Razo were the last things she heard.

"Mama!" Muirne shook Greer. Her body went limp. "Mama?"

She heard voices and the Dorchadan accent. Someone was looking for them. She scrambled up the ladder to the hayloft and hid. Her heart pounded as the voices came closer. Then they were under her.

"Here is Wybren, where I said she would be."

"Here is *one* Wybren. Where is the second?"

Someone scoffed. "Dragons do not have two Wybrens."

"There were two riders!"

"So you say. The rest of us focused on the dragon, as we were told. Come. Help me move the body."

Muirne heard scuffling and muted swearing and choked back a sob. They killed her mother and Razo. Why did they do that? Huddling in the hay, she tried to decide what to do. Her mother had said to find Moira, but how? Wouldn't it make more sense to go to the palace to tell Raca what happened? This must have been a terrible error. Raca would be the one to get her justice.

She heard more voices. One sounded familiar. She edged to the window overlooking the pasture. Having never visited Mevan before, the lack of horses in the pasture surprised Muirne. She looked for the voices and saw a group near large shelters. Dragon-sized shelters. Two people carried a body to the group, and when they moved, she saw Razo. He lay under bare trees, his scales glittering in the sun. She ducked down, hunched in the hay, and covered her face with her scarf, sobbing into it.

Chanting cut through her sorrow, and she looked out the window again. The larger part of the group stood over Razo's body, and three people stood over her mother's. Though she couldn't make out the words, the spell's evil purpose was clear.

"No," she whispered to herself. "No, not that."

Razo moved, and Muirne moaned. He rolled from his side to his belly and lifted his head. The group parted and moved apart. One figure stood beside him. She lifted her arms, and Razo laid his chin on the ground before Evanna.

The realization was like a splash of cold water. She'd thought Evanna was her friend. Hadn't she harvested Peio and Juvela as retribution for Muirne? She'd said she had.

Muirne sank back into the hay as the group chanted, "Hail, Raca" over and over. She swallowed a fresh wave of grief. She'd wait until dark, steal a horse, and find Moira.

Muirne jerked awake as the horse she rode stopped. It had wandered off the road to graze near the edge of the woods where the snow hadn't covered the grass.

She slid out of the saddle and looked around, looking for landmarks. It looked very different on the ground at night rather than from the air during the day. She had no idea where she was or how long she'd been asleep.

Panic rose, and she tried to push it down. She'd never traveled alone. She'd barely left the Keep before now, and she still didn't know how to find Moira.

Shivering, she leaned against a tree. Clouds obscured the moon and stars, so she didn't even know if the horse had turned off the road going the right direction. What if it was going home?

Closing her eyes, she took a deep breath. She only had to decide what to do first. Waiting until dawn to decide her direction seemed the logical course of action. Holding the reins loosely in her hand, she guided the horse further into the woods, where there was more grass. She sank to the cold ground, looping the end of the rein over her wrist, and pulled her legs up, huddled against the cold. Leaning back against a tree, she let the horse graze and closed her eyes.

CHAPTER EIGHTEEN ~ COMMAIN

Aithne went from darkness to agonizingly bright light. It pierced her head through her eyelids. "Am I dead?"

"Not yet, sweetling," answered a familiar voice. A warm hand cupped her cheek.

Saphir?

When Saphir didn't answer, Aithne forced her eyes open. Everything was blurry, and she blinked, trying to clear her vision. Someone sat beside her. They turned, and she heard liquid being poured.

"You must be parched," said the person.

Saphir?

Aithne's heart pounded against her ribs, and she felt faint. She squeezed her eyes closed. When she opened them, her vision was clear enough to recognize Sine.

Panic slammed into her like a wave, and she threw back the blankets covering her, scrambling to get out of the bed. "No! No! Saphir!"

Sine grabbed her shoulders, pushing her back gently. "She's alive! Aithne, Saphir is alive!"

Aithne struggled to get away, smacking Sine in the face. "I can't hear her!"

Sine pushed her back again. "Aithne! She's alive! The healers had to sedate you, and it's affecting your telepathy. It will wear off in a few hours."

Aithne stopped struggling. "She's alive?"

"She's fine. Mostly. A little banged up, but not nearly as bad as you were, thank Laoch, or she might not have gotten you to the rendezvous point."

She stuttered around a sob. "Where is she?"

"In a sheltered courtyard with Vask and Isidro."

"But she's here?"

"She's here and safe."

Aithne sagged against the pillows, exhausted and weeping, and Sine picked up a cup.

"Here, drink. It's bitter and cold, but wet."

She let Sine hold the cup to her lips, and she sputtered at the bitter willowbark but forced down a couple of gulps.

Sine put the cup down. "It's been sitting there steeping and cooling for hours, so it's no wonder it tastes terrible. Here's some water."

Aithne gulped it. "I wish you'd led with that."

"You needed the willowbark more."

Aithne wanted to say something cheeky, but a strangled sob came out as the emotion she'd suppressed for days erupted. She barely noticed when Sine shifted to the bedside to pull her into her arms. The wave of sorrow and terror consumed her, and all she could do was wail. She was vaguely aware of the door opening and closing, of Sine stroking her hair and murmuring incomprehensible words, of someone building up the fire in the fireplace.

It felt like hours before the waves crashing through her smoothed, and she fell against the pillows, spent.

Sine bathed her face with a cool cloth, and a woman in green homespun came in with a teapot and a covered pitcher.

"Thanks, Tara," said Sine.

Tara put them on the table beside Sine and picked up the old teapot. "I put some herbs in with the willowbark that will counter the sedation faster. I'll be back to check on you later."

Sine took the cover off the pitcher, and Aithne smelled the rich scent of beef broth. It triggered the memory of dragon fire and burned flesh, and she gagged, turning away.

"Aithne?"

"Just tea for now."

Sine replaced the cover and poured the tea.

She took the cup, inhaling the scent of peppermint and lemon balm with the underlying bitterness of willow bark. Her stomach calmed, and she sipped.

"I thought the broth would be more appealing."

"Not now." Aithne looked toward the glazed window. She couldn't look at the fire or Sine. "Saphir had to use fire to save me. We've probably caused an international incident. I don't know what side of the border we were on, but we were still too close according to the treaty."

"Aithne, you both did what you had to do to survive."

She nodded slowly. "But I have more blood on my hands. Now it's human and fae."

"I'm afraid it's not the last of the blood that will be shed."

She turned to look at Sine. "I know."

Someone tapped on the door, and Briant looked in. "Vask said Aithne's awake."

Sine stood and picked up the broth. "Yes, come sit with her while I get her something to eat."

Briant stepped in and dropped into the chair as Sine left. "I guess Sine told you already? I'm really sorry, Aithne."

She leaned back against the pillows. She was barely awake, but already spent. "Sorry for what?"

His face went blank. "Oh. Umm, it will wait. It's, well, I saw you'd been crying."

Fear lanced through her. "What happened?"

"Maybe it's best to wait—"

"Briant!"

He bit his lip. "Liam didn't survive the attack on the Western Keep."

Aithne closed her eyes. "Praise be to the Goddess. I thought you were going to tell me my mother died, too."

Briant paused. "Vask confirmed she's alive and well. They got the dragons out of the lair."

She allowed a tiny trickle of relief in. "That's good news. I wonder what's going to go wrong next." She shifted her focus to the far wall. "Seems like there's a lot I missed. It's probably for the best Saphir didn't say much about what's happened."

"It might be that Quillon told the others not to tell her until we were sure you were out of danger."

She nodded. "Am I out of danger?"

"For now." He moved back to the chair. "You look better now that you're not covered in blood. How do you feel?"

"Awful." She gulped the last of the willow bark tea and shuddered as she handed the mug to Briant. "Everything that isn't throbbing itches."

"That's to be expected. You have stories to tell, but you don't need to now."

Aithne sank back against the pillows. "Where are we? And why are you here?"

"We're in Commain, at the temple."

Aithne frowned. "The temple? Not the palace, or whatever they call the king's residence?"

"That's a long story. It's probably best if I save it for later."

"Uh huh. Okay, well, is everyone here, or did you come here to see me?"

He hesitated and looked away.

"Briant?"

He sighed and turned back. "They're dead. They were on their way here from the abbey, where we were staying, and they were attacked during the eclipse."

Aithne's jaw went slack. "Dead? But you and Sine—"

"I was still at the abbey, and Sine was saved by her bladder."

Aithne wanted to laugh, but she couldn't. "So everyone? Finley? Cadell?"

He nodded. "Sine saw it."

She stared at him, trying to make sense of what he was saying, and he took her hand.

"Aithne, a lot has happened with us, but you need to get your strength back before we get into that. I promise I won't keep you in the dark, but telling you everything now is more than you need."

She swallowed hard against tears. How could she have more already? "Thanks. You're right, I can't take any more right now." She took a deep breath. "Did you find someone to help with your magic?"

"Yes, sort of."

She blinked. Why was everything a surprise all of a sudden? "Me, too. I don't know why I had to go to Annwn. The magic is teaching me herself."

Briant's eyebrows raised. "The magic? Herself? Is it Lledrith?"

"How did you know that?"

"I have Lledrith, and she's teaching me, too."

A wave of dread rolled over her. "We both have the same magic?"

"It sounds like it. Do you have one of these?" He pulled up the left sleeve of his tunic to reveal a tattoo of a large tree on his arm.

Her mouth went dry. She pulled up her right sleeve and held out her arm. The lines had darkened and increased in size. It looked like a tree. The roots grew toward her wrist, and the top stopped near her elbow. "Goddess preserve us, they match."

He nodded, and his face paled. He put his arm against hers. "Are you up to having another visitor? The woman in charge needs to see this."

"I don't know, but get her anyway. It sounds important." She gulped the last of her tea and handed it to him to refill. "Why do I have a bad feeling about this?"

He filled the cup and passed it back to her. "I don't know, but I have it too."

Briant closed the door to Aithne's room and strode toward the far wing, where Adrienne's study was.

Vask, does Saphir know everything that happened?

Not yet, answered Vask. *Isidro and I plan to tell her only what she needs to know, and Quillon agrees.*

Does she know about Finley and Gautier?

No.

A tiny drop of relief rolled through Briant, and he took a deep breath. *I know it's a matter of time, but right now I'm glad they don't know we will probably have to deal with Gautier's tanad.*

It could be worse than that. Beseech the Goddess that the enemy can not make multiple dragon tanad like they can human.

Briant's chest clamped, and he gasped. *I hadn't thought about that.*

I kept silent intentionally. You need to focus on what is, not on what could be.

You're keeping things from me, Vask?

I am sharing all you need to know, beloved, and only with-holding possibilities you do not have time for at the moment. Leave the dread to me and the other dragons.

Briant's chest loosened a little. *You'll tell me if I need to know, though?*

Without hesitation.

He turned the corner to the far wing. The door at the far end of the hall was guarded by two women. He took a deep breath and squared his shoulders. When he was a few paces away, he said, "I need to see the Bealban Dia. It's important."

One of the women sneered. "We're not to call her that until she tells us otherwise, and *Adrienne* is busy."

Briant nodded and side-stepped left to lean against the wall. "Uh huh. Fine. I'll wait."

"She's likely to be some time," said the other guard. "We can have someone fetch you when she's ready."

"It's fine. I'll wait."

The first guard snorted, and they both turned their gaze down the hall.

Vask, could you ask Raya to come?

Vask's voice was laced by annoyance. *Isidro has already asked her to. It is good I cannot see through your eyes or I would immolate those guards. They have to come outside sometime.*

Briant laughed out loud to annoy the women. When they looked at him, he grinned widely and said, "Didn't mean to distract you. My dragon said something funny."

The one on her left arched a brow at him as Raya turned the corner. Three steps down the hall, she called, "Is she in?"

The guards snapped to attention. "Yes, Wybren."

Raya nodded curtly. "We need to see her." She gestured to Briant as the guard on the right started to protest. "*Both of us* need to see her. He's a Wybren, like I am, and the dragons have sent us."

The guards looked at each other skeptically but opened the door. Raya gestured for Briant to precede her, and he passed between the guards into another room. Kevia looked up from the pile of documents on the table in front of her.

She put aside the scroll she was reading, and it rolled up as she stood. "Wybrens? What's wrong?"

"Nothing that I know of," said Raya. "I'm only here because the guards wouldn't let Briant in."

Kevia snorted and rolled her eyes. "They do that with Oswin, too. I'm sorry you had to come here for nothing."

"No worries, I wasn't busy."

Kevia shook her head and knocked on the inner door. Briant heard a murmur and Kevia opened the door. "Briant is here to see you." She nodded at Briant, and as he walked past her, Kevia said, "Adrienne, may I have your permission to adjust the guard schedule? Riona and Sorcha should not serve together."

Adrienne's brow rose. "Did they keep you out, Briant?"

"They did, and it annoyed Vask. Luckily, Raya came to the rescue."

Adrienne looked up. "Goddess, give me strength. Go shake up the schedule, Kevia, and tell Riona and Sorcha that if they trade schedules to guard my door together, they will not like the consequences." The side of her mouth quirked up. "I might decide the dragons need to be guarded."

"At night," added Briant.

Kevia chuckled as she closed the door.

Adrienne stood and stretched. "I'm sorry about that, Briant."

"It's not your fault. Aithne is awake."

"How is she?"

"Battered, but that's not why I'm here." He pulled back his sleeve and held up his arm. "She has one of these."

"What?" She strode around the desk. "Where do they have her?"

"I'll take you." He opened the door so she could pass through.

"Kevia, I'm going to see Aithne. I'll take Riona with me."

"Yes, Adrienne."

Adrienne jerked the outer door open, and Briant saw the guards jump. She strode past, pausing for Briant to catch up. "Riona, you're with me."

Briant led them to Aithne's room. She was reclining against a pile of pillows with her eyes closed when he entered. "Aithne?"

She raised a hand and took a deep breath. "I'm not asleep."

He heard Adrienne order Riona to guard the door as he grabbed a second chair, gesturing for Adrienne to sit in the first. "This is Adrienne, the Bealban Dia. She's the spiritual leader of Commain."

"Nice to meet you, or at least it's nice under the circumstances."

"The Goddess gives us perseverance," said Adrienne gently. "It seems you've needed it as much as any of us."

Aithne shrugged. "I suppose I have. Briant said you need to see this." She extended her arm.

Adrienne frowned at it. "It is the mirror of Briant's." She sat back. Her eyes were wide. "I will have to consult the Goddess about this." Her brow furrowed. "I don't understand. Aithne, unless I am greatly mistaken, this mark means you have Lledrith."

"I do have Lledrith."

Adrienne shook her head. "You are, more or less, the Lavban Dia we expected. We assumed you would be a prophetess, of course, but we expected a woman with Lledrith."

"So, how did you get Briant?"

"That's exactly what I'm wondering."

Briant leaned his forearms on his thighs. "When you and Oswin examined my magic, when you realized it's Lledrith, I saw a woman made of light in our meditation."

"As did I," said Adrienne.

"Was that Lledrith, or Cruthadair?"

"Based on the message, I think it was Cruthadair."

Briant nodded and looked at Adrienne. "And people are made in her image?"

Adrienne blinked as if she hadn't expected such a simple question. "Yes."

"Well, she had two arms."

Adrienne nodded, waiting for the rest. Her jaw dropped when she saw what he meant. Laughing, she said, "The Goddess has two arms!" She sat back in her chair. "This must be why you came to us first. We'd never have believed it otherwise."

Aithne rolled her eyes. "Welcome to my world."

Chapter Nineteen ~ Western Keep

Tanwen pulled the strap of her backpack further up her shoulder and crossed her arms, tucking her hands under them. It was getting colder. Not good.

Lassair came to stand beside her, shoulders hunched against the wind. "Are you sure this is the right thing to do?"

"We don't have any good choices, I'm afraid."

Lassair hummed in agreement. "I wonder where my mother and Muirne are?"

"Razo didn't come out of the lair."

"He wasn't here; he took the hatchlings hunting. But none of them have come back yet." She sighed and looked at the sky. "There hasn't been much love lost between us lately, but I'm worried about Muirne. If

Razo hasn't come back, that means my mother might be dead. Maybe Muirne, too."

Tanwen put an arm around her shoulders. "You know your mother is too mean to go down without a fight."

Lassair laughed as she blinked back tears. "Muirne, too."

Lucas walked over. "We're ready."

Tanwen nodded. "Let's go."

Shaw, Dara, and Tarian joined them, and Tanwen turned north. Dinsmore's group had already gone south, and Siril led his group east. She suppressed the fear of never seeing them again.

Quillon, we're on the move.

Good. You are going north?

Yes.

I have found a place for you to shelter.

She glanced at the gray sky and smelled snow. *How far do you think? We don't have long before it gets dark.*

I will look for you and guide you in.

Shaw stepped up beside her. "I know where we can find shelter."

"Quillon said he found a place, but we'll keep yours in mind. Do we go due north for yours?"

"Yes, it's a fairly deep cave with a natural chimney, but we'll have to climb."

That describes what I have found, said Quillon.

One side of Tanwen's mouth curved up. "It seems like you and Quillon think alike, Shaw."

Shaw's eyebrows shot up. "I'm not sure what to think about that."

Dara leaned in. "It's best not to think about it."

They passed through a meadow, and Tarian gasped, looking at the sky. Everyone reached for their swords and looked up.

"What do you see?" asked Shaw.

Tarian smiled and pointed. "Is that Quillon?"

Tanwen felt Quillon chuckle and put a hand on Tarian's shoulder. "It is, but we need to keep moving."

"Will you take me for a ride after we are safe?"

Tanwen saw the color drain from Shaw's face. "Let's talk about that later, Tarian. Right now we need to get to shelter. Shaw, lead the way."

He gave a curt nod and strode away. Tanwen fell into step beside him, followed by Dara and Tarian, with Lucas and Lassair last.

Shaw glanced over his shoulder. "What does it mean that he wants to ride a dragon, Tanwen?"

"I can't say for sure, but we have evidence that the curse is weakening. You know Briant has been an asset. If we have one male Wybren, there are bound to be others eventually."

Shaw swallowed hard. "How do you do it? How did you let Aithne get on a dragon?"

"It's difficult, but raising a child is not for the faint of heart. I don't think there's been a day since Aithne was born that I haven't worried about her, especially now, with her so far away."

"So you're telling me it's going to get harder."

"It will, but you'll get used to it. You'll see him doing risky things and come out alive and well, and you'll gain confidence in his abilities. Eventually, he'll start to worry about you."

Shaw chuckled and shook his head. "Is that all we do? Worry about our loved ones every day until we die?"

Tanwen shrugged. "Maybe, but it's good that we have something to lose. It makes us fight to be the best we can be." The wind gusted, blowing tree branches. Leaves fell around them, and she shivered. "Let's pick it up a little. The weather is going to turn, and we need to be sheltered before it does."

Tanwen held her hands up in front of the fire and wondered if she'd ever be warm again. Outside, the wind gusted, blowing snow past the opening of the cave they sheltered in. Dara sat opposite her, watching as Lucas and Lassair taught Tarian how to use a sword.

Shaw walked toward the fire, and Dara smiled at him. He walked around her and sank to his haunches, where he could see the training. "When the storm passes, I'm going to take Lucas to collect some pine limbs to make some kind of cover for the entrance. We're going to be here for a while."

Dara hummed in agreement. "I'll come with you, and we should take Tarian. He'll be ready to get outside for a while, and we need to collect firewood."

"We'll all feel better if we go outside," said Tanwen. She jumped at a ping of alarm from Quillon. She saw Lassair freeze, not noticing when Tarian whacked her in the leg with the stick he wielded.

Tanwen, Razo sent a distress call. The enemy captured him.

Tanwen's mind went blank for a moment. *Is he—*

Yes. They killed him.

She saw Lassair's jaw drop, and her hand covered her mouth. She looked around and ran to Tanwen.

Tanwen got up to meet her as Lassair collapsed in her arms. The others gathered, unaware of what had happened.

Lassair's legs gave way and she wept in shock. Tanwen sank with her, still holding her, and looked up at the others. "They got Razo, her mother's dragon." She ignored the reaction of the others as Quillon continued.

Muirne was with her. Razo heard Greer tell her to find Moira before he died.

Lassair stiffened in her arms, and Tanwen murmured, "We'll look for her. We'll all be looking for her."

As Lassair wept, Tanwen looked at the others. "We need to look for Muirne. Greer told her to find Moira."

"Muirne was there?" gasped Dara.

"Apparently."

"Did Razo say where they were?" asked Shaw. "Greer hasn't been accounted for."

Lassair sat back and wiped her face with both hands. "He didn't have time. Venka listened for clues to their location, but only heard chanting."

Beloved, said Quillon, *I cannot say for certain, but I suspect Razo was working against us. The hatchlings he had with him are dead, too.*

Uffern. Do the others know?

I have told Raine and Vask. It seemed prudent to limit knowledge, since I have no proof.

Good. Let's keep it that way until we know something. She stood, scanning their surroundings. "There's not much we can do now except keep an eye out for Muirne. The dragons will look for her. The only thing that's safe to assume is that Razo and Greer are *tanad* now."

Lassair hiccuped, and Tanwen crouched beside her. "Sweetling, I'm so sorry."

Lassair swallowed hard and nodded. "You're right, though. We need to assume the worst, so we need to be careful if we find Muirne."

Tanwen pulled a dead branch from the snow and added it to the pile she held. The snow had stopped. It sparkled in the sunlight, and the wind didn't feel as cold.

Nearby, Lucas hacked the lower limbs off a fir tree with his dagger. It started to give, and he yanked it.

Lassair motioned for them to be quiet, and Shaw hissed at Lucas. Tarian froze beside Dara. Tanwen reached for her sword but didn't grip the hilt.

Lassair hooted and, in the distance, someone hooted back. Tanwen dropped her wood and strode forward to stand beside Lassair. She saw several people threading between trees and shaded her eyes with her hand. Relief flooded through her.

"I see Briant's brothers," she said, walking toward them through the snow. "Aengus! Hamish!"

They looked up, and their shoulders sagged in relief. They turned to the others in the group, and she heard voices murmur.

Tanwen looked back. "Tell the others. I'll take them to the cave." She turned back to the group. They looked cold and dirty, but not wounded.

Aengus pulled ahead of the others. "Tanwen, am I ever glad to see you."

She met him, and they clasped forearms. "I'm glad to see you, too." She squinted at the rest of the group. There were several children gathered around one woman and a few other men. "Is this the rest of your family?"

"The ones that made it," he said. "Hamish's wife died, but the younglings are safe."

She counted the others as they approached, mentally figuring how far their supplies would go with a dozen extra people. "Come on. I'll take you to our shelter to rest."

"We'd appreciate that."

She led them back the way she'd come, stopping to pick up her firewood. Dara and Tarian joined them.

Tanwen turned to Aengus. "We've been sheltering in a cave. It hasn't been ideal, but we're making it a little more comfortable."

Two of the men broke away from the group and waded through the snow toward Shaw and Lucas.

"Looks like we might be able to help," said Aengus.

"Any help is welcome."

Muirne startled from sleep when someone touched her.

"Sorry," said a male voice. "I didn't mean to startle you."

Muirne scrambled to her feet. "You touch a sleeping person and expect to not startle them?"

He stepped back. "I wasn't sure you were asleep."

"What else would I be?" she demanded, her heart pounding.

"Dead."

Her breath caught, and her mouth went dry. "I guess that's fair." She looked around and noticed for the first time that the horse was gone. Why hadn't she tied the rein to her clothing? "Well, I'm not dead, so I guess I'll be on my way."

"Where are you going?"

She squinted at him. As the sun rose behind him, shadows hid his face, making it difficult for her to see him clearly. "What do you care?"

He shrugged. "My group is heading to the Western Keep; join us, if you like."

She shifted and started to say she wasn't, but a familiar voice called her name. Evanna spoke to the others in the group before turning her horse toward her. "Muirne, what are you doing out here?"

Muirne froze, and something inside her said not to tell Evanna where she'd been. "I went hunting with a few others, and we got separated. It's embarrassing but I got turned around, so I was waiting for the sun to come up so I'd know which way to go."

"Then it's a good thing we found you," said Evanna. "Hop up. You can ride with me."

Muirne forced a smile. "Thanks." She climbed up behind Evanna as the man—she recognized Tiernay now—walked back to his horse.

"Why have you left Mevan?" asked Muirne.

"We followed a dragon to the landing site. Raca was so pleased with the gem she's sending us to Western Keep to see if we can find more adult dragons."

"You're not afraid of being incinerated?"

"Sure, but I'm more afraid of Raca." Evanna shivered. "I'll die before I fail her, or at least I hope I will."

"Why?"

"Have you seen her? She has power rolling off her in waves. I've heard she can cause people to waste away for years, suffering, because they failed her. That's not for me, thank you very much."

"I guess I'd face a dragon too," said Muirne. Evanna's actions made sense. She didn't like them, but clearly, if anyone was to blame for her mother's death, it was Raca. Her aunt had killed her mother.

Chapter Twenty ~ Commain

On the third day, Aithne woke to milky sunshine. She looked around and saw her clothes folded on a table across the room.

She sat up gingerly, pushing one leg and then the other off the bed. For a moment she sat still, waiting for dizziness or weakness. When there was none, she stood carefully and walked the three steps to retrieve her clothes. She took them back to the bed and sat down carefully.

She took off the nightgown and saw her body for the first time. The stitched wounds on her upper left arm and left leg itched. Bruises and scrapes covered her body. The tattoo on her arm was darker and better defined. Her body ached, but she knew she had work to do. Pulling her tunic on, she let it fall to cover the worst of it. She threaded one foot into the leg of her trews and then the other, standing long enough to pull them up and sitting again to tie them. The door opened as she pulled on her second stocking, her jaw clenched and a sheen of sweat on her brow from the exertion.

"What do you think you're doing?"

Aithne glanced over her shoulder.

Sine stood in the open doorway with a tray, her head cocked, with a look Aithne had seen on her mother's face many times. "Why are you dressed?"

"I need to get to work."

Sine put the tray on the table. "You need to rest. You could have died three days ago."

"But I didn't, and I still have work to do. Look, let me eat and meditate before you tell me I can't get out of bed."

"If I tell you that, will you go back to bed?"

Aithne's face warmed. "Maybe."

Sine snorted and brought Aithne the tray. "Lean back against your pillows." She shook her head. "The berry didn't fall far from the bush."

Aithne wanted to smile, but it hurt. Instead, she picked up the steaming mug and blew on the tea to cool it. Minty steam billowed in her face, laced with the bitterness of willow bark.

Sine pulled the chair next to the bed and sat. "We've heard from your mother. She is relieved to hear you're safe and wants you to know she is, too."

Aithne's heart skittered. "What did you tell her?"

"That you and Briant are here, and you were wounded escaping from Annwn." She raised a hand when Aithne opened her mouth to protest. "We had to tell her something. Your communication with Saphir was weak at that point and we didn't want her to have to lie to Quillon on top of everything else."

Aithne grunted and sipped her tea. "I guess that makes sense. Quillon would see through it anyway."

"Exactly."

Aithne ate the eggs and fruit under Sine's watchful eye. When she'd finished the food, Sine refilled Aithne's tea and took the tray. "Do not get out of bed until I come back."

"Don't dawdle, then," said Aithne with a cheeky grin. She leaned back against the pillows, cradling the cup in both hands, and closed her eyes. *Saphir, is there anything else I need to know that Sine didn't tell me?*

Her report was accurate. I relayed everything I know to Quillon, Vask, and Isidro. They had heard the Southern Keep fell, but we confirmed it.

Aithne snorted. *That would have been good to know in advance. Any news from home?*

Nothing you do not already know. I sense you are still fatigued, but Sine seemed over-protective.

She's mothering me since Mama isn't here. She still sees me as a little girl.

Saphir scoffed. *You are not. You are a grown woman with magic, and I sense time is short for you to control it.*

I feel that, too. I'm going to meditate for a while, and then I'll get to work.

Perhaps meditation will give you rest. I will consult Vask to see if he has further insight.

Aithne shifted her focus to the meadow, and dragon voices buzzing became insects in the flowers. The air smelled fresh, as if blood and death did not exist. The sun was warm on her body, and the aching eased. She lay back in the tall grass, waiting for prompting from Lledrith. She had a vague urge to work, but it seemed far away. The breeze ruffled the grass around her, seeming to whisper Briant's name. She left her meditation, reluctant to return to the cold and pain.

When she opened her eyes, she felt better. A moment later, someone tapped on her door and opened it.

Briant peeked in. "Are you decent?"

"As much as I can be."

He came in and dropped into the chair beside her. "Vask told me to see if you're ready to work."

She paused. "Yes, I think, but I almost didn't want to leave meditation."

"I understand that. What is yours like? Mine has a meadow where Lledrith uses butterflies to teach me."

"I have a meadow, too, but Lledrith looks like a woman made of light, and she whispers the spells in my head."

Briant cocked his head. "Interesting how we have similarities, but it's not the same."

"We should see if our magic works the same way. Can you bring me my boots?"

He got up to fetch her boots. As she put them on, he pulled a wool sweater from her pack. "You'll want this, too. My practice room is large and difficult to heat."

She pulled on the sweater and stood gingerly.

"Do you need to hold on to me?" asked Briant.

"I think I'm fine if we don't go too fast." She opened the door and took a few steps down the hall when she heard Sine sputter behind her.

"Briant, she does not need help getting into trouble!"

Raya poked her head out a door behind Sine. "What's going on?"

Sine turned. "Aithne has it in her head that she needs to get back to work, and it's too soon. She needs to rest for a few more days."

Aithne sighed. "Sine, I feel fine. Let me try a little bit. I'll come back if it's too much."

Sine sputtered again, and Raya stepped into the hall to put a hand on Sine's shoulder. "I'll go with them.

Movement will do her some good, and I'll stop her before she does too much."

"And how will you know where to stop her?"

"The dragons will monitor her."

Sine threw her hands up. "Fine. Have it your way." She turned on her heel and stalked back down the hall.

Raya grinned. "Let's go before she comes up with another argument."

They wove through corridors, and Aithne's aching eased as she moved. Arriving at the ballroom next to the courtyard with the dragons, strength and clarity returned to her. She saw Saphir outside. *I wonder if we can practice out there with you?*

I would like that, but you should stay in. It is cold out here.

Briant nudged her, and Raya sat on the cold hearth. "Let's try shielding. We both know how to do that."

"Sounds like as good a place to start as any." They stood facing each other, and Aithne began her spell, tracing the shape of her shield with her hands. Briant murmured, his hands weaving a pattern in front of him.

She frowned. "Why is your way different?"

"No idea. Keep going," Briant answered.

She started again, and her shield formed, but it was thin enough for air to penetrate. She felt tension in the back of her head as she repeated the spell.

"Try increasing your hand motions."

She made her motions bigger, and the tension became a twinge, but the shield strengthened.

Beloved, said Saphir, concern tinting her voice, *you should stop.*

I almost have it. She spoke the spell again, increasing both her hand motions and her volume.

Briant frowned. "Aithne, that's enough."

She ignored him. As she finished the spell, Raya stood and walked toward her.

Raya, Briant, and Saphir shouted together. "Aithne, stop!"

Her shield snapped into place, stronger than ever, before pain spiked through her head. Her shield crumbled, and she fell into darkness.

Voices murmured, luring Aithne from sleep. Her whole body throbbed, and her eyelids felt weighted. *Saphir?*

Beloved! Saphir's voice boomed in Aithne's head, but her relief was palpable. *It was too soon for you to work, but I do not know why you lost consciousness.*

She forced her eyes open. The shadows in the room were long, and two women stood near the fireplace, talking in low tones.

Aithne blinked and moved her arms to sit up, but they felt heavy, too. The woman in green robes glanced her way. "Oh, good, you're awake." She strode to the side of the bed and felt Aithne's forehead. "No sign of fever. Are you in pain?"

Aithne tipped her chin down, nodding, and groaned.

"That sounds like yes," said the other woman.

The healer poured a cup of tea and held it to Aithne's lips, supporting her head with the other hand.

Aithne sipped, for once not caring that the willow bark tasted awful. She drank half the cup before the healer took it away. "I think you're going to need something stronger. Can you tell me what hurts?"

"Everything," croaked Aithne.

"I'll see to that," said Adrienne. "You go and get the tea. Oh, and please send Kevia to fetch Oswin and Briant."

The healer nodded and slipped from the room, and Adrienne sat in the chair beside her. "I can't do a lot, but maybe this will help." She laid one hand on Aithne's chest and cupped the top of Aithne's head with the other. Closing her eyes, she took a deep breath and began humming a low, soft melody.

Aithne closed her eyes as her body relaxed. A gentle breeze caressed her skin as she smelled green grass and loam. Her meadow was recognizable even with her eyes closed. She felt Lledrith stir, and her body warmed, chasing cold she hadn't realized was there from her bones and muscles. Shivering, she sank deeper into the meditative state.

When Adrienne finished her song, she removed her hands, stroking Aithne's hair.

Aithne opened her eyes. "How—" Her voice rasped painfully.

Adrienne poured a cup of water and helped her drink. "How did I do that? It's one of my gifts from the Goddess. I can't actually heal, but I can help reduce pain and inflammation. You'll be able to do more when you've recovered."

Aithne cleared her throat, wincing at the soreness. "Recovered from what?"

Adrienne put the cup aside. "Lledrith opened your magic channels. It's a gradual process normally, but apparently there isn't time for that. She did the same with Briant, but for you it was more acute because of your injuries. It will take you longer to recover than it took him."

Aithne frowned. "What does that mean?"

"It will make more sense when the men arrive. We will go to the Goddess, and She will show you. Do you feel better?"

"A little. Thank you."

Adrienne smiled and got up to open the door. Briant and another man, presumably Oswin, came in with large cushions under their arms. As they passed Adrienne, she leaned out the door. "Kevia, see that we're not disturbed."

Briant dropped two cushions on the floor and stepped over to the bed. "How are you?"

"Everything hurts."

He nodded. "It will get better." He started to say something else, and then changed his mind and turned to the others. "Are we ready?"

"Waiting for you," said Oswin.

Briant walked a few steps and sank onto a cushion.

"Aithne," said Adrienne, "relax and do what you do to meditate. Don't participate; we will petition the Goddess for guidance."

Aithne closed her eyes as Adrienne prayed, and then the room went silent. She breathed deeply and soon smelled the woods again. The smell calmed her, and she felt her body relax more. In her mind, she opened her eyes and found herself sitting on the ground with the others. A glow came from the woods, floating toward them and coming to rest on Aithne. She recognized Lledrith as warmth spread through her, and she felt calm for the first time in weeks.

She heard a voice, but its source was unclear. *You must follow my lead, no matter the circumstances. You have an important job. Danger necessitates imperfection. This task will require force more than precision. You must rest and gather your strength for seven sunrises. On the eighth, you may begin.*

She felt a ripple of relief from the others, and her brow furrowed.

You must follow me. Do not stray to the left or the right, but do only what I say, no matter how odd it seems. I see what you cannot. You must allow me to guide you in the coming battle if you are to survive. Time is fleeting, and you have much to learn.

The glow dimmed, and Aithne opened her eyes. The shadows had lengthened, but it felt like they had only been meditating for a moment.

Adrienne stood and scooped up her cushion. "Briant, I need to talk to you privately for a moment."

Briant nodded and leaned to squeeze Aithne's hand before retrieving his cushion and walking out behind Adrienne.

Oswin stood and stretched. "Well, that was interesting. I'm Oswin, by the way."

"I assumed as much. Are you one of Adrienne's advisors?"

He chuckled and sat in the chair beside the bed. "Not exactly. I'm her brother."

"Oh. Younger or older?"

"Younger, by an hour."

"You're twins?"

He nodded. "She's the first Bealban Dia to have a twin. It's caused consternation."

"New things do that. Except for Briant, he complains that we do things the same way because we've always done them that way. We can't shift our paradigm fast enough for him."

Oswin laughed. "I haven't run into that, but it makes perfect sense."

"It's probably because everything here is new to him. Why was everyone relieved when Lledrith told me to stay in bed?"

"Because Briant's channels opened the day before the attack. He had to recover quickly because he had to shield us from the enemy."

"Everyone? The entire building?"

"No, we were with the dragons—Raya, Briant, and I. They were asleep, or something, during the eclipse, and we couldn't leave."

She nodded. "I lost contact with Saphir, too. It was so scary."

"I'm sure it was. So, what had Lledrith taught you before you got here?"

"To make and extinguish fires, and I used wind to cover our tracks when we escaped Annwn."

"We?"

"I had a guide. Quinn. He died when we escaped."

"I'm sorry. Were you friends?"

"Not really. We might have been if we'd had time, but we'd barely gotten past the non-aggression pact. He held me prisoner for several days before the attack, but then he helped me escape. He said it was his job to protect me, but he never explained why."

"Is that when Lledrith started teaching you? When you were a prisoner in Annwn?"

"Yes. Frankly, I wish she had started in Slan. I don't know why I had to go to Annwn and be separated from Saphir."

"Perhaps that will become clear later. That happens often."

"Does it?"

"Yes. That's probably why your next job is to learn what Lledrith is telling you to do, and do it."

She sighed. "I don't do well with cryptic. Or imperfection."

"I hope you learn fast."

Chapter Twenty-One
~ Commain

Aithne woke to sunshine filtering through the melting snow on her window. She rolled over so her back was toward the window and pulled the covers up to her chin. The room was chilly, but it was too much trouble to get up and add a log to the banked coals.

As she had every morning for a week, she slipped into meditation. She couldn't explain how her mental meadow made her body feel warmer, but it did. In her mind, she sat on the ground, eyes closed, breathing in the scent of grass and wildflowers as the breeze caressed her face.

She heard a hum in the wind, but she wasn't sure what it was. She tilted her head, focusing on it, and heard laughter. Her laughter. And Briant's. Frowning, she opened her eyes and saw an image of herself next to

Briant. They were weaving shields, trying to meld them. Oswin sat on the right side of the hearth, watching them. On the left was a bright light. It bobbed toward her, past the image of herself. It circled around her, warm and inviting, before drifting back to the hearth.

She blinked, and when her eyes opened, she was in her bed. Her head didn't hurt for the first time in a week. She got up to add wood to the fire, and her body didn't ache. Instead, she left the fireplace banked and got dressed.

She stepped into the corridor, following the sound of voices coming from a room further down the hall. The door was open, and she saw the healer in what looked like an apothecary, sitting at a high table with Sine. They were chatting, hands cupped around steaming mugs. She tapped on the door with one knuckle, and they looked over.

"Well, look who's out of bed," said the healer. "How do you feel?"

"Better than I have in weeks, honestly. I can't remember the last time nothing hurt."

Sine frowned. "Nothing? Are you saying that so we'll let you get back to work?"

"Hey, there you are!" Briant strode down the hall. "Feeling better? Lledrith told me to come get you."

Sine went to the door to stand beside Aithne. "Hmm. Well, your color is better, and what I see looks healed.

But the last time the two of you worked together, it didn't turn out well."

Aithne's stomach growled. "But I know what backlash feels like now, and I don't want to repeat it."

One of Sine's eyebrows arched. "Fine. But go eat first."

"I was going to." Aithne leaned to kiss Sine's cheek. Saying you don't have to worry about me is like telling the sun it doesn't need to rise. I'll be careful, I promise." She strode down the hall.

Briant caught up with her. "Does she always treat you that way?"

"No, but Mama isn't there. Sine figures someone has to keep me in line, and she's been my mother's best friend since Wybren training."

They walked into the dining room, and Aithne saw Oswin at a table by himself. She headed toward it. "Are you saving these seats for anyone?"

Oswin looked up. "No."

"Good," said Aithne, dropping into a chair. "I'm starving."

Briant sat beside her as she helped herself to the food in the serving dishes. She asked for the Goddess' blessing before she started eating, looking up in time to see Oswin nod in approval. Her face warmed, and she focused on her food. As she ate, she felt her focus and energy increase. "So, are you working in the same place?"

"Yes," said Briant. "Are you good to get to work?"

She nodded and drank the last of her tea. "Lledrith made it clear it's time to get started again."

Oswin nodded. "I'll come with you."

Briant opened his mouth to protest, but Aithne shrugged. "Sure, if you don't have anything better to do. Let's go!"

In her head, Saphir chuckled. *Vask says Briant and Oswin are too much alike, and they rub each other the wrong way.*

Aithne bit back a smile. *That explains a lot. Are you all right?*

Fine, said Saphir. *Our shelter is adequate, and we are taking turns doing hunting recon flights. So far, we have seen no threat in this area, but there is evidence of a failed attack.*

Please be careful.

Saphir scoffed. *The same applies to you.*

Aithne followed Briant and Oswin through a series of corridors to the ballroom. Someone had prepared a fire, but the room remained cold.

Oswin frowned. "I'll have someone light that."

"I can do it," said Aithne.

"Light a fire?" asked Briant.

"Sure. You can't?"

"Not successfully, but I can put one out."

Aithne laughed. "Of course." She crouched in front of the fireplace and recited the fire spell. Embers appeared on the kindling, and she sent a tiny breeze to fan it.

Briant stood behind her, watching as the flames grew and caught. He nodded when she stood. "Using magic to fan it instead of blowing on it? That's cool."

She shrugged. "Saves my eyebrows from singeing."

Oswin laughed and reached for a log to add to the fire. "Now, if only you could levitate the wood."

She frowned, crossing her arms. "Maybe it will work with wind." She spoke the wind spell, directing it at the woodpile. It blew over, and a couple of round logs rolled across the floor.

Briant grinned. "We'll have to think through that later. Come on, let's start with shields."

Aithne recited the spell, and her shield formed around her as Briant wove his hands in a pattern. "You don't say the spell?"

"It's faster if I don't."

Oswin re-stacked the wood. "Combine your shields."

They moved closer together, and the shields bumped against each other. Aithne heard Lledrith whisper something, and she said the words as Briant moved his hands in a different motion. Another shield formed around them.

Briant looked at it for a moment. "Let's try dropping our individual shields."

Aithne dispelled her shield as Briant dropped his, and all of the shields disappeared. "Well, that didn't work. What if we both say the spell and do the motions?"

"It's worth a try. What are the words?"

Aithne recited them, and her shield appeared.

Briant repeated them, and nothing happened. "That's so weird. Try it my way."

Aithne dropped her shield as Briant began the hand motions. She copied them, and Briant's shield came up, but hers didn't.

"Did I not do something right?"

"It looked right to me," said Briant.

"Maybe you need to be touching," said Oswin. He'd taken a piece of kindling from the pile and sat on the right side of the hearth with a knife in his hand.

Briant extended his hand, and she took it. "How are you going to do the motions if you're holding my hand?"

He blinked and let go of her hand. "Like this." He held his hands out, palms up, waist high. "Put your hands on top of mine."

She frowned, but did as he said. His hands were warm, and she felt the magic pulse in his fingers. As he started the motions, she said the spell, and a shield formed around them. She got to the end and started again. After the second time, the shield went up. Something bounced off the top, and a small log hit the floor on the other side and rolled toward the doors.

Oswin nodded. "It's solid. Now you have to do it faster."

"Do we?" asked Briant. "If we're both shielded, why do we need to do this faster?"

"Because if one of you is injured, the other will help while still being protected. If you have individual shields, you'd have to drop them both, leaving you vulnerable."

Aithne nodded. "But if it takes both of us to make the shield, won't it drop if one of us gets hurt?"

Oswin shrugged. "I don't have Lledrith, so I don't know. If you learn both parts, maybe you'll be able to make and maintain it separately."

Aithne rolled her eyes. "Oh, sure, it's that easy, Mister I-Don't-Have-Lledrith. For that matter, why do we need a shield that takes both of us to make? Protecting a person is a simple extension of the shield work we've already done for our dragons."

"But a combined shield would be stronger, at least theoretically."

"He has a point," said Briant. "Let's try it again. Even if it's not stronger, it will help us learn to combine our magic." He pointed at Oswin. "But no throwing wood at us until we get it right!"

Oswin grinned and started whittling the kindling. "Better get to it."

Briant shook his head. "Let's coordinate words and movements without physical contact."

Aithne shrugged, and they started together. The first time, Briant finished before Aithne, resulting in a partial shield around Briant. They tried again, and Aithne spoke faster. The lower part of Aithne's shield formed.

Briant ran a hand through his hair. "Oswin, can you clap a steady beat or something? Maybe the movements correspond to words."

"Sure," said Oswin. "Good idea." He tapped the kindling he was carving with the knife.

Aithne listened, and when Briant nodded, she chanted the spell, timing the syllables to Oswin's beat. Briant had a harder time. She stopped at the end, and Briant continued a few more beats. Starting again, she did the motions with him, coordinating the words more exactly. The shield formed slowly, increasing in speed when Briant picked up the chant.

Briant grinned when they finished the second round. They stood together in the same shield. He dispelled it and his half dropped, and he frowned. "What was that?"

Aithne sighed. "More work, that's what."

The next day, Aithne and Briant waded through knee deep snow. "Do you think it will really work?"

Briant shrugged. "It's hard to say with the way things have been going."

Aithne snorted. "No kidding. It's so frustrating to keep failing."

"It is for me, so it must be for you. I think we're far enough away now."

Aithne used her wind spell to clear the snow, stopping after a minute to smack her forehead with her palm.

"What's wrong?" asked Briant.

"Why did we slog through the snow? I could have cleared a path."

He grinned. "I was going to suggest that, but we've been cooped up for so long I wanted the exercise."

She snorted and cleared away more snow. When she was satisfied with the space, they sat side by side, and she increased the heat. Taking Briant's hand, she channeled it into him, and he passed it to the earth. The cold from the air and the ground dissipated.

"Are you doing okay?" she asked.

"Fine, but we're going to need more heat to turn the sand in the soil to glass."

She nodded and closed her eyes, channeling more heat through Briant. When she opened them, his hand hovered over soil that glowed red. It appeared shiny, and the red glow spread across a larger area. Part of her felt like they had enough area and heat, but her worry for her mother smoldered inside her. Aware of her powerlessness and the detrimental effect of anxiety, she redirected her worry into channeling to Briant.

"Aithne, that's enough," said Briant.

She tried to pull it back, but it had built up momentum.

"Aithne!"

"I'm trying," she growled, gritting her teeth.

Briant made a strangling sound and jerked his hand away from hers.

Gasping, she raised her hand and aimed her palm across the open field. Flames shot out of her hand, melting the snow and setting fire to the fringe of trees nearby.

Briant jumped to his feet, yelling a spell to summon a rain shower from thin air. The rain doused the fire and chilled the area they'd been heating. Steam hissed from the earth.

Aithne rolled to her feet, jaw slack. "Wow. I didn't see that coming. Are you all right? Did I burn you?"

He shook his head, surveying the shiny black soil in front of them and the swath of bare earth beyond. "No, I felt the magic but not the heat. Your hand felt warm, and not much more than normal."

She nodded. "So, what do you think? Did it work?"

He bit his lip. "Looks like it, but does it look strange to you?"

"I have no idea. I've never done this."

He laughed. "I don't think anyone has." He picked up a rock and threw it into the shiny spot. The earth splintered like ice on a pond, and the rock sank, taking the broken shards and splintering more until the entire area was thick and black with a sheen of water. He crossed his arms and shifted his weight to his left foot. "Nope. It didn't work. I don't know what that is."

Aithne picked up a fallen branch and leaned over to poke it into the edge. It slid toward the middle, and she had to let go of it. As it sank, she said, "That's a lot deeper than it should be."

Briant nodded. "We need a rope."

"How about a vine?"

He shrugged. "If it's not too fragile."

Aithne went into the woods and pulled a vine out of a tree. It broke, but it touched the ground with her arm extended.

With some work and magic, they tied a rock to one end and infused the whole thing with magic to strengthen it. Briant tossed it toward the middle while Aithne held the other end. The rock sank as if going through oatmeal, taking the vine with it. Aithne's end tugged, and she released it with a cushion of air underneath to keep it out of the muck. When it stopped, only a foot remained visible.

She released the air, and the vine drooped and sank. Clearing her throat, she asked, "How do we fix this?"

Briant shook his head. "Without knowing what went wrong, we may do more harm than good."

This looks like an opportunity to practice your wards to keep animals and small children from encountering it, said a faint male voice in Aithne's head.

Briant nodded. "Vask says—"

Aithne's jaw dropped. "That was Vask?"

Briant frowned. "You heard him?"

"Did he say we should ward it?"

Briant's eyes widened. "Yeah. How did you hear it?"

"I don't know. I don't understand any of this. But he's right."

"That happens a lot. You take this side, I'll get the other side."

The heat was excessive, said Saphir. *I heard the rock break something, followed by splintering.*

The film on the top broke, answered Aithne.

Briant spun to look at her. "I heard you!"

"Me? Or Saphir?"

"Both!"

There was a moment of stunned silence from the dragons. It felt like a weight to Aithne.

This ... this could be useful, said Saphir.

Indeed, Vask agreed.

Aithne's legs felt weak, and she sat on the ground. "Briant, I think life is going to be more complicated with you *and* two dragons in my head."

Chapter Twenty-Two
~ Western Keep

Tanwen sat by the fire, sharpening her sword, when Aengus strode into the cave. He squinted into the darkness, stomping the snow from his boots, and headed toward her. "I need a word with you."

She nodded, looking at a chip on the edge. "Sure, what's up?"

"Come with me."

She frowned, sheathed her sword, and followed him out of the cave into the woods. The sun glittered on the snow, and she shaded her eyes. She didn't know how far he'd walked before he stopped. He nodded at a tree. "Have you ever seen a bird like that before?"

Tanwen's eyebrows raised. He'd brought her out to look at a bird? She scanned the branches, and her breath caught. It was huge. Had it been on the ground, it would have reached her knee. Its body was white, but the back and wings were bright blue, and it had a crest of blue feathers on its head. It had a predator's curved beak, and it looked down at them with dark brown eyes.

She tore her eyes away from it to glance at Aengus. He was looking at the bird with a strange look on his face, his head cocked to the right.

The bird fluffed its feathers, spread blue wings that rivaled the span of a small hatchling dragon, and launched from the branch, circling above the trees and turning east. It screeched once as it flew away, and Tanwen shivered.

Aengus shook his head. "He's a royal messenger bird."

"He?"

"His name is Cythral." He took a ragged breath and let it out. When he turned to Tanwen, he was pale. "He relays messages between, in his words, the queen in the land of the dragons and his companion, the king of the east. I asked what message he carried, and he told me the message was, "Send a courier with a full report about Commainish defenses that protected Gynhalion, and how much of Annwn is under our control."

Tanwen stood there for a moment. "It was that clear?"

"That's how my magic works. When I saw him, I knew he wasn't from here. I summoned a squirrel for him as an offering."

"Do you think he'll be back?"

Aengus turned back to the cave. "I hope so. Intercepted communications will be useful."

Quillon, would you tell the others?

I have relayed the conversation. If you are able, altering the messages he carries would aid our cause.

"I've sent this through the dragon network so the other cells know to watch for him. I wonder if they're using other birds for communication?"

"Now that we know about Cythral, I'll pay more attention."

Muirne's mouth dried out when she saw the Keep. The horse whinnied and increased his speed, eager for food and shelter. Evanna let him have his head, and the group cantered through the gate as the sun set.

At the stable, she slid off the horse. "Thanks for the ride. I'm going to see if the others are back, and my mother will be worried about where I am."

Evanna and Tiernay looked at each other.

"Muirne, there you are. I've been looking for you."
Muirne turned. Gallia walked toward her.

"Why were you looking for *me*?"

"Berengar wants to see you. He said something about a special assignment."

Muirne wanted to run, but there were too many people around. "Let's go, then." She walked with Gallia into the Keep to what had been Dinsmore's study. Every step felt like she was walking to her doom. She hadn't realized Berengar even knew who she was.

He was alone when they arrived. He nodded to Gallia, and she closed the door behind them, leaning on it casually.

Muirne tried to moisten her mouth, but it remained dry; she shook out her hands. "You—you wanted to see me?"

Berengar smiled. "Thank you for coming. I've had word from Raca. She wants you to accompany Evanna's group south to harvest a water dragon."

"Why me? How does Raca even know who I am?"

"Your mother told her about you."

"Raca knows my mother?"

Berengar looked at the floor and leaned against his desk. "Raca is your aunt, Muirne. Surely you know that."

Muirne's face burned. "When do we leave?"

"In a couple of days. Evanna is to find a dragon here first. We'll rotate some different mages to her team, and she'll need fresh supplies."

"I'll help with that after I find my mother. She'll be worried."

He gazed at her like a cat watches a mouse. "Your mother was summoned to Mevan. You didn't know about that?"

She froze, shaking her head. "How—how would I?"

Gallia snorted. "We saw you leave with her, Muirne."

Panic flowed through her, and she turned to Gallia. "If you know I went to Mevan with her, why aren't you surprised to see me? Why do I suddenly have a special assignment? Do you know what happened to my mother?" She turned again, stepped back to keep them both in view. "Evanna killed her, that's what happened! She drained Razo's strength into a dragon gem, and my mother died, and she turned them both into *tanad!*" She choked on a sob and covered her mouth with her hand.

Berengar looked almost sympathetic, but not surprised. "I'm sorry about that, but we all have our role to play."

Muirne's jaw dropped. "Murdering my mother was *planned?*"

"Of course not. It wasn't my doing. Evanna gets her orders from Raca, and she doesn't explain them to me."

Anger displaced Muirne's fear. "So why would I want to do anything to help Raca when she had my mother—her own sister!—killed?"

"No one asked what you wanted," said Gallia. "Raca knows better than we do how to use our individual strengths."

Muirne sobbed. "She thought being a *tanad* was my mother's strength?"

Gallia shrugged. "She wanted the dragon." She looked at Berengar. "Is this going the way you anticipated?"

He pinched the bridge of his nose. "Absolutely not."

"Shall I manage it?"

He snorted. "Please."

Gallia strolled around him to the corner of the room where the bell pull was.

Muirne bolted for the door. As she reached for the doorknob, something hit her from behind. She slammed face-first into the door, and everything went black.

Beloved, said Quillon, *Peio observed Cythral flying west. He is near the Western Keep.*

Tanwen's breath caught. *Can Peio still see him? We need to know if he lands there and how long he stays.*

I will ask him to monitor the situation.

Tanwen looked around. Aengus and Shaw sat with their children near the fire. She walked over and joined them. "What are we up to?"

"Avoiding naps," said Aengus.

Tanwen snorted and arched an eyebrow at the children. "I'd take the naps for you if I could."

Tarian sighed. "Are you giving us an order?"

"Yes," said Tanwen. "Yes, I am. Go take naps and make me jealous."

The children grumbled and went to find their bedrolls.

Aengus and Shaw looked at her, jaws slack. "How did you do that?" asked Shaw.

Tanwen shrugged. "I don't know. Mother magic?"

Aengus snorted. "It didn't work for Fiona."

"Maybe it only works with other people's children. Or it might be because I'm in charge." She crouched near the fire. "Listen, I got word that Cythral may be heading to Western Keep."

Shaw frowned. "That bird we're looking for?"

"Yes. Peio is watching to see if he lands, but he was near the Keep, flying west."

"Why would he be going there?" asked Shaw.

"To give a message to whoever is in charge at the Keep, most likely," said Aengus. "If he lands there, I could sneak into the mews and find out what news he's carrying."

Tanwen looked at the fire. "If you do, a couple of us will go with you. We're running low on supplies, and even with your magic we have had no luck hunting. We could raid the salle. Hopefully they haven't moved the travel rations from the armory."

He has landed at the Keep, said Quillon.

"We'd better plan this fast. He landed at the Keep."

Chapter Twenty-Three ~ Western Keep

An hour before dusk, Tanwen walked out of the cave with Aengus, Lassair, Lucas, and Hamish. "Hamish, are you sure about coming with us?"

Hamish pulled up the hood of his cloak. "I'm sure the children will need food, and I'll be able to get us past locked doors." He glanced behind him at his children. "Fiona will look after them."

Tanwen nodded. "Let's go, then."

They started through the woods, traveling south toward the Keep. They arrived in darkness, halting at the woods' edge. Tanwen turned to them, pitching her voice low. "Everyone is clear on the plan?"

They nodded, and she looked at Lassair. "Don't wait for us. You and Aengus get the information you need and go back."

"Yes, Wybren Tanwen," murmured Lassair. She nodded to Aengus, and the two of them headed for the mews.

Tanwen started toward the salle with Lucas and Hamish. It was dark and overcast. The air smelled like snow. Again.

The salle was unlocked and empty, and apprehension tingled Tanwen's nerves. Lucas headed for the armory in the back, and they followed. She saw Lucas' light wisp bobbing in the enclosed room as she crossed the sawdust-covered floor.

Lucas' light went out, and he came back out the door. "They've cleared everything out."

Hamish muttered a curse.

Tanwen put a hand on his arm. "I know another place to check."

They left the salle and headed toward the Keep.

"Are we going to the building by the guard shack?" whispered Lucas.

"Yes. It's risky, but less so than going inside the Keep." She headed to the wall and followed it to the gate.

Lucas cast his shield to hide them as Hamish used his magic to open the wicket gate. They slipped inside and headed for the rock sided building beside the guard shack. Hamish opened the door, and they went in, closing it softly. Soft candle light glowed from a row of cells around the corner from the main room.

Tanwen grabbed backpacks, and they filled them with travel rations, blankets, and water skins, working quickly and quietly. Tanwen motioned to the door when a voice made her jump.

"I hear you out there. Have you finally brought me some food?"

Lucas' eyes went wide, and he mouthed, "Muirne?"

Tanwen's heart pounded, and she leaned to look around the corner. Muirne's tear-stained face peered between the bars of the small window in the door. Her eyes widened, and Tanwen raised a finger to her lips. She motioned to Hamish, and he muttered a spell. The hasp holding the lock on Muirne's door broke, but the lock remained shut.

Voices outside made her freeze, and she shoved her packs at the men. "Lucas—shield," she murmured. "Take these and go. I'll get her and be right behind you."

Lucas opened his mouth to protest, but Hamish nudged him. Lucas said a few words, and they disappeared. Tanwen didn't wait to see what they did. She closed the distance to Muirne's cell in a few long strides. She felt a draft as the men left, leaving the door ajar. Her hands trembled as she grabbed the lock and pulled. Nothing happened. Muirne gestured towards the hinges, mimicking a pull on the lock. She did, and the door swung open.

Muirne darted out and ran for the door, knocking the candle over.

Tanwen cursed under her breath as the light went out, and she had a few seconds of gratitude that it ignited nothing until she heard someone notice the darkness. The man told someone to go replace the candle, and someone else protested that it shouldn't have burned down already.

The door opened, and Tanwen pulled Muirne toward the corner, away from the cells. When a guard entered with a fresh, unlit candle, they crept toward the door.

The guard muttered to himself that he should have lit it before he came in. He fumbled, knocking something over, cursed, and said a short spell. The candle lit, and he saw the open cell door.

Tanwen dragged Muirne toward the door and they ran for the gate. She jerked the wicket gate open and stopped short. A man blocked the doorway.

He cocked his head as Tanwen reached for her sword. "Going somewhere?"

Something hit her head, and she dropped into darkness.

Tanwen?

She groaned, head throbbing. She touched the back of her head and felt stickiness.

Beloved?

I'm here.

She felt a trickle of relief from Quillon. *Where is here?*

She opened her eyes to darkness. The wall behind her felt damp. It smelled wet and musty, and she frowned as she stood clumsily. *I don't know. A cave?* She took a couple cautious steps, and her hand brushed wood. A cold draft wrapped around her as she felt the surface gingerly. It felt like a door, and her mouth went dry. She continued feeling her way around and touched the damp rock again. Her hand trembled. *Quillon, I think I'm in the dungeon.*

Alarm that wasn't her own pinged through her. *Take out your beacon!*

She reached for it and stopped. *Not yet. How close is dawn?*

It is the third watch.

She tried to take a calming breath and managed half. Someone groaned. "Muirne?"

"Where are we?"

Tanwen closed her eyes as a mixture of relief and annoyance flooded through her. "I'm not sure."

A moment passed, and Muirne whimpered. "Did they throw us in the dungeon?"

Tanwen's head throbbed, and she sank to the floor before her legs gave out. "Maybe."

Muirne started to cry. "Why did this happen? Why does she hate me?"

"Who?"

"Raca. She had Razo and my mother killed, and now she wants Evanna to use me as bait for a water dragon."

Tanwen squinted in the darkness. "What are you talking about? Who is Evanna?"

"The necromancer killing dragons and channeling their strength into magic gems."

Beloved, pull out your beacon. Venka and I will find you.

No. If someone is killing dragons, you need to stay away. I won't be the bait that gets you—gets us both—killed. Give me some time to get out of this. She felt fear and anger from Quillon. *I don't like it either, but it won't help anyone if we die, and it certainly won't help us rid the Keep of whoever has it. Do you want to be tanad?*

No, he said grudgingly.

Neither do I. Tell Venka that Muirne is with me, and then figure out a way to help without swooping in, torching everything in your path. She pulled up her knees and leaned her forehead against them.

"What are we going to do?" asked Muirne.

"I don't know. Quillon will tell the others. Between us, we'll figure something out."

Tanwen shivered in the damp, drafty cell. She and Muirne had discovered, through trial and error, where the warmest spot was, but that wasn't saying much. They each had a thin blanket and enough food and water to keep them alive.

She felt Quillon brush her mind.

Tanwen, Lassair and Aengus are safe. Aengus talked to Cythral and two ravens, who were also carrying messages. They allowed him to place a beacon spell on them. He promised to feed them when they are nearby.

That's good news. Everyone else is safe?

They are. Shaw assumed command and moved them to another spot.

Relief flooded through her. *I knew I could count on them to carry on.*

Do you want to know what he learned from Cythral?

No. Don't tell me anything strategic. So far, they've left us alone, but I expect that will change.

Quillon paused. *What if I pass along fabricated intelligence?*

Tanwen smiled for the first time in days. *You want to lie to me?*

Essentially, yes.

If it will help, do it, but only tell me things I can divulge to the enemy without risk.

I will coordinate with the others.

She closed her eyes, building boundaries in her mind so Quillon wouldn't realize how miserable she was. Part of her felt she deserved to be imprisoned since she'd killed Liam, even if it was self-defense. That did nothing to ease the grief of losing him. She was a widow. Again.

Beside her, Muirne coughed, long and ragged. "Are we going to die here?"

"Not if I have anything to say about it."

Muirne sighed. "How you can prevent it when you're stuck in here?"

"The others are working on that. We need to stay alive in the meantime."

"I wish they'd hurry."

"Me, too."

Chapter Twenty-Four ~ Commain

Aithne woke the next morning to find her window half obscured by snow. Yawning, she got up and went to look out the window. Snow fell in curtains, blurring the outside world.

She sighed and reached for her clothes. *Saphir, do you have shelter?*

Of a sort. The porticos are more than wide enough to keep the snow off, and our hosts are constructing walls for us.

Good. Today would be the perfect day to curl up with a book and a mug of arda in front of a fire, but I guess I'd better get to work.

Perhaps there will be time later. There are no signs of this stopping soon.

Aithne dressed and went in search of breakfast.

Briant met her on the way. "Hey, what's up with this snow?"

She grinned. "I don't know, but it's pretty. We should clear some paths, though. Make ourselves useful."

"Good idea. We can figure out how to use your wind with my earth."

Aithne snorted. "Are you sure you want to do that? Earth and fire didn't work out so well."

"We have to do something. It stands to reason not everything will work, but we still have to try."

Oswin has warded the area from yesterday, said Vask.

Aithne shivered. "That is definitely going to take some getting used to."

Indeed, said Vask.

I concur, agreed Saphir.

Aithne laughed, but a ping of alarm from Saphir cut it short. She and Briant stopped walking in the middle of the hallway. Someone behind them tsked and walked around them, and they moved toward the wall.

News from Quillon. The enemy has captured your mother.

Aithne's heart slammed against her ribs, and she saw a look of shocked horror on Briant's face.

What do you mean? Is she all right?

She says yes, but she told Quillon not to attempt a rescue for fear that she is being used as bait.

That makes sense, said Briant, *but I bet Quillon is ready to torch everything.*

Indeed.

She looked at Briant and asked, "What do we do? Do head for Slan?"

No, said Saphir.

Quillon ordered us to remain here, said Vask.

Aithne's heart pounded, and she touched the wall for support. *We're going to listen now? When Mama is in danger?*

Beloved, said Saphir, *Raine has also ordered us to remain in place and for you both to continue working while they devise a plan to rescue her.*

But —

Saphir's voice took a hard edge. *Aithne, we are staying here. Keep working. Vask and I will not fly in a blizzard. It is too dangerous. The best way to help your mother is to practice harder. Your magic might be needed to rescue her.*

Briant took a step back and ran his hand through his hair. "I don't know how I'm going to focus."

Aithne nodded and shivered. She closed her eyes, fighting the urge to cry. "I'm not really hungry anymore. Are you?"

"No," Briant answered, "and I'm not sure eating is smart now anyway."

"Let's get to work then."

"Good idea." He followed her through the hall to the ballroom. "Wow. Aithne, I'm sorry. Are you all right?"

She shook her head. "Not at all. I don't know what to do."

He squinted in the dim light. "How about if we find a warm place and meditate for a while? Maybe the Goddess will send guidance."

She shrugged. "Is this your way of making sure I don't take off on my own?"

"Would you do that?"

"I don't want to do anything else, even though I know it's wrong."

"Then let's go meditate. If nothing else it will calm your mind so you can think without panic."

She nodded. "Let's go."

When they got to the Sanctum, Aithne paused in the doorway. "I haven't spent much time in here."

"Me neither," said Briant. "It's pretty, though."

Aithne nodded. The stone walls had large transom windows. Snow fell in fat flakes past them, and it looked more peaceful than Aithne felt. Milky light shone down from a skylight in the vaulted ceiling onto a round, raised dais. The support beams were painted pale yellow and arranged in a starburst pattern. Against the dark wood of the ceiling, they looked like sunbeams coming from the skylight.

Briant walked in ahead of her, taking two cushions off the shelves on the wall by the door. The fireplace in the nearest corner had a banked fire. The ones in the other three corners were laid but not lit. Aithne walked to the banked fireplace, reciting the wind spell as she walked. She sent a gentle breath of air toward the fire, and it licked the smoldering wood.

Briant smiled. "That's handy."

Aithne added more wood from the stack beside the hearth. "Quinn taught me the one they use, and I ended up spraying water over the snow I was clear. Lledrith's spell works much better."

Briant dropped the cushions in front of the hearth. "Funny how that works."

They sank onto the cushions and faced the fire. Cold ran down Aithne's spine as she warmed, and she thought about going to the kitchen for a hot cup of tea.

Time enough for tea later, said Saphir.

Aithne sighed and closed her eyes, directing her attention to her mental meadow, but anxiety clouded her mind and made her heart pound. She took several deep breaths.

Stop trying to force it, said Lledrith.

Aithne clenched her jaw. *Easy for you to say. It's not your mother in the enemy's hands.*

I am part of you. She is my mother. There is work to do and no time for overthinking. Go to the meadow.

Aithne took an extra deep breath and smelled grass. When she opened her eyes, she was in the meadow. She could feel Briant nearby, but couldn't see him. Oddly, she didn't feel like she had to look around for him. Instead, she focused on the rosebush that hadn't been there before.

Is that the rose from the cave?

It is. You need something to focus on. Empty your mind to learn the next step.

Aithne closed her eyes again, inhaling the scent of the rose even though the bush was several feet away. She saw herself in a large space, but she couldn't tell what or where the room was. She was going through a series of movements, repeating them over and over. Her view changed, and she seemed to circle around herself, watching from every angle. She felt her hands lift as she stopped beside the image of herself, repeating the movement, stepping when the other Aithne did.

Now you do it, said Lledrith.

Aithne stood, still mentally standing beside the image in her head, and began the pattern. It felt natural. Power flowed through her body, but dissipated into the air doing nothing. Peace bloomed in her gut, and for the first time in weeks, she felt calm and confident. She got the impression from Lledrith that this was not so much working magic as gathering magic for larger spells, and she smiled a little when snow fell from the sunny sky. *So do the actual magic outside?*

She heard an amused chuckle from Lledrith. As the sequence drew to an end, the meadow faded, and she stood a few feet from her cushion, her back to the fire.

Briant was in a similar position. He blinked and turned to look at her. "Gathering magic for larger work to do outside later?"

Aithne's stomach rumbled. "Yes, but I think we should eat first."

That evening, Briant sat in front of the fire in the library. Outside, the wind howled and lashed snow against the windows. He'd gone out to check on Vask and found the dragons in the same portico. Their hosts had constructed wooden walls of a sort, and they assured him they were warm and dry.

Now he sat in a padded chair, his stockinged feet on the heart, holding a cup of tea, replaying his last conversation with Tanwen in his head. He'd been cold, angry, formal. He had resented her apparent change of heart where he was concerned, and now he might not have the chance to make things right. Why had he left it like that? Didn't he learn anything from losing his family without warning?

The door opened, but he paid no attention, assuming a servant had come to add wood to the fire.

Instead, Adrienne took the chair beside him. "If you'd rather have cold tea, they can prepare some for you."

He frowned and looked at her, and she nodded at the cup in his hand. Sighing, he leaned forward to put it on the hearth. "Aithne could warm it for me, but she's gone to bed, thank goodness."

"Did your practice wear her out? I'm sure she's worried about her mother."

"You heard about that?"

Adrienne leaned toward him. "I have eyes and ears everywhere."

He nodded, turning his attention back to the fire.

Adrienne sat back. "Huh. I thought that might make you smile. Do you want to talk about it? And don't ask what I'm talking about."

"Eyes and ears everywhere, even in my head?"

"I don't need spies to know you're fretting about something. Are you worried about your family? Is the training not going well?"

He shook his head. "I had a falling out with Tanwen—Aithne's mother—before I left Slan. I'm worried about her."

"Why did you fall out?"

"My partnership with Vask didn't develop the normal way. Really, nothing has been normal since I met him, and the other Wybrens resented that. Not Aithne or Tanwen, but the others. It's a long story, but we had a necromancer killing people in Slan, even some of my family. We tracked him down and he fought back with a big *tanad* army."

"Like at the abbey?"

"Exactly like that. I saw the mage in a tree and threw a lightning bolt at him as Vask torched the tree. I killed him and avenged those he'd slain, and they treated me like a hero. When things settled down, I became an ordinary Wybren. They didn't listen to my ideas, or when they did, they told me why the way they'd always done it was better."

"Why did you fall out with Tanwen specifically?"

"She's in charge of the Wybrens."

"Ah, I see. You were angry at your boss."

"Yes, and now I'm worried I won't have an opportunity to say I'm sorry. And she's Aithne's mom, so I can't talk to her about this."

"Are you sorry?"

He frowned and looked at her. "Of course I am."

"Why? She's the one who didn't follow through on what you expected. What do you have to be sorry about?"

"I don't want our last time together to be angry. She helped me a lot, and I never thanked her."

Adrienne leaned forward and turned toward him, tucking her leg underneath her. "Nobody wants to leave it like that. If you do, there's something wrong with you. But that doesn't mean you have to feel guilty. So really, what's the reason?"

Briant couldn't meet her eyes, and his face warmed. "Well, maybe I was being unreasonable in my expectations."

Adrienne smiled. "Ah, yes, there you go. I hoped you'd get around to that."

Heat flared in Briant's face, and he sat up. "What does *that* mean?"

Her eyebrows raised. "Exactly what you think it means. You feel guilty because you were focused on your perceived reality, and it didn't match the real world."

Nicely said, Vask interjected.

Frustration popped inside him. *You too?*

I've been telling you that for weeks. I didn't phrase it like she did.

Briant snorted, shaking his head. "Vask agrees with you, for whatever that's worth."

She laughed. "I knew I liked him for a reason."

"Don't!" He pointed at her. "Don't encourage him! He hears you!"

Her eyes went wide, and she put her hand on the side of her face. "He *does?* I had *no idea!*"

Vask laughed in his head, and Briant started to stand and storm out of the room, but something in Adrienne's eyes quelled his anger. He shook his head, rubbing a hand over his face. "Of course, he's going to side with the girl. Why should this be any different?"

Sorry, Briant, she is prettier than you are.

You could have picked a girl!

I knew you were the one to do what needed to be done even before I knew what the task was, and I was right.

"Is there a party in here I wasn't invited to?"

Briant looked up as Oswin walked into the room.

"Not at all," Briant said. "Adrienne and Vask are beating up on me."

Oswin rubbed his hands together, grinning, and sat on the hearth. "Oh, good! I haven't missed it all!"

Adrienne's jaw dropped, and then she covered her mouth to stifle a giggle.

The last of Briant's anger melted away, and he shook his head, laughing. "Fine. You're right. You're both right. I was a jerk."

"Wait, could you say that again?" asked Oswin.

Briant snorted. "No. You already knew that."

"I suspected it," said Oswin. "As usual, my sister confirmed it."

Briant scrubbed a hand through his hair. "I honestly don't know how you've managed this your whole life. Does she beat you up like this?"

"No, not always. She mostly does that to people she likes." His face went blank, and he looked at Adrienne. "Wait. Do you—"

She sat up straight. "That's none of your concern." She stood. "Now that we have that sorted out, I'm going to bed."

"Quitter," said Oswin.

"Half the battle is knowing when to quit. Good night!" She swept out of the room.

Oswin shook his head. "I have a feeling you might be in big trouble."

Chapter Twenty-Five
~ Commain

The next morning, Briant was pulling on his boots when Vask startled him.

Briant, said Vask, *all of you must seek guidance from the Goddess immediately. Quillon received credible intelligence about another attack on Gynhalion, and Saphir verified that there appears to be an army en route.*

Briant's mouth went dry. *I'll gather the others.*

We will continue to monitor.

Briant headed toward Adrienne's study and saw Aithne several feet in front of him. "Saphir told you?"

She looked over her shoulder and stopped. "Yes. Do you think Oswin will be with her?"

"I don't know. Go tell her, though. You'll get in faster than I will."

Aithne snorted and jogged down the hall.

Briant followed, stretching his stride. He wanted to give Aithne time to get in the door, but he was too anxious to slow down.

She waited for him in the open doorway, and the guards at the door glanced at him. He followed Aithne into Adrienne's study. She stood behind her desk, and an acolyte scurried out, eyes on the floor.

Adrienne walked around the desk. "I only have a few minutes. I'm gathering everyone in the Sanctum. The acolytes felt something disturbing."

Briant nodded. "Good. We'll go with you."

"Do you know something?"

Aithne glanced at Briant. "The dragons have spotted an army heading this way. Saphir thinks it's a couple days out."

Adrienne's face paled. "Come."

They hurried through the halls. When they arrived, Oswin, a few of the priestesses, and the acolytes were there.

Adrienne scanned the room. "Let's begin. The others can join when they arrive."

Briant grabbed two prayer cushions and passed one to Aithne. They dropped them outside the circle that was forming.

Adrienne looked at them. "No, you need to be beside me." She looked around. "Oswin, you too."

The others adjusted their positions as Briant settled to Adrienne's right, Aithne to her left, and Oswin beside Aithne.

Briant closed his eyes and sank into the meditation. Instead of finding himself in the meadow, his surroundings looked like thick fog. He saw those closest to him and sensed the presence of the others. He felt a weight on his shoulders, and he closed his eyes again.

Images coalesced in his mind—snow-covered mountains, the northern hunting site, fields covered in patchy snow with sheep grazing on brown grass. He saw others in his vision—Aithne and Oswin, which weren't surprising, but also Adrienne, Raya, and Sine. Underneath the images, he got the strong impression that he was supposed to seek those things out, and he needed to do it soon.

He opened his eyes when he heard Adrienne's voice. The sun shone through the windows from a higher angle, but he wasn't surprised they'd been there longer than it seemed.

"The Goddess is gracious. We have four days to prepare to defend Gynhalion again. Milani, go give the queen a status report. I will go myself and meet with her at the start of the afternoon watch." She turned to Aithne and Oswin. "I need all of you in my study."

"I'll get Raya," said Aithne. She rolled to her feet and scooped up her cushion, dropping it on the rack as she jogged out the door.

"I'll find Sine," said Briant.

Adrienne nodded. "Hurry."

He strode out of the Sanctum, leaving his prayer cushion beside Aithne's, and jogged toward the infirmary. Sine had been spending a lot of time with Mercia, and he hoped to find her there. As he passed the dining room, he heard a familiar laugh and stopped to look in the door. Sine stood in the kitchen, cradling a mug in both hands.

He took a deep breath and strolled in, peeking through the serving window. She was talking with a man who stood at a high table, cutting vegetables. "Sine? Sorry to interrupt, but you're needed."

Sine put down the mug. "What's happened?"

"I'll explain while we walk." He strode out of the dining room, and a moment later she fell into step beside him.

"Is it Aithne?"

"She's involved, but she's not hurt." He lowered his voice, pausing when people passed, and told her what he knew. A moment later, they arrived at the open door of Adrienne's study. Oswin, Aithne, and Raya were already there. Adrienne and Kevia stood in the back corner, heads close, talking in low voices.

Sine went to Aithne and Raya. "Anything new from the dragons?"

"No," said Raya. "Right now, that seems like a good thing."

"I doubt we'll get much more of that," said Sine as Kevia hurried past them, closing the door.

Adrienne joined them. "I hope you're wrong, but I suspect you're not." She motioned to the sitting area, and they settled there. "First, let's make sure we saw more or less the same thing." She described her visions, which mirrored Briant's.

Aithne agreed. "That's more or less what I saw, too, but I also saw the Spire at Mevan. I ran past it in the dark, and I think Briant was with me."

Raya sat back and let out a breath. "It's about to get real, isn't it?"

"I think we're past that," said Oswin. "I got the impression that we need to leave in the next day or two."

"I can be ready," said Sine. "How are we traveling?"

"Dragon," said Briant. "Hopefully, Saphir is strong enough to carry double."

Aithne nodded. "She said she is."

"Good. Kevia will oversee supplies," said Adrienne. She paused for a moment and then turned to Aithne. "I think you and Briant should come with me to tell the queen. I'm not sure why, but it seems important."

Aithne nodded. "I'll see if I have something decent to wear."

"Under normal circumstances, that would be fine. This time, I want you both to wear riding gear. If it looks like you are ready to leave, it will make more of an impression."

"Do we need to make an impression?" asked Briant.

Adrienne raised one shoulder and let it fall. "She rebuffed the first attack more easily than anyone thought. It's likely she'll think it will be that easy again, which we know it won't be. Perhaps learning about my absence will spur her to action."

Briant leaned forward. "We'll do what it takes, but our focus needs to be on getting ready to go. Do you have the resources to feed the dragons before we go?"

"The Goddess has provided generously in the last few years. Tell the kitchen what you need."

"I'll see to that," said Sine.

"I'll come with you," said Raya.

Adrienne let out a long breath. "Good. Let me know if they give you any problem, and be sure they understand that the order is from the Goddess, not from me. If they withhold what any of us need, there will be consequences." She stood. "Let's get going."

Briant stood at the bottom of the main staircase with Aithne and Oswin.

Aithne shifted. "I hope this doesn't take too long; it's going to be dark soon."

The sound of boots on the stairs made Briant look up.

Adrienne ran down, her blonde hair braided in a less elaborate style than the plaits of her office. "Sorry. I didn't want to waste time proving who I am because she didn't recognize me without the braids." She pulled up the hood of her cloak as she reached the bottom. "Oswin, you're armed, right?"

He nodded. "We all are."

She released a slow breath. "Let's get this over with, then."

Briant followed her out of the temple and down the steep hill. "Should we expect trouble?"

"I doubt that, however, it's risky to assume any-thing."

"Makes sense," said Aithne.

"It does," agreed Oswin. "Besides, we will need to be vigilant while we travel. Best to get into the habit sooner rather than later."

The palace was one tier down from the temple, and they reached it quickly. The palace, made of white marble, stood three stories high with a dozen wide, age-worn steps leading up to it. Marble columns supported the upper floors, adorned with arched windows and balconies. Briant estimated it was half the size of the temple.

Oswin preceded Adrienne up the steps to the guards at the door. "The Bealban Dia will have an audience with Queen Elisaid."

One guard looked him over while the other looked past him. Adrienne pushed her hood back, lifting her chin, and gazed back at him.

The second guard blinked. "You're not in the gold," he said.

She arched an eyebrow at him. "You are correct. Let us in, please."

The second opened the door while the first moved to block Oswin, Briant, and Aithne. "You said the Bealban Dia needs to see the queen. She has no need of bodyguards in the audience chamber."

Adrienne paused inside the door and turned. "Why would I need bodyguards when the Goddess Herself protects me? Stand down and let them in."

The guard's eyes rounded, and he stepped back. Briant nodded at Aithne, who followed Adrienne. He and Oswin followed her, and Briant held the eyes of the second guard as he walked past. He hoped the man saw the simmering anger on his face.

They proceeded down the hall to the audience chamber. Adrienne set a pace fast enough for her cloak to billow around her. Briant ignored those who gathered to watch their entrance. Instead, he kept his eyes on the enormous, guarded double doors at the end of the hall. Something about their appearance sent a shiver down his spine, and he took care not to let it show.

A dozen paces from the door, Adrienne called, "Open the doors."

When the guards paused, Oswin barked, "Open the doors to admit the Bealban Dia!"

The guards pushed the doors open, and they walked in without pausing. As they entered, the queen approached her throne and sat. She wore a deep blue gown, and her long black hair was loose, pulled away from her face with a jeweled tiara.

She glowered at the group and looked at the door. "What is the meaning of this? I was told the Bealban Dia demanded an audience."

"I did," said Adrienne.

Queen Elisaid looked back at her as Adrienne swept her cloak off. Aithne stepped forward to take it, even though they hadn't discussed it as far as Briant knew.

The queen squinted and lifted her chin. "You're not wearing the gold."

"I am not. I've already been targeted for assassination by the enemy. The Goddess instructed me to give them a harder target to hit."

The queen shifted. "Why have you come? Is this to do with the nonsense Milani reported?"

"It is far from nonsense. Multiple sources have alerted us to a second attack on Gynhalion. This time, the enemy will be better prepared."

"Given our decisive victory, why would they risk another attack?" Queen Elisaid scoffed. "It makes no sense to throw more lives at a city they can't take."

Briant narrowed his eyes. "It makes no sense to you. The enemy doesn't abide by our logic."

The queen looked down her nose at him. "And you are?"

"Wybren Briant. I was on the diplomatic team from Slan. Some of us were heading your way the day of the eclipse. They didn't arrive because the enemy attacked them. They are, no doubt, *tanad* by now, as is the dragon of the Wybren with them."

"*Tanad?*"

"Undead fighters," said Briant.

Queen Elisaid rolled her eyes. "What are your sources, *besides* the Goddess?"

Adrienne's voice was icy. "Intelligence from intercepted messenger birds, and the dragons who are housed at the temple. This morning, they observed a large army heading this way."

The queen scowled. "How large?"

"Several thousand," said Briant, telling her what Vask said. "The dragons did not take the time to count them, but mine said the column extended into the trees on both sides of the road and stretched a third of a league. They have several ballistae and a robust battering ram."

The queen gasped. "Surely not!"

Aithne shrugged and looked at Adrienne. "We've come to say what we were sent to say."

"And who, pray tell, are you?" asked the queen.

Adrienne took a step forward, motioning to Aithne and Briant. They moved to flank her. "Wybren Aithne and Wybren Briant are the Lavban Dia—the arms of the Goddess. Their presence here is the reason you have four days to prepare. The three of us are her instruments, and I tell you this now, Your Highness, if you do not heed our warning, Gynhalion will be no more."

"Surely the Goddess will protect the city with you in it."

"The Goddess has given me a task elsewhere. Mobilize your troops. All of them. And may the Goddess have mercy on you."

She turned and strode out the door, Aithne and Briant still flanking her, Oswin following two steps behind.

"Wait!" called the queen. "What does that mean, Gynhalion will be no more?"

Adrienne ignored her. Outside the audience chamber, Adrienne took her cloak and put it on without pausing. She didn't slacken her pace until they got back to the temple.

"Do you think it worked?" asked Briant as the door shut behind them.

Adrienne shrugged. "Only the Goddess knows. It is not our concern. We have much to do before we leave the morning after tomorrow."

Chapter Twenty-Six ~ Western Keep

Tanwen jerked awake when the cell door opened. Two large men in livery she didn't recognize strode in and pulled Tanwen and Muirne to their feet.

"What are you doing?" shouted Muirne. "Get your hands off me!"

The guard holding her arm smirked, but said nothing as they dragged them from the cell.

Tanwen's heart pounded. *Quillon, they're moving me.*

If they question you, tell them what you know.

It's safe?

It's outdated, and they will assume that. They will also not likely consider your continued communication with me.

Tanwen's guard opened a door further down the hall and shoved her into a room flooded with light. She gasped and shielded her eyes. Someone whacked the back of her right knee, and she dropped to the floor. They grabbed her hands and tied them behind her as she squirmed to get free.

"You might want to stop fighting, unless you like pain," said a female voice.

Tanwen squinted in the light. The woman sat on a wooden chair. She wore a robe that covered her feet and her hands to her fingertips. It was the same color as the livery the guards wore, and was embroidered with a strange symbol. Brown hair curled over her shoulders, but the light obscured her face.

"What do you want?" asked Tanwen.

"Oh, I'm sure you can guess—let's start with the location of your dragon."

"I don't know. I haven't seen him in a week."

The woman scoffed. "Are you suggesting a Wybren would be away from her dragon?"

"It's not ideal, but it is preferable to having him turned into *tanad*."

"How did you and Muirne come to be together?"

"We came to get supplies, and we found her locked up near the guard shack."

"Yes, she was there for a reason."

Tanwen shifted as her knees ached on the stone floor. "To be bait for a water dragon. She told me."

The woman shrugged. "We didn't need her for that after all, but it has made her significantly less important to us. What about those who were with you on your supply raid?"

"What about them?"

"Where are they, and how many others did they return to?"

"I assume they returned to our camp in a cave northwest of here. We had about a dozen others with us, mostly children."

The woman nodded. "Good. Now, how will you get your dragon to come here?"

Tanwen snorted. "If you think I'm going to do that, you clearly don't know anything about Wybrens."

"I know more than you think. For instance, I know the necklace you're wearing is a beacon that will summon him."

Tanwen allowed her jaw to drop and took her time collecting herself. "I'm sure he's too far away."

"Let's test that theory." The woman got up and strode across the room.

As she reached for the beacon, Tanwen dodged away. The guard behind her grabbed her shoulders, and the woman pulled the beacon out of Tanwen's tunic. She held it up in her palm for a moment. "How long does it take?"

Forever, said Quillon.

Tanwen closed her eyes. "If he's nearby, he'll have sensed it already."

"Good," said the woman. She dropped the beacon and went back to her chair. "We'll see if he responds. In the meantime, let's chat about how you freed the dragons."

"Why? They're gone, and they aren't coming back."

"Indulge me. The information might come in handy sometime."

Tanwen snorted and shook her head. "We used magic to open a tunnel. I'm surprised you haven't figured it out yet."

"Wybrens can't use magic."

"You're right, but men do."

The woman smiled. "Why would men help you? Aren't they afraid of dragons?"

"Some are, but not all. Haven't you heard? We have a male Wybren now."

The woman and the guard laughed. The woman sat back and said, "Thank you for that. Let me show you what happens when you lie."

The guard kicked Tanwen in the back. She yelped and fell over, barely keeping her head from hitting the floor. She squirmed and sat upright. "Good to know."

The woman stood and looked out the transom window. "Where on earth is your dragon?"

"I told you, he's out of range. Perhaps he doesn't know I've been taken."

The woman turned and scowled. "Why did you keep that from him?"

"Our communication is limited by distance, and even if it wasn't, I wouldn't tell him. I won't be the bait that draws him to his death."

"Oh? Well, we'll see about that." She nodded to the guard and left the room.

The guard kicked her again, and she tumbled over. He stepped over her and kicked her in the abdomen, and she gasped in pain, curling into a fetal position. He kicked her twice before punching her in the face and slamming her head against the floor.

"That's a small sample," he growled, grabbing her arm and hauling her to her feet. He dragged her back to her cell and shoved her in.

Tanwen landed on her shoulder and cried out again. *Beloved?*

She bit back a sob as tears streamed from her eyes. *Don't come.*

Chapter Twenty-Seven ~ Commain

Aithne adjusted the strap of her pack. *Are you sure you're all right to carry double?*

I am fine, beloved, and even if I were not, we do not have an alternative.

Would you tell me if you weren't able?

She sensed exasperation from Saphir. *No. But Vask and Isidro will keep a close watch on me and make us stop to rest if they sense my strength is flagging.*

Aithne sighed and pushed away her trepidation. *I have a bad feeling about this.*

Whatever happens, we will face it together.

Sine stepped up beside her. "Vask says I should ride with you. They decided to shift saddles every time we stop, and I'll ride with whoever doesn't have one."

Aithne gestured to Saphir. "Makes sense." She rolled her eyes when Sine crossed her arms. "Sine, please, ride in front of me the first time. You haven't flown in a while, let alone bareback."

Sine huffed and pressed her lips together, but climbed onto Saphir's back. "I'm only giving in because we need to leave."

"I understand," said Aithne as she mounted behind Sine. They shielded their faces from snow and wind as Isidro launched. When he circled up, Saphir's muscles bunched. Aithne pressed herself to Sine's back as Saphir launched.

The wind hit them, taking Aithne's breath away, and she formed a shield from Saphir's nose to the dorsal spine behind her. Beneath them, the ground blurred in an endless carpet of evergreens and snow. The sun was a dull glow hidden by clouds and snow, giving them a vague idea of the time as it rose.

It felt like weeks when Saphir signaled to the others to land. The snow had become less patchy, and they landed in a snow-covered field with a copse of evergreens.

Briant walked over as Aithne dismounted. "Aithne, we need a fire. Hopefully, we can find enough wood here."

"I have something better." She opened a saddlebag and took out one of Quinn's fire laurels. "I don't know if they are reusable. Goddess willing, they are, because I only have three." She walked into the trees with the others as the dragons arranged themselves around the copse, each facing a different direction.

"What is that?" asked Raya.

"The fae call it a fire laurel." She kicked a spot clear of snow and put it down. Crouching beside it, she whispered the fire spell, and a small flame licked the inside edge furthest from her and spread.

Raya crouched beside her, holding her hands out in front of her. "You know you don't have to whisper, right? None of us is bothered by your magic."

The side of Aithne's mouth curved up. "That's not why I whispered. Volume plays a part in the intensity of the spell. If I shout it, I could set fire to the copse."

Raya's eyebrows raised. "That's—interesting."

Sine walked over with two pieces of waxed canvas. "If we're going to rest and warm up, sitting in snow won't work." She kicked snow away from the fire, and Raya got up to help her. A few minutes later, they huddled together with blankets and jerky. Aithne warmed their water skins one by one so they didn't have to drink cold water.

Adrienne looked around. "Perhaps we should fill our water skins with snow before we go?"

Aithne nodded. "Filling them at a water source will be faster, but snow will do. It takes more space than water, so I will warm them and add more snow until they're full."

"Will that deplete your magic stores?" asked Sine. "The last thing we need is for you to get backlash."

Aithne shook her head. "It won't be a problem."

"That might depend on how many times you have to warm the skins," said Oswin. "If you get them warm enough the first time, the snow we add will melt, and we can use body heat to keep them warm."

"It's a good idea," said Briant, "but we aren't dependent on our own power for spells. Lledrith allows us to gather it from the earth."

"And the air," said Aithne. "I get more from the air than the earth."

Briant cocked his head. "Interesting. I get some from the air, but not as much as from the ground."

"Why?" asked Sine.

Aithne shrugged. "It sort of makes sense. I'm better with wind spells, and you do more with water. Maybe the magic you gather from the air is actually moisture from the wind."

"That's logical." He held his hands out to the fire. "I'm glad you're here, though. If I was in charge of fire, it would take a while."

Oswin snorted. "You wouldn't be in charge of fire. I'm better at it than you are. For that matter, Raya is better."

Adrienne punched Oswin's shoulder. "Oswin!"

Briant chuckled. "No, he's right. Goddess willing, we'll never have to find out."

They stopped for the night at an outpost on the border. As Adrienne went inside to talk to the commander, Aithne and Briant unsaddled the dragons beside the building.

"I wish we had something to build a shelter with," said Aithne.

Briant crossed his arms and leaned against Vask. "We'd need a lot of whatever material we use. Unless—"

A shout and the sound of swords leaving their scabbards made them jump. Briant ran for the door with Aithne close behind, and the dragons spread out to cover the outside. Adrienne stood in a corner with Oswin in front of her. Raya and Sine fought back against six men. Aithne began to chant.

One man lunged at Sine, and he flew back in a gust of wind. Aithne directed the next gust between Sine and Raya, blowing two more away.

Incoming! shouted Vask. Briant heard dragon fire and a meager amount of screaming.

"Uffern," he muttered.

Adrienne said something Briant didn't pay attention to, and Oswin shouted, "Briant! Cover Adrienne!"

Briant backed up, weaving his hands to cast a tremor spell. He directed it at the enemies' feet, and they stumbled back. Sine stabbed one, and Raya partially decapitated another.

Raya growled as blood sprayed over her face and clothing. Running for the ones Aithne blew back, she shouted, "Wybrens!"

Sine echoed her, and they attacked the four remaining men.

Aithne ran forward, flames dancing on her fingers. When she drew even with Sine, she tossed a fireball onto the nearest man, sending a breeze after it to spread it to the one beside him.

Adrienne gasped behind him. "Briant! We have to help Oswin!"

She grabbed his hand and pulled him out the door. He had enough time to realize her tattoos were glowing when a wave of hot power rushed through him. Pulling his hand away from Adrienne, he wove an earthquake spell in large motions before he noticed the sea of tanad rushing toward them. He released the spell with a shout, and a large crevice opened, swallowing several dozen people. They fell without a sound as the dragons blew flames on the ones in front of them.

"Holy Goddess, preserve us!" shouted Adrienne. She put a hand on his shoulder, and power surged through him again. He wove his hands without thinking about what he was doing, and a geyser erupted from the earth near the tree line. Bodies and trees flew up in the torrent, crashing to the ground.

The dragons blew more fire, and Briant heard Aithne's voice behind him. Storm-force wind blew the dragon fire through the tanad ranks, but he hadn't heard Aithne cast the spell. As the enemy soldiers, human and tanad alike, fell to the inferno, Briant cast another earthquake spell aimed at the crevice he'd made. The earth shook under their feet and filled it in. He followed with a rain spell to put out the fires as Raya and Sine came out. The water did little to quench the smell of blood and burned flesh, and Briant's heart skipped a beat. He looked away from the bloodshed so he wouldn't see his mother's face.

Beside him, Adrienne was pale and dazed. He scratched an insistent scratch on his arm. "Adrienne, why are your tattoos glowing?"

She turned her face toward him, allowing her hands to drop to her sides, but she said nothing. Behind her, Aithne dragged her sleeve up, and Briant saw light glowing from her tattoo. Frowning, he pulled his own sleeve up. His glowed, too.

"What happened?" gasped Aithne.

Adrienne's shoulders sagged. She fell, and Briant caught her, lifting her off her feet and taking her inside. Sine followed.

The main room was bloody and littered with body parts. The stench was overpowering in the enclosed area. He carried her down a hall and found sleeping quarters. In the main room, Sine called Aithne to come in and blow the stink out.

He laid Adrienne on the nearest bed, and Oswin came in to kneel beside her.

Adrienne's tattoos dimmed, and she looked around the room. Her eyes widened, and she sat up. Oswin protested, and she scoffed. "I'm fine. We need to petition the Goddess quickly. Queen Elisaid needs to know this outpost is compromised."

Oswin moved to sit on the foot of the bed.

Adrienne crossed her legs in front of her, leaning against the pillow. "Briant, you should see to the dragons."

He wanted to ask why their tattoos were glowing, but he left them to their meditation. In the main room, the windows were open, and Aithne directed a gentle breeze. The smell improved even in the short time since he'd passed through. "I'm going to shield the dragons."

"Good idea," said Aithne, not pausing her work.

The dragons held their positions surrounding the small building. Briant dispelled the rain, and the water glazed over with ice. Raya walked past him, dragging the top half of a man's body, adding it to a pile of corpses.

"Raya, let me help you." He followed her in, and they dragged the rest of the bodies out as Sine set to work cleaning up the blood. As they got the last of the bodies out, Briant used his earth magic to open a hole under the pile and pushed the dirt over them as they sank down.

Raya shook her head. "You're handy to have around, kid."

"Glad to help." He stared around at the remaining bodies and buried them, too. "Vask? Do you think it's safe to gather on the downwind side? I will shield the three of you from the cold."

"I will enjoy that, but perhaps after we ensure there is not a second wave."

Oswin strode out, muttering under his breath. He glanced at Briant. "Shield the dragons. I'll set wards."

He felt a wave of relief from Vask, and the dragons moved to the south side of the building. Briant built the shield, extending it around the west corner. "When Oswin gets back, I'll move the shield around the door."

"Good idea," said Aithne. "Adrienne said we will need to swap watches to keep the shield up through the night."

"That was the plan. They're done meditating already? I saw Oswin come out. He was scowling."

Aithne nodded, glancing over her shoulder at the door. "They were going to warn the queen, but the Goddess told them the queen has known for a few days that the outposts are compromised."

Briant's eyebrows raised. "All of them?"

She shrugged. "They didn't say, but they're understandably livid that she said nothing to us about it. If we'd known, we could have avoided this."

"No kidding." He leaned against Vask's side, drawing magic from the earth. "This is going to be a long trip."

"No doubt. But I have the impression that the Goddess knew this was going to happen. I'm not sure why."

"I know," said Adrienne, walking around the corner.

"You've stopped glowing," said Briant.

"We were glowing because I was channeling power to you."

Aithne sagged against Saphir. "That explains that power surge I felt when you touched me."

"You got that too?" asked Briant.

"I don't know why," said Adrienne, "but I have the feeling she is teaching us something, and we don't have the luxury of time." She squinted, her face turning toward Oswin, who walked back toward them. "We need to be more alert than ever. This will be a trial by fire."

"Great," groaned Briant.

Oswin nodded as he approached. "Good, you have the shield up."

"I'll wrap it around the door when we are ready."

Oswin nodded and looked at Adrienne. "You told them?"

"I did."

"Good. Go back inside and rest. Don't argue with me, sister. You're not the Bealban Dia out here." He turned to Aithne as Adrienne went back inside. "I will help with the watch. Even if I only hold the shield for a few hours, you two will rest a little more. I have a feeling we'll need it."

"As long as you stay within your limits. Sine was right earlier—we don't need to deal with backlash."

"Agreed," said Oswin. "I'll go tell Adrienne."

Briant sighed and went back to Vask.

Aithne watched him. "What? He's helping."

"Oh, yeah, he is. Absolutely." He examined his fingernails. "And if he gets to watch you sleep, all the better."

"What does that mean?"

Saphir blinked. "It means you should get to know Oswin better, beloved."

Aithne narrowed her eyes. "I don't know if you mean what I think you mean, but no one has time for that right now."

"Not now, perhaps," said Isidro. "But if we live through whatever trial is to come, there will be time."

CHAPTER
TWENTY-EIGHT ~ SLAN

Tanwen woke, shivering. She was cold and wet, and the wind blew over her. Opening her eyes, she saw bars and a wooden board on the other side. Something cold fell on her face, and she looked up to see the gray sky and snow.

She tried to sit up but found the cage, which was on the back of a wagon, too small. Two men sat in front of her, and several walked beside the wagon.

She took out her beacon and held it up. *Quillon?*

I see you, he answered.

She frowned, looking around. He was behind her, far above weapons range. He looked like a bird, but she recognized him.

Which way am I going?

East on the West Road.

She gulped and curled into a ball. *Mevan, then. Are they moving Muirne, too?*

I do not see her. I do not know if she left the Keep. It is likely you are going to Mevan. We are already considering options.

She suppressed a stab of fear.

Quillon scoffed in her head. *Tanwen, we are aware that we dragons must keep our distance. That does not stop us from helping the humans plan.*

It's not only that. She closed her eyes and coaxed air into her lungs, but Aithne and Liam lingered in her thoughts.

Beloved, Aithne knows you love her and will fight to stay alive. As for Liam, you defended yourself. There was nothing that could be done.

I wish I knew what happened to him, though.

As do we all. Perhaps a healer could find his body and examine it?

She swallowed hard. *We don't have the time or resources for that. And it wouldn't change anything, anyway. He will still be dead.*

But you saved me.

She couldn't stop the sob and the rush of anger. *But why did I have to choose?*

You didn't. He did. Your only choice was to live. He sent a wave of love and empathy through their link, and she clung to it as she covered her head with her arms and wept. *Does Aithne know?*

Saphir told her Liam died. She needs to know nothing more now.

Tanwen swallowed hard. *You're right. There's a chance none of us will live through this.*

That is correct. Saphir suggested you attempt to meditate. Aithne has found comfort and instruction from the Goddess with that tool.

The Goddess? Like Cruthadair, the mother goddess?

The same.

Tanwen's mind went blank. *She's real?*

Saphir has seen the form she allows mortals to see, as has Vask. According to them, Brigid and Laoch were mortal and are no more.

Tanwen took a moment to let it sink in. *Are Vask and Saphir convinced?*

They are.

Did they tell you how to do it? The meditation?

I will relay the procedure when they are able.

Tanwen dried her face with both hands. She leaned against the bars as the sky lightened. They crested a hill, and she saw Mevan in the distance. Her heart pounded. *Sooner will be better.*

Tanwen jolted awake without having realized she'd fallen asleep. Darkness enveloped her; a shiver wracked her body, and she did not know where she was. She heard men's voices, and a moment later, the wagon jolted. She groaned as it jarred her.

They passed through a gate, and someone held a torch up to the wagon. She flinched, shielding her eyes from the bright light, and the person shouted, "You are lucky she still lives! Raca does not want her dead yet!"

Her heart jolted. Raca. She curled tight again.

Raca wants you alive. That is something, said Quillon.

Tanwen snorted. *She wants me alive because they won't know where to look for your body if I'm dead. They don't care about me—it's you they want.*

That is logical, but perhaps not the only reason.

She struggled to focus. *What do you mean?*

If it is dragons they want, why have they only taken you? And you, specifically? Did they target you?

Since when do dragons overthink? She groaned as they started up a steep hill and the cage slid back against the wagon gate. She gasped at the impact. *They don't know for sure who I am. How did they target me?*

They have not indicated that they know who you are. Dorchadans have a history of deceit. Perhaps they sought you, or perhaps they recognized only that you are a Wybren. We must wait and see.

She closed her eyes and clenched her jaw against the vibration of the wagon wheels on cobblestones. *Has Saphir told Aithne what's happened?*

Aithne and Briant both know. Saphir suggests you picture a calm, peaceful place in your mind. It does not have to be a real place or conform to the world we know. Imagine with your senses. That is the beginning of meditation.

Imagine with my senses? Sure. I have nothing better to do right now. She considered and rejected several ideas of ideal spaces before thinking about the warmth of Quillon's lair. From there, she went to a small, warm room with sunlight streaming in glazed windows, a mountain view, and a fireplace. She imagined herself on a large, soft chaise with a cup of arda, a plate of her favorite pastries and fruit, and a stack of books. Leaning her head back, she smelled lavender, but it didn't seem odd.

She jolted and gasped. The wagon had stopped moving. She heard voices, footsteps, and the creaking of door hinges. She tried to sit up to see where they were, but she couldn't move. The cage opened, and rough hands dragged her out. She wanted to scramble away, but her body felt oddly stiff and refused to cooperate.

They pulled her out of the cage, and one man dragged her over his shoulder. Her head and arms dangled down his back, and he held her legs as he walked into a building. He went up one flight of stairs and through a door, where he dropped her on a narrow bed. Her heart pounded as he leaned over her, but he turned and walked out. She heard the lock click, and her body relaxed.

Moving carefully, she got up. The room was small, but it had a table and a chair in front of the barred window. She smelled food and arda, and went to the table. The arda and stew steamed, and the bread was hot. She sank into the chair, nibbling a crust of bread to avoid getting sick.

She felt a cautious trickle of relief from Quillon. Picking up the mug, she leaned back and looked out the window. *This is an improvement, at least. There's some good news to share with the others.*

Let us be grateful for small blessings, he answered.

When Tanwen woke, the sun shone in the window. She sat up and squinted. It neared the top of the casement. Her head ached, and she groaned, pinching the bridge of her nose. She smelled cinnamon and glanced toward the window again. A tray sat on the table, and she frowned. How did they get in to put food on the far side of the room without her knowing?

With a touch of regret, she left the warm bed. She lifted the cover on the tray to find an assortment of fruit, cheese, and boiled eggs, accompanied by a large pitcher of water and a covered carafe of arda. Guilt crept in as she ate. Her friends slept in the cold and ate when they had food.

They are also free to go where they will, reminded Quillon. *They would tell you to eat and rest, regain your strength, and escape.*

You're right. She poured arda and cradled the mug in both hands, taking a deep smell of milk and spices. *It's not Sine's arda, but it will do.*

I will relay the message.

She lingered over her food, watching the activity out the window. It overlooked a cobbled courtyard surrounded by stone on three sides. The fourth wall was white stone. Her room had a curved wall. A tower at the palace, then, but only one floor up. *I guess they're not afraid I'll escape,* she told Quillon. *The window is small. Even if I figure out how to get the bars out, I'm not sure I'd fit through it.*

I am too far away to sense your exact location, but the others are working on a plan to free you. Sine said to gather your strength and whatever information about the enemy you can get, and be ready.

She smiled. *Of course she did.*

She was about to go back to bed when a door from the castle opened. A woman with a long white braid, wearing brown trews, a blue tunic, and boots, strode out and crossed the courtyard. Everyone stopped what they were doing and bowed, and a shiver ran down Tanwen's spine.

Quillon, I think I'm about to have a visitor, and I need to be sure you're listening in.

I have not stopped.

She felt a small surge of relief, followed by another spike of anxiety, when she heard boots coming down the hall.

When the door opened, the woman came in, and Tanwen's blood ran cold. She did her best to maintain an appearance of calm, almost boredom.

Tanwen smiled a little and reached for the tray. "Have you come for this? I appreciate the food."

The woman's eyes widened. She smiled, but it didn't reach her eyes. "That is not why I've come. I have questions."

Tanwen nodded and leaned back. "Sure. Ask me anything."

"You are a Wybren?"

"I am."

"Where is your dragon?"

Tanwen shrugged and waved a hand at the window. "Out there somewhere. I really have no idea where he's hunkered down, but he won't come here."

"No? Why?"

Tanwen cocked her head as if she didn't understand the question. "Why won't he come here? I'm not sure if you get out much, but whoever invaded us can turn animals, even dragons, into *tanad*. We are avoiding that, and if he comes here, he will undoubtedly be shot at."

"I guarantee he will be." The woman leaned back against the door and crossed her arms. "So we're at an impasse already. You won't call your dragon, but that's the only thing keeping you alive."

"It's not a matter of won't. It's a matter of can't. He's too far away to communicate with."

The woman chuckled. "You wouldn't know this, but I had a Wybren helping me until recently."

Tanwen allowed her skepticism to show. "A Wybren? Helping you?"

"Technically, she's still helping me, but in a different capacity. In any case, I know you are able to communicate with your dragon over longer distances than you'll admit to. I also know the dragons talk to each other, so he can spread the word that I am actively crushing the resistance. We'll find your dragons—all of them—and you won't have a choice but to bend the knee to me."

"To you?" Tanwen nodded slowly. "So our Wreiddons were deceived in Dorchada. They were told Raca is a man."

The woman smiled. "They believed what I wanted them to believe, Wybren Tanwen. I suggest you reconsider summoning Quillon. It will save you a lot of pain."

"I'll think about."

"Good. Let me leave you with a small incentive." She took a large amethyst from her belt pouch, closing her hand around it and waving her hands in a pattern.

Tanwen's gut clenched suddenly and painfully. She crossed her arms over her abdomen as the pain took her breath away. It felt like when she'd birthed Aithne, but worse, and she groaned, falling from her chair.

She heard the woman's feet move. "Huh. That is interesting. You have deep potential for magic ability, but it's buried so deeply, waking it will kill you. I've never seen the like." The door opened. "That's a small sample, Tanwen. I can do worse with a thought."

The door closed, and Tanwen fought to take a breath, and then another to quell the pain. *Don't even think about it, Quillon.*

I am not, but perhaps you should try the meditation technique again.

She groaned and pushed herself up, crawling onto the bed. *Good idea.*

Chapter Twenty-Nine
~ Commain

Aithne shivered as they left the outpost, angling west, when the sun melted the snow off the top of the shield. They flew against the wind, snow pelting their shields like tiny pebbles. The weather forced the dragons to fly low, nearly skimming the sparse tree cover. They fought for every wing flap.

Aithne pressed herself to Adrienne's back. Her shield covered Saphir's head and extended over her neck like a blanket that ended behind Aithne. It protected them from the snow, but the bottom, left open to accommodate Saphir's wings, let the cold in.

Ahead of her, Oswin shielded Isidro while Raya huddled behind him. Vask flew to her left with Sine riding behind Briant with no saddle. She lost track of time. Gray, snow-laden clouds blocked the sun.

She heard Vask signal Saphir and Isidro to land, and they followed him down toward a snow-covered clearing at the edge of the thinning evergreen forest. Her stomach growled, and she realized they had been flying longer than they thought. She tightened her grip on the saddle pommel in front of Adrienne, who stiffened as they descended.

Aithne pressed closer to her and said, "Move with me and push your feet into the stirrups. We'll be on the ground in a few minutes, and we'll get some food and rest."

Adrienne snorted. "Food is the last thing on my mind right now." She flinched when Saphir descended after Vask, ducking her face sideways and clutching Aithne's wrists.

Saphir circled gently, landing as if the ground would break beneath her. As her muscles relaxed, Adrienne took a breath and let it out.

Aithne sat back. "If you let go of my arms, I will unbuckle the straps."

Adrienne released Aithne's wrists. "Sorry. I must seem so cowardly."

Aithne let the straps fall one by one. "Not in the least. You'll get used to it. Flying doesn't come naturally to any of us. Wybrens learn younger, when things are less scary."

Adrienne slid out of the saddle as Aithne released her shield. "It's not flying I mind; it's taking off and landing that scare me."

Aithne chuckled. "Maybe we will get where we're going fast so you don't have to endure it too many times."

"Or we'll get there more slowly and I'll get used to it."

Aithne jumped to the ground and reached for the girth strap. "If that happens, you'll get used to flying, and I'll get used to the cold." She patted Saphir's shoulder. "Are you well?"

Yes, but I am glad for a brief respite.

Aithne pulled the saddle off, shivering as cold hit her lungs.

Raya walked over to take it as Adrienne walked toward Oswin. "That's strange. It feels like the temperature is dropping, but there's no wind."

Saphir shifted uneasily.

"What is that?" gasped Raya.

Aithne turned to look at where Raya pointed. A creature melted from the woods, and her breath caught. "Is that a grimalkin?"

"Too small," said Oswin.

"Not by much," said Sine.

"It looks like a wolverine, but they're not white," said Oswin.

The creature stalked toward them, followed by dozens more. They had short legs and were covered by something that looked like white armor. Their eyes glowed blue and cold. The first one was bigger than the others by half. It snarled, and Aithne saw long, sharp teeth. It reared up on its hind legs, raising its front paws in the air. With a barked yip, it slammed its front paws down.

Fear raced through Aithne. She dropped the saddle and grabbed Adrienne, pulling her away from Saphir. "Up!"

Before the dragons could respond, the ground trembled.

Aithne stumbled as walls of ice shot from the ground with a deafening crack. Raya yelped, stumbling back and dragging Aithne back in time to avoid being crushed. Crystalline walls three times Oswin's height surrounded them. Through the ice, she saw the blurred shapes of the others. Adrienne and Oswin were trapped together at the far end, separated from Briant, Sine, Vask, and Isidro by another ice wall.

Raya fumbled with her sword as the cold intensified.

Aithne threw a shield around herself, Raya, and Saphir, but it felt thin. She followed it with a fire spell aimed at the nearest wall. Flames licked the surface and flickered out.

Saphir growled in pain as frost formed between her scales.

Through the ice, Aithne saw the creatures advance and spread out, surrounding the walls.

Dread coursed through Aithne. "They're hunting us," she said, her breath clouding heavily. She turned left when she heard a scratching sound. Two of the creatures scaled the wall as easily as if they walked uphill, leaving scored claw marks in the ice. The cold was so intense her teeth ached, and Saphir's body heat faded.

Alarmed, Aithne looked at her. Saphir looked back, anger in her eyes, groaning as she turned to the nearest wall. She blew fire at it. The ice didn't melt.

The two creatures reached the top of the wall and sat on their haunches. They raised their front paws and moved them in tandem. Balls of frost formed, and the creatures threw them at Saphir. Her wings clamped close to her sides. She gasped as the frost crept over her scales.

Aithne squinted through the distortion at the next cell. Something swirled around Briant's feet. Were they freezing him in place?

She didn't have time to wonder as the two creatures launched themselves into their cell. Raya grunted as she swung her sword clumsily at one. Saphir snapped at the other, but the movement was slow, and the wolverine stepped aside.

Aithne cast fire at the nearest one, and the spell sputtered a small flame and went out. She shouted a wind spell to blow them into the wall, and the breeze pushed one back.

"A little harder," shouted Raya.

"That should have blown it completely out!"

Adrienne and Oswin positioned themselves back to back, hands raised, chanting something Aithne didn't recognize. They began to glow, but the wolverines didn't give her time to wonder what they were doing.

Three more dropped into their enclosure. Movement caught her eye. She recognized the movement of Briant's hand—he was casting a water whip, and her heart sank. Why didn't he pick something stronger than a cantrip?

When he raised his hands, a surging torrent spiraled out, laced with clumps of dirt.

Aithne stepped in front of Raya, pushing her toward Saphir, and shouted a simple fire spell. A cyclone of flame crashed against the wall.

In the far cell, light swirled around Adrienne and Oswin. It refracted through the ice walls, filling every chamber with colored light.

Aithne reached for the power in the air and it burned through the numbing cold as Lledrith roared through her. She shouted the fire spell again, and the fire punched through the inner wall.

On the other side, Briant's water whip churned mud, freezing and thawing in quick succession, driving the wolverines back.

The creatures fled back over the walls but stopped outside.

Briant's magic became a wave of mud that toppled the wall as the other walls vibrated in harmony with Adrienne's and Oswin's combined chanting. Their spell transformed the remaining walls into power channels that shimmered and pulsed like heartbeats, using the wolverines' frost barriers against them.

Briant's mud avalanche pulsed toward the creatures, freezing and thawing.

Aithne shouted a wind spell that lifted three wolverines into the air and blew them toward the trees. The remaining ones yowled in surprise as their frost armor shattered.

Oswin's and Adrienne's voice rose in unison, their hands high in the air, their tattoos glowing. The walls vibrated with the resonance, and it sounded like singing. The pure note made the remaining wolverines flatten their ears, and they fled.

Behind her, Aithne heard Raya shout in surprise as Saphir reared up, the frost falling from her scales. On the other side of the maze, Isidro and Vask appeared over the top of the walls. Saphir's natural body heat returned rapidly, slamming into Aithne like a wall, and the dragons breathed flame at the retreating creatures.

The walls melted as suddenly as they'd appeared, and the clouds opened to allow a shaft of light to fall on them.

A veil of smoke blew off Aithne's clothes, and Briant's hands dripped mud. Adrienne and Oswin laughed, turning to each other and hugging.

Sine's eyes were wide. "What—what was that?"

Adrienne's glowing tattoos faded. "The Goddess helped us."

Aithne's arm itched, and she pulled her sleeve up. "I think it's more than that. Briant, is your tattoo glowing?"

He pulled up his sleeve and held up his glowing arm.

Oswin looked at the three of them with wide eyes. "That's... unexpected. We need to figure out what that is."

Sine looked around. "Yes, but not here. I don't feel safe here."

"We are unlikely to be safe anywhere," said Vask. "Let us shield and rest for a bit, and then we will move on."

They huddled together, and Briant layered his strongest shield over Aithne's.

Raya said, "I sure hope those critters stay away. They got past your shields without too much trouble."

"Not really," said Briant. "They build their magic dampening spell around the shields."

Raya snorted. "Either way, they got past them. How do we fight against that if they come back?"

"We know to watch for them now," said Oswin, "and when we stop for the night, I'll put up wards to warn us. Adrienne, do we need to do anything else?

Adrienne blinked. "Sorry. What?"

Aithne leaned to look at her. "Are you all right? Were you hurt?"

Adrienne shook her head. "No. I feel—strange. Hollowed out, like something in me eroded, but also so peaceful."

Briant moved to crouch in front of her. "All of our tattoos were glowing at the end. Could there be a connection?"

"I don't know. I'll ask the Goddess when we stop for the night."

Near dusk, the dragons landed near a stone outcropping at the base of the mountains. They made camp, and the dragons lined up in front of the opening, facing out and looking different directions. They let their tails rest inside the outcropping, sharing body heat with the humans.

Aithne and Briant made their combined shield around them, and it kept the wind away from everyone. Aithne sat on the ground between Saphir's paws, holding the shield, and Sine brought her some jerky and dried fruit. She leaned against Saphir's chest as she ate.

Are you sure you don't need to hunt, Saphir?

I am fine, beloved. The three of us gorged before leaving Gynhalion. Adrienne's people were generous.

Aithne sighed, trying to push her anxiety aside.

"That was a big sigh," said Oswin, coming between Saphir and Vask to sit with Aithne.

"We're close to the Annwn border. I don't know if the fae are still looking for me, or if they have scouts this far north. For that matter, I don't know if water dragons hibernate."

Oswin frowned. "Why did you think about that?"

"We have three fire dragons, and the river is on the other side of the mountains. I don't know if a water dragon could sense them from far away."

"Are you sure they exist? The only stories I've heard about them were centuries old."

Aithne shivered. "They exist. One attacked me. That's when Quinn captured me."

"The man who captured you helped you escape?"

"He observed me long enough to know I'm the Lavban Dia. Well, one of them. We didn't know about Briant. The fae were going to kill me as a false prophet, and he know that would be a disaster."

Oswin squinted into the dark. "That's an understatement."

Aithne chewed a piece of jerky, listening to the murmur of voices behind her.

"I wish I knew where we were going."

"We will find out when the time is right."

Aithne nodded. "That doesn't help much now."

"You get used to that. I did, anyway. Trusting the Goddess is easier than fretting over potential problems."

Aithne looked at the sky. The clouds had parted but lingered. They left streaks of darkness between the stars. "It seems so peaceful. Will it ever be again?"

"Has it ever been, really?"

She heard the dragons talking to each other before a wave of emotion from Saphir she couldn't quite decipher.

Beloved, Tanwen has been moved to Mevan.

Aithne's mouth went dry, and she was glad she'd finished eating. She tried to ask for the details but couldn't think how of the words.

"Aithne? What's wrong?" asked Oswin.

Briant came around Saphir's other side. "She told you?"

Aithne looked at him and felt the burden of the shield lift from her. "Yes, but I don't know what it means."

Quillon observed her in a cage on a wagon. They took her to the castle. He knows where she is, but she still insists he stay away.

She heard Raya relaying the information to the others.

Aithne's hands shook. *Did she look all right?*

Yes, and they allowed her to keep her beacon. Dinsmore, Siril, and Moira are formulating a plan to rescue her.

Do they know Sine is with us?

They do, and they will consult her through us.

A trickle of relief steadied her, but her stomach still churned. "Briant, can you hold the shield for a while? I need to go lie down."

"Of course."

Stay here with me, said Saphir. *I will keep you warm.*

As she curled against Saphir's chest, she heard Adrienne say, "Tomorrow we turn north."

"To Mevan?" asked Sine.

"Yes. We need to leave at dawn," said Adrienne. "The Goddess was explicit."

Briant couldn't shake the feeling that something bad was going to happen. He scanned the ground as Vask led the other dragons north. The wind gusted, buffeting them. Behind him in the saddle, Adrienne squeaked and grabbed his waist. Briant gripped with his legs, and the single strap holding him in place in front of the saddle creaked against his coat. It had been his idea to ride in front to break the wind, but he missed the saddle.

Vask, when this is over, remind me to tell whoever is in charge the trainees need to practice riding bareback more.

That is a sound idea, said Vask.

Briant yawned. He kept his shield minimal, conserving his energy after keeping watch most of the previous night. Oswin took a turn, and they let Aithne sleep. She was perturbed when she woke. That almost made it worth the effort.

Adrienne huddled against his back, shivering. He moved the shield from himself to wrap around her, and a few minutes later, he felt her relax.

The sun was high behind milky clouds when they approached the woods where the Mevan road split off the South road. A trickle of relief dripped into him when he saw movement, and something slammed into his shoulder. He looked down to see an arrow sticking out of his chest.

Adrienne screamed, and another arrow bounced off Vask's scales. A ballista bolt soared over his tail and Isidro banked to evade it.

Saphir dove past them in a blue blur, breathing fire on the ballista. The crew scattered, and Briant felt Vask's sides expand with air before he blew flames on the flee-ing men, setting the grove on fire.

Briant grit his teeth as he wove his hands through a water spell to extinguish the flames. He saw Aithne cast a wind spell, using it to direct the fire to the running men. Briant raised his shield around Vask, ignoring the pain from the arrow, and the dragons turned west.

The dragons landed, and Sine ran toward him as Adrienne slid out to the saddle. Briant fumbled with the strap, but it wouldn't come loose. His mind muddled as the pain set in, and he noted that Adrienne's leg was bleeding. Raya and Oswin ran over as Sine climbed into Vask's saddle.

"Sit still. I'll get the strap," she said. He felt a tug, and the strap loosened. He let himself fall off Vask's back. Oswin and Raya caught him, lowering him to the ground.

Sine joined them. "I don't know if it's good or bad that the arrow didn't go through."

"I guess we'll find out," said Raya. "Oswin, can you pull it out? You have the best chance of getting it in one go."

Oswin knelt beside him, and Briant felt Adrienne's hands on his head. She chanted, and Briant closed his eyes. He felt the others grip his body, holding him down, and pain tore through him. He yelled, convulsing, and the others pressed down harder.

Steady, growled Vask in his head. *Focus on your breath.*

He dragged air into his lungs. They inflated far too slowly, and fear flooded through him.

Someone unfastened the top of his coat and slipped a hand inside, covering the wound. He whimpered at the pressure, but the pain dulled. His body relaxed.

His lungs loosened, and he opened his eyes. Adrienne crouched over him, eyes closed and praying with her hand in his coat. The wind blew a lock of hair loose from her braid. He wanted to tuck it back in, but his shoulder throbbed.

She took her hand out. Blood covered it, and she wiped it on the dead grass behind her.

The dragons had arranged themselves around the humans, and the wind died as Aithne shielded the group.

Adrienne stared into his eyes for a moment before her cheeks turned pink. "I closed the wound, but you'll need to immobilize your arm until it heals more."

He nodded. "Thanks."

"You're welcome," said Oswin. "We should make camp here."

"Here? Really?" asked Raya. "We're an hour from Mevan."

Adrienne stood. "We have cover here, and the dragons need to stay clear of the city. Briant needs a sling, food, and rest."

"Agreed," said Vask.

Raya raised her hands in surrender. "Fine, Vask, if you want to stay, we'll stay, but let's move into the part of the woods that isn't burned."

Chapter Thirty ~ Slan

Aithne looked around at the sound of leaves crunching underfoot. Behind her, Saphir dozed, her breath a warm breeze as Aithne held the shield around the group.

Sine walked around Saphir and handed Aithne a few water skins. "We did our best to fill them with snow."

Aithne sighed and took them. "I hoped you were bringing arda and pastries."

Sine chuckled. "I'd rather be bringing those, too."

Aithne whispered the warming spell, pushing heat through the leather until the snow inside was warm water, and handed them back. "The snow you add will melt, and I can reheat them if they get too cold."

"I think we'll want you to warm all of them before we go. We'll have to fly higher today, and warm water skins will keep the cold away. Sort of."

"Do we know where we're going?"

"Besides north? I haven't heard."

Saphir stirred. *Quillon wants us to go to the place Vask and Briant met.*

Aithne frowned at the stab of surprise from Briant and shook her head. "We are going to Briant's home."

"You don't seem happy about that," said Sine.

"It's not that. Lledrith has given Briant and me telepathic access to each other and our dragons, so I have a person and two dragons in my head now. It's a lot."

Sine stared, wide-eyed, for a moment. "We must be heading into a fight of epic proportions if you need that."

Aithne snorted and rolled to her feet. "Thanks for that, Sine. So encouraging. We need to get going."

Saphir landed in a clearing shortly before midday. She waited for Sine to dismount before sliding off Saphir's back, protecting her head against debris as Vask landed. She felt a mix of happiness, sorrow, and trepidation wash over Briant, followed by a jolt of surprise from Saphir.

Beloved, did you get a look at the Dorchadans who helped you in Annwn?

Not really. Why?

I saw two men who looked like them.

What? Where?

At the homestead beyond the trees.

Aithne took a deep breath to steady herself. "We need to be careful when we approach the house. Saphir saw men who could be Dorchadan."

Raya pulled the saddle off Isidro. "Could be Dorchadan? Why do you think that, Saphir? Do you see a substantial difference in their appearances?"

"No," said Saphir. "They look like men I have seen before, and they wore Dorchadan uniforms the last time."

"They had a grimalkin, too," said Aithne with a shudder.

"Great," said Oswin.

"We will remain here until we know you are safe," said Vask.

"Raine says those men have been there since her group arrived," said Saphir.

Oswin snorted. "That doesn't mean it's safe."

Isidro turned to look at Oswin. His voice rumbled as he said, "Raine would not lead us into danger, *human*."

"Not intentionally, I'm sure, but what if the men are holding people hostage?"

"They'd tell their dragons," said Sine. "Come on, Oswin, let's go before you really irritate him."

Aithne pressed her hand into Saphir's shoulder. *Be safe.*

You as well, beloved, answered Saphir.

Adrienne put a hand on Aithne's shoulder. "The Goddess would have told us if we were walking into a trap."

"Are you sure?" asked Aithne. "Even if the trap puts us where she wants us?"

"If that's the case, it will still work out according to her plan."

Aithne snorted. "I know, but what if the plan is for us to die?"

"Then we will be with Her," said Oswin. He touched her arm. "Come on."

They followed Briant through the trees to the clearing. Aithne saw a fenced area with a large cabin and four smaller ones with a garden in the middle. Standing next to the fence, watching the woods, were the men Aithne had seen in Dorchada. They wore different clothes, but a sensation deep in her gut told her Lledrith confirmed their identity.

"Is that them?" whispered Sine.

Aithne nodded. "Yes. Lledrith confirmed it."

Briant stepped out of the trees before anyone stopped him.

The men's eyes widened. They leaned together, talking.

Briant stopped several paces from them and rested his hand on his sword pommel. "Why are you at my homestead?"

The men strode forward with joy on their faces. "Blessed be the chosen ones of the Goddess!"

Aithne felt Briant's surprise, and it mingled with her own.

The men stopped a few paces away. The younger one looked awestruck, and the older one said, "I am Anton, this is Ivan. We are the Dorchadan resistance. Please come inside."

She looked toward the house when she heard voices. Moira and Dinsmore came out of the main house and jogged toward them.

"It's all right, Anton," called Dinsmore. "They're with us."

Anton turned. "We know. At last, it is beginning!"

They turned and walked toward the house as Moira jogged to them. "Briant, Raine said you were shot."

Briant lifted his sling as much as his shoulder would allow. "Of all the places to take an arrow. I need my arms to cast spells."

"Astrid and Eoghan are here. Between us, we'll fix you right up. I'll take you to them, and the rest of you should go inside. Raya, you're not going to believe who we found."

She led Briant toward the smaller cabins.

"Come on in," said Dinsmore. "It's warm inside."

The front door opened and a woman in a Wybren riding coat ran out.

"Raya!"

Raya stopped, her jaw hanging slack. "Ceann?" She laughed and ran to meet her, Sine on her heels.

Aithne paused in surprise. She'd heard the name from her mother but had never met her.

"Who is that?" asked Oswin.

Raya stepped back, wiping tears from her face. "Isidro told me you were still alive, but he didn't know where you were. Where have you been?"

Ceann grinned. "That's a long story. Come inside." She paused and looked at Aithne. "You must be Tanwen's daughter."

Aithne nodded, a stab of anxiety shooting through her at the mention of her mother's name. "I've heard a lot about you. It's nice to finally meet you, but I hoped the circumstances would be different."

Ceann turned back to the door. "None of us saw this coming." She led them into a large cabin. The main room had a long table in front of a fireplace, with a couple of rocking chairs in front of the hearth. "Sine, go through there and check on Agnes's pantry."

Sine's eyes went wide, and she strode through a doorway. Ceann grinned as she pushed a pot over the fire. "I'll have tea ready in a few minutes. You must be frozen through, and sadly, there aren't any baths here. At least, not like we have at the Keeps." She looked at

Oswin and Adrienne. "Looks like I'm not the only one who picked up new friends."

"That's one way to put it," said Aithne. "This is Adrienne, and her brother, Oswin. They're from Commain."

Ceann sank onto the hearth. "Commain. Goodness. Now we need someone from Annwn."

"No! No, we don't," said Aithne. "There's a chance any fae will attempt to kill me." She told Ceann the short version of her story.

When she was done, Ceann ladled hot tea into mugs. "That explains why you're here and not with Shaw's group."

"They're here?"

Ceann nodded. "Several from the Western Keep have gone scouting."

Sine came back. "It's well-stocked, which is what I'd expect from Agness. Where have you been, Ceann?"

"I was visiting my sister near the Southern Keep when everything fell apart. I knew something terrible had happened, but it was a few days before Dyratrisse recovered. We learned the dragons from Eastern Keep were dead, so I knew we couldn't go back there. I was going to head for the Western Keep, but I wanted to make sure my family was safe. I went to the Southern Keep to see if they could take them in." She looked down. "Everyone there is *tanad.* They almost got me, but Anton, well," she looked at Anton and Ivan, who stood near the window, "I didn't expect to be saved by a Dorchadan."

Aithne's face heated, and she looked at her hands in her lap. "They saved me, too, but I didn't know they were friendly. I didn't know until now that there is a Dorchadan resistance."

Ivan shuffled his feet. "Shall we explain?"

"Yes," said Ceann. "The sooner we get everyone on the same page, the better. Come sit by the fire."

Anton and Ivan exchanged a look before moving to the table. Ivan pulled a bench out, and they sat on it.

Anton looked at Ceann, and then at the others. "The foe we face has been building strength for centuries. She is daughter of your King Fergus and Wybren Ailin."

Raya choked on her tea. "You mean great granddaughter a few times, right?"

Anton shook his head. "No. Daughter. The most powerful of all, she survives by stealing the bodies of others. When she takes body, the magic adds to hers. It is great honor for Raca to choose one's body. The families are given high status. They think their daughter becomes Raca, that her knowledge transfers to new person, but it is not so. The owner of body dies as sacrifice to Maccha."

Adrienne's eyes grew wide, and Oswin hissed.

Anton looked at them. "This is why she must be stopped. She will kill all who worship the true Goddess. Already in Dorchada, no one admits to it. Many have fled, but there are still a few who gather information to aid in our calling. Ivan's cousin is one such. Ivan, tell them what Griegor told you."

Ivan shifted on the bench. "I hope my cousin is wrong. He is servant to one of Raca's advisors and overheard him talking to another. There is fear that Raca is no longer content with stealing bodies. She is gathering power to become a goddess."

Raya snorted. "A goddess? So, she's delusional?"

"It is possible," said Adrienne. She stared at the fire. "The Goddess has been hinting at it my whole life and I didn't understand until now. There is a combination of spells that will allow a person to transcend humanity. In theory, it's not possible because it needs all the magic forms, and one is rare." She looked at Aithne. "Only two known people have Lledrith."

"Who is Lledrith?" asked Anton.

Aithne felt faint and grasped the edge of her bench. She felt a jolt of shock from Saphir. "Holy Goddess. That's why they were taking me to Raca."

Sine's jaw dropped. "When you summoned Saphir?"

Aithne jumped up and took a few steps away from the others. "How? How did she know I have Lledrith? I didn't even know then."

Saphir sent her an image of Liam, and Aithne stopped pacing mid-step. "Papa?" She sank to the flagstone floor.

"Sweetie, what are you talking about?" asked Ceann.

Sine got up and walked to Aithne's side, kneeling on the floor beside her. "We need to get everyone together. This goes deeper than we thought."

Briant opened the door for Moira and followed her into his mother's cabin. He'd never seen so many people in her main room, and he sensed Aithne's fear. The leaders of the Western Keep refugees talked with one another. "I wonder what we missed," he whispered to Moira.

Dinsmore stood, and the others fell silent. He summarized what had happened, ending with, "Aithne, please tell us what you know."

"It's not much," she said, standing. "On my way home from my stone quest, after my magic woke, two women tried to capture me. I didn't know anything about them, but something told me not to allow it. I escaped, but they found me again when I called Saphir. They kidnapped me before she arrived. They said they were taking me to Raca, and I knew I couldn't let that happen."

"Why?" asked Ceann. "How did you know what Raca was?"

"When Papa was a prisoner in Dorchada, they were interviewed by a man called Raca. That's where I heard the name. Or title, I guess. The mages who had me kept referring to 'her' when they spoke about Raca, but I didn't have time to figure out why." She looked at Adrienne and Oswin. "My stepfather was held prisoner with Ruan and another Wreiddon, Colin."

Oswin's brow furrowed. "Did he have the same spell cast on his brain?"

"He must have. All three of them had horrible headaches when they got home."

"He had a spy spell," said Adrienne. "That's how Raca found out about Lledrith."

"But we didn't know about Lledrith until later," said Briant.

"Raca would know," said Anton. "There is no hiding from her eyes."

"Tell me if I have this straight," said Briant. "Raca saw Lledrith through Liam and sent mages to bring her to Dorchada to steal Aithne's body?"

"Yes," said Anton.

Briant frowned. "How did she know about it before Liam saw her? The mages tried to get Aithne before she even got home from her stone quest."

"They were perhaps not same people," said Ivan. "That does not matter now. We must decide how to defeat Raca before she gets Lledrith. If that happens, there will be no hope."

Dinsmore turned to Ivan. "How do we do that?"

Lledrith stirred in Briant's gut as Aithne walked over to him. "Is there a quiet place to meditate?"

He nodded. "That's what I was thinking. Dinsmore, I'm going to take Aithne, Oswin, and Adrienne to meditate. Maybe the Goddess already has a plan."

Dinsmore nodded and turned back to Ivan. Adrienne and Oswin joined them.

They took their coats and walked outside. "Let's go to the barn," said Briant.

Oswin said, "You three go. I'll keep watch." When Adrienne protested, he held up a hand. "Something tells me we need to be vigilant, and I have the distinct feeling that you three need to do this together."

Adrienne pressed her lips together, and Briant knew she wasn't happy.

A few minutes later, they settled in the barn's hayloft.

"Did you spend a lot of time up here as a boy?" asked Adrienne.

"No, not really, but that's what makes it the perfect place to meditate. There aren't as many memories attached to the space." He settled in the remaining hay. His breath puffed white, and he wrapped a blanket around himself. The girls did likewise, and a moment later, they sank into meditation as one. He felt Adrienne's surprise and happiness, and a vague sense of not having had people around her who hungered for the Goddess as much as she did.

Briant's mouth quirked up as he opened his eye to gold-tinged fog. He saw his confusion mirrored in Aithne and Adrienne. The air vibrated with a sense of urgency. Without knowing why, he stretched out his arms and felt the girls take his hands. Power thrummed through them, wild but controlled, bigger than the three of them combined, and utterly silent. He got the strong impression that the three of them needed to enter the castle together for a small work with the Goddess, and that it needed to be the next day. Deep in his bones, he knew delay would be the end of everything.

An unseen force pushed him out of the fog and opened his eyes. Adrienne's were wide and fearful. They still held hands, and Aithne gripped his tighter.

"We have to go tomorrow," said Aithne.

"We can't delay," said Adrienne.

Briant nodded. "I know. That means the others have to be ready tomorrow. We'd better go tell them."

He loosened his grip on their hands, but Adrienne pulled him back. "Wait. This task we're called to—did it seem too easy?"

"I didn't get any details," said Aithne.

"Nor I," said Adrienne, "but it's almost like she downplayed the magnitude. A small act that will affect everyone?"

"Maybe it starts small," said Briant. "Regardless of the size of the task, or the risk it poses, we all have to stay focused on what She wants us to do, and watch out for each other."

"We have to make sure I don't fall into enemy hands," said Aithne. "If I get captured, one of you needs to kill me. That's the only way to stop her from getting Lledrith."

"She can't get it from me?" asked Briant.

Aithne paused. "They didn't come after you. Has she ever taken a man's body? I don't know, but we have to protect Lledrith at all costs."

Briant looked at Adrienne, and she nodded. "All costs. We should tell the others that the timetable got more urgent."

"Adrienne!" Oswin peered into the loft from the ladder. "I had a vision. We have to go tomorrow."

Briant looked at Aithne as she shivered. "We know. Did anyone else get it?"

"Ivan."

"Good," said Adrienne. "The Goddess is spreading the message. We won't have to fight about that, at least. Let's go get the plans finalized. We need a meal and some sleep to face tomorrow."

Briant rolled to his feet and followed the others down the ladder. *Vask, that goes for you, too. Go hunt and sleep.*

We are already working on that.

Good. If there's one thing I don't have to be told, it's that this won't be easy.

The sun was setting as they rushed to prepare for the following day. Aithne helped Sine prepare their evening meal with what remained in Agness' stores. Sine seemed quiet, and Aithne didn't mind. She had enough on her mind without adding Sine's worries.

Ceann came in and leaned against the wall, out of their way. "It feels strange not to have my sword on."

Sine nodded. "It does. How are they coming?"

"They found a way to make our weapons lighter, at least. I wish we had time for some training sessions."

"Me, too," said Sine. "But then, what *has* gone our way in the last few weeks?"

Ceann hummed in agreement and crossed her arms. "Dyratrisse told me Tanwen won't let Quillon rescue her. She doesn't want to be bait."

"Sounds like her," said Aithne.

"It does, but what if she's not bait for Quillon?"

"Does it matter?" asked Sine. "Whether the enemy is getting him to come or not, they will kill him if he does."

"I know, but what if *he's* not the target?" She bit her lip. "What if she's bait for you?"

Aithne's jaw dropped, and her hands stilled. "What?"

"The enemy needs your magic, right? And she doesn't use men's bodies, so it's likely Briant would be the target."

Sine turned away from the onion she was dicing. "Holy Goddess, you might be right."

Aithne's heart pounded, and she fought to maintain her composure. "If that is the case, I don't see how it changes our plan." Sine sputtered, and Aithne clenched her hands. "What can we do differently, Sine? Leave Mama there? Refuse to give the enemy what she wants? Even if I did agree to that, it's not what the Goddess wants. She was clear, not only with me, but with Briant, Oswin, Ivan, and Adrienne, too!" She stalked to the window and looked out at the snow, taking a few deep breaths.

"Did the Goddess say specifically that you need to be there?" asked Sine, her voice trembling.

Aithne closed her eyes and dropped her head. "Yes, Sine. I have to be there."

"Look, I wasn't trying to start trouble," said Ceann. "Tanwen is my friend, and I won't leave her to die if I can help it. But even if you do have to go, Aithne, you don't have to go out of your way to confront Raca tomorrow. The plan is for the three of you to cause a distraction, so do that and get out. Avoid Raca. When we get Tanwen back, we will figure out how to take her down."

In her heart, Aithne knew things wouldn't be so straightforward. She turned around to say so and saw fear in Sine's eyes. "I'll try. I can't make promises. Not knowing what she looks like makes things complicated, and the Goddess will lead us where we need to go. Surely the last thing she wants is for my magic to fall into the wrong hands."

Sine dashed tears away with the back of her hand. We can only ask for that much. Aithne, will you see if there is anything else in the smokehouse?"

"Of course." Aithne ducked out the door and strode to the smokehouse. She was sure Sine knew nothing remained, but she went in and leaned against the wall for a moment.

She heard footsteps outside. She froze, holding her breath until Oswin peeked in.

"Do you need any help?"

"No, Sine sent me to make sure we got everything."

He walked in, and his presence filled the rest of the space. "I overheard Ceann. She's not wrong."

"It doesn't matter."

"No, it doesn't. The Goddess will use us as She sees fit." He took her hands. "But that doesn't mean we have to be reckless."

She looked at him and realized for the first time how blue his eyes were. "I know. And I will avoid Raca if possible, but I have a feeling that won't be an option."

"Me too. I can't blame Sine for wanting you to stay back."

"Me neither, Oswin, but we both know—we *all* know—I wasn't given this burden to stay back out of fear."

"Is it a burden?"

She sighed and leaned against the wall, closing her eyes. "It's torn my life to shreds. I have Saphir, Briant, and a few friends left from my old life. I can't stand back and lose my mother because of it." She swallowed the lump in her throat. "Besides, if I kill Raca, I'll avenge my stepfather."

He stepped closer and wrapped his arms around her. She hesitated for a moment before returning the hug and allowing herself to relax against him, just for a minute.

His voice rumbled in his chest. "I'm sorry. We are raised to think Lledrith is a great honor. I never thought of it as a burden."

"It's not to your people, but Commainish women use magic. Slannish women can't."

"I know, but maybe that will change after tomorrow."

"Maybe, but at what cost? And who will still be here to see it?"

Chapter Thirty-One ~ Mevan

Tanwen whimpered as pain spiked through her torso. Doubling over, she seized the chair for support, her knuckles turning white from the force of her grip. Breathing, let alone moving, got more difficult with every bout. The worst of the pain passed, and she gasped. Sweat rolled down her face, and she collapsed onto the chair.

Quillon, is this affecting you too?

His voice had a hard edge. *Only in that I am aware of your suffering.*

Have you heard from anyone?

They assure me our loved ones are well. Raine will not allow the others to tell me anything more.

Despair washed over her. *That's smart.*

Perhaps, but it irks me to be treated like a security risk.

Tanwen smiled despite the pain. *You haven't been irked since the water dragon incident.*

I was past that. I was angry.

Tanwen took a breath as deep as her lungs would allow. Blowing it out, she stood, supporting herself on the table, and limped to the far wall. She had to move in case the chance to escape presented itself. *That galla does not know she's about to deal with an angry dragon.*

It is not only me, beloved. Saphir and Vask are angry also, although they will not say why.

Tanwen took a deep breath. It hitched in her chest as pain lanced through her again, and she put her hand on the wall. *They're angry on our behalf. Whether or not that's true, it's what I'm sticking with.*

As will I.

Breathing shallowly, she tried to stretch. Her body protested, but she pushed on. *Maybe it's a good thing they're treating you like a security risk. Without something to lose, would they do that?*

Quillon paused for a moment. *That is as good a theory as any. Perhaps we should hold on to that.*

Whatever it takes at this point. Please ask Saphir to be cautious.

I will. He was quiet for several minutes. When he replied, his voice was calmer. *I have endured a diatribe from Saphir about humans arguing and not doing any-thing. She was quite convincing.*

Tanwen sighed and trudged back to the window. *So they're either coming or they're not.*

You did not have to put it that way. Take heart, beloved, and keep fighting.

It's getting difficult.

Open your mind to me. I will create a scenario wherein I find Raca and immolate her and everything around her.

Tanwen snickered. *You're going to tell me a story?*

Indeed. I will do whatever I can to distract you from your suffering.

She was about to lie down when she saw a maid with a tray step into the courtyard. When she headed for the tower, Tanwen grabbed the chair and limped around the bed, positioning herself behind the door.

A moment later, she heard footsteps in the hall and adjusted her grip on the chair. The door opened, and the girl came in. Tanwen clenched her jaw as she picked up the chair and swung it at the maid's head. The tray crashed, covering Tanwen's grunt. She dropped the chair and darted out the door. The only way out was down the stairs and through the courtyard. *Goddess, help me!*

She limped down the stairs as fast as she could. As she reached for the doorknob, someone grabbed her around the waist. She screamed, flailing, and a man's arm pinned her arms to her sides and tightened his grip on her torso. He murmured something she didn't recognize, and her body froze.

He picked her up and started back up the stairs. "Nice try, Wybren. I'll make sure you don't get that chance again."

She wanted to scream, but it froze in her throat. He passed her room and took her to another one, further down the hall. She saw a bare stone floor and walls, and a window smaller than the last, set higher in the wall.

He dropped her in the corner, and pain ripped through her. Before she could think, he'd shackled her hands and chained her to a ring on the floor.

Standing to admire his work, he crossed his arms and nodded. "There, now. You'll be far less comfortable in here. I suppose I'll reward your effort, though." He walked out and came back with a blanket and some fruit. "Make that last. Raca might decide you won't get more."

He walked out, and the lock slid closed with a loud click. When he walked away, the spell released, and she fell sideways, catching herself with her arm. Lowering herself onto the cold floor, she squeezed her eyes shut to stop tears falling as the pain wracked her body. *Quillon, tell them they need to hurry.*

I already have, beloved.

Aithne, Briant, and Adrienne stood together at the edge of the woods as the sky lightened. Aithne's mouth was dry, and she tugged at the collar of the stolen guard uniform Ivan had given her the night before. She didn't ask how he got them.

Briant and Adrienne wore uniforms, too, and Adrienne had braided Aithne's hair and coiled it into a tight bun. Not having the braid bouncing on her back felt as foreign as the clothes.

She forced air into her lungs and reached for Saphir.

Not much longer now.

I know, answered Saphir. *We must trust the Goddess to keep you from harm.*

We don't know that's what her plan is. If the worst happens —

We will still be together, beloved.

The wind gusted and blew sharp snowflakes into her face. The trees creaked in protest, and Aithne shivered.

I think I've figured out why Mama doesn't like the woods.

Ask her when you see her next.

Adrienne broke the silence. Pitching her voice low, she said, "Let me ask the Goddess' blessing for our mission." She reached for Aithne's and Briant's hands, linking the three of them together.

Aithne's breath caught in her chest as magic thrummed into her, and she saw Briant's eyes widen.

Adrienne's palms were damp with sweat, and her voice trembled as she prayed. The dread in Aithne's gut faded.

When she finished, Briant looked across the cleared area at the gate nearest to the castle. "It's not too late to turn back."

Aithne scoffed. "You know that's not true. That stopped being an option months ago, at least for me." She let go of their hands and squared her shoulders.

"You're right," said Adrienne. "We do the bidding of the Goddess regardless of our fear. I guess I know why the Goddess picked me now. Sagart would never do this. She'd assign it to someone else."

"Sagart is too old anyway," said Briant. "Ready?"

"No," said Aithne and Adrienne together.

Aithne allowed herself a small smile and stepped out of the trees as the watch guard passed their location. They ran across the grass to the gravel road. Aithne's sword bounced against her leg.

Adrienne whispered a spell and touched the wicket gate beside the main gate. The lock clicked, and she pushed it open. They slipped through, staying in the shadows as they threaded through alleys to the main road.

When they stepped out of the alley, the sun broke through the clouds. A beam of sunlight fell on the castle.

Adrienne gasped. "That's a good sign."

Briant grinned. "Are you ready to wake people up?"

"Let's go," said Aithne.

They ran toward the castle. Aithne whispered the spell for a flame arrow, directing it at the hinges on the right side of the tall entry doors. It hit the bottom corner and licked up the outside. As they neared the steps, she pitched her voice low and spoke a wind spell, shoving her hands at the flames. The wind slammed against the wood, and the fire shot up, spreading across the surface to the other door. Guards looked over the parapet, and Briant shot a stream of water at them.

The door groaned as the hinges broke. It sagged in but remained upright, still locked to the door on the left. As Briant threw a shield around the three of them, Aithne sent a stronger wind, and the door blew in. They ran through the opening, allowing the shield to protect them from the fire.

The doors led to an oversized foyer that opened to a short staircase with a wide hall beyond, and a smaller passage to the left. Guards ran down the passage, and crossbows twanged. Bolts bounced off the shield, and someone rang the alarm bell as the sun broke the horizon, painting the clouds outside the windows red. Aithne turned, shouting a wind spell. The wind whipped around them, lifting the guards off their feet and throwing them back down the passage.

Adrienne gripped the back of Aithne's sword belt, guiding her backward to the hallway. Power surged through her, and she pulled her hands back as they reached the steps.

Grinning, she turned and ran up the stairs into the castle.

CHAPTER THIRTY-TWO ~ MEVAN

Oswin, Moira, and Lucas followed Ivan through the woods toward the castle as the sun came up. The woods were kept cut back around the castle wall, giving the watch time to see invaders. They paused near the tree line, and Lucas cast a shield spell Oswin didn't recognize. Alarm bells rang, and Ivan said, "It is signal! Let us go!"

They ran across the clearing and to a door in the castle wall. One guard on the parapet looked down, and Oswin was sure he could see them, but the guard moved on. He made a mental note to get Lucas to teach him the spell if they lived through the day.

Ivan tapped a code on the door, and the peephole slid open.

"Truth at all cost," he murmured.

Oswin frowned as the peephole closed again. He rested his hand on his sword, and the door opened. Ivan led them in with a nod to the guard, a young man who seemed to be at most fifteen.

"Truth at all costs," said the boy. He shut the door and leaned his back against it. He motioned with his hands, pointing in a quick pattern Oswin didn't understand.

Ivan nodded and led them down the narrow corridor meant to bottleneck any enemy who breached the door. Oswin searched the murder holes above, expecting arrows, but saw none.

Ivan led them unerringly through the labyrinth to a staircase leading up. Pitching his voice low, he said, "You must use the dragons' directions from here."

"How do you know this is the right place?" asked Moira.

Ivan cocked his head. "The boy—my nephew—he told me." He quickly repeated the pattern the boy had used, and Oswin realized it was the directions they'd used to navigate the labyrinth. "I must find Anton for our next step. May the Goddess walk beside you."

"And you," said Oswin. He led the others up the stairs. At the top, he turned to Moria. "Which way?"

She pulled out her beacon and held it up. "Right."

Oswin nodded. "Lead the way. Lucas, that shield would be helpful."

Lucas whispered the spell, and they stepped out of the shadows into a corridor lined with torches. It spiraled up, and they saw a guard near a torch.

Lucas looked at the others, putting a finger against his lips, his steps silent.

As they neared the guard, he scanned his surroundings. His eyes widened as they drew closer, and his jaw clenched. "No, this tower isn't haunted. Not at all." He gripped the hilt of his sword and pressed his back against the wall.

They slipped past him. When he was out of sight, Moira paused and looked around. She pointed left, and Oswin saw another flight of stairs.

He sent Moira and Lucas ahead of him. At the top, they emerged from a door on the right into another narrow corridor with several doors. Another guard stood in front of the first one and turned to face them.

The guard snorted. "Impressive shield. Lucky for me, I see through magic." He and Oswin pulled their swords.

Moira had hers ready, and she lunged, ready to slice across his torso. She gasped as her sword flew up faster than she expected and arced over her head. Oswin caught it clumsily, his eyes widening at the light weight.

He shouldered Lucas out of the way and charged at the guard, his sword in one hand and Moira's in the other.

The guard turned and ran to yank a bell cord. The bell clanged and Moira cursed, but Oswin chased the boy down and ran him through. As he fell, he pulled Moira's sword out of him, turned, and handed it back to her. "Which way?"

"Up!"

They ran past the dying guard to another staircase, racing up the steep stairs two at a time. They heard yelling, and Moira lunged, grunting at the top. Lucas followed, and when Oswin exited the stairs, Lucas and Moira were pulling a body toward him. Its head, partially severed, dragged on the floor. They tossed the bleeding corpse down the stairs. Oswin heard something bounce, but he didn't look at it.

Moira ran down the hall, her beacon held out in front of her, and stopped at a door. She pounded on it. "Tanwen!"

Oswin heard an answer from the other side as Moira motioned to him to hurry. Sheathing his sword, he muttered the spell to break the lock. Ignoring the shouting from downstairs, he touched the door and heard a snap.

Moira shouldered the door open. "Tanwen!"

Oswin shoved Lucas in and followed, pressing the door closed, already muttering a spell to block it shut.

"What are you doing?" hissed Lucas.

"We can't go out that way." He strode to the small window past Moira and the person he assumed was Tanwen. She was in a shadow, and he got little more than an impression of red hair.

"Oswin, she's shackled."

"Good." He dropped to his knees beside her. "Lucas, get the rope out of my pack." He said the spell to open the lock on her shackles, but it didn't work. He heard someone exclaim over the body on the stairs and resisted the urge to curse.

"Oswin!" hissed Moira.

He held Tanwen's hands up, casting a freeze spell on the chain. Pulling out his dagger, he smashed through the frozen iron, and Tanwen fell back.

He turned for the rope, tying it through the eye that held the remaining chain.

Lucas cast a concussive spell, and the bars in the window splintered.

Oswin looked up. "Good lad. Moira, you go down first and hold the rope steady."

She nodded. Grabbing the rope, she ran and jumped. The rope went taut as she rappelled down.

Oswin stood and pulled out his sword. "Lucas, I hope you can rappel with a load. We don't have time to get you down separately."

"What about you?"

"I'll hold them off."

Lucas nodded and reached for Tanwen, pulling her up. She murmured, and Oswin glanced at her. She was unrecognizable. Bruises and swelling covered her face as Lucas put his head through her still-shackled arms.

"Sorry, Tanwen, I need you to hold on." He took the rope and backed out the window as footsteps pounded toward the door.

Oswin readied a spell, one he had never used, had never wanted to use. He backed toward the window and looked down. Lucas was halfway down, holding Tanwen with one arm and the rope with the other. He had another ten feet to safety.

The door smashed open, and Oswin unleashed his spell. A whirlwind of fire hit the first man through the door. He screamed and fell back. The door caught fire.

Oswin cast a second one, reducing the first man and the two behind him to ash.

Lucas yelped, and the rope went slack.

The fire spread inward.

Oswin grabbed the rope and launched out the window. His stomach lurched, and he bounced off the wall. "Run!" He couldn't watch to see if they obeyed. He plunged, trying to get down before the fire reached the rope. It went slack in his hands. He looked up to see the burning end slide out the window as he fell the remaining five feet, landing on his feet, stumbling, and rolling.

Moira and Lucas, who carried Tanwen, ran around a corner. He rolled to his feet and followed them through an alley and then another.

He caught up in time to see Moira hold up her beacon, turn, and look both ways at the end of the alley before grabbing Lucas' arm and sprinting across the street. Oswin followed. He heard fighting outside the city wall. Good. The diversion worked.

Moira ran to a house next to a tall tower and pounded on the door. It opened, and she ran in, holding the door for Lucas.

"Hurry!"

Oswin ran faster, bolting through the door. She slammed it shut in time to see Lucas running up the stairs with a limp Tanwen.

Moira took his arm before he followed. She panted as she barred the door and led him down a short hall to a room with a long table. On his right, he saw cluttered bookshelves. They ran around the table and through another door into a large kitchen. Moira opened the door to a butler's pantry and yanked open a cabinet at the end.

"Go!" she hissed.

He stopped. Had she lost her mind?

"Oswin!"

He stepped closer and saw an opening. Casting a light wisp, he saw a hole.

Moira pushed him, and he tumbled in. She followed, pulling the door shut. He dimmed the light wisp, shielding it with his hand, moving back as far as he could. Moira scooted back beside him. Outside, someone pounded on the door, and he heard footsteps stride down the hall.

Voices murmured before he heard several pairs of feet pounding above them. Doors opened and slammed shut, and Oswin pulled his dagger. The boots receded, and the house fell silent. A moment later, he heard a door open, and a feminine voice said, "Your friends are safe, for now. Remain there, and I will come for you soon."

Oswin let his head fall back against the earthen wall, not caring that he dislodged dirt and pebbles that fell down the back of his shirt. "Blessed be the Goddess," he murmured as Moira began to weep.

Aithne used her wind to create as much havoc as possible, blowing people against walls and down corridors. Art tumbled off walls and pedestals. Briant tore the marble floor to shreds, and together they used the stone as projectiles against everyone who stood in their way.

Power from Adrienne pulsed through Aithne. Part of her thought of telling Adrienne to keep it in reserve, but it felt too good. She shouted her spells, and for the first time, she enjoyed her magic.

At the far end of the corridor, she saw another pair of tall doors. They were closed and guarded. They came to a perpendicular corridor, and she heard a noise to her left. A crowd, filling the entire width of the corridor, shambled toward them. She recognized several faces—Finley, Cadell, Greer, Muirne—and her stomach clenched.

"*Tanad!*" she shouted.

"I see them!" yelled Briant. Aithne glanced over her shoulder. Briant wasn't looking her way; he was looking at the crowd coming from the right side.

Aithne cast a whirlwind, directing it at the *tanad*. They slowed but didn't stop. From somewhere in the shuffling crowd, she heard several voices shouting spells she didn't understand. Saphir stirred in her mind, and Aithne cast a wall of fire, closing off the corridor and pushing it into the mass of bodies. She heard screaming, but not enough to account for the stench of burned bodies.

The floor shook. She stumbled, jostling Adrienne. They grabbed for each other as Briant erected a barrier of broken marble to block his side of the corridor.

Turning back to the corridor ahead of them, Aithne noticed one door at the end of the hall hanging open. The guards were gone. She grinned. "Come on!"

They ran down the hall as a couple of *tanad* climbed over Briant's barrier. When they reached the doors, no one stood in their way. The room beyond was dark.

Adrienne put out her arms to stop them. "This is too easy."

"Is She telling you something?"

Adrienne nodded. "Go."

They strode in, conjuring light wisps they sent up and ahead. The inky darkness made their light appear dim. The door slammed, and Aithne jumped. Their light wisps went out.

They froze, reaching for each other. Aithne heard one footstep.

Adrienne let go of her hand. Her tattoos glowed as she raised her arms. With the rustle of velvet, the curtains over the windows fell, flooding the throne room with the first rays of the sun.

A woman stood beside the throne. She wore brown trews and a blue tunic, and a white braid hung over her shoulder. She clapped slowly. "If that isn't an entrance, I don't know what is." She sat, crossing her right leg over her left and leaning her elbow on the arm of the throne. You've shown an ability to destroy corridors and drapes. I do hope that's not the best you can do."

Aithne shivered. The woman's voice compelled her to take an involuntary step. "It's her," she murmured. "It's Raca."

The woman chuckled. "I knew bringing Tanwen here was the right choice. It brought you right into my hands."

Aithne's heart raced. "Ceann was right," she whispered.

"That doesn't mean we've lost," growled Briant. He grabbed her arm, reinforcing the shield.

The woman covered her mouth. "Oh! Oh, my! A shield!" She waved her hand, and the shield crumbled around them. She laughed. "What's next?"

Briant raised his hands, pulling moisture from the air. It coalesced into mist as the room brightened. A small part of Aithne's mind noticed that all of their tattoos were glowing.

Adrienne cast a cold spell as Briant rebuilt the shield, and Aithne blew the frozen mist into shards toward their opponent.

Raca waved her hand, and the shards blew back, ricocheting off the shield Briant had finished only just in time. Adrienne took the shield as a thick cloud blew toward them, stinking of sulfur. Aithne coughed as she cast wind and blew it back. Raca stood, laughing, in her own poison.

Adrienne grasped Briant's arm and sang praises to the Goddess. Briant shouted a spell, flinging arrows made of holy water toward the throne. Raca waved her hand, and the arrows exploded, bursting into flashes of blue, red, and purple. As the magic flared, Adrienne choked. She gasped twice, remaining steady, and muttered prayers in a low voice.

Aithne reached for her link with Briant. *Make steam!* When he did, she added a swirling wind, sending a steam cyclone rushing toward the throne with a deafening roar that made the windows rattle.

Raca said something Aithne didn't hear and waved her hand, turning their cyclone into shards of ice that shot back at them, shredding their shield. Aithne ducked, turning her back and gasping as ice pierced her skin and clothing. She threw another shield around them and ice pinged off it.

Briant grabbed Adrienne's hand. He raised their arms in the air, gesturing widely and shouting a spell under-girded with Adrienne's prayer. A stone wall rose from the marble floor in front of them, giving them cover.

The floor trembled, and the wall fell as the ground beneath it turned to lava, which spread toward the door and behind them, forcing them to move forward and closer to the windows.

Aithne felt panic creep around the edge of her consciousness as they moved away from the blast of heat. Adrienne touched her shoulder, and the fear dissipated. Adrienne took the shield from her, praying more loudly.

Briant forced water through the lava, creating explosive steam directed toward Raca. It engulfed the dais where she stood.

Aithne held her breath, waiting for the steam to clear, praying under her breath to see Raca's corpse.

Instead, she heard Raca's laughter before. A sudden crack of thunder made them jump, and a black hole formed in the air. It absorbed the heat and energy, and the floor solidified. She raised a hand toward them, flinging back the fiery whirlwind filled with glass shards they'd sent toward her.

Trusting the shield to protect them, Aithne cast several fire-wrapped wind pockets from multiple angles. They raced toward Raca, leaving trails of light behind them.

Raca raised her hands and absorbed the fire.

Aithne trembled with sudden anger as Briant cast a spell that sent a wave of mud toward Raca. She yelled a tempest spell to push it faster.

Raca shouted a spell, and in a single blink, she stood in front of the shield Adrienne struggled to hold.

"I've enjoyed this, but unfortunately, I have to work today." She touched the shield, and Adrienne dropped to the floor, screaming.

Raca waved a hand, turning the spells back. Aithne's wind threw her back against the wall. The stone softened long enough to encase her hands. Her ears rang, and the back of her head throbbed. She noted absently that Adrienne writhed on the floor, and Briant's mud wave had frozen around his legs halfway to his knees.

Raca smiled, surveying her work. "Now I have a spell for you. My people think there has to be a ceremony for this, and I didn't see a reason to correct that." She turned to Aithne. "Soon it won't matter what anyone thinks, but I'll know every thought, every feeling, every motive. Once I have Lledrith, no one will stop me."

She began reciting a spell as she prowled toward Aithne.

Pain lanced through Aithne, leaving her breathless. Her vision blurred, and her heart pounded with fear she'd never felt before. She heard Saphir shriek. Was it outside, or was it in her head?

She squeezed her eyes shut against the pain. Her lungs constricted, and she couldn't scream. A sound caught her attention. She opened her eyes. Dark smoke appeared to shroud everything. Briant's hand moved in a spell behind Raca's back, and Adrienne struggled to her knees, her lips moving and her eyes closed.

For a second, Aithne relaxed and reached for her connection with Briant. *Thank you for protecting Lledrith. Tell Mama I love her.*

Briant scoffed in her head but didn't reply. She closed her eyes and waited for her death.

Saphir shrieked again, and she heard fire. Another dragon roared: Vask. The sound startled her, and her eyes flew open. He breathed fire, too, the sound somehow deeper than Saphir's. Burning bodies fell past the windows from the parapet, the fire cutting their screams short.

Raca stepped in front of her. Her form blurred, but everything around her was in sharp focus. Aithne's breath caught, and she felt a pull she couldn't describe. Pain ripped through her. Was Raca tearing her in half?

Raca shouted the words of her spell, her arms raised wide, a note of triumph in her voice.

Words flooded into Aithne's head. She whispered them, increasing the volume when she was able.

Briant's movements widened, and Adrienne stood, shouting the same words Aithne did.

Raca's eyes widened, and she backed up a few paces. She shook her head in disbelief, but continued her spell. Her body came into focus. The words stopped, and she stumbled, gasping. Her mouth dropped opened. She screamed, and the wall released Aithne's hands.

Aithne stepped forward. Her body felt strong as she followed Raca, yelling the words she didn't recognize so loudly her throat hurt.

Raca tried to run, but colors started exploding in clouds from her body, forming into feminine shapes. They reached for her, pushing her toward the windows. She ducked and tried to run, but the colors surrounded her. Aithne kept screaming, following Raca, pouring the grief and anger from the past weeks into the spell.

The colors lifted Raca off her feet and exploded. Raca flew back several feet into the far wall, partially collapsing it.

Aithne stopped, swaying, watching to see if she rose. A column of fire fell on Raca's body, followed by two more.

Aithne took a step back as heat blasted through the hole. A shield she didn't cast rippled around her. She saw a flash of silver scales. Her strength evaporated. She felt her body fall as everything went black.

Oswin didn't know how long they hid in the small dark hole, but they heard fighting outside. Part of him wanted to go join the diversion, or to tell them they were done and could retreat. But something kept him still, waiting.

He jumped when a dragon shrieked, and Moira grabbed his arm.

"What are dragons doing here?" he whispered.

The dragon shrieked again, followed by a deep roar and the sound of fire.

Moira gasped and crawled to the entrance. "Come on! Quick!"

He followed her, and she ran out of the kitchen.

"Lucas! We need your help!"

Dragons roared as Oswin ran out the door, nearly crashing into Moira. She was standing by the door, looking up at several dragons.

Lucas ran out and turned to see what they were watching. When he saw the dragons, his face went white. "Laoch, preserve us," he muttered. He turned and ran back inside. "Tell me when they're gone."

Moira gasped as two dragons engaged, one green and one silver. "Gautier," she moaned.

Oswin squinted as they passed in front of the sun. "Blessed Goddess, they got her?"

Moira nodded, her hand pressed to her mouth as tears spilled down her cheeks.

The dragons spiraled around each other in a deadly dance. From below, it looked like a violent storm in dragon form—claws flashing, wings buffeting, occasional bursts of flame illuminating the smoke of the burning city. The silver dragon bit Gautier. She didn't bleed.

A red flash caught his attention, and Moira stiffened.

"What's wrong?" asked Oswin.

"The red one—Raine—is mine," she murmured. "The bronze one is Razo. Greer must be dead."

Raine darted around Razo. Oswin heard a twang, and Moira screamed. The bolt pierced Razo's wing at the shoulder joint. He roared, breathing fire toward Raine as he banked, flapping his good wing to keep from falling. Raine flapped hard, climbing steeply, and the fire passed under her tail, hitting the one remaining ballista. It burst into flames, and Raine shot fire at Razo. It hit him in the chest, pushing him back. Vask swooped in and bit Razo's good wing, tearing half of it off. Razo plunged. Vask and Raine blew fire at him together, and he crashed into the shrine of Laoch in a shower of splintered wood and tiles that burst into flames.

Oswin heard dragons shrieking in the distance. Another formation approached.

The silver dragon bit Gautier's throat, tearing out a chunk of flesh, and she dropped from the sky.

Vask and Raine banked, flying toward the newcomers as the silver dragon blew flames, setting Gautier and half a city block on fire. Screaming rent the air.

Moira grabbed his arm. "Raine says we have to get to the castle! Lucas, let's go!" She sprinted away, and he followed. Lucas caught up as they ran. They wove through alleys, avoiding pockets of fighting in the streets.

A loud explosion shook the ground. Debris shot into the air as he reached Moira, and grabbing her arm, he pulled her into an alley; they ducked down, pressing their bodies against the wall nearest the explosion. Lucas rounded the corner, sliding in beside them, constructing his shield as he ran. Lumps of rock and brick rained down, bouncing off the far wall and pelting the shield.

Suddenly, everything went quiet. He heard only the sound of debris falling around them.

Moira's eyes widened. "Come on!" She bounced off the inside of Lucas' shield. "Lucas!"

He waved his hand. "Go!"

Oswin pelted after Moira, ducking out of the alley and running to the end of the street. A dragon shrieked and fell, burning, onto the remaining part of the castle roof that hadn't been burning. It roared to life, completely engulfed. He choked on the stench of smoke and burning bodies.

More bodies, hundreds of them, lay on the ground, and he saw a gaping hole in the wall.

They ran around bodies as best they could, jumping over and stepping on them when necessary. Something told Oswin they needed to hurry, but he didn't know why.

When they reached the hole, they paused, weapons drawn. Oswin peered around the wall. Three bodies lay sprawled on the floor—two women and a man. One woman had red hair.

He jumped over what was left the of wall and ran, the others close behind. "No! No!" He dropped to his knees between Adrienne and Aithne. Aithne lay in a pool of blood, and her face and hands were red and welted. Though bruised and bleeding from minor cuts, the others otherwise appeared unharmed.

Moira crouched beside Briant. She touched his neck as she squinted through the dust at Aithne.

"Oswin, is Adrienne breathing?"

He nodded, fear and relief roaring through him.

Moira stood. "We have to get them back to the Spire. Lucas, can you manage Briant?"

"Yes," said Lucas.

Moira hoisted Aithne onto her shoulders with a grunt, and Oswin scooped up Adrienne gently. As he ran back to the Spire, he muttered, "Don't die, don't die," to both his sister and the Goddess.

The woman who had met them before was waiting outside again. She held the door open. "Take them in the sitting room," she said as they approached. Someone had pushed back the furniture in the room to the left of the door, and Oswin eased Adrienne to the floor before turning to help Moira with Aithne. He avoided looking at her pale, blood-covered face.

Two more people in black robes came from somewhere in the house. One knelt beside Aithne and began cleaning the blood off her. Oswin backed away, joining Lucas beside the wall as Moira and the other two tended the wounded.

Lucas was pale and fidgeted with the hem of his tunic. "What happened out there?"

Oswin shook his head. His voice was rough as he answered, "Right now, only the Goddess knows." He reached for a cushion from the nearest chair and dropped it on the floor. "If you pray, this is a good time to do it."

Chapter Thirty-Three ~ Mevan

Everything hurt. Tanwen floated out of the darkness toward a vague light. She heard something explode and felt an alarm from Quillon. When she opened her eyes, the light pierced her skull, and she groaned. She ignored the pain and struggled to get up.

A woman in black robes turned away from the window, placing her hand on Tanwen's shoulder. "Be still."

"What's happening?"

"One of the castle walls blew out. You can do nothing about it in your condition."

Pain ripped through Tanwen. "Quillon!"

Stay there, beloved. Saphir and Vask are still flying.

Tanwen swallowed a sob and lay back against the pillow. "Where am I?"

"At the Spire."

She blinked at the woman, who picked up a mug, holding it in both hands. She whispered something and the tattoos on her hands glowed faintly. Leaning forward, she put one hand under the pillow and tilted Tanwen's head up, bringing the mug to her lips. "Drink this. It will help restore the vitality stolen from you."

Tanwen drank as well as she could. The liquid was warm and a little viscous, tasting of mint and rosehips. It soothed her throat. When the woman took the cup away, she asked, "What does that mean? Restore the vitality?"

The woman poured more water into the mug. Her back was to the window, casting a shadow over her face. When she sat on the stool close to her head, Tanwen saw her clearly.

"You're not Neva."

The woman smiled. "I'm not. I am Catriona. Neva is downstairs. You had a powerful wasting spell cast on you. The Goddess had to work through two of us to counter it. Now we need to fix the damage it caused, which will help you heal better and faster."

There was a commotion downstairs, and Catriona glanced at the door. "I am needed downstairs, but I will send someone to sit with you." She picked up the mug. "Can you hold this?"

Tanwen's arms trembled as she raised them. Catriona whispered over the cup again, placing one hand on

Tanwen's forehead. Her skin was warm, and a shiver ran down Tanwen's spine as if Catriona chased cold from her bones. She placed the mug in Tanwen's hands and left the room.

The sounds of fighting outside ceased. She frowned, wondering what happened, but too tired to care. Sipping the remaining tea, she rested the cup against her chest, allowing the warmth to seep through her skin.

The door opened, and Lucas came in. He had blood on his clothes.

A whisper of concern pinged. "Is that yours?"

Lucas cocked his head, looking at her before glancing at his clothes. "Oh, the blood? No. Actually, it's Briant's."

Panic shot through the fatigue as Lucas sat on the stool by the bed. "He'll be fine. The Seers are healing them, but they'll have a long recovery."

"They?"

He nodded. "Briant, Adrienne, and Aithne."

Tanwen's breath caught in her chest. "Aithne? She's here?"

"She's downstairs. Neva told me to come tell you she is safe and being cared for, and there's nothing for you to do. She said Quillon might get details from Vask and Saphir."

"Did you see which way the dragons went?"

"They're here, surrounding the Spire. When the castle wall exploded, a lot of the *tanad* dropped, and the rest were easy to take care of. Saphir burned the weapons on the roofs, and the focus now, out there, at least, is putting out the fires." He took her hand. "They're safe. Aithne is safe. You need to rest."

She nodded and squeezed Lucas' hand as tears filled her eyes. "Thank you."

"I didn't do much, really. Grunt work, mostly. But you're welcome. I'm glad you're safe, Tanwen. We were worried about you." He put his other hand on top of hers. "Rest. I'll stay with you."

She closed her eyes. *Quillon?*

He is correct. We are safe. I am outside your window. Vask and Saphir guard the other sides.

Have they told you anything?

Only that Aithne and Briant were in grave peril until the full power of the Goddess surged through them, and they killed Raca.

Relief made her muscles feel weak. *She's dead?*

She will no longer hurt anyone. The threat is significantly less severe now. Only human fighters who remain loyal to her remain, and the three of us will see they do not bother you.

Tears burned in her eyes. *It's really over?*

It is. Soon we will rebuild, which may have troubles of its own. We will deal with that when the time comes. Rest, beloved.

She sniffed, and Lucas dried her tears as she suc-
cumbed to sleep.

Pain jolted Briant from utter darkness into blinding
light. He gasped and squeezed his eyes shut.

Someone murmured, "You're going to be fine, Briant." The voice was familiar, but he couldn't place it.

It is Moira, said Vask in his mind. *We are at the Spire.*

Briant's brow furrowed, and his head pulsed as he
tried to figure out what that meant. Someone wiped his
face with a damp cloth and then laid it over his eyes.
More voices murmured, but he couldn't make out the
words.

Sensing his confusion, Vask sent images into his
mind: Aithne trapped with her hands embedded in a
wall, Raca stalking her and chanting, and then flying
across the room into a wall, Vask breathing fire to destroy her body, black ash in the wind.

Briant let the knowledge filter through his sluggish
brain, dredging up his own memories of the battle, the
fear, and the determination not to let Raca win. Chanting the words from Lledrith, joined by Adrienne and
Aithne.

Panic lanced through him, and he sat up.

"Whoa, steady on, Briant!" Raya put a hand on his shoulder. "You're safe!"

"Adrienne—" His voice sounded raspy, and speaking burned his throat.

Raya reached for a cup and helped him drink. "They're fine. Adrienne, Aithne, Tanwen—they're here and on the road to recovery."

Briant gulped the water and looked around. He was on the floor of what looked like the front room of a house. His head swam, and he lay back down, reaching for Vask as he covered his eyes with his hands. *This is the Spire?*

You are in the Seers' living quarters. The tower is next door.

Raya nudged his hands aside and laid the cloth over his eyes. She'd dampened it with something that smelled lemony, but also bitter.

Are the others really well?

Well is an overstatement. Their injuries, like yours, will take time to heal, but they survived and are out of danger. Tanwen is awake. Aithne and Adrienne as still unconscious.

Briant's head throbbed, but he felt his body relax. *What of the others?*

Oswin and Lucas have minor injuries. Ceann reports injuries but few fatalities in the diversion group. She has not answered queries about your family, but several are unaccounted for.

Fear edged in, and he pushed it aside. Worrying about them would change nothing, but prayer might. He sent his mind to his meadow. A wave of pride and love from Vask followed him, and he let himself smile as he reached for the Goddess.

He expected to find himself in the meadow. Instead, he opened his eyes on top of a mountain overlooking the rest of the range. He turned and Vask joined him. "Do you know where we are?"

"Not precisely, but somewhere in the northern reaches."

That is correct, said Lledrith. *This is where your next task will be.*

Briant shielded his eyes from the sun as a black dragon soared toward them. When it got closer, he saw deep red scales. He felt a jolt of shock from Vask. "What's wrong?"

That—it cannot be. She cannot still live.

She does, said Lledrith. *You must find her. Your task is to rebuild the Wybrens, and they will require dragons.*

"Vask, who is that?"

"Hedda. My mother. Ailin's dragon."

Well done, my child.

Adrienne squinted in the dark at a distant glow. Something about it looked odd, and she couldn't tell what it was.

The glow dimmed and enlarged, and she felt a hand caress her hair. A human shape appeared in the light.

You have proved yourself worthy of the office, Bealban Dia. History will remember not only your bravery but also your faith and wisdom. We have much to do, and the work has only begun.

Adrienne's heart thudded. *Holy One?* Her answer was a wave of love and assurance, with a hint of amusement.

Do not fret, Adrienne. I have been with you in every trial. You will face nothing as arduous as the battle against evil you won. The challenges you endured have shaped you into the person I need you to be for the future. Much has changed, and you will lead our people into the new age. First, there must be a season of rest and healing.

Holy One, what of the others?

They live and must also heal.

Relief flooded through her, and she released the tension she hadn't been aware of. *And the purge?*

It proceeds according to My plan. You will learn more in time. Rest, child.

Adrienne smiled as her weariness lifted. Her eyes fluttered open, and she squinted at a plaster ceiling.

"She's awake," called a strange voice.

"Thank the Goddess!" Oswin appeared beside her and took her hand. "Adrienne?"

She blinked. "It's over. Now it begins."

Chapter Thirty-Four
~ Mevan

Three days later, Lucas came to Tanwen's room. "Ceann and Moira are here to see you. Neva said you can come downstairs to see them if you want, or I can bring them to you."

She pushed back her covers. "No, I'll go down. Give me a minute to dress. I'll probably need help on the stairs."

Lucas stepped out and closed the door. Tanwen stood, gritting her teeth against the pain, and pulled on a tunic, trews, and wool stockings. Her boots sat under the window, but she shuffled past them. Lucas waited in the hall, and she followed him to the stairs. Leaning on him and holding the stair rail, she reached the bottom floor without falling.

Lucas led her to the sitting room. Ceann and Moira stepped forward, wrapping their arms around her. For a moment, she clung to her friends. Then her legs weakened, and they helped her to a chair.

Moira took her hand. "You look better than the last time I saw you. How do you feel?"

"Better than the last time you saw me, which isn't saying much."

"We'll take whatever improvements we can get," said Ceann. She bit her lip and leaned forward. "Things are in flux right now. The king and the heir are dead, and no one knows where the queen and the other children are. Two councilors are still alive, but they're the two who were most vocal about dragons staying at the Keeps. They're recruiting like-minded men."

Tanwen's mouth went dry. "That doesn't sound good. Are the Keeps habitable?"

"Not the Eastern Keep," said Ceann.

"The Western Keep is for people, but not for dragons until we get the rest of the tunnels open," said Moira.

"If we can," said Tanwen. "There's no lair at the Southern Keep, even if we could go there. Do they have a solution?"

Ceann bit her lip and glanced at the floor. "They want us to ask if they can go to Commain."

Tanwen's breath caught, and she sat back. "They want to banish the dragons?"

Moira snorted. "According to them, the dragons didn't do much to protect Slan, and in some cases, they were weaponized against us. Vask, Raine, and Quillon defended us against *tanad* dragons, and between them, two thirds of the city burned. It's all rhetoric, but it's gaining ground."

"But Wybrens are part of the fabric of Slannish culture," said Tanwen.

"We know that, but everything is in shambles. We only have seven grown dragons and a handful of hatchlings left. Their logic is if we have to build society again from the ground up, let's have it the way we want it, and that means no Wybrens."

"Do I need to come talk to them?"

"No," said Moira, clenching her jaw. "Sullivan was one of their first recruits. He told them what happened to Liam."

Tanwen's mouth dropped, and she sat back feeling like she'd been gut-punched.

Footsteps and murmuring voices made them turn their attention to the hall on the other side of the arch.

Adrienne stepped in. She wore a loose robe, and her blonde hair was loose. Her bruises were fading, but she still walked slowly. "I don't want to interrupt."

"No, come in," said Tanwen. "Your timing is good, actually."

As Adrienne sank into a chair, Tanwen told her what they'd discussed. When she finished, Adrienne smiled. "Interesting. During my meditation, the Goddess made it clear she wants Wybrens in Commain."

Ceann frowned. "That seems too easy."

Adrienne shrugged. "Sometimes when there is a push, there is also a pull. Slan had a societal shift during the last wandering darkness, and it appears ready for another. Our royal council has begun assembling a regency for our princess. If the Wybrens are effectively being banished, I have the power to offer asylum per the wishes of the Goddess."

"I wouldn't say we're being banished," said Moira.

"Wouldn't you?" asked Ceann. "They want the dragons confined to Keeps. I made it clear that the Keeps cannot shelter them, and I got the impression that it was up to us to figure it out."

"Even better," said Tanwen. "Tell them if they don't have a viable solution, we'll leave. Adrienne, do you have a place big enough for us? We can shelter here for a while, but there isn't enough space or resources for us long-term."

"Several villages in the northeast were razed by the invasion from the north. It appears Aramach was in league with Dorchada, and we are already taking steps to secure that border more tightly. It seems an ideal place for Wybrens."

Moira tapped her chin. "I don't know how much help we'll be. Our numbers are way down."

"For now," said Adrienne. "There are Commainish children interested in training."

"That's great," said Ceann, "but we don't have enough dragons. The only ones alive are bonded, with the exception of a few hatchlings who won't be ready for decades."

"The remaining dragons will give us protection we don't have currently," said Adrienne. "Would it help if I talk to the men taking control?"

Ceann laughed. "I doubt it. They barely listen to Moira and me."

"What about Oswin?" asked Moira.

Ceann squinted. "Maybe. I'd feel better knowing we have a place to go before we give them an ultimatum."

Tanwen leaned forward. "How about this? Moira, Raya, and Sine go to Commain to look at the area and assess its viability. Ceann, you handle the council. If we need to buy time, you can be the good guy and I'll be the bad guy. They won't trust me anyway. If we need a man to speak for us, we can bring in Oswin or Briant. We can work out training details later. It might be that we do ground training until we figure out the dragon situation."

Moira nodded. "Adrienne, can you or Oswin guide us where we need to go? It probably won't be good if we just show up."

"I don't know if I can, but I can arrange for an escort," said Adrienne.

"Moira," said Ceann, "how fast do you think you can decide about the new site?"

"With travel time? Four days? Five? It depends partly on what we find."

Ceann bit her lip. "We need an interim solution, then. Right before we left, Sullivan told me the dragons need to leave Mevan."

Moira nodded. "That's what we're working on."

Tanwen, said Quillon, *Venka has passed a message from the council. They want us gone tonight, or they will not guarantee the safety of dragons or Wybrens.*

Tanwen gasped, her shock mirrored on Ceann's and Moira's faces.

Adrienne frowned. "What is it?"

"We have to leave tonight," said Tanwen.

Ceann stood. "I'm going back. They're being ridiculous. We can't go to the Keeps, so where do they expect us to go?"

"The landing site?" asked Moira.

That is acceptable for the short term if you and Aithne can go, said Quillon.

Tanwen pushed herself out of the chair. "I'll talk to Neva about moving Aithne."

"Ceann," said Adrienne, "shall I send Oswin with you, or is it better to keep Commain out of the equation for now?"

Ceann looked at Moira. "What do you think? I don't want to give them an easy out. But if we take Oswin, he can approach it from a diplomatic standpoint."

Moira crossed her arms. "I say we take every male willing to go. They've threatened our safety."

Tanwen nodded grimly. "A show of force might send a message that they don't have as much power as they think they do."

Ceann rested her hand on her sword. "If Oswin is willing, we'd welcome him. Tanwen, go find Neva. Moira and I will gather bodyguards, and we'll have Quillon keep you updated."

Tanwen found Neva in the kitchen and told her what had happened.

Neva's face hardened. "Have they agreed to the landing site?"

"It hasn't been suggested yet."

She took the pot she'd been stirring away from the fire. "I'll get someone to see to this. I'm going to the castle with them."

"So you think it will be all right to move Aithne?"

"It sounds like it will be more dangerous if she stays, but I mean to make sure we transport her as safely as possible. They will agree to my demands or answer to the Seers. Go upstairs and rest. One of us will pack your belongings, and we will leave before dark."

"We?"

"If Aithne must go, so must I. I doubt there's anyone at the landing site, let alone a healer." She gripped Tanwen's arm. "Aithne is the Lavban Dia. She will get the best care we can give her."

Tanwen's eyes filled with tears. "Does she still need to be that? It's so dangerous."

Neva's face softened, and she touched Tanwen's cheek. She'll be Lavban Dia forever. History will remember her, and it will not be dangerous for much longer. We will protect her. Go on now and rest."

Tanwen hobbled to the stairs as Briant came down.

"I was coming to find you." He descended the remaining stair. "Are you coming up?"

Tanwen nodded. "I've been ordered back to bed. We leave for the landing site in a few hours."

Briant frowned. "That sounds ominous." He offered his arm. "I'll help you up."

Tanwen took his arm and repeated the news again as they climbed. They'd reached her room when she finished. "So that's what I know. Why were you looking for me?"

"Vask and I will have to head north for a while. Perhaps the Goddess knows how to solve the dragon shortage. I keep dreaming about Vask's mother."

Tanwen sank onto the bed. "How do you know she's Vask's mother?"

"He was with me during the first vision."

"When do you leave?"

"I'm not sure, but not before we move to the landing site. We might go with the others to Commain first."

"Don't over-do it."

He chuckled. "I'll do my best." He paused in the doorway and looked back, his face serious. "Tanwen, I want to apologize for how I left things between us before I went to Commain. It felt like I suddenly became unimportant, and I acted like a selfish child."

Tanwen sighed. "That feels like a hundred years ago, and I knew you were having difficulty, but I didn't know how to fix it."

"If there's anything I've learned lately, it's that you never leave things unsaid or unresolved."

"You've gotten wiser. I'm glad we're friends again."

"Me too. I'll let you rest."

***

The sun was high when Raya stalked into the castle with Ceann, Moira, Neva, Briant, Oswin, and a dozen Wreiddons. They carried weapons, and the men wore leather jerkins.

Much of the castle was in ruins, and the damage took Raya's breath away. "What happened here?"

"Aithne, Adrienne, and me, mostly," said Briant. "We didn't set anything on fire—that was the dragons—but we left a trail of destruction."

Raya snorted. "This doesn't seem like overkill?"

"We were a diversion," said Briant, "or that's what we thought. We had to make noise to be effective."

Ceann led them through the corridors to the residential wing, issuing orders to gather the council as she went. Most of them had gathered in the room they'd chosen as a council chamber when they arrived.

The two oldest men, both dressed in finery, were the last to arrive. One looked down his nose at the group. "Wybren Ceann, why have you brought a mob?"

"They're not a mob. They're our protectors."

"Against what?" asked Sullivan.

"You," said Moira, "or whoever decided to threaten us with harm if the dragons don't leave."

"Threaten you?" asked the first man. "Nobody threatened you."

"That's not the message we received, Councilor Odran. Someone here told Wybren Lassair our safety is not guaranteed if the dragons don't leave by tonight. We are responding according to the information we have." She raised her hand as several men protested. "Whether you meant to convey harm is irrelevant. What is relevant is that you have demanded the dragons leave, but you did not propose a place for them to stay. Neither of the Keeps can house them. Do you expect them to remain outside, exposed to the elements, while we clear the tunnels at the Western Keep, or do you have another suggestion?"

"I, for one, have no idea what you're talking about," said Odran. "Lomman, do you know what this is about?"

"Enough!"

Raya jumped as Briant, Oswin, and Neva stepped forward.

Speaking in unison, they said, "Cruthadair, Mother Goddess, grants your wish. The dragons will depart. When you seek their protection, you will not find it. I will remove my blessings from you and give them to one more worthy. You will seek my face, and I will turn from you. You will cry out to me, but I will not answer until your hearts forsake your false gods and turn to me. Listen to the prophets I send to instruct you. If your hearts learn the truth, I will know, and I will gather you to myself. If you fail, there will be no relief from your troubles. They will follow you to the grave. Heed my words, mortals, and repent!"

The three of them turned as one and stalked out the door, leaving the council blinking in disbelief. Ceann watched them go and then turned back to the council. "We require a carriage for transporting our wounded to the landing site and a provision wagon. We need them at the Spire within two hours to reach the landing site before nightfall. Make it happen, or face the Seers."

Raya glared at the speechless men as they left them. She strode out of the castle with the others. When they got outside, fat snowflakes fell. She snorted. "Great. More snow. Ceann, what just happened in there?"

Ceann shook her head. "No idea, but I hope I never see anything like that again."

Chapter Thirty-Five ~ Slan

The darkness surrounding Aithne felt warm and soft. She'd gotten there in a wave of agonizing pain. Now she basked in the relief, content to let her mind remain blank.

Lledrith stirred.

Good, Aithne thought. *At least you didn't fall into the wrong hands.*

I would not let that happen, answered Lledrith. Her voice was warm and soothing, rolling through Aithne like a healing balm.

Aithne sighed. *Am I dead?*

Not yet.

Her brow furrowed. That wasn't Lledrith's voice. *Saphir?*

I am here, and I will be here when you wake.

When I wake? What if I don't want to?

If you die, I will die with you.

Aithne let the information roll around in her head for a while.

Is there anything worth living for? Can't I be done?

A period of silence followed before Lledrith said, *You have accomplished the most difficult tasks, but you are not finished. The remaining work will be less arduous, but still must be done.*

A wave of disappointment flowed through her. *But it's so comfortable here.*

Do not fret. You will stay here until it is time for you to return.

She tried to put her disappointment aside. Returning meant pain and conflict. The thought alone proved debilitating.

Rest, said Saphir. *I will rest as well.*

Aithne sank into her previous oblivion. When it lightened again, she saw herself teaching a group of children about dragons. This version of herself was older, and when she looked closer, she saw contentment, even happiness. But she leaned on a walking stick, and years of pain had lined her face.

While most children scattered, two stayed put. Twins, a boy and a girl, with blond hair. They hugged her and called her Mama. The scene expanded to include Saphir and a silver hatchling.

We have work to do, whispered Saphir.

Let it begin, Lledrith agreed.

Aithne felt a gentle push from behind, and an equally gentle pull from ahead. Despite her desire to resist, she found herself unable to. She felt her fingers twitch. Her chest rose as she inhaled, and her lower back throbbed. She groaned, protesting at the pain.

A man's voice said, "Aithne?" A hand took hers.

Her eyelids felt heavy, but she forced her eyes open. A blurry face appeared. She blinked to clear her vision, and Oswin squeezed her hand.

"Aithne?"

Her heart skipped a beat, and she tried to smile. "Hi."

"Welcome back."

"Th-thanks," she stammered.

He smiled. "You must be parched." He let go of her hand and turned to pour a cup of water. "Adrienne drank a whole pitcher when she woke up."

He helped her sit up, propping pillows behind her. She felt stiff and sore, and something deep inside ached. "How long have I been here? Where are we?"

Oswin handed her the cup. "Five days, and we're at the Spire."

Aithne sipped the lukewarm water. She couldn't muster the energy to be surprised.

The shutters on the window across the room were closed, the slats propped half open, and she saw snow falling in fat flakes.

"Is it over?"

"Raca is dead, so that part is over. But we have to leave Mevan sooner than expected. The men who stepped into the power vacuum want the dragons gone, and Saphir refuses to leave without you. Neva isn't pleased about moving you."

"Is my mother alive?"

"She's here. She hasn't left your side in days, so we made her go to bed for a while. Not that it did much good; she went downstairs with Lucas a while ago. I'll get her."

"No, if they got her out of bed, there's a reason. You promise she's whole?"

"Physically, she's on the mend. Emotionally? Well, I don't think any of us will be whole for a while. I'm glad you're awake, though. I was starting to worry."

Her face warmed, and she held up the cup. "Why?"

He took the cup and refilled it. "You were unconscious for longer than I thought you would be. It scared me." He gave her the cup. "That can wait until later."

She heard rushed footsteps on the stairs.

I told Quillon you are awake, said Saphir as the door opened.

Tanwen looked in. "Aithne?"

Aithne choked on tears, and Oswin took the cup from her. Tears blurred her vision, and she felt her mother's embrace. The fear she had shoved aside for months burst out in hoarse sobs that wracked her with pain. She felt Tanwen's arms tighten, and her hand cupped the back of Aithne's head. When the pain became too great, she breathed deeply to bring it and the tears under control. Sniffling, she pulled away and leaned against the pillows. Oswin was gone, and she wondered when he'd left.

Tanwen blinked away tears, and Aithne saw yellow and purple bruises. Her breath caught, and she reached a trembling hand to touch Tanwen's cheek. "Oh, Mama."

Tanwen covered her hand. "It's better than it was. The swelling is almost gone."

Tears filled Aithne's eyes again. "What did they do to you?"

"It doesn't matter now. It's over. As soon as Neva clears you to fly, we're going to Commain and starting a new life."

"How? Why aren't we going back to the Western Keep?"

"The Keeps were damaged. We can't go back there anytime soon, there isn't room for all of us at the landing site. We're moving the Wybren training to Commain, where they aren't hostile to dragons." Her voice hardened. "Things are different now."

"I know," said Aithne. She looked at the bedspread. "It's not your fault."

"What?"

"Papa. You didn't kill him. You released him from Raca's bondage."

Tanwen's eyes brimmed with tears, and she pressed her lips together. "I hoped it wasn't him, that it was the *tanad* who tried to kill me before. But I knew in my gut he wasn't *tanad*."

"We've lost everything except each other and our dragons."

"Not everything. We still have friends left."

"Will you be able to liaise with Mevan from Commain? Or will you have to stay here?"

Tanwen clenched her jaw. "Everyone is going. Following Liam's death, a rumor began that I was either too foolish to notice Raca's influence over him, or that I killed him to prevent exposure that I knew. Moira said it would die, but it spread, and some of the new councilors believe it."

Aithne picked up the cup and drank. "Who is going?"

"Everyone."

Aithne shook her head. "Who is left?"

Tanwen stilled, and her voice caught. "We lost Finley, Gitta, and Alina. Eilis too, most likely. No one has heard from her or Umha."

The door creaked open, and Neva looked in. "Oswin said you're awake."

Tanwen turned. "She is. Do you need to look her over?"

"Yes, but I need a word with you first."

Tanwen leaned forward and kissed Aithne's forehead. "I'm going to get Sine to make you some arda."

"I'd love that."

They stepped out, and Neva pulled the door shut. Aithne leaned back against the pillows. *Saphir?*

Love and joy flowed through their bond. *I am here.*

What did Raca do to me? I feel like half of me is missing, and it hurts so much, I wish the Goddess had let me die.

Beloved, you remain whole. Raca was trading bodies with you. I saw her pulling you out of your body, and I was powerless to stop it. The part that was torn has not healed yet, but Lledrith assures me it will.

She sniffled. *So that spell we cast together killed her?*

No. Lledrith told me it bound your souls to the correct bodies. The interruption of her spell caused it to backfire, and that killed her. Centuries of stolen magic erupted from her at once, destroying her body and part of a wall.

How did we not die with her?

I do not know. The important thing is that you did not die, even if you think you want to now. Your wounds are deep and raw, the pain is intense. It will take time to overcome, but you will.

The door opened, and Neva stepped in. Her steps were silent as she walked around the bed. "I see your pain." She sat on the stool and took the cup from Aithne's hand. "Let me help you with that."

Aithne nodded.

Neva laid one hand over Aithne's hand, and the other hand on her head. She closed her eyes and said, "Relax. This won't hurt."

Aithne closed her eyes. Sorrow and disappointment still dammed inside her. The tears began again, and she didn't stop them.

A wave of something that felt like warm oil rolled through her body, dulling the edges of her emotion, cooling the simmering anger. She hissed as it touched the raw edges of her soul, burning like salt.

Neva hummed, easing back the magic away from the pain.

"How do you have magic?" Aithne murmured.

"The Goddess bestows it on who She will, and she provided safety for those of us who carry it." She took her hand off Aithne's hand, and the stream stopped. It pooled in Aithne's core like a warm bath.

Aithne kept her eyes closed. "Are you the only one in Slan?"

"No, there are several of us. There have been since before the curse."

"You're not an apprentice."

"That is correct. I am a Seer."

"I thought the Seers were men."

She removed her hand from Aithne's head. "That's what we let people think. It gave us more protection. She protected you, too. The enemy could have inflicted more harm than she did. Going in alone would have resulted in your death, but the three of you, blessed by the Goddess, survived the ordeal."

Aithne opened her eyes. Neva leaned forward as she took both of Aithne's hands. "I know it hurts. I know the last several months have been an uphill battle, and you want it to stop. It will. You will heal, but it will go faster if you share your burden."

"Who should I share it with?"

Neva smiled. "You will know when the time comes. Are you hungry?"

"Not really, but I will eat if I need to."

"Ordinarily, I wouldn't rush it, but you need strength for traveling. We must leave today."

Aithne's brows rose. "Why? Are there enemies left?"

"It's not that. The new council has expelled the drag-ons from Mevan. We will go to the landing site, and from there to the abbey in Commain."

She felt resolve and stubbornness from Saphir. "I'll do my best to be ready."

The snow had stopped when Aithne heard activity downstairs. One of Neva's colleagues had come up to help her dress and pack what little she had. Her pack sat on the chair beside the door.

Aithne sat up, clutching the mattress as her head swam, and pushed one foot into a boot. Gritting her teeth, she paused as pain swept through her.

"Let me help with that."

She looked up as Oswin came in. He knelt on the floor, holding her leg steady with one hand and pushing the boot on with the other. The room tilted as he put her other boot on, and she squeezed her eyes shut.

"Sorry, I didn't mean to hurt you," said Oswin.

"You didn't. I'm dizzy."

"I heard you hit your head, so it's not surprising. We're almost ready to go. Do you mind if I carry you down the stairs?"

Aithne's face warmed. "Yes, I do mind, but it's the most expedient way short of falling down them. I don't know how I'm going to stay in the saddle."

"You're not," he and Saphir said together.

Oswin lifted her off the bed, and she kept her eyes closed. "Ceann demanded a carriage. The ride will be bumpier, but there is no risk of you falling off."

"Lovely. At least it's only two leagues."

"Today. Tomorrow Neva will decide if you take the carriage to Commain."

She listened to Oswin's footsteps on the stairs. *Saphir, am I going in a carriage so I don't fall off, or because you're hurt too?*

For you, mostly. My wing has not healed from being shot at the Southern Keep. I would carry you, but Moira has advised against it.

The wind was icy as Oswin stepped out of the door, and she gasped. His arms tightened, and a moment later, he lifted her. Two pairs of hands touched her, and she opened her eyes. Adrienne and Neva helped her sit on the opposite bench, and Oswin climbed in behind her. The bench had green velvet cushions, and red curtains covered the windows.

Pain ripped through her, and she gasped as the carriage moved forward. Neva and Adrienne leaned forward, but Oswin waved them back. "I'll do it this time." He took Aithne's hand and touched her shoulder with the other one. A current of magic flowed through her, and she relaxed against him.

"I should learn how to do this," she murmured.

"You will when you've healed," said Neva. "For now, we will take care of you."

She nodded as the magic warmed her body and she fell back into sleep.

The next morning, Aithne curled in a soft chair in front of a fireplace, tucked in a light blanket. Her head ached, and she rubbed her temples. She looked up at the sound of footsteps and Briant handed her a mug.

She breathed the steam and smiled. "Sine's arda."

Briant sat in the chair beside her. "No one makes it like she does."

She sipped, noting the richness on her tongue. "You'll be in Commain tonight. Goddess only knows how long it will be before I get to the abbey."

"I'm not going to the abbey yet. I'm heading north with Vask."

She held her mug in both hands to warm them. "North to where?"

"I'm not sure yet. The Goddess hasn't given me many answers, but it seems like we're looking for Vask's mother."

"She's still alive?"

"Lledrith says she is, but Vask is in denial."

Aithne sipped her arda. "Was she old when he hatched?"

"No, but she'd be over 700 years if she's still alive. Vask said she was Ailin's dragon."

Aithne's eyebrows shot up. "*The* Ailin?"

"That's what he said. Anyway, you'll be in Commain when we get back from whatever this is. Raine and Moira are on standby to join us if Hedda really is alive."

"When do you leave?"

"In a few minutes. We're taking Adrienne home to take her seat on the regency council, and I'll go on from there. Raya and Moira are going to Gynhalion with us so they can check out the new training site."

Aithne sighed. "Do we really need a training site? It's not like the Wybrens will be around much longer. There's a handful of adult dragons and a few hatchlings, but who knows if they'll be suitable to bond?"

"It looks dire. That could be the reason we're searching for Hedda. Are you feeling better?"

"The pain isn't as bad. Neva says it's going to take months to recover."

Briant drained his mug and leaned forward to put it on the hearth. "You'll have time now that the fight is over."

"Is it? Or have we exchanged one fight for another?"

"That's how life works. You conquer one mountain only to face the next one."

"I guess so."

He squeezed her arm. "Hang in there. Let Oswin keep you company."

A gust of cold wind whipped the flames in the fire-place. Briant stood. "Do you have everything ready?"

"Yes," said Oswin. "Ceann and Lassair have left with the hatchlings. Saphir will fly over us and watch for trouble. Aithne, are you ready?"

She drank the last of her arda and stood, holding onto the chair to steady herself. "Briant, have a safe trip." She stepped forward and hugged him.

"You be safe too," he said and stepped back, taking her mug. "I'll take these back to the kitchen, and then we'll be off."

"Take care of my sister."

Briant grinned. "Since Aithne might as well be my sister, I will if you will." He pushed the kitchen door open and walked through.

Aithne chuckled. "He's not that far off. We've bick-ered like siblings since we met."

"I found something that might be helpful." He held out a slender tree branch stripped of bark. "I'll have to smooth it out so you don't get a splinter, but I think it's long enough."

She took it and let go of the chair, leaning on the stick. It was almost her height and had a small knot below the spot where her hand gripped. "This will do nicely. Thank you. Is the carriage ready?"

"It is."

She took a deep breath and hobbled to the door, leaning on the stick with Oswin at her side. "Three days in the carriage isn't going to do much for my back."

"Two, hopefully," said Oswin. "I cast spells on the carriage and wagon to lighten them so the horses can go faster. We'll still have to stop for the hatchlings and to rest the horses, but hopefully we'll get there quickly. There's a storm coming and I don't want to get caught in it."

Neither do I, said Saphir.

If it looks like we're going to, you'll go on to Commain with the hatchlings. Don't argue with me, Saphir. I'll be safer if I'm not worried about you.

We will deal with that if the time comes.

As she crossed the threshold, she heard a child laugh. Tanwen stood with a group of people, but she couldn't make out who they were in the dim morning light.

One of them broke away and walked toward her. "There she is!"

She squinted. "Siril?"

"Aye, it's good to see you, lass." He hugged her gently. "A little worse for wear, but on your feet, like a true warrior."

"I'm really glad to see you, too. Why are you here?"

He motioned to the people talking to Tanwen, and she saw Adrienne in the group. "We're coming with you. Well, not with, exactly. We'll give you a head start and follow along behind. Not too far, mind, with the weather about to change, but far enough to let the dragons stay ahead."

Aithne blinked away tears. "I'm glad you'll be there. The more friends I have around me, the better."

Oswin touched her arm. "We'd better get going."

Aithne nodded. "Siril, have you met Oswin?"

"I did last night. Go on, then. We'll be behind you."

She nodded and let Oswin help her into the carriage. Blinking away tears, she pushed the red velvet curtains open. "It hasn't hit me yet that we're not going home."

"Not your old home," said Oswin. "But now you'll have a part of home with you in your new life."

"The most important part."

They traveled northwest across farmland rather than detouring to take the road north. Many of the farms looked abandoned, and Aithne pushed aside thoughts of how that came to be.

The day was gray and cold, and the carriage bumped over frozen ruts. Aithne's head throbbed. The motion of the carriage made her dizzy and nauseated. She closed her eyes and leaned her head back against the seat, staying as still as possible.

It felt like they traveled for days when they stopped to rest the horses, even though she knew only a couple of hours had passed. She left the carriage to stretch her legs. Her head throbbed, and stopping didn't help the nausea. She drank some water and ate a handful of berries. Her stomach settled a little, but not much.

She saw Neva chatting with strangers, but her head hurt too much to care. She got back in the carriage and curled up on her bench. A moment later, Neva and Oswin returned.

Aithne clenched her jaw as the carriage jolted forward. Pain shot through her, reminding her of Liam's headaches. Fear stabbed her.

Saphir, did you see any of the battle with Raca?

No. Why?

My headache reminds me of Papa's. Do you think Raca cast that spell on me while we fought?

I do not know, but I sense only wounds from the fight. Would I be able to sense a spell as well?

I don't know, but what if she did?

If she did that, we will address it, but not until we confirm its presence. Rest, beloved. Worrying will fix nothing.

I know you're right, but I don't know if I'll be able to.

CHAPTER THIRTY-SIX ~ COMMAIN

"Aithne."

The voice pulled her from sleep, and she struggled to open her eyes.

Adrienne knelt beside her. "Welcome to the abbey."

"Already? How?"

Adrienne smiled and helped her sit up. "The trip goes faster when you're asleep."

Aithne yawned. "Did I sleep the whole day?"

"You did, and while Oswin was concerned, Neva was relieved. Rest will help you heal. Come. It's warm inside."

Aithne nodded and slid to the end of the seat near the door. Adrienne exited ahead of her and offered her hand to help. Aithne concentrated on not falling out as her head throbbed. When she stood outside, Neva handed her the walking stick, and they flanked her toward a looming gray stone building.

Aithne's back spasmed, and she gasped, leaning heavily on the walking stick.

Neva stopped. "What is it?"

Aithne clenched her jaw, afraid to move. She touched her back with her free hand and squinted at the door where her friends entered. The building tilted, and she stumbled. Adrienne and Neva caught her, and she squeezed her eyes shut so she didn't see the world spinning. She heard someone running and Oswin's voice.

"Take her stick," he said as he lifted her. "Let's get you inside."

She wrapped her arm around his shoulders and kept her eyes closed. A moment later, she heard a commotion but didn't open her eyes to peek. Oswin lowered her into a chair, and she felt a fire in front of her.

When she opened her eyes, Oswin was crouched beside her.

"How are you doing?"

"I don't know," she whispered. "I'm afraid, Oswin. When Papa came back from Dorchada, he had headaches like I have now."

Oswin cocked his head and shifted to sit on the hearth. "Were Dermod and Ruan with him?"

"Ruan was, and Dermod was one of their rescuers."

Oswin looked at the floor.

"Is she all right?" asked Adrienne from behind her.

Oswin stood. "For the moment, but she needs to see Mercia and Geralt." He held up his hand. "I'll explain later."

"I'll see to it."

Grief washed through Aithne, and tears blurred the fire. Swallowing hard, her voice wavered. "Oswin, I don't want to be a bother. Whoever Mercia and Geralt are, I'm sure they have things to do."

He sat in front of her and took her hand. "They're healers, and they're familiar with the spell Ruan and Dermod had."

She frowned. "Dermod had it?"

Oswin nodded. "Both of them had the same spell."

"But Dermod didn't go into Dorchada at all. Papa and the others were in Slan when they found them."

"I don't know how it happened, but they had the same spell, and they disappeared together."

"Disappeared?"

"When we moved from here to Gynhalion, yes. Raya might tell you more later. Right now, you're going to get warm and fed."

Aithne rested on a bed, eyes closed. She breathed in the scent of herbs and did her best not to think about anything. Firm hands rested on her head and feet, and warmth coursed through her. Voices murmured, and the hands lifted.

She opened her eyes. Mercia stood on one side of the bed, and an elderly man she'd introduced as Geralt sat on a stool on the other side.

Aithne blinked as Geralt patted her hand. "You do not have a spell in your brain. The dizziness is caused by an injury from the battle, but it will heal in time."

Aithne released her breath. "If my stepfather hadn't been afflicted with a spell, I never would have thought to be afraid of one."

"Rightly so," said Geralt. He stood with a groan. "I have work to attend to. Check with me in a few days, and I will evaluate the healing." He shuffled away before Aithne could respond.

Mercia took her hand and helped her sit up. Pain flared through her back and hips, and she hissed. "I hope you have good news, too."

"Mine is much the same. The injuries from the battle will heal, but they certainly were not helped by traveling here all the way from Mevan."

Aithne arched her back slowly to ease the ache before pushing her feet into her boots. "We knew that would be the case, but Neva insisted we needed to beat the weather."

Mercia hummed skeptically. "What's done is done. You must rest and not fly while you heal."

"Saphir needs a long rest, too. Goddess willing, there won't be a need to fly until spring."

Someone tapped on the door, and Aithne twisted, hissing as pain shot through her. Oswin walked in, and something inside her softened, making her smile. He caught her eye, and for a moment, the pain stopped.

"Healer, the Bealban Dia would like an update on Aithne's condition."

Mercia chuckled, and Aithne's face warmed. "Tell the Bealban Dia the Wybren is healing, and Geralt confirms the lack of spells. It will be several weeks before she is able to do anything strenuous. Geralt and I will continue to monitor her."

Oswin's shoulders relaxed. "Thank the Goddess. Aithne, I'll wait outside for you."

"There's no need," said Mercia. "I'm done with her for now, but Aithne, come back before evening meal. I'll have a tincture ready for you."

Aithne nodded, and Oswin offered his hand to help her stand. She gripped his wrist, and when she was steady on her feet, she took her walking stick from Mercia.

Hobbling slowly, she left the apothecary and followed Oswin down the hall. He offered his arm, and she took it. His muscles were hard under her hand and she leaned into his body, noting that he was rock steady and smelled good.

Snow tapped against the windows they passed as they made their way to an alcove near the dining hall. He nodded to the cushioned chairs. "Take a seat. I think Sine made arda."

Aithne smiled and limped to the chair nearest the fireplace. "That sounds perfect."

He grinned and strode further down the hall.

She released a shaky breath and propped her feet on the front of the hearth.

Leaning her head back against the chair, she closed her eyes and focused on the sounds of the wind and fire. Her head throbbed, and she massaged her temples.

Saphir stirred in her mind. *Beloved, shall I have Quillon relay the news to Tanwen?*

That's a good idea.

She smiled, grateful to hear the dragons' voices buzzing. After losing contact with Saphir, she doubted she'd take that for granted again.

Oswin came back with a tray. "It's good to see you smiling." He set the tray on the hearth and handed her a mug. "When I told Sine the arda was for you, she made me bring pastries, too."

Aithne blinked back tears. "I missed that so much." She sipped the arda.

Oswin sat in the chair beside her and handed her a plate of pastries. "So, good news from Mercia."

"Really good news. I was scared."

"I know."

She turned to him. "I tried to hide it, but I knew I could trust you. You didn't seem surprised when I told you."

"You did hide it well. Neva and Adrienne thought the pain was getting to you. But I recognized your fear because I've felt it, and I knew you'd protest when I said you needed Mercia, so I did it without telling you."

"You didn't think it might backfire and I'd be angry?"

"Sure, I thought about it. You can't conquer a fear unless you face it. Denial makes it worse. It was worth the risk."

She leaned forward and put her plate and cup on the hearth, then turned in her chair to face him. "Why was it worth the risk?"

"I care about you enough to risk your wrath for your own good." He reached for her hand. "Aithne, we've faced terrible things together. I've seen you when you're angry, and I'm not afraid of it."

"Maybe you haven't seen the worst of it yet."

"You haven't seen the worst of me. Does that scare you?"

"No."

"Then maybe we have something special."

Aithne's heart stuttered, and an emotion she didn't recognize rose inside her. She heard Saphir sigh, and it made her laugh.

Oswin scowled. "Why are you laughing?"

"The first thing you need to know before we go any further is you don't get me without Saphir."

"Why would I want that? Your bond with her is part of who you are."

Yes! Keep him! shouted Saphir.

Aithne groaned as Saphir's words jolted her headache, and she pressed her fingers to her forehead. "Sometimes she expresses opinions I don't expect. Odd reactions from me are something you'll have to live with. She approves, by the way."

His face turned pink. "She's always in your head?"

"She hears everything I hear, but we have ways to keep things private."

"Will I be able to tell when that is?"

"Doubtful. You'll probably want to take some time to think that through."

Oswin nodded and turned his attention to the fire. For a moment he was quiet, and then he nodded again. "I'm in."

Chapter Thirty-Seven
~ Commain

One month later

Aithne turned her face to the sun as the humid air rushed past. Saphir banked, and she saw their new home laid out before her. Rolling hills stretched to the river to the north and the sea to the east. From their altitude, she located Aramach across the river, a day's march away.

Work on the new Keep and the lair had begun; progress hastened with magic. The fields south of the Keep and north of their village were being prepared for planting. The trees sprouted new leaves, and flowers blossomed far below.

I'll never take this for granted again.

Nor will I, beloved, answered Saphir. *The coming of spring truly feels like a new beginning.*

It does. A wave of grief passed through her. *Not that we have a choice about beginning again.*

She felt surprise from Saphir, and her heart skipped a beat as she banked. *What's wrong?*

Nothing at all. Look to your left.

She turned to see several dragons flying toward them. *Is that Vask and Raine?*

It is! I don't know where they found more dragons, but look at them!

Aithne laughed, her grief covered by Saphir's joy. She held onto the saddle as Saphir spiraled to the ground. As she landed, Aithne saw Oswin striding toward them. Adrienne ran after him, her blonde hair partially braided, as if she'd left in the middle of Kevia's work.

Saphir landed, and Aithne unbuckled her straps. Taking her walking stick from the spear holder, she slid out of the saddle and hobbled the three steps into Oswin's arms.

"He did it," he whispered into her hair. "He found them."

Adrienne panted as she grabbed Oswin's arm, and he pulled her into their hug.

"Is it really him, Aithne?"

"It's him." She pulled back enough to look at them through tears. "Briant has saved us again, and now he's home."

AUTHOR NOTES

In Western myths, dragons often symbolize challenges to be overcome, testing the hero's courage and skills. I have found this to be true as I've written this series. In many ways, The Dragon Rider Chronicles as challenged me as a writer and a person. It's made me take an honest look at situations, to let go of what didn't work and move in a different direction.

When confronted with a dragon, you have three options—fight, run, or learn. You can kill the dragon if you want to, but there will be another one, and another until you learn what they're trying to teach you. For me, facing the fear and learning the lesson has been pure gold. I leveled up as a writer and a human, shedding doubts and insecurities along the way.

I hope you've enjoyed this series. The dragons tell me I'm not done with Balphrahn despite the face that I've committed to another project. If you want insider news about future books, please sign up for my free newsletter at www.wendyblanton.com.

Until next time, enjoy your coffee and listen to your dragons.